ALL GOOD THINGS

A Jack Hart Mystery

by Rosemary Reeve

Cover designed by 100 Covers
Back cover photograph by Busath Photography:
Used by digital and print license to Rosemary Reeve

Quote by Nathan Bransford reprinted by the kind permission of Nathan Bransford.

Rosemary Reeve
Visit my author's pages at amazon.com/author/rosemaryreeve
https://www.goodreads.com/goodreadscomrosemary_reeve

Printed in the United States of America

First Printing: April 2018
Independently Published

ISBN: 9781980960263

To my mom, Dawn Reeve, who made everything better.

CHAPTER 1

There wasn't enough blood. That was the problem. If it had spattered across the clean, white pages of her brief, everyone would have agreed that her disappearance was suspicious. But as it was, the stain on her office carpet was only a little larger than a quarter. It should have been easy to overlook, easy to step over, but I couldn't take my eyes off it. I was sure I hadn't seen it there before.

It happened Monday morning. Harmony's door had been closed when I got in. Nothing unusual there. Harmony stayed late and came early. About nine, I knocked to see if she wanted to run downstairs for a latte. She didn't answer. I figured she was on the phone. About ten, Bob from the mailroom came by to ask me if Harmony had been around. He hadn't seen her all morning, either, he said, and she hadn't touched the stack of faxes he had left on her chair.

Bob and I walked into her office. It looked like she was there. Her computer was humming, but the screen was dark. I touched a key, and the blue screen leapt to life. She was in e-mail. I logged her out, mindful of the e-mail bandits who liked to sneak into unsuspecting associates' offices and send messages - sometimes humorous, often stupid, usually cruel - from their computers. As I turned around, I saw the thick brief spread on her desk, peppered with edits and revisions in her round, precise handwriting. Her fountain pen lay across the paper, uncapped.

"I left her the first fax just after seven," Bob said. "I've been back three times with the rest, but she's not picking them up."

Bob seemed upset. He took his delivery duties seriously. More than once, he'd tracked me down in the men's room to bestow the latest urgent message from someone who was just too busy and too important to use overnight mail.

Now his face was pinched. "She always tells us if she's going to be out," he said. "She tells us; she tells Janet; she puts it on her voicemail. She's the only one who does." He reddened a moment, embarrassed by his unintentional reproach. "But Janet doesn't know where she is, and I don't know where she is, and it's just not like Harmony to let people down."

"It certainly is not." Bob and I jumped at the voice from the doorway. Janet Daniels, Harmony's secretary and a much-feared fixture of the 42nd floor, was staring at me with disapproval, as if it were my fault that Harmony was late and hadn't called in. "You wouldn't happen to know where Ms. Piper is this morning, would you, Jack?"

Ms. Piper. Geez. Harmony was twenty-nine-years old. Janet was somewhere between fifty and death, an iron-voiced lady with rusty white hair and a surprisingly - and deceptively - sweet face. She terrorized the staff and associates, but she was always nice to Harmony. Maybe it was because Harmony's grandfather had been Humphrey Piper, the original Piper of Piper Whatcom & Hardcastle. Maybe it was because Harmony's father was Humphrey Piper II, the current Piper of Piper Whatcom & Hardcastle. Or maybe it was just because Harmony was easy to like.

"She was here late last night," I told Janet. "I left around midnight, and she was still here." When I saw Janet's expression, I added, "I offered her a ride, but she said she was going to put in a few more hours and take a cab home. I'm sure she's just sleeping in. She's been working awfully hard on all this stuff."

As I tapped the brief on Harmony's desk, the fountain pen skidded off the papers and spun onto the floor. Janet made a disgusted, guttural noise. I got down on my knees to assess the damage. The pen had rolled underneath Harmony's desk and out the other side, by the two chairs she kept for visitors. There was a dark stain by the nib. I crawled further under the desk to get the pen, but Janet was too fast for me. From beneath the desk, I saw Janet's cruel high heels by the chair legs, her thin, ringed hand grasp the pen. I heard her hiss, "Really, Jack," and saw her handkerchief daubing at the stain. And then Janet took the handkerchief away, and I heard nothing at all.

Puzzled, I crawled out, straightened up, and faced Janet across the desk. She was holding the pen in one hand, her handkerchief in the other. Her thumb was pressed against the pen nib, but it hadn't left so much as a shadow of ink on her skin. On her handkerchief was a brownish smear. She was looking from one hand to the other in bewilderment. Without speaking, she suddenly thrust the pen and handkerchief at me.

The nib of the pen was dry. I tried it on the corner of one of Harmony's papers, and it left an exhausted, chalky trail. When I touched the stain on Janet's handkerchief, no one had to tell me it was blood. It was flaky and copperish, and it seemed perversely alive.

ALL GOOD THINGS

CHAPTER 2

The police were not impressed. Not with the bloodstain, not with the dry pen, not with the missing attorney who never missed anything. The West Precinct officer was patient but firm. Sorry, Mr. Hart. No missing persons reports until an adult had been gone forty-eight hours without explanation. The stain might be blood. It might not be blood. But an uncapped pen and a dark spot on the carpet were not sufficient grounds for an investigation. Not given the current existing circumstances. Not at the current existing period of time.

Mr. Piper was in Tokyo, presiding over the firm's annual seminar for Asian clients. Janet left a message at his hotel. The current Mrs. Piper was sure she had heard Harmony come in around three that morning and almost sure she had heard her leave again a little while later. The Pipers' house was so big, I wondered how Mrs. Piper could have heard anything. Mrs. Piper seemed annoyed with me for calling. Harmony seemed to inspire protective feelings in everyone, even her procession of ever-younger stepmothers. "Don't you think Harmony deserves a day to herself?" Mrs. Piper asked. "That law firm doesn't own her, you know."

I knew. I knew that Harmony would, at any moment, come by my office, settle into one of my visitors' chairs, stretch luxuriantly, like a happy dog, and - for a moment - make me feel lucky that I worked for her father's firm. I knew that Harmony was at a client's office, the county law library, or an emergency hearing, and had - for the first time in her responsible, considerate, ever-so-polite life - just forgotten to alert those around her. I knew that nothing bad ever happened to Harmony.

The day wore on. No Harmony. No calls from Tokyo. No calls from the police apologizing for being such bureaucratic, rule-bound, unthinking paper pushers and promising to bring in the bloodhounds. Just periodic, anxious visits from Bob. I couldn't keep my mind on my work. I read the same paragraph three or four times before I gave up and went next door to Harmony's office. I wouldn't touch anything. I wouldn't move anything. I just had to take another look.

My eyes riveted on the bloodstain. It was indeed small: unobtrusive but unnerving. I tried to imagine how it could have gotten there. Maybe Harmony cut herself. Maybe she had a bloody nose. Or maybe she was bleeding from a gunshot wound. I shook myself. That was ridiculous. I had seen Harmony myself at midnight. All the security systems had been in place. Only people with firm pass cards could have come up on the elevator. The young guard with the bristly black crew cut had been at his post. The enormous arched doors in the main lobby had been covered with their night-time portcullis. No one could have gotten in to hurt her. And no one could have taken her out without going by that guard.

I jumped to the door and nearly ran into Bob, who was barely visible behind an enormous bouquet of roses. He turned his back on me in alarm, sheltering the red blossoms with his body. "These just arrived," he said, "for **her**." He set them on the desk, ignoring my protests that he shouldn't touch anything until we knew where Harmony was.

Both of us stared at the flowers. The vase was a narrow, black glass tower, above which loomed masses of roses. These weren't buds; they were full and deep and unfurled, a red sea unrelieved by baby's breath or greenery. The arrangement perched on Harmony's tidy desk like an exotic, fragrant bird.

A small white envelope in the top of the blossoms snagged my attention. It was addressed in a flamboyant teenage hand, with little circles over the "i"s. The clerk at the florist, no doubt. Bob was staring at it, too. I reached for it, and Bob clucked anxiously. "You can't open that, Jack," he said.

"Indeed you cannot." Janet made her second unsettling appearance at Harmony's door. "But I can." To my astonished face, she added, "I open all of Ms. Piper's mail in her absence. You never know when something will be urgent."

She picked open the envelope. We crowded around her to read the card, which was written in the same round, pubescent hand.

"My dear," it said, "I have been counting the days."

by Rosemary Reeve

CHAPTER 3

An embarrassed silence filled the room. Janet cleared her throat and said, "Well, I suppose this puts a somewhat different slant on Ms. Piper's absence." She crumpled the envelope and tucked it into her pocket, then perched the card back among the blooms. Sneaky bitch. She smoothed her dress, cleared her throat again, and left.

I glanced at Bob and wished I hadn't. He looked simultaneously sheepish and disappointed. I was sure my face mirrored his crestfallen expression. What was the matter with me? From the looks of things, Harmony was safe and probably having a really good time. Did I want her to be in danger so I could rescue her? No, I decided, after a moment. But I sure as hell didn't want her off who knows where doing who knows what with some clown. I glared at the scarlet riot on her desk. I wished I had sent it to her.

The day crawled by. Jeremy Smith, the head of the litigation department, walked into my office without knocking and tossed a thirty-page case storyline that I had prepared for him back on my desk.

"Is there a problem?" I asked.

"The margins, Hart," he said, pointing an accusatory finger.

I stole a glance at the margins. They looked perfectly uniform to me. I cocked a questioning but, I hoped, not challenging eyebrow at Jeremy.

"I can't stand to read it like that. You should have put it only on the left side of the paper." He sliced his hand through the air, as if dividing my offending document. He glared at me and stalked out, slamming the door behind him.

I said a few choice words toward the door, then brought up the storyline, changed the margins, and sent it to print. That storyline had taken about 45 hours of my time, including one all-nighter. Now, no matter how good the content was, Jeremy would see the storyline as a failure because I hadn't known about and pandered to his margin fetish. I slipped the now-60-page document on Jeremy's desk with appropriately obsequious apologies. He didn't even look up.

My phone was ringing when I got back to my office. I snatched it. Maybe it was Harmony.

It wasn't. It was Dan Bradford, the partner in charge of international litigation. He was calling from the client seminar in Tokyo, and he sounded edgy.

"Jack, I need you to write a speech for me right away."

I almost groaned. More nonbillable work. That meant I'd be staying extra late tonight to make up the lost billable time. But if I didn't play along, I'd get no more international litigation cases from Dan Bradford. I forced myself to say brightly, "OK, Dan. What about?"

"Hell if I know. New frontiers, synergistic partnerships, a future to build on, puppies, kittens, the next millennium, hands reaching across the sea, whatever. Just your patented bullshit, Jack. I have to give our Korean clients a bit of individualized attention before the final banquet tonight. Humphrey Piper was supposed to do it, but the bastard's not here."

"Where is he?" I asked, before I realized how stupid it would sound.

"Knowing Piper, he's off knocking up a geisha girl. Entertainment hostess, I mean. Actually, the weasel is always slipping into a dark room to seal some nefarious deal or other. He'll probably appear in a puff of smoke at the podium right as I'm getting up to speak. But just in case, I want to be prepared. Silver-tongued, even. So get cracking. E-mail me the speech right away, Jack. I mean within two hours tops. I want to have a chance to look it over so I can appear sincere. OK? Good. Bye."

I stared at the blank computer screen. What was I going to write for Dan to say to our Korean clients? "Thank you very much for letting us bleed your economy dry with high-stakes, no-win, civil litigation. There's just not that much money left in our own"? It would be different, at least. Different, but not popular. I needed something patriotic and inspiring. I couldn't recycle the rising sun metaphor that all our Japanese clients had enjoyed so much. What did the Korean flag look like?

I thought about my geography teacher at good old Franklin High, whose idea of instruction was to have us color maps and flags of different countries. I had found this surprisingly helpful in later life. I screwed my eyes shut and it appeared: the Korean flag was white with a yin-yang symbol. Oh, that was good. I pounded out a ten-minute speech on the theme of balance between different but complementary forces - East-West, import-export, attorney-client, and plaintiff-defense. I read it over once, e-mailed it to Dan, and let myself relax for a minute.

Dan had said Humphrey Piper was missing. Was this coincidence or a trend? Harmony was missing. Harmony's father was missing. I wondered if I should call the police back and let them know. I decided against it. Dan hadn't sounded at all worried. I knew what he meant about Mr. Piper's ability to appear and disappear as if in a puff of smoke. Both Mr. Piper and Harmony seemed not so much to walk as to glide just above the ground. In Harmony, it looked sinuous and graceful. In her dad, it looked sort of creepy and gelatinous.

I tried to concentrate on my work, but I couldn't get Harmony out of my mind. Finally, I gave up and slipped on my jacket. I would just walk around the block a couple of times to clear my head.

I paused at the security desk in the main lobby. Chris, the guard on duty, and I had a nodding acquaintance, and I decided to give it a shot. Did he know Harmony Piper? Of course. Little lady, black hair, blue eyes, big smile? Chris himself had a big smile as he described her. The smile faded fast as I described the events of the morning. He was solemn and intent as I wound into my request: was there any way of telling when and in what condition Harmony left the building?

Chris shook his head slowly, thinking it over. "It depends how she, um, left," he said. "There aren't cameras in the elevators, but each floor has a camera where the elevators open. I'll review the tapes from the six floors of your firm and see if she took the elevator down. If she walked down the fire stairs, though, there's not much I'll be able to tell you - unless the night guard noticed her going across the lobby to the parking elevator or one of the exits."

I bought Chris a double-tall mocha. He was already starting to fast forward through the tape of the fortieth-floor elevator bank when I handed him the steaming cup. Back in my office, I tried to concentrate on the thirty-six interrogatories I had to answer by tomorrow. I was on number four when Bob walked into my office.

"Jack," he said, "there's something weird about Harmony's flowers."

You're telling me, I thought.

"If she's off with some guy," he continued, "why would he send flowers to her here?"

The point had not escaped my notice. With a little condescension, I said, "It doesn't mean anything, Bob. She might be meeting him tonight. She might have taken the day off to plan their evening or buy a new outfit." Or rest up, I thought bitterly.

Bob nodded but didn't look convinced. I started to say something false and encouraging, but the telephone cut me off. It was Chris. He wanted me to come down right away.

At the security desk, Chris introduced me and Bob to Frank, the bristly-haired guard who had been on duty from midnight to 8 a.m. Frank said that Harmony had not crossed the lobby while he was at the desk. When I asked how he could be so sure, he reddened, then said, "I kind of keep an eye out for her." Chris confirmed that Harmony hadn't taken the elevator down to the lobby: she hadn't shown up on the tapes from any of the floors. If Harmony had left the firm last night, Chris concluded, she must have walked down forty-two flights of fire stairs to the lobby and exited the building while Frank was on a break.

"What about the freight elevator?" Bob said. "There's a camera in the freight elevator."

"She couldn't take the freight elevator," Chris explained, in the same condescending tone I had used with Bob a few minutes earlier. "Her pass card wouldn't work. She'd need to know the security code to select a floor and open the doors."

Bob said nothing but was clearly skeptical. "Could we just take a look at the freight elevator tape from midnight on?" I asked. "She might have gotten the code from somebody."

Now it was Chris's turn to look skeptical, but Frank was already off fetching the tape. Bob and I hunkered down behind the security desk while Chris and Frank discussed the shift change and Frank's duties for the night. The blue-gray image of the empty freight elevator trembled before our eyes as we fast-forwarded. I stopped the tape and noted the time at which the custodians left the building. Could Harmony have been hiding in one of those trash carts? Could Harmony have been hidden in one of those trash carts? I pushed the thought out of my mind.

Just as the tape sped past 2 a.m., I saw the flicker of a familiar face. Bob and I hit the stop button simultaneously. Chris and Frank crowded around, rewound the tape, and let it play at normal speed.

At 2:11 a.m., Harmony Piper had entered the freight elevator at the 42nd floor.

She was alive.

She was alone.

She was crying.

ALL GOOD THINGS

CHAPTER 4

I couldn't sleep that night. Whenever I shut my eyes, I saw Harmony's trembling, ghostly face, contorted with sobs and glistening with tears. She had looked like a kid who is lost or hurt bad. What she hadn't looked like was a lady who was off to meet her boyfriend. She had taken the freight elevator down to the loading dock. Then she had fiercely wiped her eyes, stepped into the shadows, and, as far as I knew, just disappeared.

Bob, Frank, Chris, and I had rushed to the loading dock, but we had found nothing to explain why or how Harmony had left that way. As I had worked on the interrogatories until late into the night, I kept reaching for the phone to call the police. My common sense intervened. What was I going to say? That an attorney I knew only casually hadn't come to work today? That in her absence she had received a bunch of flowers that the mail guy and I found highly suspicious? That she had left the firm in tears, by a circuitous route that almost ensured she wouldn't be seen?

I could almost hear their patronizing response: No missing person complaints until forty-eight hours had elapsed. Besides, sir, isn't it clear what must have happened? The young lady must have been upset with a boyfriend because he'd been neglectful. She must have left in tears and have chosen a roundabout route so as not to attract attention. She must have reproached her boyfriend for his neglect. When he said that flowers were already on their way, she must have been touched, and they must have spent the day making up from their misunderstanding. Mustn't they, sir?

I admit that it all made perfect sense. That is, it all made perfect sense until I thought about Harmony. She wasn't like that. She never talked about a boyfriend. Even if she had one, she wouldn't have cried because she felt neglected. She was direct – amazingly direct. If she felt her mythical boyfriend had been neglecting her, she would have told him so, and asked him what he was going to do about it. But how was I going to explain that to the police?

I had my chance sooner than I thought I would. I spent all morning and part of the afternoon at a hearing, hot and tired from my sleepless night. I grabbed a sandwich and was just beginning to attack the day's paperwork when a call from the receptionist interrupted my finishing touches on the interrogatory answers. A Detective Anthony and Officer Oden to see me. Now.

Detective Anthony was tall and broad-shouldered, with the ruddy face and gray crew cut of a high school football coach. He seemed to take up all the space in my small office. I had offered to find us a conference room, but Anthony said he'd rather talk in my office - so as not to cause me any trouble, sir. Right. Officer Oden was a big guy, too. Cramped beside Anthony, Oden looked like he was fighting for air. He was about my age, I guessed, and good-looking in an Elvisy way. He seemed familiar to me. High school? College? Anthony started to talk, and I gave up trying to remember where Oden and I had met before.

Anthony didn't waste time. I had called the police yesterday morning regarding Ms. Harmony Piper, hadn't I? Yes, I said. I had. And I'd been informed that the police could do nothing until Ms. Piper had been missing for forty-eight hours, correct? Yes, I agreed, still trying to figure out why they were there now. My tired mind stumbled over the hours since yesterday morning. Had Harmony been gone two days? Or just one? It seemed like forever.

"Why were you so concerned when Ms. Piper didn't come in yesterday morning?" Anthony asked.

I opened my mouth to tell them about the freight elevator videotape, but something in Anthony's manner made me suspicious. He knew something I didn't know. And until I knew what it was, I was going to play it safe and answer his questions like a lawyer.

"Because she's the most responsible person I know," I said. "There's no way she would have just skipped work without letting somebody know."

"And she didn't let anybody know?"

"No, " I said. "At least not that I know of. She didn't tell her secretary, she didn't tell the receptionist, she didn't tell the mailroom. She didn't tell me. In fact, when I said goodnight to her when I left at midnight, she said she'd see me tomorrow."

"How did she seem when you said good night to her?"

"Tired."

"How could you tell?"

I paused, remembering. "She had dark circles under her eyes. And she'd been here all day. She said her stepmother had dropped her off right after church in the morning."

"Did she say anything else?"

"No. I don't think so. Nothing that I can remember."

"What did you do when you left the firm?"

"I went home and went to bed."

"Did anyone see you?"

Geez. What was this all about? First I couldn't get the police even to take me seriously, and now Coach Anthony over there was asking me for my alibi. Then I thought: alibi for what? My stomach lurched, and my hands felt cold. When I looked up, Anthony and Oden were watching me closely.

"Detective Anthony, has something happened to Harmony?" My voice seemed to come from somewhere far away.

Anthony looked at me sharply, then looked away. "We don't know, Mr. Hart," he said. "But we are very concerned about her disappearance."

"Why? Yesterday, you guys wouldn't even come over to look at the blood on her carpet." I tried and failed to keep the accusatory note out of my voice. "Look, all I want to do is to find Harmony. If you need to check me out first, fine. I left here at midnight. I said goodnight to the security guard on my way out. His name is Frank. He'll remember me. It took me fifteen or twenty minutes to drive home. I live by myself near Green Lake, but my dog barked up a storm when I got there. I don't know whether she woke up the neighbors, but if she didn't, it will be the only time ever. I'm always getting complaints about her. You guys are, too."

Oden looked self-conscious. I bet he had checked me out before he came over here. I continued, "I went right to sleep, and I can't give you an alibi until the next morning, when I stopped at the Honey Bear Bakery on the way to work. They'll remember me, too. I'm the oatmeal raisin scone and espresso to go guy. Now will you please tell me what is going on? Why are you suddenly so interested in Harmony's disappearance?"

Oden looked at Anthony. Anthony looked at Oden. I wanted to throw something at them. Then Anthony leaned across my desk. His voice was suddenly quite soft. "Jack, Officer Oden and I met with your managing partner a little while ago, before you were in. Everything I'm about to tell you is or will be public knowledge, but for the moment, I'd like you to keep this information in confidence."

I nodded.

"Ms. Piper's father has been in Tokyo for your client seminar, hasn't he?"

I nodded again.

"The seminar concluded Tuesday evening. Mr. Piper apparently planned to take an early morning flight to Fukuoka to visit an, um, friend."

He stopped. I tried to encourage him: "But?"

"But when Mr. Piper did not get off the plane as scheduled in Fukuoka, his friend became concerned. The airline checked and confirmed that his luggage was on board. The gate agents located the bag, and, well, to make a long story short, they located Mr. Piper."

I shook my head, not understanding. Anthony tried again.

"Mr. Piper's body was crammed into his suitcase," he said. Now I was really shaking my head. Anthony and Oden looked at me sadly.

"It was a big bag," Anthony said. "And he was a little man."

ALL GOOD THINGS

CHAPTER 5

I t took me a moment to absorb the news. Harmony's father was murdered. Harmony was missing. And the police obviously thought there was some kind of connection between the two. A thousand questions spun around my mind. How was Humphrey Piper killed? When was Humphrey Piper killed? Why was Humphrey Piper killed? And what did all this have to do with Harmony? Anthony wouldn't answer. He said he had told me all he could. Anything more would "jeopardize the international investigation."

You mean you don't know, I thought. Anthony was speaking again, and I forced myself to pay attention.

"How well did you know Mr. Piper?"

"Not well. He spent most of his time abroad."

"What can you tell us about him?"

"Mr. Piper's father started the firm. Mr. Piper was the managing partner when I got here. He stepped on some toes, and they replaced him with Marshall Farr, the current guy you saw earlier. Harmony told me that he thought about leaving the firm, but he decided to make them indebted to him instead."

"What do you mean?"

"He opened up our Asian practice. I don't know how many tens of millions of dollars he's brought into the firm from Asia, but it's got to be a lot. He's the highest-paid partner at the firm; I mean, he was. And thanks to him, we now have an office in Tokyo, a presence in Shanghai, and a really good reputation in Korea, Hong Kong, Taiwan, Jakarta, and Singapore."

"You said he stepped on some toes. Whose?"

"Well, some of the partners didn't like him because he opened a lot of offices all over the country. They weren't profitable at first, and people resented having to subsidize their losses. And most of the associates didn't like him because he made their lives a lot harder."

"Harder how?"

"This used to be sort of the family-style firm. It was small and supportive, and there wasn't any requirement that you bill a certain number of hours. People here made a little less than at other Seattle firms, but they didn't mind because it was understood that they could work a little less."

Anthony waited, and I continued: "Mr. Piper changed all that when he was managing partner. He put in a high billable requirement for associates, and he froze our pay. During my orientation session, he told my class that our work satisfaction would be the result of our reality divided by our expectations. He said that the best way of increasing our satisfaction would be to lower our expectations. It didn't play well among the associates, especially because the partners had no billable requirement and their pay skyrocketed."

"Why didn't you leave?" It was the first I'd heard from Oden, and both Anthony and I were startled. Oden's voice sounded awfully familiar to me.

"A lot of associates did leave," I told him. "But most of us graduated right into the teeth of the worst recession in years for lawyers. The senior associates, the ones who had already been trained and were most profitable, left almost to a person. I think maybe one guy stayed. But the younger associates didn't have much to go to. As we've gotten training and experience, though, people have left as soon as other opportunities opened up. Now that we're profitable, the firm doesn't want us to leave. The associate committee keeps holding meetings about associate morale and trying to make us feel guilty for being disloyal to the firm. But it's too late. There aren't many associates who wouldn't leave if a better offer came along."

"And the associates blame Humphrey Piper for all this?" Anthony asked. I realized suddenly that he was looking for suspects and that I had just implicated all my peers in the murder of the man most of us referred to, without affection, as the Antichrist. I decided to back-pedal.

"I don't know if they blame him. But he was the most visible symbol of the changes."

"What about Ms. Piper? How did she get along with her father?"

At last, an easy question. "Harmony adored him," I told them. "She never said one bad thing about him. She stuck up for him when other associates criticized him."

"Do you know of any tensions in their relationship?"

"No, none at all. She still lives at home. They have a huge house, and she probably has all the privacy she could want, but I think she just likes to be around him. When he's in the office, they go to lunch and coffee together. She asks his advice on things. She actually takes it. She keeps his picture on her desk. She quotes him to me. I mean, like all the time."

"What sort of quotes?"

"You know, maxims, words to live by. Advice for when I'm stuck or in trouble: 'All hard decisions are the client's.' It's true. If you can't make a decision, it probably means that the decision isn't yours to make."

"Did they ever disagree?"

"I don't know. They must have. I never saw it, though."

"Has Ms. Piper seemed upset or tense over the last week or so?"

"Well, no." Anthony heard the hesitation in my voice and cocked an eyebrow. "She's seemed preoccupied," I said. "She's up for partnership this fall, and she has to put together a summary of her achievements and experience by next Monday. She's getting ready for a trial in a really big case. She's also been working on an appellate brief, and both of them are taking a lot out of her. She was here late every night last week, and she didn't really want to take breaks, even just to chat. She just seemed like she wanted to get her work done. She was really focused."

There was a pause. Anthony seemed to be hesitating. Oden looked at him, and he looked at Oden. I tried to prompt him. "Why do you ask, Detective?"

"Last weekend, one of the hotel maids entered Mr. Piper's room," Anthony said. "He was on the telephone with someone he called Harmony. The maid told the Japanese police that Mr. Piper appeared agitated. He would raise his voice, then whisper fiercely, then pace around the room. When he turned around and saw her standing there with the tea, he dropped the phone and shouted at her to get out."

I was open-mouthed. I tried to picture sleek-haired, mirror-eyed, silk-suited Humphrey Piper shouting and pacing. I tried to imagine him whispering fiercely to anyone, much less Harmony. I failed utterly.

Then Anthony dropped the real bombshell. "The maid speaks a fair amount of English," he said. "She is quite sure that Mr. Piper was refusing to give Harmony a large amount of money." He tapped my desk to underscore what he was saying. "Three million dollars, to be exact."

ALL GOOD THINGS

CHAPTER 6

I couldn't help it. I laughed out loud. Anthony cocked an eyebrow.

"That's amusing?"

"It's impossible. It's ludicrous. The maid must have misunderstood. Harmony doesn't need money. She's a trust-fund baby. Her mom was some sort of timber heiress. She left her millions."

"Of which Mr. Piper was to be trustee until his death?" Anthony looked awfully smug.

"I don't know," I said after a pause. "I don't know anything about anything like that."

"You were fond of Harmony Piper?"

"I **am** fond of Harmony Piper."

"And you can't imagine her doing anything wrong?"

"No," I said. "I can't. I can't, and I won't."

Anthony stood up. Oden stood up too, hastily, as if he had missed an important cue. I kept my eyes on my desk. "Look, son, no one is trying to railroad your friend," Anthony said. "But we've got a man who's murdered a few days after he angrily refuses to give a lot of money to his daughter, a daughter who goes missing right before her father's body is found, and a will where the daughter assumes full control of her multimillion-dollar trust fund on her father's death. Now, we have to eliminate all the possibilities; you understand?"

I nodded without looking up.

"We don't have a time of death for Mr. Piper yet. It may turn out that Harmony couldn't have gotten to Japan in time to have been involved in her father's murder. At least, not directly involved. But until we know that for sure, we have to treat it as possible. And that means that we need to take a look at Harmony's office. Will you step next door with us, Jack? Our criminalists have been in there already, but we'd appreciate your telling us whether anything has been moved since yesterday morning."

I blinked. Had they kept me talking in here so I wouldn't realize they were collecting evidence next door? The bastards. I wished they'd go away. My ears were buzzing, and my eyes burned. I wanted to go downstairs and immerse myself in a mocha grande. I wanted to go home and play keepaway with my dog. I wanted to go to sleep, wake up, come into work, and find that Harmony was happily writing her brief in her office, and Mr. Piper was off happily kissing wealthy industrialists' butts in Japan. Instead, I got up and walked with them next door.

The air was thick with roses and something chemical. From the greasy, gray-green smudges around the office, I guessed it was fingerprint powder. It looked like a messy extraterrestrial child had gone around touching everything just for the joy of making everything sticky. I showed them the bloodstain first. Then I pointed out the computer and explained why I had logged out of e-mail. No, she wasn't in any particular message, I told them, just at the screen that listed all her received mail. The faxes were no longer on her chair, and the brief was missing from her desk. I explained about the pen. I explained how the roses arrived yesterday. Anthony was looking at the card.

"No envelope?" he asked.

"You'll have to ask her secretary," I replied. "She opens all Harmony's mail." Let Janet deal with the ramifications of destroying evidence. I felt I was in deep enough already.

The picture of Mr. Piper was missing from her desk. Had it been there yesterday morning? Anthony asked. I couldn't remember. At midnight when I left the office? I couldn't remember that, either. They looked around a little, asked a few more questions, then shook my hand and thanked me for my time. I walked them to the elevator and pressed the button. As far as I was concerned, they couldn't leave soon enough.

I stood uncomfortably with them in the reception area. The elevator came, and they walked in, turned, and nodded goodbye. Just as the door was closing, Anthony stopped it with his hand. As if it had just occurred to him, he said, "Jack, do you know when Harmony left the firm on Monday morning?"

It was the question I had been dreading since I realized they suspected Harmony of her father's death. I hesitated. I didn't know when Humphrey Piper had been killed. I didn't know when Harmony would have had to leave Seattle to get to Tokyo. I didn't even know how long it took to fly from Seattle to Tokyo. But I did know that lying would take more energy and intelligence than I could muster at the moment.

More from exhaustion than nobility, I said, "I think so. I asked the security guards to check the elevator tapes. According to the security camera, she got on the freight elevator at 2:11 in the morning. She took it down to the loading dock. But that's all I know."

Anthony looked me right in the eye for a moment. Then he removed his hand from the elevator door and gave me an incongruous little wave. "Thank you, Jack," he said. "We'll keep in touch."

The door slid closed. I walked back to my office with the weird feeling that I had passed some sort of test. I closed the door and breathed deeply for a moment. Then I pulled out the telephone book and started calling airlines. We had a firm travel agent, but she had a big mouth and a short attention span. I wasn't even going to try to explain this to her. I got lost in voicemail hell a couple of times, but half an hour later, I had the information I had needed at the elevators.

There had been a 3 a.m. flight from Seattle on Monday, October 23, the continuation of a red-eye from the East coast. After a layover in Hawaii, it had landed in Tokyo just before 6 a.m. on Wednesday, October 25, Japanese time. There was no one named Piper on board.

I hung up the phone, leaned back in my chair, and covered my eyes with my hands. I felt sick. At that time of the morning, it would have taken 20 minutes tops to get from downtown to the airport. It would have been close, but she could have made that plane. Anthony had said Mr. Piper's body was on board an "early morning" flight to Fukuoka. Depending on how early, it was possible that Harmony could have arrived in Japan before someone stuffed Mr. Piper into his luggage.

It was possible. It was ridiculous, preposterous, and patently incredible - but it was possible. And it was my stupid meddling with the security camera tapes that had proved when Harmony left the building, that had proved that it was possible for her to get to Japan in time. I swore and hit my desk so hard that my interrogatory answers slid into the garbage can. I made no effort to retrieve them. Who cared if they weren't served in time?

I felt like I'd betrayed my best friend.

ALL GOOD THINGS

CHAPTER 7

It didn't help much to learn that Anthony had known about the freight elevator video long before he questioned me. Both Chris and Bob had told him about it. Anthony was just testing me, trying to see whether I would lie to him to protect Harmony. Hell, I would have if I could have thought of anything even halfway convincing to say.

I still felt bad. If I hadn't made a fuss about it, maybe Chris never would have thought about the freight elevator. We would never have known for sure when Harmony left the building. Actually, it was Bob's bright idea to look at the freight elevator tape, wasn't it? Sure, I said grimly to myself, blame it all on poor old Bob.

I sulked in my office for quite a while, my timesheet forgotten, my phone unanswered, my work undone. At 3 p.m., I stirred myself. I finished the interrogatory answers and gave them to my secretary for service. I answered my mail, checked a couple of books out of the library, and left several cryptic voicemails that made it sound like I was working on projects that in reality I hadn't touched. The voicemail trick was the best technique I had found for surviving at Piper Whatcom & Hardcastle. The workload required you to juggle and prioritize, but the partners had such eggshell egos that you had to fool them into thinking that you were putting their projects first. Not everyone can come first, Harmony had explained to me. You just have to make them feel like they do.

Harmony. Even when I was trying to concentrate on work, she was on my mind. By 5 o'clock, I had had enough. As I started to log off my computer, an e-mail notice caught my eye: "HUMPHREY PIPER." I pulled it up. It was a firm-wide message from Marshall Farr, our managing partner:

> It is my unpleasant duty to inform you all that Humphrey Piper, former managing partner and current partner in charge of PWH's Asian operations, died yesterday, while serving the firm's interests in Japan.

Marshall went on to recap "Humphrey's" accomplishments and contributions to the firm. A memorial service was scheduled for noon on Thursday. He encouraged everyone to attend. The firm's deepest sympathies and condolences went out to Humphrey's family, particularly his daughter, Harmony, an associate in the Seattle office. It was expected that Harmony would be out of the office for a while, he wrote, but sympathy cards for her and her stepmother would be at each reception desk if people wished to extend their personal condolences. The firm would send flowers to the memorial service.

Marshall concluded:

> This is a sad day for PWH, and a sad day for our Asian clients. As Humphrey would have wished, PWH will do whatever is necessary to ensure that our Asian clients continue to receive the same prompt, sterling service that Humphrey provided to them, so long and so well.

It was odd to see someone, even the formidable Marshall Farr, refer to Mr. Piper as "Humphrey." Even partners usually called him "Mr. Piper." Maybe Marshall used Mr. Piper's Christian name to try to make us feel close to him or properly bereaved. If so, it hadn't worked. I skimmed through my remaining e-mails, and Marshall's eulogy was followed by a string of mocking messages from associates. There was one from Charlie Snow, a first-year associate who was always sure to plumb the depths of bad taste. "So the Antichrist is headed for his last satannical . . . er, **sabbatical**," it read. I logged out quickly. It just didn't strike me as funny right then.

Outside at the bus stop, I was amazed to see the throngs of people on the street. Usually I waited for the bus amid a few sullen winos and a beehive of crack dealers. What was going on? As I watched people stream out of the office buildings up the block, I realized that for the first time in a long time, I was leaving work at a normal hour. I looked at all the happy, relieved faces. This was what it was like to have a regular job.

The bus was packed. I found a seat near the back, next to a wispy girl with magenta hair and a pierced eyebrow. The bus wound through its grimy, downtown stops. The city had torn down porno theaters and adult bookstores to make space for a shopping center, a park, and our office complex, but the change hadn't disrupted the original occupants of the area. All the dealers, drunks, pickpockets, and prostitutes were still there. They were just joined by office workers and shopkeepers, most of whom kept looking over their shoulders.

by Rosemary Reeve

At the last free stop, an old woman with two shopping bags boarded slowly and painfully. She looked in vain for a seat. Nobody else budged, so I swung myself up. She took my seat without a word or a look in my direction. I found myself swaying from a railing as the bus charged up Aurora. The kid swaying opposite decided to make my bus ride even more pleasant.

"Hey, man, whaddid you do that for?"

"What?"

"Give your seat to that old lady. You're tired, man."

So it showed. "Everybody's tired," I told him. "It's just that she's old and tired, and I'm young and tired."

"Huh." The kid twiddled his nose ring. Then he started toward the door as the bus lurched to a stop. He said over his shoulder, "I dunno. You don't look so young to me, man." And he went on his way, laughing.

That did it. I elbowed a few smaller guys out of the way and found myself a seat. The night turned the bus window into a mirror, and I could see what the kid had seen. I looked like a lawyer. I looked like a middle-aged lawyer. My suit was neat, my shirt was pressed, but my face was haggard. I had bags under my eyes. My cheeks were sunken, and my hair looked brown and flat. How had this happened? I was only 28.

Stress, I thought. No sleep. Bad diet. Limited exercise. Loss of a friend. I had never recoiled from my reflection when Harmony had been around. When she and I had played for the firm soccer team this summer, I had, I flattered myself, looked pretty good. The sun had lightened my hair and darkened my skin. I lost a little weight, ate a lot, felt better. It had been nice while it lasted.

I had balked when Harmony suggested soccer. Although I had two years of college football under my belt, I had never played soccer before, and I didn't relish the thought of making a fool of myself in front of our managing partner, Marshall "Shinkicker" Farr.

"Harmony, no," I had said. "I get humiliated enough in the litigation department. At least there I can bill it." But she kept asking, and one Saturday afternoon, when I was so tired of working that anything else sounded good, I gave in. To my surprise, I had a great time. The restriction on use of hands struck me as unfair, but I discovered an untapped talent at keeping goal. I was big and solid, and I thought nothing of throwing my body in front of a speeding ball. With me as goalie, our team, "The Artful Dodgers," went undefeated in our division, and we were going on to tournament play when the accident happened.

A vicious kick had crashed the ball into my chest. The collision stopped the goal but broke two of my ribs and collapsed one of my lungs. They had to call the paramedics, and I was carried off the field. Harmony rode with me to the hospital, holding my hand and begging my pardon. She was beside herself. It was all her fault, she cried. I hadn't wanted to play soccer. She had badgered me into it. And now I had gotten hurt. She would never forgive herself.

I couldn't stand to see her so upset. My own pain I could handle, but not hers. After I had been treated and was resting and breathing oxygen in a hospital bed, I told her things I had never told anyone before. I told her why my ribs were so fragile that a soccer ball could shatter them. I told her why my nose was crooked. I told her why I had a cigarette burn on my arm. And I told her why I had adopted the starving, mistrustful, half-psychotic dog that had followed me home one day from a walk around Green Lake.

I knew what it was like to be beaten up and abandoned.

by Rosemary Reeve

CHAPTER 8

I steeled myself as I turned up the path to my house. Already, I could hear her barking. As I got closer, I could hear her snarling and grunting. I paused at the front door. The first time this had happened, I had nightmares. Even now, it was not the most enjoyable way to come home.

I threw open the door and braced myself against the frame. Just in time. Ninety pounds of bone, muscle, and teeth leapt from the entryway, aiming right for my throat. My loyal dog, Betsy. I grabbed her front paws in midair and flipped her over on her back. Then I jumped on top of her and held her down. I counted to ten out loud while I avoided her snapping jaws. After she'd been down ten seconds, she suddenly stopped snarling and struggling. I had won. I had earned the right to enter my house. There would be no more attacks unless I tried to come in again. Betsy might be nuts, but at least she fought by Marquess of Queensberry rules.

I let her up, and she scampered off into the kitchen. Bets was not a conventional dog. It had never occurred to her to be man's best friend, probably because men had never done much for her - at least until I came along. She had never fetched a newspaper. She looked with disdain upon the balls, sticks, and Frisbees I threw for her. She played only one game: keepaway, which occurred quite naturally whenever either of us had something the other wanted, and which involved a lot of barking, swearing, and running around. No wonder the neighbors were always calling the police. If I had had any slippers, Bets would have eaten them, urinated on them, or buried them in the backyard.

It wasn't that she didn't like me. She did. Sometimes she'd let me scratch her ears for minutes at a stretch. We were just trying to get used to living together. She had followed me home in late June, and until late September, she had spent most of her time in my backyard. She came into the house to eat, drink, and watch television. We watched Mariners games together. She'd sit with me on the couch - just out of reach. If I had some Cheetos and was willing to share, she might come over to me once and a while, but the minute the game was finished, she would be out the door, happily digging up my yard.

Except for the atrocities to my lawn, it had all worked fine. But now it was too cold and wet for Bets to stay outside. She had moved into the house, and the last few weeks had been a period of adjustment. Bets had chewed holes in my walls, ripped up part of the hall carpet, and attacked me every single night I came home. I walked through my house, assessing the day's casualties.

The bananas were missing from the kitchen counter. Just gone, even the skins. She had taken the soap from its hiding place, high on the ledge of the bathroom window. I groaned. The last time Bets ate the soap, I ended up showering with dishwashing detergent. It was not an experience I wanted to repeat. In the living room I found the damp shreds of a letter asking for alumni contributions to the University of Washington law school. It looked as if Bets had eaten both the reply envelope and the pledge form. *Good dog.*

All in all, Betsy had done pretty well. Maybe she was getting used to staying by herself in the house. To tire her out so I could sleep, I took her for a run around the neighborhood. I kept the leash slack, and she kept close. I knew from experience that if she felt the slightest tug, she would dig in her heels and refuse to budge. So long as the leash was a mere formality, however, she enjoyed a good run.

I stopped at the Puget Consumers Co-op and bought some soap. When I noticed Betsy watching me through the market's glass doors, I bought her a box of her favorite treats, "Mr. Barky's" vegetarian dog biscuits. She sniffed the bag knowingly when I came out. She was such a strange and handsome dog. Even the vet wasn't sure of her heredity, but she had the shape of a beagle, the size and power of a Rottweiler, and the coloring of a chow: a smooth, bright orange coat and a startlingly purple tongue. Her tail arched high over her back. She was fantastic; she looked like she had wandered out of a Crayola commercial.

At home, I sat on the kitchen floor, held her food dish in my lap, and petted her while she ate. The vet said it would help her trust me, but all it had done so far was stain several pairs of pants with bits of kibble and doggie slobber. As I leaned back against the stove and rubbed her ears, I thought about Harmony. Betsy adored Harmony. Harmony had brought over a chew toy while Betsy and I were still keeping a respectful distance between us. Bets - proud, reserved, diffident Bets - had gone mad with joy, running around Harmony in circles, bringing her the squeaky toy over and over again for her to throw, and flopping down on her back and waving her paws in the air until Harmony knelt down and rubbed her belly.

If Betsy's behavior was unexpected, Harmony's had been astonishing. Up to that point, I had known Harmony only from our interactions at the firm. She was always kind, calm, and cheerful, but she had been a little intimidating. She was lovely; she was rich; she was smart; and she was the boss's daughter. She had seemed very proper. But within ten minutes of meeting Betsy, Harmony had been down on her hands and knees chasing my mad dog through the house. Betsy had danced ahead of her, her tail wagging so hard it looked like she might take off, glancing back now and then to make sure Harmony was in hot pursuit. Then she had had the bright idea of chasing Harmony, and the two little maniacs had careened around my living room with abandon.

This might have gone on all night, but one of them got confused while they were dashing around my coffee table, and they crashed head-on. By the time I got to them, Bets was standing on top of Harmony, licking her face and wriggling with excitement. I extricated Harmony and helped her up. She was sweating, gasping, and roaring with laughter. For just a moment, she leaned against me and I put my arms around her. She put her arms around my waist and bent her head against my shoulder. Then she slipped off to the bathroom to wash her face and smooth her hair.

When she emerged, she looked more or less as proper as always. But she seemed different to me after that. I didn't find her intimidating any more, for one thing. And for another, I nourished a faint hope that she might like me as something more than just her friend and her next-door neighbor at the firm.

But that didn't really matter now, did it?

Harmony was gone.

by Rosemary Reeve

CHAPTER 9

When I woke up, I was still sitting on the kitchen floor. I had fallen asleep feeding Betsy and feeling sorry for myself. I was cold but not as cold as I should have been. Betsy was curled beside me, her nose tucked under my chin. Amazing. Maybe it was just because I was still holding her food dish, but this had to be Betsy's record for affectionate behavior.

I stroked her nose. She licked my hand. I tried to pat her on the back with my other hand, but that was too much togetherness. She slipped over my lap and stood a few feet away, watching me and wagging her tail.

"You could at least help me up," I said to her, but she didn't move. I hoisted myself stiffly to my feet and gave her one of the Mr. Barky biscuits I had bought at the Co-op. She ran off with her prize, and I turned to the task of feeding myself. It was eight o'clock, and I was starving. I made myself a peanut butter sandwich and settled down at my desk.

I tried to think through the last few days. Nothing had made sense since Harmony disappeared. Maybe if I put the events in order and separated what I knew from what I had been told, a pattern would fall into place. I made a chronology:

Weekend: Maid overhears Humphrey's agitated phone call
                   "with Harmony"

10/23 12 a.m.   I say goodnight to Harmony.

10/23 2:11 a.m.   Harmony in freight elevator, crying.

10/23 3 a.m.   Mrs. Piper hears Harmony come home.

10/23 3 a.m.   Flight leaves for Tokyo.

10/23 4ish a.m.   Mrs. Piper hears Harmony leave.

10/23 7 a.m.   Bob leaves fax for Harmony.

10/23 10 a.m.   Janet, Bob, and I find bloodstain.

10/23 12:30 p.m.   Flowers arrive.

Noonish 10/24 PST   Mr. Piper's body discovered in Japan.   (Early 10/25 in
Japan.)

I studied it. If Mrs. Piper was right, Harmony could not have arrived in Japan
before her father's body was discovered. She would have missed the last flight to
Tokyo. But I imagined the police probably had the same reaction I had: in that huge
house, how could Mrs. Piper hear anything? All right, I'd assume that Mrs. Piper
didn't hear Harmony come in. Then did the chronology make sense?

No, I decided after a few minutes. The flowers were still troubling, for one thing.
Maybe I could believe that Harmony had skipped out for one stolen day of making up,
but now she had missed two days of work without calling in. Passion had its limits.
So did self-control. I couldn't imagine that Harmony wouldn't have at least stopped
by the office to take a look at the roses. Any mythical boyfriend must have mentioned
them. A guy wouldn't drop a hundred bucks or so on flowers without using them for
maximum effect.

So where did the flowers come from? The obvious answer worried me. What better
way to throw us off the scent? Janet, Bob, and I had been ready to start dredging
Elliott Bay until those roses showed up. If someone had taken Harmony - or if
someone had hurt Harmony - that confusing bouquet probably bought him a day to
get away or cover his tracks. Or - and I didn't believe it for a minute - if Harmony
had vanished on purpose, she could have sent herself the flowers to obscure her
disappearance. Either way, the roses looked like a dodge.

I shivered. The roses added a sinister, premeditated element to this puzzle. I
needed to find out who sent them, but I couldn't even remember the name of the
florist. I made a note to ask Janet and Bob about it tomorrow.

I took a bite of my sandwich and looked at the chronology again. The other
troubling part was the period between midnight and 2:11 a.m. on Monday, October 23.
Harmony had been fine at midnight. Tired, preoccupied, and overworked, but fine.
Her door had been half-open. She had been tapping away on her brief. When I stuck
my head in to ask if she wanted a ride home, she had smiled and waved good night.

Two hours later, she had been sobbing her heart out in the freight elevator. I
wouldn't have believed the change in her if I hadn't seen it myself on the security tape.

She had looked hopeless and broken. She had looked, well, she had looked like her father just died.

I didn't know when Mr. Piper had been killed. Maybe he had been dead when Harmony had left the firm. But no one except his murderer had known that Mr. Piper was dead until sometime around noon on October 24 - early morning October 25 in Japan - almost a full day and a half after Harmony had got on that freight elevator.

I tried to imagine Harmony's Sunday. Church in the morning with her stepmother, who dropped her off at the office. A long day of work. A long night of work. And then, around two in the morning, something must have happened. A phone call, probably. A late-night phone call, which she would have answered immediately, fearing that something was wrong. And someone, someone she trusted, must have told her that something indeed was wrong. Her father was ill. Her father was dead. Her father was in trouble, far away in Japan, and she needed to go to him. She had to hurry; there was a flight to Japan leaving in a few minutes. Just go right away to the loading dock. Someone would pick her up.

And someone did. I shut my eyes. A lot could happen on the way to Sea-Tac. I thought of all the dark curves and steep embankments where someone could slow down and push a body - a small body - out of a car. And then what would someone do? Well, for one thing, someone would try to get an alibi. Someone would pretend that Harmony had come home that night.

Mrs. Piper. She couldn't have heard Harmony come in. Why else would she lie, except to cover her tracks? Who else would profit from both Humphrey's and Harmony's deaths, except the wife and stepmother who probably stood to inherit millions? How else would someone have lured Harmony down to the dark loading dock, except by telling her that there was an emergency, that something was terribly wrong? I remembered the anger in Mrs. Piper's voice when I had called about Harmony, and I wanted to throttle her. A few hours after I talked to her, I remembered, the flowers had arrived.

I was pacing around the room. I stopped suddenly. If Mrs. Piper had been luring Harmony to her death and lying about it in Seattle, who had stuffed Mr. Piper into his suitcase in Japan? She must have had a confederate. Who? How? I tried to picture Mrs. Piper and failed. Had I ever met her? Did I know anything about her?

My mind was racing. Bits of conversations were swirling into something I needed to remember. I remembered Mrs. Piper's voice: annoyed, but with a kind of lilt. I remembered last year's Christmas party, with all the partners gleaming and affable in their tuxedos. I remembered standing by Mr. Piper near the bar, while he tossed off champagne and said to someone else's spouse that he would ask Mieko to give her a call.

Mieko. I remembered. Mrs. Piper was Japanese.

by Rosemary Reeve

CHAPTER 10

called the police. They put me on hold. As I fretted, I became uncomfortably aware of a big flaw in my theory. If Mrs. Piper had killed her husband and her stepdaughter for money, she would have wanted everyone to believe that Harmony was dead, not to think she had just disappeared. If they never found Harmony, Mr. Piper's estate would be tied up in probate for years until Harmony could be declared legally dead. Plus, Mrs. Piper probably would have wanted it to be very clear that Harmony had predeceased Mr. Piper. That way, any bequests to Harmony would have been of no effect.

Before I could hang up and rethink my theory, a tired voice came on the line. Detective Anthony was not available, the voice said. Would I like to leave a message? I debated with myself until I could feel the tired voice growing restive. Finally, I asked her to tell Detective Anthony that Jack Hart had called and wanted to talk to him about Mrs. Piper. Not Ms. Piper. *Mrs.* Piper. I thanked her and hung up. When Detective Anthony called, I would just ask him how Mrs. Piper had heard Harmony come in. If he seemed suspicious of her statement, I'd share my theory with him. If not, I wouldn't. Good plan.

I was suddenly weary. And starving. My sandwich had vanished, and a trail of tell-tale crumbs led to a contented and peanut-buttery Betsy, who was dozing in front of the television. Sneakynosed little thief. That sandwich had taken my last two pieces of bread. I was too tired to go back to the Co-op for more. Besides, Betsy would attack me again when I came in, and I just didn't feel up to that.

I had a bowl of cereal and went to bed.

The telephone shattered my sleep the next morning. Detective Anthony? I fumbled for the phone and mumbled a thick hello. When I realized who it was, I immediately wished I hadn't bothered. My mother's gravelly voice always set my nerves on edge, but it was particularly unpleasant first thing in the morning.

"Jack, what are you doing there? Why aren't you at work?"

I looked at the clock in horror. 9:45 a.m. I should have been in the office hours ago. "I overslept, Mom," I said lamely. I hated having to explain myself to her.

"Ah," she said. "I *see*."

Three words, and I was blindly furious. A personal best for Mom. "No, you *don't* see," I yelled. "I overslept because I hadn't gotten any sleep the night before. And I didn't get any sleep the night before because I was working, Mom. Did you hear me? I was *working*. I wasn't - I wasn't -"

Mad as I was, I couldn't bring myself to say the word. It was a simple enough word. Drunk. I wasn't drunk. Unlike somebody else in this conversation I could mention. Unlike somebody else who had been "oversleeping," having "migraines," and feeling "indisposed" since I was five years old.

"What? You weren't what?" She was goading me.

I was so angry I could have sworn up and down for ten minutes without repeating myself. I struggled to get myself under control. I pretended she was a client. A demanding, horrible, megabucks client that I couldn't afford to cuss out.

"What do you want, Mom?"

"You forgot to send the rent. The landlady's mad. You need to send me the check right away."

Ah. I *see*. It was an old trick of hers. I had been paying her rent for a couple of years. For the first few months, I had sent her the money directly. Then I found out that she was living in a flophouse in Pioneer Square. Who knows what she had done with the rest of the money. Booze, drugs, sharp clothes, sparkly things. Mom liked them all. Now I sent the rent right to her landlady, which is exactly what I was going to do when the rent was actually due. Next week.

Still pretending she was a client, I explained to my mother that the rent wasn't due, that the landlady couldn't be mad, and that I would send the landlady the check directly, "so as not to inconvenience you, Mom."

I could almost hear her thinking it over. When she spoke again, she sounded tired. She muttered something about the landlady's being really mad, but her heart wasn't in it. The gambit hadn't worked, and she didn't have the energy to waste on saving face. There was a pause. I could hear a voice in the background. The TV? A "friend"? Then there was a smothered sound, as if Mom had put her hand over the receiver. What was going on?

"Jack, I have to go." Her voice was even harsher than usual. "Send me the check."

Click. I stared at the phone. A sudden wave of revulsion rolled up from my stomach, and I gasped. I threw the phone across the room - and nailed Betsy right on the nose. Good grief. I hadn't even seen her.

I leapt out of bed, dragging the sheets behind me. Betsy was looking at me in shock. Her eyes were huge. When I got within a few paces of her, she took a step back, raised her hackles, and growled. Then she dropped her head and whined. She was shaking.

She had just started to trust me. All those Cheetos. All those baseball games. All those walks. All those spit-stained slacks. All wiped out because I had hit her on the nose with the phone? I had never spanked her. I had corrected her, scolded her, and wrestled with her, but I had never once raised my hand to her. I figured she had had quite enough of that. I couldn't stand her to think that I'd hurt her on purpose.

I put my arms around her. She dragged her paws unwillingly. I rocked her. "I'm sorry. I'm sorry." I said over and over again into her ear. "I didn't see you. I didn't know you were there. I wasn't mad at you. I'd never hurt you. I'd never, never hurt you." She whimpered. My mother had a lot to answer for.

Betsy stopped shaking after several minutes of rocking and apologies. She let me rub her nose. I rubbed it very lightly, in case it still hurt. Poor girl. Then she tucked her nose under my chin again, and we sat quietly together. What did it matter? I was already late for work.

We both jumped when the phone rang. It took some searching under the bedclothes before I located the receiver. Betsy looked at it warily as I pulled it out from under the sheets. I think she had decided to mistrust the phone instead of me. Fair enough.

If it was my mother again, I was going to yell at her. I was actually getting ready to yell at her, and I was sort of looking forward to yelling at her. I was taken aback when a strong male voice answered my curt "hello."

"Jack! Jack, is that you?"

Who was this? "This is Jack," I said cautiously.

"Jack, this is Marshall Farr." Our managing partner. Our managing partner was calling me at *home*? I was in medium-deep shit. "Are you all right?"

"I'm fine," I said. "I'm fine, Marshall. I just overslept." Trust my luck that the one morning I slept in, I would have to explain myself both to my mother and my boss.

"Oh." I could hear the relief in his voice. "I'm sorry, Jack. It's just that we were worried about you. When your office was dark and you hadn't called in, I thought, well, I thought -" He didn't finish the sentence. We both knew what he thought. He tried to sound lighthearted. "I mean, when we lose associates to other firms, it's mismanagement, but when we simply lose them outright, well, that's sheer carelessness."

I laughed nervously. "I'm OK, Marshall. I haven't gotten a lot of sleep in the last couple of days, that's all."

"I know how you feel." He paused. "Jack, do you need a few days off? We can cover for you. I know that you and Harmony were - are - good friends."

I was touched. The thought of going back to bed shimmered in my mind like an oasis in the desert. I could sleep, buy some groceries, fix actual food, make the phone incident up to Betsy. But I had to talk to Janet and Bob about the florist. I had to sound out Detective Anthony about my suspicions of Mrs. Piper. And I'm sure I had some real lawyer work to do, although exactly what escaped me at the moment.

"That's really nice of you, Marshall," I said. "But I'd rather keep busy. I'll be there in an hour."

I was wrong, but I didn't know that at the time. I rushed around my house getting ready for work. I fed Betsy her favorite breakfast of cottage cheese. I showered vigorously, working up masses of lather with my new bar of soap. I played conciliatory keepaway with Betsy, who had decided that it would be fun to put my underwear on her head. I ironed my shirt. I put the hot iron in the kitchen sink, where Betsy couldn't tip it over and burn herself. In fact, I was all ready to go - looking clean, pressed, and rested - when the phone rang again.

It was Detective Anthony. He sounded out of breath. I had called? Yes. I wanted to talk about Mrs. Piper? Yes. He was silent. I found myself babbling my theory into the phone, heedless of my intentions to play it cool and sound him out. When I finished, there was another long silence.

"Jack," he said finally, "the reason I didn't get your message until now is that I was over at the Pipers' house."

Now it was my turn to be silent. I waited for him to continue. "The maid arrived this morning and found the security gate and the front door wide open. Mrs. Piper hadn't slept in her bed. There weren't any dishes in the sink. The maid got scared and called us. She thought that Mrs. Piper had disappeared too."

The maid *thought* Mrs. Piper had disappeared, he'd said. "But you found her?" I asked.

"Yes, we found her. She was sitting on the couch in her husband's study."

He sighed. I held my breath.

"She'd been dead for hours," he said.

ALL GOOD THINGS

CHAPTER 11

had asked Anthony whether Mrs. Piper had committed suicide. He said that unless it was possible to strangle yourself and then prop your body up with sofa cushions, she hadn't. That was really more than I wanted to know.

I left Marshall a message that I had changed my mind and would take the day off after all. Then I sat on my couch and waited for Officer Oden to come by. Anthony had said that the police needed my help. I wasn't exactly clear on why and how, but Anthony's cordial tone left me pretty sure I wasn't going to be arrested. Even I didn't look dumb enough to kill somebody and leave a message about them with the police.

Oden was late. I passed the time watching Betsy. After waiting patiently by the door for me to leave, she seemed to forget that I was there and go about her midmorning schedule. First she sprawled in the sunny patch in front of my bay windows, her orange coat gleaming. Then she got up, shook herself, went over to the television, and turned it on with one expert swat of her paw. Pretty soon, she was engrossed in a Mexican soap opera. She didn't even notice as I put together a treasure hunt. I slipped a Mr. Barky biscuit partway under the sofa, secreted a rawhide bone in her blanket, and left a crazy trail of liver snaps up to her box. I hoped she'd find them all and have a wonderful afternoon.

When Oden rang the doorbell, Betsy let out a dutiful bark but didn't take her eyes off the set. When I patted her goodbye, she gave my hand a quick lick and stepped to the side, so my body didn't block her view. I left her to daytime TV, and stepped out into the soft October light.

Oden was driving an unmarked car. It was dark blue and relatively sporty. Only its oversized mirrors and radio antenna suggested law enforcement. Without Anthony by his side, Oden seemed larger and more relaxed. He asked a lot of questions about me, my family, my schooling, and my work, which I answered in as few syllables as possible. Twenty-eight. Single. Just a dog. The University of Washington for a marketing BA and law school. Four years at Piper Whatcom & Hardcastle. General litigation, mostly corporate defense.

I was getting suspicious. When he asked me why I had gone to law school, I had had enough.

"Officer Oden, do we know each other?" I asked.

He pulled up at a red light and looked over at me. "We did."

"How?"

"I'll give you a hint." Without any warning, he struck me across the face with the back of his hand. It was only a glancing blow. It didn't hurt, but it shocked me into silence.

He slid the car into gear and accelerated. "Remember now? I hope you do, because otherwise, I just hit the wrong Jack Hart. Internal investigations will have my badge."

I remembered all right. I remembered things I never wanted to remember, things that I had pushed as far down in my mind as they would go. I remembered my second - or was it third? - foster home, a run-down bungalow in Tacoma. Three foster kids, a youngish couple as the resident adults. She had long blond hair and narrow, darting eyes. He had one leg shorter than the other, huge hands, and thick arms webbed with swelling veins.

It had seemed pretty nice at first. A real bed, not a cot or a bunk. My own chest of drawers. Macaroni and cheese and Hawaiian Punch for dinner. But when I was upstairs putting my things away and getting ready for bed, he had walked into the room. He hadn't said a word, just backhanded me across the face and sent me sprawling to the floor. I had hit my head on the open drawer on the way down. Then he had kicked me in the side and flipped me over on my back. He had put his foot on my throat and said, "You just remember who's in charge around here."

It was Oden who had helped me up; Oden who had stopped the bleeding from the gash; Oden who had told me that I had experienced my new foster father's way of welcoming me to the family. Mark Oden. I remembered him now. I remembered everything. We had shared a room for about six months. After lights out, we had schemed about killing our foster father, two scared, battered kids whispering in the dark. Mark was going to distract him. I was going to clobber him with something heavy. I don't think we would have done it even if we had had the chance. But thinking about it made us feel powerful.

Mark had gotten in trouble for stealing something at school and been shipped off to a group home. I suddenly remembered the sight of him getting into his caseworker's car, clutching a black garbage bag of his clothes and shoes. I had never expected to see him again. Now we compared notes eagerly. He lived with his divorced older brother in Seward Park. He had been engaged last year but had broken it off because his fiancée was sure she wanted kids and he was sure he didn't. He had come to the police department through a non-traditional route. He had been in trouble from the day he left the Tacoma bungalow. Burglary, car theft, drugs. It wasn't until he was almost eighteen that he had decided life looked better and safer on the other side of the law. It had taken him a long time because of his juvie record, but he had made it. He was a cop, and he loved it.

"So now you're a big-time lawyer," he said. "I should have figured. You loved school."

"That's because I didn't want to spend any time in that home. Or any of the homes after that."

He grunted sympathetically. Since we were getting along so well, I decided to ask a personal question.

"Mark, where are we going?"

"The Pipers' house."

"It's in Magnolia."

"I know."

"We're nowhere near Magnolia."

"I know that, too." He laughed. "I'm taking you via the police garage. We're going to drive in, hop in another car, and drive out."

"Why? To confuse me?"

"You're already confused enough, I think. No. Just in case someone's trying to follow you."

That was a new one. "Why do you think someone's trying to follow us?"

"Not us. You. We don't think someone's trying to follow you. We just want to make sure no one does." He looked at my puzzled face and relented. "Someone was parked outside your house for a couple of hours last night. It might be nothing. Just a coincidence. Someone cooling off in his car after a fight with the wife. But on the other hand, you can't be too careful."

"How do you know someone was outside my house?"

"Your charming neighbors, of course. You and your mad dog are famous around there, you know." He raised his voice in an uncanny imitation of the lady to the east. "'That dreadful lawyer next door has had someone sitting in a car outside his house for hours.' Like you had planned it or something. The North Precinct sent a unit by, but the car was gone."

He drummed his fingers on the steering wheel. "Look, Jack, I'm not trying to scare you or anything, but I want you to be careful. Keep an eye out for a dark, boxy car. I'm sorry, but that's the best description your neighbor could give us. Do you have a cordless phone?"

I nodded, thinking regretfully of hitting Betsy in the nose with it that morning.

"Don't use it anymore. Get a real phone. The kind that plugs into the wall and stays there. OK? At least until we get this mess sorted out. Your calls on a cordless can be tapped too easily."

We were at the police garage, row after row of marked cars in the murky light. Mark put his hand on the door handle, but I stopped him. "I'll get a real phone. I'll be careful. But I have two questions."

"Shoot."

"First, what is it that you're not telling me?"

"Oh, pretty much everything." He tried to laugh it off, but his eyes were serious. "We're still waiting for the pathologist's report, but the timeframe we're working on looks pretty clear. You had someone in a car outside your house for a couple of hours. You made a call to Anthony and said you needed to talk to him about Mrs. Piper. A unit drove by your house shortly afterward, and the car was gone. And not too long after that, well, someone strangled Mrs. Piper."

My heart was racing. "You think someone was listening in when I left the message for Anthony?"

"It's possible. It's not hard to do. You can get everything you need at Radio Shack for a few bucks."

"Did my neighbor get a good look at the person in the car?"

"No. She thinks it was a man. Doesn't know why. And she thinks she saw a flash of light in the car now and then. Could mean he was wearing glasses; could mean he was using a lighter; could mean he was drinking a Coke. Not very helpful."

I was seething. My house. Someone had been outside my house. Someone had been watching through my bay windows as I talked to my dog. Someone had been listening in that dark car as I talked on the phone. I felt robbed. After a string of foster homes, I finally had a home of my own. I had a car, and a dog, and a house, and no one was supposed to mess with them. It didn't matter to me that my car was a clunker, my dog was a stray, and my house was, charitably, a fixer-upper. They were mine. They were mine, and no one could take them away from me. But someone had. I wasn't going to feel secure in my house tonight. I wasn't going to be able to shed the outside world like a jacket when I walked through the door.

I swallowed my anger and started to get out of the car.

"Wait," Mark said. "What about your second question?"

"Oh." I had forgotten. "Does my neighbor really call me 'that dreadful lawyer next door'?"

Mark smiled at me. "Yes," he said. "She does."

by Rosemary Reeve

CHAPTER 12

Mark and I parked behind a line of police cars on Magnolia Boulevard. The Pipers' security gate was wide open. We walked on planks up to the house, so as not to muddy any tire tracks or footprints. I wasn't looking forward to this.

On the way from the police station to Magnolia, Mark had explained what Detective Anthony wanted me to do. I was aghast. "You want me to look through Harmony's *clothes?*" I said. "You have got to be out of your mind. I'm a guy. I won't know whether anything is missing. Get a woman to look in her closet."

"We tried that already. We asked Mrs. Piper about it yesterday afternoon, when we had to come in here to tell her that her husband was dead. She said she never went into her stepdaughter's room, was rarely up when she left for work, and usually spent her evenings at the Seattle Tennis Club, so she seldom saw Harmony come home. She said she had no idea what kind of clothes Harmony had. Has. I got the feeling that if they were the same size, Mrs. Piper would have been able to account for everything. But they weren't. Harmony is bigger." He glanced at me. "In the nicest possible way, of course."

"The housekeeper?"

"No good. She's new. Only been with them a few weeks. We're looking for the old one, but we haven't had a lot of success. We think she's gone back to the Philippines."

"What about Harmony's secretary, Janet Daniels? She saw Harmony every day. She loves clothes, and she'll remember what Harmony wore. I won't."

"Ah, Janet Daniels. Scary lady. We tried her, too."

"And?"

"She flunked Detective Anthony's credibility test. He took a suit, a dress, two pairs of shoes, and a couple of shirts out of the closet before we brought her in. Janet looked at everything and swore that all the clothes she could remember Harmony wearing were there."

"Maybe she was just mistaken."

"Maybe so. But that still means we can't rely on what she thinks. You, on the other hand, passed Detective Anthony's credibility test. You didn't lie about the freight elevator videotape. Besides, you probably spent as much time with Harmony as anyone else."

We were in the sunny entryway of the Pipers' grand house. On one wall was a huge photograph of Harmony and her father on the deck of a white boat. Harmony was wearing a royal blue dress. She looked beautiful. Her hair was very black, and her eyes were very blue. She had her arm around her father, and it looked like she was laughing. Beside her, Mr. Piper looked like a wealthy and well-groomed ferret.

On the opposite wall was an oil portrait of an exquisite Asian woman wearing a creamy, sleeveless dress. Mrs. Piper? Mark nodded. Then he steered me past the picture and up a few marble steps that led to the main staircase. Over his shoulder he murmured, "She doesn't look like that anymore."

Guilt hit me as we climbed the stairs. If I hadn't left that message last night, maybe Mrs. Piper would still be alive. I was bad luck. I shouldn't be here. Mark seemed to be reading my thoughts. "It wasn't your fault, Jack," he said.

I had never been in Harmony's room before. More accurately, I had never been in Harmony's suite before. We passed through a study lined with bookshelves, a sitting room, complete with a fireplace, and a sunroom with a view of the Sound. It sparkled below us, a brilliant blue.

Harmony's corner bedroom had the same beautiful view – two walls of windows over the Sound. I wondered how Harmony could stand to spend so much time at the office. If I lived here, I'd never leave. The thought struck me with a pang. Harmony couldn't have left all this voluntarily. She had to be in real trouble. Or really hurt. Or worse. Much, much worse.

When Mark slid her closet open, I could smell her familiar perfume. I had always loved Harmony's perfume, but now it stung the back of my throat. I took a deep breath and walked into the closet, which was about the size of my bedroom. I started sorting gingerly through her clothes. This was going to be impossible. I might have recognized them on Harmony, but I wasn't going to recognize them on a hanger. I had looked at Harmony a lot, and I had liked looking at Harmony, but I had looked at Harmony in the clothes, not at the clothes on Harmony. I said as much to Mark.

"Well, we're not going to be able to find her to model for you," he replied. "Not unless we can figure out whether someone snatched her from your office or whether she came back here, packed a few things, and took off on her own."

I poked my head around the door. "You still think Harmony had something to do with Mr. Piper's death?"

"Not directly, no. She couldn't have. In fact, we think Mr. Piper may have been dead by the time she left your office. He'd been in that suitcase quite a while before they found him, probably more than a day."

"But you still think she might have been indirectly involved?"

He paused. I went over and sat on Harmony's bed. "Look, Mark. I want to find her. You want to find her. I've told you everything I know. I'm trying to help. But if you don't tell me what's going on, I'm not going to know what to look for."

He considered that, then shrugged. "She came back here that night, Jack," he said. "At least, someone who knew the code to the security system went through the gate and disarmed the burglar alarm at 2:45 Monday morning. Someone reset the burglar alarm and opened the gate again at about 3 a.m. We got the computer data from the security company."

"So Mrs. Piper was right?"

"A little off on the timing, but yeah, she might have heard someone come in and leave again. You can, you know. We were suspicious, too, but the alarm system beeps if a door is opened. And the buttons you press to disarm it make clicking sounds. We tried it out, and you can hear them even in Mrs. Piper's bedroom. I'm not sure whether it would have been enough to waken her, but if she had been awake anyway or just dozing lightly, yeah, she could have heard Harmony come in."

I felt like a fool. "I was so sure she was lying," I said. "I was so sure she had killed Harmony. If I hadn't left that message –"

Mark put up his hand and stopped me. "First, we don't even know if someone was listening to your call. It just fits in with the estimated time of death. Second, you may have been right." I looked at him in surprise. "The inheritance angle occurred to us, too, you know. Mrs. Piper didn't have any money of her own, and Mr. Piper was a tomcat. She may have been afraid of losing him and his fortune. She's got a ton of friends and family in Japan who could have done the overseas dirty work for her. Not all of them are exactly on the scrupulous side of the law."

He rubbed his eyes. I wondered how much sleep he had been getting since Tuesday morning. He continued: "Just because Mrs. Piper's dead now doesn't mean that she wasn't involved. She would have had to have an accomplice in Japan, and a joint crime is the most dangerous act in the world. If you're going to do something wrong, Jack, do it by yourself. She could have gotten cold feet, and her accomplice could have silenced her. Or her accomplice could have gotten greedy and decided to knock her out of the way."

"But the security system," I said. "How could Mrs. Piper have gone to pick up Harmony without its showing up on the computer data?"

"Easy. The data don't show whether she was coming or going. All we know is that at certain times of the night the gate opened and the burglar alarm was disarmed and reset. You can open the security gate remotely from the house, so all Mrs. Piper would have to do is open the gate before she opened the front door, and leave all security systems off until she came back. Then she'd just go into the house, open and close the front door, reset the alarm, and open the security gate remotely. From the computer data, it would look like someone came and left, but it just as easily could have been that someone left and then came back."

I was silent, thinking it over. "And that's why it's so important to know whether any of Harmony's clothes are missing, and if so, what. It looks like Harmony left the firm, came back to her house, spent a quarter of an hour here, and took off. What would she have wanted here? If she meant to disappear, she probably took something inconspicuous to wear. On the other hand, maybe someone just wants us to think that Harmony came here and got something. If so, there might still be something missing. But it will be something that just screams 'Harmony,' something that everyone would identify with her if we were, say, to find it in an abandoned suitcase at the airport." He stopped for breath. "Now do you understand what you're looking for?"

"Yes."

"And will you do the best you can?"

"Yes." I was already halfway to the closet. Mark followed me. "OK, Jack, we checked all over the house, in her office, and in her locker at the gym. All her clothes that we could find are here. When you think about everything you've seen her wear, what outfit would just scream 'Harmony'?"

"Her black suit," I said after a moment.

"Is it here?"

"Yeah." I fished it out and held it up for his inspection.

"And that screams 'Harmony' to you?"

"Yes, she wears it all the time."

"It's just a plain black suit. How can you be sure that she wears this particular suit all the time?

"Because I watch for it," I said, a little self-conscious. "I watch for it because it's short and shows off her legs."

Mark laughed. "OK," he said. "You know, this is the suit Detective Anthony removed before your good friend Janet Daniels swore up and down that everything was present and accounted for. He chose it as a test because it smelled more strongly of Harmony's perfume than any of the other suits. He figured she must have worn it a lot."

Downstairs, someone shouted, "Oden! You up there?" Mark headed for the door, giving me my marching orders over his shoulder. "Yell if you find something. Or yell if you don't find something." He shrugged. "You know what I mean."

I don't know how long I spent looking at Harmony's clothes. I visualized Harmony coming into the office, hovering over the printer, sitting across from me at lunch. Then I looked for whatever outfit she was wearing in my mind and moved it to the other side of the closet. I found every outfit I looked for, except for the black wool dress and black wool coat she had on when she disappeared.

When I couldn't picture Harmony in any more clothes, I took a look at her shoes. Blue, white, gray, cream, green, tan, and red high heels. Geez. Just call her Imelda. Flat shoes in the same colors, plus purple and black. I couldn't remember, but I assumed that she had been wearing black high heels with her black dress. Slippers. Boots. Cleats. Birkenstocks. Black velvet party shoes. Spike heels with gold sequins. *Harmony.* That was a side of her I hadn't seen. Revealing, white, strappy sandals, which I had seen and which I remembered fondly. That was it.

I rocked back on my heels and looked at the shoes again. Something was missing. I crawled far back into the closet but didn't find anything else. I sat on the floor thinking about Harmony's feet. There were worse ways to pass the time, but I wasn't enjoying it. This really was impossible. Usually I didn't even see her feet. They were under a desk or a table or elsewhere out of sight.

Then it hit me, and I scrambled up so fast that I knocked my head on the closet's built-in chest of drawers. Even with the bump on my head, I could picture Harmony on all fours chasing Betsy around my living room, her hair flying, her T-shirt riding up, and her white tennis shoes kicking at the air.

But there weren't any tennis shoes in her closet.

No running shoes. No walking shoes.

None of the Nikes or Reeboks that everybody had.

None of the shoes you would grab if you were running away.

by Rosemary Reeve

CHAPTER 13

I t was a good news/bad news type of thing. The good news was that if Harmony had come back to the house, she probably had disappeared on purpose and most likely was alive. The bad news was that if Harmony had come back to the house, she probably had disappeared on purpose and most likely was in trouble. Deep, deep trouble.

The big question was, was I going to tell Mark Oden and Detective Anthony? No, I decided. Oden and Anthony would interpret the missing shoes as evidence of a deliberate disappearance. And, with some justification, they would think that innocent people just didn't go around deliberately disappearing. No matter what, I wasn't going to do anything to incriminate Harmony.

Then I changed my mind. I had to tell them. The missing shoes might be another credibility test. If I didn't mention them, Anthony and Oden would consider me either a fool or a knave. I would lose any chance for input into and influence on the investigation. And there was another, more important reason. Even the police believed that Harmony could not have killed her father in Japan. Someone else would have had to do the dirty work, and I took Oden seriously when he said a joint crime was the most dangerous act in the world. If Harmony was out there somewhere, she was in danger. Two people were dead already, and I wasn't taking any chances that Harmony would be the third. I could get Harmony a great lawyer if she were found and charged with a crime, but I couldn't protect her from a murderer if I didn't even know where she was.

I fidgeted in Harmony's leather chair. I wished Oden would come back so I could squeal and slither away. I wandered around her room, looking idly at everything and nothing. The design on the rugs wasn't just an abstract pattern, I noticed. It was a picture of fruit, flowers, and leaves. The colors were repeated in a bowl on the mantelpiece: black glass shot through with strands of purple, green, blue, and pure gold. Next to the bowl was a gold frame. I picked it up with a start. Harmony had a picture of me on her mantle.

Well, not of me alone, although half my face and most of my right arm were visible. It was a photo of our soccer team the day we won our division. There we were, muddy, red-faced, and exhausted, grinning like idiots, flexing our muscles, stabbing the air with our index fingers, and generally looking like we all really needed a beer.

by Rosemary Reeve

All except Harmony. She was at the edge of the group. She was turned away from us, facing the frame with her hand out and her mouth open. An orange foot at the very bottom of the photo explained why. We had persuaded Betsy to sit at the front of the group with her paw on the soccer ball: our loyal mascot. Betsy had looked proud and triumphant. She had held the pose, too, throughout the time that Marshall needed to shout us into an appropriate configuration, fiddle with the automatic timer, and run back to his place in front of me. Right before the shutter snapped, however, Bets had sauntered out of the picture, leaving one orange foot on the print as a memento of her presence. Harmony had tried to stop her, but it was too late.

In spite of everything, I laughed out loud at the memory. It had been such a contrary, willful, Betsy-like thing to do. Then my throat tightened, and I sat down. In the frozen moment of the photo, Harmony didn't look like she was chasing my impossible dog. She looked like she was trying to find a way out of the photograph, like she was trying to escape. Escape from us, from the field, from our whole little world. I looked at the picture for a long time. Harmony, I thought. Where are you?

I may be slow, but I'm not dumb. I may have sat there in misery for quite a while, but when I realized the significance of the photo, I was back in Harmony's closet like a shot. I had been wrong, wrong, wrong about the black suit. Maybe it would have screamed "Harmony" to me, but not to anybody else. Even Janet hadn't remembered it. But there was something that would have been even more closely identified with her. I was digging furiously through her closet when Mark Oden entered the bedroom.

"It's OK, Jack," he said. "You can come out of the closet now."

Mark walked over and considered the jumble on the floor, where I had dumped the contents of the chest of drawers: primarily underwear. Mark dangled a particularly lacy something in front of me. "Having fun?"

I snatched the bra from him, tossed it back on the pile, and told him about the missing tennis shoes. He cocked an eyebrow. "They're not missing," he said. "They're right there."

"Those aren't tennis shoes. Those are cleats, for soccer." I turned one over and showed him the studded sole. "See? But I know she had some sneakers, and I know they're missing."

I saw his expression harden, and I knew what was running through his suspicious little policeman's mind. "Wait," I almost shouted. "There's more. Her soccer shirt is gone."

Mark obviously thought I'd lost it. He pulled out her jersey and waved it at me. "I saw her in the picture, too, Jack," he said. "And the shirt she's wearing is still here."

"Not that one. That's just her team jersey. We were the division champs, Mark. That's our victory photo over there. Every player on the winning team gets a special shirt from the league. I got one. Harmony got one. I've seen her wear it. It's like a polo shirt. It's purple, and long-sleeved, and it has the league's logo on the pocket."

54

I paused for breath. "The firm paid to have our names and team numbers embroidered on the sleeve." I grasped my wrist. "Right here, like a bracelet. Hers would say, 'Piper #5.' You can't seriously believe that she would have taken that shirt if she had wanted to get away without attracting attention. You don't commit a crime and slip into oblivion in a bright purple shirt with your name embroidered on the cuff."

Mark rubbed his chin and hmmed a few times, but he didn't argue. "And the shirt's gone?" he asked.

I surveyed the wreckage I had made of Harmony's closet. I had searched every inch.

"Yes," I said. "It's gone."

by Rosemary Reeve

CHAPTER 14

I t was almost 5 p.m. when Mark and I left the Pipers' house. Detective Anthony arrived right after I realized Harmony's purple shirt was missing, and he took over our investigation. He looked grave as I told him about the shirt. There was a long silence.

When I couldn't stand it anymore, I said, "Don't you think this shows that Harmony isn't guilty of anything? She hardly would have taken that shirt if she was trying to get away without attracting attention."

Anthony rubbed his red face. "She either took it innocently, or she hoped we'd realize the shirt was missing and look for it. If someone was with her, and she was either forced to leave or suspicious of the person, she might well have grabbed that shirt. She might be able to leave it somewhere to help us find her trail. It's also possible, of course, that someone else took the shirt to make it look like she had disappeared."

My head ached, and I was tired. When Anthony dismissed us, I was glad to leave the Pipers' beautiful house. I looked up at Mrs. Piper's portrait on the way out. She looked malevolent in the dying light. Harmony's picture was almost entirely in shadow. I could barely discern the outline of her face.

On the drive back to town, I told Mark my thoughts about the roses Harmony had received. He was way ahead of me. He had traced the florist and had become even more skeptical when he learned the circumstances of the transaction. Someone had ordered the flowers and the gift card by phone first thing Monday morning, then had come in a little while later and paid for them with cash.

"That bouquet had four dozen long-stemmed roses in it, Jack," he said. "With the vase and delivery fee, we're talking more than $300. It was worth a lot to someone to throw us off the scent."

The clerk who had logged the order and written the card - the one with the flashy handwriting - was on the road with her band somewhere in Oregon. I wasn't surprised to learn that both the clerk's and the band's name was Juliet. Oregon police would question the clerk when the band turned up at its next gig. Maybe she would remember something about the person who had placed the order and paid for it.

I started to say how conspicuous an Oregon policeman would look attending a concert by a band named Juliet, then considered my present company and fell silent.

Fortunately, Mark thought I was talking about the eye-catching quality of Harmony's missing purple shirt. I told him I would borrow the firm's championship photo of our team for him. I still had my shirt, too, if he'd like to take a look at that.

"Thanks," Mark said. "I'll stop by your house tonight and pick them up. Want me to use the lights and the siren? It will give your neighbors something to talk about."

"I don't think they need anything else, thank you."

"Suit yourself. I've got a bunch of paperwork to do before I take off. How about I come by at 8ish?"

I nodded. Then Mark said those three little words that single guys everywhere long to hear: "I'll bring dinner."

The office was quiet when I got in. Most of the staff had gone home, and the associates were holed up in their offices, billing away. I spotted only one partner as I walked to my office. Jeremy Smith was down at the other end of the hall, tall, angular, and severe in an ill-fitting black suit. The associates didn't call him the Vampire for nothing. I ducked into my office before he could see me.

I had ten voicemails. Four were client questions I could answer with return voice messages directly to the clients. Three were messages from partners forwarding client questions. That meant I had to respond to the partners so they could look informed when they called the clients back. Two were from my mother, alternatively threatening and begging for "just a little check." She had dropped any pretense that I hadn't paid the rent. She needed the money, she said, "for expenses." One was from Janet Daniels, who was blathering about a missing file.

Janet could wait. I'd find the file tomorrow morning. My mother could definitely wait. I'd stop by her apartment tomorrow at lunch. No, that was Humphrey Piper's memorial service. OK, I'd stop by her apartment tomorrow night. The clients and the partners couldn't wait. I answered the clients' questions first, leaving voicemails all over town. I got a simple pleasure from the thought of the phones ringing in their darkened offices, of their message lights going on and signaling that I had been on top of things and left them the advice and information they needed.

With less good humor, I turned to the partners' questions. Marshall Farr's was easy. If he had read the letter I had written for his signature, he would have been able to answer it. Oh, well. Marshall was a busy man. Details - like what court a case was in - often escaped him. Dan Bradford's question was entertainingly profane but didn't make sense. I left a tactful return message asking for more information. And Jeremy Smith's was a damn good question. It was going to take some research before I could give him a damn good answer. On the way to the library, I detoured to the lunchroom and took down our soccer team picture. I'd get retroactive permission tomorrow.

The library was deserted. The stacks were quiet, the study tables empty. This was my favorite time of day. The lights reflected off the high glass arches, shutting out the world and turning the windows into mirrors. It made the library look twice as big as it really was, as if the study lamps and shelves of books just kept going forever, a golden orb against the night. My research led me to the Washington reporters. I was standing in front of the shelf of the squat, tan volumes when I heard a noise, very close to me but somehow muffled. Thoughts of Mr. and Mrs. Piper raced through my head. I called out in a tense, sharp voice, "Who is it? Who's there?"

No answer, except for a muffled shuffle and a kind of snicker. A book right by my arm suddenly leapt off the shelves and crashed into the wall behind me. I jumped and almost yelled, but then I saw the satiny flash of gold and green through the hole left by the missing volume. I reached through the hole, grabbed the garish necktie, and pulled with all my might.

A satisfyingly panicked squeak and gurgle confirmed my suspicions. I pulled and pushed a few more books off the shelves. I bent down to glare into the pale and perspiring face of Charlie Snow. Charlie was a first-year associate who had been a class clown since kindergarten, when he had innocently broken wind just as the teacher was bending over. It was a watershed moment, he had told me seriously, a moment when he earned an undeserved but inescapable reputation for being incorrigible and a reprobate, a moment when he became addicted to the raw power of disobedience. Some have greatness thrust upon them.

Now Charlie was in a most undignified position. Rump in the air, head stuck through two rows of metal shelving, wedged between the Washington reporters, Charlie sniveled a bit as I wrapped his tie around my hand. I slid my other fist up the unabashedly polyester fabric until it pressed against his Adam's apple.

"Charles Westcott Snow, it would serve you right if I kept going until your face turned the same ugly colors as your tie. Out concern for the aesthetic sensibilities of the firm, I am going to let you go. But if you ever jump at me, lie in wait for me, or in any other way attempt to mess with my mind, I will take this very necktie and use it to dangle you from the chandelier in the largest conference room during a Governing Committee meeting. Understood?"

"Understood," Charlie whispered. I let go of his tie, and he backed out of the shelf. I could hear him on the other side of the shelves, breathing hard and clearing his throat. Then he came around to my side and leaned against the Washington reporters, some of his usual insouciance returning as the color flooded back to his face.

"Geez, Jack," he said, rubbing his neck. "What would you have done if I had turned out to be a partner?"

"Fainted because you were in the library so late. What would you have done if I had turned out to be a partner?"

"Fainted because you were in the library at all. Actually, I would have just told 'em I was you. We fungible billing units all look alike."

I gave Charlie a document review assignment and kicked him out of the library. I found a pleasant study carrel and settled down to work. A few hours later, I was pretty sure of the relevant statutes and cases, but the applicable volume of the Washington Administrative Code was missing from the shelves. When I brought up the on-line catalog, I found that it was checked out to Harmony Piper.

I didn't want to go in her office again, not with those creepy roses and that bilious powder. But I needed that book. I pushed open her door and was relieved to see that someone had cleaned up the fingerprint powder. The roses, however, looked creepier than ever. They were drooping and shedding petals. They had the grotesque effect of bending under a great weight.

The book was on her desk. I picked it up and was almost out the door when something made me pause. There was something different about her office tonight; something had changed since Monday morning. I looked around. As far as I could tell, the only change was that someone had turned off her computer. Its warm hum was missing.

I leaned against her credenza and thought about her computer for a minute. She had been in e-mail, and that suddenly struck me as odd. Harmony had been working on her brief in WordPerfect when I saw her last. Why would she have gone into e-mail before she left? Only the real night owls - essentially, me and Harmony - sent e-mails in the wee, small hours of the morning. I hadn't sent any messages that night, and I hadn't received any messages sent that night, either.

I called our evening computer systems assistance and was lucky enough to get Pete, a wiry computer wizard who had played soccer with me. I needed some stuff from Harmony's e-mail and didn't want to bother her because of her dad, I told him. Could I have her passwords? And Pete - gentle, trusting, brilliant Pete - said, "Sure, hang on." Then he came back on the line and said, "Harmony's system password is J-A-P-A-N. Her e-mail password is B-E-T-S-Y."

I treated myself to a moment of giddy pride in my dog as I logged into Harmony's e-mail. I couldn't find any messages either sent or delivered on Sunday, October 22, or early Monday, October 23. I scanned the stored messages, not really knowing what I was looking for. She had saved a couple of my messages. That was nice. There were a few old messages from her dad. He had sent one from Tokyo in August. It wished her happy birthday: "I can't believe my baby is 29." A couple of messages about partnership caught my eye. She was supposed to have her first partnership interview two weeks from today.

I was almost ready to log out when I remembered about purgatory. Deleted messages went into a queue and were purged from the system at irregular intervals, whenever the system needed the extra space. Until they were purged, however, you could pull them up. I tapped in the commands and found myself at a fairly lengthy list of Harmony's deleted messages.

At the very end was a message from "PIPEHU," computer code for Humphrey Piper. My hands were cold and clumsy as I pulled it up. My whole body went cold as I read it:

> Harmony, I'm sorry, but I just can't. Not now. There's no way I can pull together that kind of money. Please don't do anything. I will take care of it - in my own way and in my own time. Please remember: it is my decision, not yours. I will talk to you next week when I get home.
>
> - Dad

by Rosemary Reeve

CHAPTER 15

I sat in Harmony's office a long time, staring at that message. So the maid had been right. Harmony had needed a lot of money. I shook myself to clear my head. Why on earth would Harmony need a lot of money? I didn't know. When I got right down to it, I guess I didn't know Harmony very well at all.

I brought up the message information screen. Mr. Piper had sent the message at 1:40 a.m. on Monday, October 23. The message had arrived at 1:41 a.m., and Harmony had opened it at 1:43, less than a half an hour before she had fled the firm in tears. This had to be what had made her so upset. Whatever the reason, she must have needed that money badly. Why in the hell would Harmony need $3 million? It was too much money for me even to comprehend. Debts? Gambling? Bad investments? I swallowed hard. Blackmail?

Then I squinted at the screen. The message said it originated from Seattle. That meant Mr. Piper must have dialed into the Seattle network from Japan. But why? Why not dial into the Tokyo network instead? He could easily have sent the message from the Tokyo office to the Seattle office, without the delay and expense of an international phone call. I flipped back to the old messages he had sent Harmony. All of them had originated from Japan.

Something was wrong. I sent myself a copy of the message. Then I printed out the message and the information screen. I tossed the printouts, the soccer picture, and the administrative code in my briefcase, put on my coat, and called a cab. It was only 7:30, but the thought of a dark, boxy car waiting out there somewhere made me leery of taking the bus.

When I threw open my door, Betsy lunged for me, barking madly. I grabbed for her paws and missed; she crashed into me and spun me to the floor. I flung my arms around her and rolled until I was on top of her. I began counting. At six, she started whimpering, and I let her up immediately. I was on my knees, anxiously examining her, when she butted her head into my groin.

The world constricted into a silent, narrow, airless cell. I doubled over. I couldn't even get a breath to swear at her. Then the little hooligan began prancing around me, barking, looking for all the world like she was doing a victory dance.

"Would you like me to arrest her?" I could make out Mark's dark figure on my front porch.

"Don't bother," I said unsteadily. "Just shoot her."

"No can do." He helped me to my feet. "She's not armed. There'd be an inquest."

"Not armed? Have you taken a good look at her teeth? That dog is a walking weapon."

Mark shut and locked the front door and shepherded me into the kitchen. He tossed two large, warm, white sacks on the table. They smelled remarkably good. Betsy trotted over to investigate. Mark patted her as she peered over the table. Then he held out his hand for her to sniff, and she nuzzled him and gave him a friendly lick.

"So the long arm of the law has caught up with you at last, Betsy. Your reign of terror is over." He scratched under her chin, and she wagged her tail. She was winning him over. "I don't think she's such a menace to society, Jack."

"You don't know her very well," I replied, still sore. "Watch this." I took Betsy by the collar and swiveled her head toward Mark. "Bets, this is the big, bad policeman who hit me in the face while I was stopped at a red light. A rogue cop, Betsy. Police brutality, Betsy. Bite him, Betsy. Kill, Betsy. Kill."

I let go of her collar. I saw Mark tense, waiting. Betsy looked at him with her head on one side for a moment, then rolled over at his feet and waved her paws in the air.

When Mark stopped laughing - it took a while - he bent down and rubbed her belly. "Watch your midsection and etc.," I advised, getting out plates and forks.

"Ah, I'm OK. I hope you like barbecue. There's two kinds of ribs, fried chicken, mashed potatoes, gravy, biscuits, and pecan pie. Sound good?"

"Sounds great. But what are you going to eat?"

"Don't worry. I brought enough for three."

"I brought you something, too." I fished the printouts out of my briefcase. "Take a look at those while I make sure Betsy can have some of the ribs. If they're spicy, the pepper will mess with her nose."

The thick, sweet barbecue sauces passed inspection, and Mark handed Betsy a rib with great ceremony. She snatched it and shot under the table, where she gnawed it loudly and sloppily. Mark licked his fingers and turned back to the printouts. He whistled.

"What do you make of this message?" he asked.

I said I thought it was fishy and told him why.

He nodded. "There's another reason, too," he said. "When it was 1:40 a.m., October 23, in Seattle, it would have been 5:40 p.m., October 23, in Japan. But according to his hotel bill, Mr. Piper's last phone call was to his wife at 3 p.m. on October 23, Japanese time. Mr. Piper couldn't have dialed into the Seattle network from his hotel room at 5:40 p.m."

"Maybe the hotel had a computer room."

"Maybe, but he still would have had to charge the call, either on a phone card or to his room."

He was right. No matter how well-appointed and accommodating the hotel, they always made sure that long-distance charges showed up on your bill.

"So this message is a fraud." It wasn't a question.

"Looks like it to me. I hate to tell you this, Jack, but it's looking more and more like someone tricked your little friend and lured her downstairs. And as much as I want to keep your spirits up, it's really hard to think of a harmless reason for doing something like that."

"Yeah." I couldn't say anything more. The food still smelled wonderful, but I couldn't take another bite. When I looked up at Mark, his eyes were sad.

He hit the table with his fist, emphasizing each word. "We will find her, Jack."

Now I really couldn't speak. Yeah, you'll find her, I thought. Dead or alive.

by Rosemary Reeve

CHAPTER 16

Mark ate quietly for a while. I got up from the table and busied myself fetching my soccer shirt and the championship picture. He tactfully studied the computer printouts.

I went to the bathroom and splashed cold water on my face. When I got back to the kitchen, I felt a little better. "Do you think it was Mrs. Piper?" I asked.

Mark laid the printouts aside. "There weren't any phone calls from the Pipers' house the night Harmony disappeared. So she couldn't have dialed into your network from home. She might have sent the message from somewhere else. We don't know where yet, though."

Betsy made a rude digestive noise under the table, and we both laughed. We laughed a bit nervously, but we laughed. I sat down again, and Mark started to tell a ribald and amusing story about the exploits - gastrointestinal and otherwise - of his neighbors' yellow Labrador, Lester. I had some trouble following the plot, but I laughed a lot and pretty soon I noticed I was eating again. The ribs were delicious. The sauce was crusted and charred. I sucked the bits of smoky meat from the bone and licked my fingers. Then I bit into a piece of fried chicken. The coating broke with a hiss.

I was ravenous. All I had eaten in the past two days was a bite of a sandwich and a bowl of cereal. I mounded potatoes on my plate and baptized them with gravy. I felt stronger and calmer with every bite. By the time I had polished off three more ribs and four biscuits, I was feeling almost hopeful again. Unless and until someone proved to me that Harmony was dead, I just wasn't going to believe it.

Mark looked at me with amusement as I dug into a drumstick. "Detective Anthony said he thought you looked a little pale this afternoon," he said. "And Detective Anthony is always right."

"What's Detective Anthony's first name?"

"Anthony."

"Yeah, what's his first name?"

"Detective Anthony's first name is Anthony."

"You have got to be kidding."

"Nope. Anthony C. Anthony."

"Geez." I thought about that for a moment. "I'd go by my middle name."

by Rosemary Reeve

"No, you wouldn't," Mark said. "Detective Anthony's middle name is Clive."
I groaned in sympathy.

Mark said, "I know. And you and I thought our parents were unfit. Actually, he's pretty cool about it. I saw him speak at some public safety whiz-bang. He got up and said, 'Good evening. I am Detective Anthony Anthony. My first name is Anthony. My last name is Anthony. It has been this way almost since I was born, and I assure you, it has ceased to astonish me.' It got a big laugh."

I laughed, too. Then I said, "You know, Mark, you're a good mimic. You sounded just like Anthony. And you can imitate my neighbor, too. It sends chills up my spine, but you can do it."

"Thanks. Impressions are my one talent. I used to use them to get out of trouble."

"How?"

"I'd call up my school or my guidance counselor or whatever authority figure I was avoiding at the moment and pretend I was my foster mother." His voice became high and fluttery. "'No, Mark can't possibly come in today. He's got a fever and a runny nose, and unless I'm much mistaken, he was exposed to the plague not long ago.' It always worked. And then, of course, I'd go off and do whatever I wanted."

"So, in other words, you used your talent to get into trouble, not out of it."

"Good point, Counselor, very keenly noted, but I used it to get out of trouble, too. I'd call my foster mother and say that I was from the school and I just wanted to apologize for all those truancy notices, which were, naturally, due to a computer error. I very seldom got caught, so long as I could remember who I was imitating. I used to get my foster mothers mixed up, though. And when I was put into group homes, well, that was just impossible. All the counselors were named Kimberly and had long, straight, brown hair. I never knew who the hell I was. Once I actually pretended to be the person I was talking to on the phone. And you know, bless her little heart, Kimberly didn't even catch on." She probably couldn't keep all the other Kimberlys straight, either."

Mark took a big bite of pecan pie. "So I guess I used my impressions to get into trouble and out of trouble. Whaddya know? I'm a multifaceted guy."

The three of us chewed companionably for a moment. Then I asked, "What was it like in the group homes?"

"It depended on the home. Mostly, they were just more supervised and impersonal than the foster care. No one pretends to be Mommy and Daddy. You're in an institution, and you know it, but there's more outside oversight. In other words, Jack, they can't hurt you as bad when somebody's not looking." He was quiet. "I never got sent to the Grange, though. I understand that was a whole different story."

The Grange was a big juvenile facility that lurked behind a high iron fence on First Hill. It had just made headlines for forty years of physical and sexual abuse of the hundreds of boys who had gone through its gates. Not all of those boys had come out

68

again. It was a huge scandal, and heads were going to roll, but I was appalled that it had taken forty years to break the story. Hadn't anyone ever talked to those kids? There had been more than a handful of deaths; hadn't anyone ever investigated? The details in the newspaper stories haunted me. They made my experience as a ward of the State look like a birthday party.

Mark seemed to be thinking along the same lines. "I was pretty lucky, you know," he said. "I wasn't molested or beaten to death."

"No, me either," I said. I looked him right in the eye. "But it's kind of hard to feel grateful for that."

He nodded but didn't speak. For a while, the only sounds came from Betsy, who was crunching under the table. Finally, I stretched and looked with regret at the heap of gleaming bones and the drifts of piecrust crumbs. All good things must come to an end.

"Coffee?" I asked, clearing the plates.

"Do you have any tea?"

"No, but I have coffee in tea bags."

"That'll be fine."

After he had drained his mug, Mark seemed to turn back into a policeman. I tried to pay him for our share of the feast, but he insisted that it was a gift from the good people of Seattle. He packed up the picture, the printouts, and my shirt, and started for the door, all the while giving Betsy a stern warning to treat me with the respect and kindness I deserved. "Or more than he deserves, but at least some, OK, Bets?"

Betsy retreated under the table with her bone. She was making no promises. I picked up her leash and was surprised when Mark took it out of my hand.

"No walks, tonight," he said. "It's too late. Just lock your door, go to bed, and don't stir from this house until morning, when your insufferable neighbor will be up and keeping an eagle eye on you. Drive to work. And when you get there and have a phone that cannot easily be tapped, call me and let me know what you want to have for dinner tomorrow night. Understood?"

I was stunned. "You mean you came here tonight to protect me?"

"Among other things. Protect you, feed you, make sure you got some sleep. I told Anthony I drew the line at reading you a bedtime story and tucking you in, but I will do both of those things if that's what it takes, Jack." He paused. "I'm serious. We need you at your best to help us catch those bastards, whoever those bastards may be. OK?"

"OK."

"Good." He saluted me, and he was gone.

I locked the door behind him, stacked the dishes in the sink, and was about to go to bed when I remembered that I still needed to answer Jeremy's question. I was full and sleepy, but the thought of getting up early in the morning to finish the research didn't appeal to me, either. Betsy had come out from under the table and was sniffing around my briefcase. I shooed her away and pulled out the administrative code I had taken from Harmony's office. I opened the thick, blue book on my desk and got to work.

As I skimmed through the incomprehensible regulations, I noticed that a couple of pages seemed stuck together. I had to pick them apart with my fingernail.

As the pages gave way, I saw what had been holding them together. One page was stained with blotches that were rusty brown. On the facing page was stuck a photograph of a sleek, smiling little man with brilliant eyes and shining hair.

It was the missing photograph of Harmony's father. The bottom half was stiff and dull with dried blood.

ALL GOOD THINGS

CHAPTER 17

The phone! Where the hell was the phone? Eavesdropper or no eavesdropper, I wanted to call Mark and tell him to get back here right away. But I couldn't find my phone. It tended to wander a bit, true, but usually it stayed in the general vicinity of my study and bedroom. I rampaged through the house, tossing pillows and clothes aside. Nothing. Then my eyes fell on Betsy, who was looking the other way and pretending not to notice my frenzy. Usually when I was searching for something, Betsy was right in the thick of things, barking wildly and getting underfoot. Now she seemed suspiciously demure.

I put my arm around her neck and pulled her close. "Bets, I won't get mad. Just show me where the phone is." She turned her head away. "Please, Betsy. It's really important. The telephone, Betsy. Find the telephone."

Betsy scampered over to the sofa and pawed the upholstery. I followed and started searching under the cushions. Then she scampered over to the fireplace. She led me on a merry chase throughout the house, but there was no sign anywhere of the missing telephone. Finally, I ignored her gallivanting and just searched room by room.

I found it at the bottom of the basement stairs. Betsy had made quite sure that no more flying telephones would come out of nowhere and smack her on the nose. It looked like she had stood at the top of the stairs and flung it to the concrete floor below. In fact, from the bits and pieces scattered around, it looked like she had flung it to the floor several times. I sat on the bottom step and stared glumly at the destruction. So much for the thought of putting it back together. This had been an execution, Betsy-style.

I wasn't going out to find a pay phone. I wasn't going to drive into work. And I definitely wasn't going over to my neighbor's at midnight to ask if I could make a call. I could hear her already: "'That dreadful lawyer next door, always coming over here in his pajamas, never a speck of consideration.'" No way. This would just have to wait until morning.

I forced myself to calm down, finished my research, and copied the relevant regulation onto a separate piece of paper. I slipped the bloody book in a plastic bag so I could make sure Mark got it more or less intact. Since I didn't have a phone anymore, I couldn't leave Jeremy a voicemail in answer to his question. I couldn't do anything except go to bed. So I did.

I felt unsettlingly isolated as I turned out the light. If something happened during the night - a heart attack, a burglary, a murder, say - I wouldn't be able to call for help. I could yell, but even if my neighbor heard me, she wasn't likely to do anything until it was too late. "'That dreadful lawyer next door, always screaming bloody murder in the middle of the night.'" There wasn't much I could do about it. I punched the pillow and pulled the covers over my head. Betsy would just have to protect me. With that uncomforting thought, I fell into an uneasy sleep.

I overslept again the next morning. What was the matter with me? My body seemed to crave unconsciousness. I was still bleary-eyed when I stumbled into work, about an hour late, with my suit rumpled and my hair sticking up. Who should I bump into, of course, but Marshall Farr, the most important person at the firm.

Marshall didn't waste any time. "Jack! Where have you been? I've been trying to reach you at home."

There would be no ribs for Betsy tonight. Bread and water were too good for that dog. "I'm sorry, Marshall," I said. "My dog ate my telephone."

"What?" Marshall looked momentarily nonplussed, then comprehension lit up his eyes, and he grinned. "Ah, yes, I remember Betsy from soccer. Quite a handful." The light went out of his eyes, and he was all business again. "Look, Jack, I'm going to be in and out of the office for the next couple of days, and I need someone to cover a hearing for me. It's a case Harmony and I were working on together, and I need someone to argue a summary judgment motion. You shouldn't feel any pressure. We know we have a slim chance of prevailing, but it's an important motion strategically. We're just trying to educate the judge before trial. Can you handle it?"

A summary judgment hearing where no one would be mad at me if I lost? What a great gig. "Sure, Marshall, I can do it," I said.

"Good." He handed me a thick black binder. "Here's the argument notebook Harmony prepared." He glanced at his watch. "The hearing's in 35 minutes."

Damn, damn, damn, damn, damn. I skimmed the argument outline and pleadings on the bus to the courthouse. I was too nervous to be mad, but my mood had not improved at all when I opened the binder and saw the name of the case: Brand v. Crabfest Seafoods, Inc. Alfonse Brand was Harmony's least-liked opponent. He lied, he whined, he threatened. He also complicated matters by developing a severe crush on her. He used to offer her candy during depositions. He also used to call her up a lot, and he got mad when Harmony told him that ethical rules forbade her to talk to him without his lawyer present.

Brand's lawyer was Harmony's least-liked opposing counsel. Boyd Tate was a sole practitioner, and a true blowhard in the classical sense. He was the guy all the lawyer jokes are about. Together, Brand and Tate had sorely tested the guiding principle of Harmony's practice: You don't fight fire with fire. You fight fire with water.

Last year, Harmony had won a partial summary judgment against these clowns. She got the judge to knock out three improper defendants and a whole slew of frivolous tort and contract claims. I had sat in during the argument. I had a legitimate reason to be there - I was waiting for an opportunity to present an *ex parte* order to the judge - but I had come down extra early so I would get to see Harmony in action.

She had blown me away. She was so calm and so controlled. I don't know how she kept her composure. Tate yelled, banged the table, kept calling her "dear," and at one point, charged toward her shaking his fist, his already ugly face an even uglier shade of puce. I was ready to punch him right in the nose, but Harmony didn't flinch. She kept her gaze fixed on him, as if he were a harmless and only mildly interesting kind of fly, and she couldn't be bothered to swat him. She never even spoke to him during the argument; all her energies and attention were focused on the judge. The more Tate raved and blustered, the more courteous and patient Harmony became. It made Tate look - unsurprisingly - like a total jerk, ill-tempered, illogical, and ill-prepared.

By the time she sat down, Harmony seemed like the only reasonable person in the courtroom, and Tate seemed like a blithering idiot. The judge granted Harmony's motion from the bench, complimented her on her brief and her performance, and then said sharply, "Mr. Tate, I trust that neither Ms. Piper nor myself will be subjected again to a debacle of this enormity?"

It took Tate a few seconds to decipher all those big words. Then he rose weakly, opened and closed his mouth a few times, and then said, "No, of course not, Your Honor . . . and Ms. Piper." Harmony smiled warmly at him and said, "Thank you." She paused just a fraction of a second and added, "Dear."

I had never seen a judge guffaw before. Everyone laughed - everyone except Tate, that is. Even Mr. Brand, who had just seen four-fifths of his case go right down the toilet, slapped his knee and howled.

As the bus pulled into Pioneer Square, I wrenched myself from my reminisces of Harmony's argument a year ago and forced myself to concentrate on the current motion for summary judgment. I wanted to argue as well as she had last year. I got off the bus, ran up both escalators, and headed down Third Avenue to the courthouse. I fumbled in my pocket for spare change as I passed through the constant gauntlet of panhandlers along the courthouse wall. I'd rather give my money away than lose it to the light-fingered kids who hung around the key tray at the metal detectors.

A daunting line curled in front of the metal detectors and revolving doors. I had only ten minutes until the argument. To keep from screaming and pushing to the front, I tested myself on the facts of the motion. After getting most of the case dismissed last year, Marshall and Harmony were seeking summary judgment on the one remaining claim: racial discrimination. Mr. Brand insisted that Crabfest Seafoods had fired him because he was white. Crabfest Seafoods insisted that it had fired Mr.

Brand because he had attacked a coworker with a 12-inch gutting knife. We were arguing that the knife attack was a legitimate, non-discriminatory reason for the firing, and that Mr. Brand could not show that this reason was a pretext for racial discrimination.

All in all, it was a solid motion, except that Crabfest had only suspended, not fired, a black employee who had attacked a coworker with a jagged clam shell. Harmony's brief argued persuasively that the greater danger posed by the knife attack meant that Brand and the black employee were not "similarly situated," and therefore, that Crabfest's decision only to suspend the black employee did not raise an inference of racially discriminatory discharge of Brand. We ought to win, but Marshall was right. If the judge didn't want to make the call - and risk being reversed on de novo appeal - he might well send the case to the jury.

I rushed through the metal detector with five minutes to spare. As always, the lobby smelled strongly of popcorn, thanks to the little snack bar in the corner. On my first trip to the court, the snack bar had displayed a disquieting sign: "Welcome to the King County Courthouse. Please unload gun and remove ski mask before entering." Then a deranged husband had burst into family court and shot and killed his wife, his unborn child, and two other women. The sign had come down - and the metal detectors had gone up - within days.

The lobby was mobbed with people waiting for elevators - jurors, defendants, court watchers, and reporters. I caught the eye of The Seattle Times court reporter and waved. I had worked with him on forcing access to the records of the Grange. After a few minutes, it became clear that I was not going to get on an elevator in time, so I ran up the stairs instead.

With one minute to go, I was outside the courtroom, panting slightly, but pumped and ready to argue. No sign of Brand or Tate. I peered inside the courtroom. There was a trial going on. I sank onto the bench outside the courtroom and thought about this for a moment. Now that I had a chance to reflect, I was pretty sure it was Thursday. That made this whole emergency argument assignment very odd, indeed. Most judges heard summary judgment motions only on Fridays. I rubbed my temples. Could it be Friday? I thought back over my weird, wrenching week. It could be Friday, I decided after a moment, but it probably wasn't.

I considered my options for determining what was going on. I could call Marshall and look like a fool. I could call Tate and look like a fool. Or I could tiptoe into the courtroom, try to engage the bailiff's attention, and look like a damn fool. What the hell? I opened the door as quietly as possible and slipped inside.

Judge Brady looked up and frowned as I entered. Great. I edged over to the bailiff and explained my predicament.

Her blank, bored expression quickly changed to amazement. "The Brand summary judgment?" she said. "We heard that last Friday. Harmony Piper argued. She won."

75

It was my turn to be amazed. I was stammering about Marshall and Harmony's father and how sorry I was to have disturbed the trial when she put her hand on my arm. "It's OK. The judge will want to talk to you. Have a seat."

I was expecting a judicial tongue-lashing when Judge Brady called a recess and waved me and the bailiff into his chambers. I was wrong.

"It's Jack Hart, isn't it?"

"Yes, Your Honor," I said, surprised.

"I remember you from the Motorhead trial. You did a fine job."

This couldn't be what he wanted to talk to me about. "Thank you, Your Honor."

Judge Brady seemed to be making up his mind. Then he said, "Jack, is Harmony Piper all right?"

I caught my breath. I'm sure my shocked look answered his question. When I had collected a few of my wits, I said, "She hasn't been to work since her father died. I don't know how she is."

Judge Brady exchanged significant glances with his bailiff. "Humphrey Piper was a law school classmate of mine. Last night, I went to the private service for his friends and family. And Harmony wasn't there. Now, I could imagine Mieko's not being there; she's always been flighty. But I couldn't imagine Harmony not coming to her own father's memorial."

He polished his glasses and continued: "When no one could tell me where she was, I became very concerned. You see, there was an incident in court last week after the summary judgment hearing. I take it she didn't tell you about it?"

"Your Honor, I'm not sure she even told anyone that she won the summary judgment. Or even that she argued it last week. The partner running the case sent me down to argue it today."

"Well, she argued it last week, all right. And she won. I announced my ruling from the bench, and Mr. Brand, well, Mr. Brand became agitated."

"He kicked his chair over, spat on the floor, and overturned the counsel's table," the bailiff chimed in. "Then he went over to Harmony, put his face next to hers, and started screaming at her. Tate actually tried to stop him, but he just kept screaming. I called security and cleared the courtroom. We tried to have Harmony escorted back to her office by the police, but she wouldn't do it. She laughed it off."

I felt sick. What if the police and I had been barking up the wrong tree for days? I should have thought about Alfonse Brand. I should have told the police about him. I knew he had had a crush on Harmony and been angry at her when she wouldn't take his calls. I was such an idiot. I was such a prize-winning, prototypical, Exhibit A idiot.

I didn't want to know, but I had to ask: "What did Brand say when he was yelling at her?"

Judge Brady and the bailiff exchanged looks again. Judge Brady cleared his throat. "He said, 'You bitch. I'll get you, you fucking bitch.'"

ALL GOOD THINGS

CHAPTER 18

I delivered Judge Brady, the bailiff, and the bloody book to Detective Anthony on the fifth floor of the Public Safety Building. Then I excused myself, went into the bathroom, and threw up.

Afterward, I leaned against the sink and washed my face and hands over and over. I rinsed my mouth with cold water until my teeth ached and my tongue was numb. My head felt leaden. I toweled off, shut my eyes, and tried to concentrate on Betsy, on work, on the weather. On anything. I wanted to crowd out any thoughts involving Brand, Harmony, and a gutting knife.

I was making myself repeat the multiplication tables when I remembered a friend from law school who had spent three ghastly years as a child advocate. Her boss, livid because she was crying in her office after a particularly grisly case, had screamed at her, "I don't ever want to see you cry again! Why can't you just go into the bathroom and throw up like a man?"

Vomiting, I thought. One of the many grand traditions of the Bar. They somehow neglect to mention it in law school. Then I staggered back to the toilet and was sick again. When I finally emerged from the bathroom, Mark was waiting for me. He handed me a can of Sprite.

"Feeling better?"

"Yeah," I lied.

I sipped the Sprite and choked. The bubbles scalded my raw throat. Mark pounded me on the back. "Don't jump to conclusions," he said, pounding pretty hard. "Brand could just have been blowing off steam in that courtroom. We don't know if he was anywhere near Harmony that night. We're going to pick him up now, and we'll know a lot more in a couple of hours. Until then, there's nothing you can do here. Go home or go back to work."

"I should have told you about him. I knew he had a crush on her, but I didn't even remember him. If I had just thought about it harder - "

"You still wouldn't have remembered him. You didn't know what he said in court on Friday. None of us did. So just calm down and stop blaming yourself. We don't have time for it." He leaned closer and lowered his voice. "This is not about you, Jack."

His intensity shut me up. I took a big gulp of Sprite and got it down this time.

"Are you feeling well enough to make it to Mr. Piper's service?"

"Yeah. I'm OK." I wasn't OK, but I was OK enough. "I just have to stop by the office on the way."

Mark retrieved my coat from the bathroom, where I had forgotten it. He miraculously produced my briefcase, which I also had forgotten. I had pressed the button for the elevator when I heard someone shout behind me.

"Hey, Oden! We got the priors on Brand." The elevator slid open. I stopped the door with my hand. The shouting continued, softer but still plenty loud enough for me to hear: "You were right. He's a rapist. Three arrests and one conviction."

I was too far away from the bathroom to be sick again. I just turned around and looked down the hall. Mark was standing next to someone who was handing him some papers, but he was staring right at me. I held his gaze for what seemed like a long time. Then I couldn't stand it anymore, and I burst into the elevator, breathing hard and shaking my head.

I ran all the way back to the firm. I must have looked like death, because even the panhandlers didn't try to stop me. When I got to my office, I shut the door and leaned against it. Gradually, my breathing slowed and my heart rate returned to something approaching normal. I sank into my chair and reached blindly for a Kleenex. My hand touched nothing but air. I looked around. Someone had moved my box of Kleenex.

When I examined my desk carefully, I could see that someone had moved a couple of things. I wasn't fastidious, but I depended on certain things being in certain places so I could do several different tasks at once without having to waste time on logistics. I could talk on the phone and complete and turn in my time sheet at the same time, for example. Now I tried to flick a time sheet toward my out-box; it fell a few inches short of the goal. There was a clean strip of otherwise dusty desk beside the box. Someone had moved it over.

Well, I knew Janet had needed a file, but I wished she'd put my stuff back where she found it. She would have a fit if I trespassed on her sacred desk, with its incomprehensible filing system and its cup of dauntingly sharp pencils. "A sharp pencil is a happy pencil," Harmony had whispered to me once, as we'd both watched Janet grind an entire boxful into barbs. I had never seen Janet use one of them; I think she kept them at her desk as a trap for the unwary. I felt like going over there, rearranging her files, and breaking every one of her points.

I took a deep breath. My annoyance at Janet had calmed me a little. It was the first time since Monday morning that I had felt my usual, mild irritation with the petty indignities of life. How I had missed mild irritation and petty indignities! I stretched and glanced at the clock. I wanted to make sure I was on time for Mr. Piper's service. If Harmony was OK, I didn't relish the thought of eventually having to explain to her why I hadn't gone to pay my respects to her dead father. And if Harmony wasn't OK

- not that I believed for a minute that she wasn't OK - then I needed to go to the memorial as her proxy.

I stopped by Marshall's office and left the <u>Brand</u> argument binder on his chair. I peered at the jumbo planning calendar by his door. Why had he thought the argument was today? Thursday, October 26, was clear except for a 9 a.m. Governing Committee meeting and a brief note about Mr. Piper's noon memorial. I looked at Friday, October 20, the day the argument had actually taken place. There was nothing about the argument, but the day had been crossed out.

On my way to the elevator, I passed my secretary and asked her to pull the <u>Brand</u> pleading and correspondence files from Janet's "Harmony" drawer. I would need them to draft the final order, judgment, and cost bill for Judge Brady's signature. My secretary grimaced, and I beat a hasty retreat. Much as I objected on principle to asking my secretary to do something I didn't want to do, in this case, it was better her than me. Janet may have hated everyone except Harmony and certain exalted senior partners, but she seemed to hate male associates more than she hated anyone else.

I was a few minutes late to the service because the elevator was slow in coming and all the church parking spaces were taken up by limousines. I had to squeeze into a pew with Charlie Snow and some other associates. The place was packed. A sea of jet-black hair near the front caught my eye. Wow. I knew the firm had flown in a lot of our Asian clients, but this was really impressive. I counted about three solid rows. As I looked around, I was struck by the number of people I had seen only in pictures. The partners in charge of each of our twenty offices were here, as well as all the members of our Governing Committee. We had about forty partners and twelve associates stationed overseas, and it looked like the firm had brought them all back to Seattle for this memorial.

I was startled to realize that all the attorneys from my firm were wearing Piper Whatcom name tags. Tacky, tacky, tacky, but it was a touch that Mr. Piper would have loved. He was the master of client development. Thank goodness I had been too late to be accosted, identified, and branded by our marketing director.

Dan Bradford was in the pulpit. "We in the legal profession must both embody and reconcile a host of competing interests and influences," he was saying, flinging his arms wide. "The adversary system itself is premised on the clash of great opposing powers - plaintiff versus defendant, justice versus mercy, the spirit versus the letter of the law." My jaw dropped. He was giving my speech - the speech I had written for the Korean clients - as a tribute to Mr. Piper.

Dan lowered his head, as if overcome by emotion. "Lesser men see opposition as something to be not celebrated, but destroyed." He threw back his head and gazed toward heaven. "But when great powers meet, they meet not in battle but in marriage. Through opposition, these great but complementary differences create balance: balance in our economies, balance in our cultures, balance in our lives. East and West, import and export, attorney and client: they are bound together in balance. They are the yin and yang, but together they make the whole."

Dan clasped his hands in front of him, as if he were praying. "Humphrey Piper understood this ancient Asian principle," he concluded. "Humphrey could see that Piper Whatcom was out of balance, that it was teetering, if you will, on the edge of this vast continent, and he, um, reached across the sea to grasp the hands of those of you who join us today from the Pacific Rim. And in so doing, he founded a synergistic partnership, he created the bridge over which this firm can travel to the next millennium. It is a privilege to pay tribute to him today."

Well, at least I didn't write that last bit. Dan sat down with a flourish. He caught my eye and grinned.

Jeremy Smith was next. He looked, as always, a little jumbled and off-kilter, as if he were not so much one whole person as a composite of every boss, bully, and teacher who ever made you feel small. His head seemed far too large for his body. His tie was crooked, and his glasses tipped at a disconcerting angle. The joke among the associates was that Jeremy was always so disheveled because he couldn't see his own reflection in the mirror.

Actually, Jeremy looked not so much like a vampire as a giant praying mantis. He craned over the microphone and hissed a few sour words of homage. Humphrey was a success because he saw work as an opportunity, not a burden, and adversity as a chance to regroup instead of an excuse to fail. All of us, particularly those just starting out, should heed Humphrey's example. While he may not have been thought of as a lawyer's lawyer, he had been an unparalleled client developer, and the firm would be the poorer for his death.

It fell to Marshall Farr to give Mr. Piper a proper eulogy. He did a good job. He told about starting on the same day as "Humphrey," and how they had struggled through their grueling first year together. Polite but strained laughter came from the associates, who were thinking, to an associate, "You had three staff members to every lawyer and no billable requirement. Tell us again how much you suffered." At least, that's what I was thinking. Then Marshall wound into Mr. Piper's many awards and accomplishments, which, I had to admit, were phenomenal. It sounded as if he'd started, directed, revamped, or conquered every prominent organization in town.

Marshall's final topic was Mr. Piper's service to the firm that bore his name. Under Humphrey's leadership, Marshall said, Piper Whatcom had rocketed from a sleepy Seattle firm to a vigorous, nationwide partnership. And thanks to his efforts in Asia, Piper Whatcom had found a cherished and much appreciated place on the Pacific Rim. Big, muscular Marshall gave an odd little bow to the front rows, which bowed back to him. He concluded by announcing that the Governing Committee had voted unanimously that morning to retain the Piper name in the title of the firm.

As he put it: "Even death cannot separate Humphrey Piper from Piper Whatcom & Hardcastle. We are the firm we are today because of him. None of us will ever forget him. The overwhelming attendance of our members, from the most junior associate to the most senior partner, is evidence of the place Humphrey held - and will always hold - in our hearts and minds. We are here to thank him, to remember him, and to say goodbye."

Charlie Snow passed me a note. I unfolded it and read: "And to make absolutely, positively sure he's dead."

CHAPTER 19

here wasn't much left of the formal service after Marshall's speech. A beautiful lady in black sang "Abide with Me," and quite a few people cried. I'm not sure whether they even knew Mr. Piper, but the lady had a thrilling voice, a voice that seemed to throb like the beating of wings. We had a moment of silence, and the priest asked whether anyone would like to share a memory about Mr. Piper.

A few partners rose to express their thanks for the help Mr. Piper had given them in building their practices. Brent Sang, a disgusting, brown-nosing associate from our Salt Lake City office, got up and said that Mr. Piper had been the second-best role model and teacher at the firm, exceeded only by the living, present partner in whose pocket he was trying to ride to the top. There were murmurings among the associates, and even some flinching among the partners. Oh, well. Brent was up for partner this year. The Salt Lake City office was new, small, struggling, and somewhat overlooked by the firm. I guessed that Brent was overjoyed to have the opportunity to brownnose firm-wide. Mr. Piper could not have died at a better time.

After Brent had finished groveling, a white-haired Asian gentleman stood and started to cry. It was the first genuine emotion I'd seen for Mr. Piper, and I strained to hear him clearly.

In soft and lightly accented English, the older gentleman said that he had lost not only one of his best lawyers but one of his best friends. They had met thirty years ago when he had been doing graduate studies and Mr. Piper had been on the Board of Regents at the University of Washington. A recent immigrant from Japan, he had had few friends. The Pipers had almost adopted him. He had lived with them for four years - rent-free - during which time Mr. Piper had introduced him to all the important people in Seattle.

The associates were looking at each other in surprise. This was a different side of the Antichrist. The man wiped his eyes and continued. He told about returning to Japan and starting his own business. I couldn't hear the name. He told how happy he had been when Humphrey had offered to be the company's outside counsel. It was a decision he had never regretted, he said. No one could have worked harder for his company than Humphrey. Even when he called him late at night, Humphrey would be in the office. Humphrey had worked tirelessly for him. Humphrey was - Humphrey was . . . . He stopped, unable to continue.

I think everyone was relieved when Marshall got up quietly, slipped an arm around the white-haired man's shoulders, and guided him with gentleness and respect to a seat of honor at the front of the chapel. Then he whispered something in the priest's ear, and the priest rose, told us that he was sure we all shared Mr. Yamashita's warm feelings for Mr. Piper, blessed us, and let us go.

Mr. Yamashita. Thirty years ago. He must have been living with the Pipers when Harmony was born. I wanted to talk to him. I looked for him in the chapel and in the church reception hall, where our marketing staff had laid out a lavish buffet. Just as I reached the door to the parking lot, I saw him slip into an enormous limousine, flanked by large, unsmiling guards, and drive away.

I went back into the reception hall. The buffet looked sumptuous and wonderful, glistening with bowls of shrimp, platters of cracked Dungeness crab, and sides of red, velvety smoked salmon. After the morning I'd had, however, I didn't dare eat. I looked for Marshall so I could explain about the argument, but he was surrounded by clients and partners, all talking at once. Mr. Yamashita's moment of tenderness and raw grief hadn't quelled the attendees' commercial tendencies. The hall rang with the braying, boasting, and fake, hearty laughter that accompanies lawyers at lunch. It was too much for me. I headed for the door again.

"Hey, Jack, where's Harmony? Why isn't she here?" Charlie Snow fell into step beside me.

The real answer was so painful that I was surprised when I heard myself respond in a perfectly normal voice: "There was a private service last night for the family. This is just a business event for Mr. Piper's clients and colleagues."

Charlie seemed satisfied and thrust a dripping chicken sate at me. "You know, you ought to try one of these, Jack. They're really good."

I declined, and Charlie wandered off. Brent Sang was heading straight for me, hand extended and face alight with a dazzling smile. The silly up-for-partner git was working the room and had mistaken me for a someone who could vote for him. How insulting. I couldn't have aged that much since Harmony had disappeared. I grabbed Brent's outstretched hand and pulled him toward me.

"I'm only an associate," I muttered in his ear. "Don't waste your time."

Brent's Miss America smile disappeared immediately. He looked almost human again. "Hey, thanks, man," he said. "Sorry about that, but I've got to make the most of this opportunity. Where do you think I should start?"

"Get to Marshall if you can. He likes to talk about sports and how he saved the firm after Mr. Piper overextended us by opening all those offices. All that nice stuff he said about Mr. Piper at the service was just fluff. He can afford to be magnanimous now that Mr. Piper's dead. Marshall likes flattery, but don't be too obvious. He's smart. You'll have to make him think you're discerning, not fawning. Don't waste your time with Jeremy Smith. He doesn't like anybody, and you're sure to say something wrong. If you know any good dirty jokes, try them out on Dan Bradford, but make sure he tells you his dirty joke first. He can only remember one, and if you tell the joke he was going to tell, he'll never forgive you."

Brent was looking at me with something approaching gratitude. "I owe you one, um -"

"Jack Hart," I supplied for him, inwardly rolling my eyes. Brent and I had met on at least six occasions, and I had had to tell him my name every single time. "Good -" Brent resumed his dazzling smile and was already off backslapping and shaking hands. "- luck," I finished lamely.

If that was you had to do to become a partner, I wasn't sure I wanted it. I turned around and almost bumped into Dan Bradford, who was devouring a jumbo shrimp. He slapped me on the back. "Jack! How'd you like the speech?"

"It sounded vaguely familiar," I said.

"Well, I stopped by your office last night to tell you to write me another one, but you had already gone home, you lazy bastard. Think the invaluable Korean clients noticed the duplication?"

"I'm sure they were all too overcome with grief," I said.

Dan cackled with laughter. "Right. As are we all, of course." Then he was off to tackle bigger fish or additional shrimp. I couldn't tell which.

I was almost to the door when Jeremy intercepted me. He was pocketing his cellular phone. One of our big real estate clients was having trouble with a major tenant that was threatening to break its lease. We needed to file pleadings for a temporary restraining order by noon on Friday. Friday, I thought wearily. That would be tomorrow. "Have the drafts on my desk by 8 in the morning, Hart," he snapped. He glared at me. "As I recall, you need some pretty heavy editing."

Finally, I escaped from the crowded hall. I checked my voicemail at a pay phone down the street, just in case Mark had left me a message about Brand. I was still mad at him for not telling me what he suspected about Brand's criminal record, but I figured he had kept silent to spare me the worry. Oddly, that just made me even madder. He had no business assuming I would freak out when I learned that Harmony had been threatened by a convicted rapist. The fact that I had freaked out was immaterial; he still should not have assumed.

Nothing from Mark. Just a bunch of client calls and a peevish message from Jeremy. In the tumult of the morning, I had completely forgotten to call him back about his earlier question. I left him a return voicemail with the answer. I didn't bother trying to explain why I was late in getting back to him: a) he wouldn't care; and b) he wouldn't believe me. Then I left Marshall a message about the argument. It was hard not to sound aggrieved, so I tried to keep it light: "Hi, Marshall. Good news about the Brand summary judgment. The judge granted it. But it actually turned out that he granted it last week. I guess Harmony took care of it before she left."

On the way to town, I stopped at Bartells' drug store and bought a plug-in, stay-put phone. I bought the cheapest one in case Betsy decided to attack it when my back was turned. As I neared the Denny Regrade, I decided to make a perfect day complete and stop and see my mother. If I could get her financial whining straightened out, it would be one less thing on my mind.

Mom lived in a restored 1920s apartment building, which was built in a U-shape around a small garden. A high iron fence topped with spikes discouraged prowlers, and Mom said she felt perfectly safe in the garden even at night. The garden had white benches, lots of trees and flowers, and a fountain in the shape of a woman stepping into a spring. The building was between two busy, downtown streets, but in the garden you could hear only the splash of water - and the occasional fire engine.

I let myself in through the front door and climbed the stairs to Mom's apartment. I knocked. No answer. I knocked again, and this time I heard a noise, as if someone were standing on the other side, waiting for me to go away. I called, "Mom? Are you there? It's Jack. I've come to talk to you." Nothing. I tried again. "Mom? It's Jack. I've come to talk to you, and I've brought my checkbook."

I heard the noise again, but Mom didn't open the door. If the checkbook didn't smoke her out, nothing would. I had a key to the place, but I couldn't bring myself to use it. There are things you don't want to catch your mother doing, and I figured that my mother had probably done – and was doing – them all. As I turned away, I heard a sigh, as if the person inside were relieved that I was leaving. It was a sad and broken little sound. It seemed way too wistful and innocent to come from someone like my mother.

I paid the rent before I left, just to save a stamp. My mom's landlady seemed unusually taciturn. She called me Mr. Hart instead of Jack. She didn't respond to my harmless inquiry about her health, and she looked the other way when I ventured a pleasantry about the weather. Strange; usually, she was a bit of a flirt, and always liked a chat. I must have lost my touch. Or maybe I still smelled like vomit. I was too worried and tired to care.

I parked in a garage a few blocks away from the firm. Partners got free office parking, but associates didn't, and most of us couldn't afford to park in the building. As I neared the firm, I began to notice police cars and firetrucks here and there on the street. I stepped up my pace. More police cars and firetrucks. There were people everywhere. Now I was running. A piece of yellow police tape was stretched in front of our vast, arched doors. A huge policeman caught my shoulder as I dashed toward them.

"Please," I panted. "I'm not trying to make any trouble. Just please tell me one thing. Are Detective Anthony Anthony and Officer Mark Oden in there?"

The policeman paused. "What is your name, sir?"

I told him. He almost lifted me up the steps, under the tape, and into the building. He pointed. "Over there."

Police were all over the place. Mark and Anthony were talking to a young man in a forest green uniform who was sitting on the floor near the freight elevator. The man's face was the same color as his clothes. A sharp, cheesy stink made me gag as I approached them. I wasn't the only person who had thrown up that day.

Mark looked up as I came closer. He put himself between me and the freight elevator. I forgot all about being mad at him. I was so scared that I didn't even care when he put his hands on my shoulders and pushed me back against the wall. The cool marble was actually kind of comforting and supportive. Mark spoke very slowly and very calmly.

"Jack, we have to ask you to do something. We found a body. It's a woman. It might be Harmony. It might not be Harmony, but we have to make sure. And there are reasons why it's going to be hard to make sure."

I opened my mouth, but nothing came out. I couldn't move. I just looked at him.

"Jack, we have to ask you: Would you be able to identify Harmony from one of her hands?"

ALL GOOD THINGS

CHAPTER 20

Mark sat with me in the lobby as we waited for the police technicians to make sure that the elevator was structurally safe and could support my weight. Everything seemed to be happening in slow motion and to someone else. I had heard myself say, "One of her hands? Her hand? What do you mean, her hand?" Then the thought of that 12-inch gutting knife had sliced through my voice, and I couldn't say anything more.

Mark was talking to me quietly, trying to calm me down. No, the body wasn't dismembered, he said. But it was stuck on top of the elevator, and all they could see clearly was one hand. As for the rest of the body, it had been seriously damaged, probably from a fall down the elevator shaft. A conventional identification was out of the question. If I didn't recognize the hand, they'd have to rely on the crime lab and dental records.

"How did you know she was there?" I asked.

"Your freight elevator started to malfunction late this morning. They checked the electronics and the wiring and finally figured out that the problem had to be some damage to the structure itself, the sheaves and the door mechanism, or something. They called the maintenance company, and when the maintenance man opened the ceiling emergency door and looked up, well, he found her."

The maintenance man must have been the green young fellow sitting in a pool of his own vomit. I swallowed hard. "Is it - is she - is the body - bad?"

"Yes," Mark said. "She's crushed."

I couldn't think about this anymore. If I thought about going into that freight elevator and examining a lifeless hand, I wasn't going to be able to do it. "Tell me about Brand," I said.

Mark hesitated.

"I've got nothing left to throw up."

"We're holding him for questioning. When we first brought him in, he insisted that he didn't mean anything by what he said in the courtroom, and that he'd been with his girlfriend all night Sunday and Monday. That alibi fell through almost immediately. We caught the girlfriend last week with some coke, and she was eager enough to swap Brand for a break on the drug charges. We told Brand that his girlfriend wouldn't back up his story, and, just to turn up the heat a little more, we told him that we had matched his prints to ones on the bars and keypad of the Pipers' security gate."

"You had?"

"Yeah. And there are footprints there, too. The tread comes from a common kind of tennis shoe, but it was in Brand's size."

"What happened when you told him about the girlfriend and the prints?"

"He got scared. We Mirandized him. He said he wouldn't say anything else until he talked to Tate." He paused. "Tate is a dick. Anyway, after about fifteen minutes with Tate, Brand came out with a completely different story."

This was torture. "What did he say?"

"He admitted that he had been outside the Pipers' gate on Sunday night and early Monday morning. He said that he just wanted to talk to Harmony about his case. Actually, first he claimed he wanted to apologize for his behavior in the courtroom, and we said, 'By waiting outside her house in the middle of the night?' Then he said that he just wanted to 'scare' her a little."

"Did you charge him with kidnapping Harmony?"

"No."

"Why the hell not?"

"There's more."

"Sorry."

"He and Tate could tell we weren't buying it, and Brand started to spill his guts. I mean, really babbling. He admitted that he had wanted to break into Harmony's house. He said he tried to crack the security code first, but couldn't. Then he tried to scale the fence, but he saw some headlights down the street and jumped off and hid in the bushes. He saw a blue BMW drive up to the gate, and a woman lean out of the driver's window and enter the security code. The gate swung open and the woman drove up to the house. Brand said he decided things were getting a little crowded for what he had in mind, so he got out of there."

"And you believed him?"

"I don't know whether I believe that he got out of there, but I do believe that he saw a woman in a blue BMW open the security gate. He got the time exactly right: 2:45 a.m."

"He could have known the time because that's when he opened the gate himself."

"Possibly, but there aren't any footprints on the other side of the fence. Besides, he described the woman in the car pretty thoroughly. He said she was 'kind of an old broad, but still a looker.' And it so happens, there is a woman involved in this mess who drives a blue BMW and who is kind of an old broad but still a looker."

It had to be Janet. Janet Daniels drove a BMW? I was in the wrong business. "You mean Janet?"

"Her Royal Highness. We're trying to get her in for a lineup and a little talk, but she didn't come to work today, and it looks like she hasn't been at her house in Leschi for quite a while. She didn't happen to be at that memorial service, did she? We had some plain-clothes guys there, but they couldn't find her."

I tried to remember. All I could picture were Dan's histrionics, Brent's brown-nosing, and a sea of puzzled, indistinguishable faces. "I don't know," I said. "I don't recall seeing her, but it was so crowded that she easily could have been there." I was quiet for a moment. "You think Janet killed Harmony?"

He looked up at the high, vaulted ceiling and sighed. "I think Janet has a lot of explaining to do."

"Did Brand see Harmony in Janet's car?"

"There was someone in the passenger seat, but the passenger side is in shadow from that big hemlock. He couldn't tell who it was, not even if it was a man or a woman."

"Or alive or dead?"

"No."

Anthony called "Oden," and gestured to us to come over. "You ready?" Mark asked.

"No. But I'm ready to get it over with."

With Anthony on one side and Mark on the other, I stepped into the freight elevator. The elevator car was painted white and brightly lighted. A woman's arm dangled through a dark hole in the ceiling. I flinched when I saw her black sleeve. The hand was streaked with dried blood and blue-black at the finger tips, but the unbloodied skin above was very white. Harmony was always very pale.

Anthony put his hand on my back. "Take your time, son."

I blinked and made myself take a step closer to the hand. The black sleeve had a nubby texture. Harmony's black dress was smooth. What had her black coat looked like? I couldn't remember.

I forced myself to scrutinize the hand, even the horrible, blackening fingertips. The palm was facing me. To see the top of the hand, I had to skirt around the dragging arm and look at it from the back of the elevator. I gasped when I saw the fingernails. They were long and pointed, polished a dull, dark red. Harmony's fingernails were short and round, always faintly pink or beige. Ladylike. I remembered her hands tapping on away at her brief around midnight.

Relief gushed through me. "It's not her. It's not Harmony," I said. Both Mark and Anthony exhaled noisy. I realized they had been holding their breath.

"Let's get you out of here," Mark said.

As I edged around the hand, a memory rustled in my mind. The woman was wearing two large rings. One was set with a deep red stone; the other was a heavily carved gold band. I had seen those rings before. The woman's fingers were curved, as if she were reaching down to pick something up.

I stopped suddenly, and Mark crashed into me. The elevator shuddered, and the woman's arm began to sway. We all stared at the arm, transfixed. I don't know what Mark and Anthony were seeing, but I was seeing Harmony's pen on the floor with a dark stain by the nib, and a thin, ringed hand, silhouetted against Harmony's white office wall, reaching down from above. The rings were the same ones I had seen on Monday, when I had crawled under Harmony's desk to get her pen. And so was the hand.

That could mean only one thing.

The woman on top of the elevator was Janet Daniels.

by Rosemary Reeve

CHAPTER 21

"Have you noticed," Mark asked, "that every time we think we have a suspect, she ends up very, very dead?"

We were up on the 42nd floor. I was standing awkwardly by the reception desk as policemen and policewomen dusted, searched, and examined. It seemed like hours had passed since I'd stood beneath Janet's dangling hand.

"Yeah, I have noticed that," I said. "It's like someone's one step ahead of us."

"Or several."

"Just promise me that you won't decide I'm a suspect again. I'd hate to be strangled, and I'm afraid of heights."

"How about being stuffed in a suitcase?"

"Nope. Claustrophobia, too."

I felt ridiculously and unaccountably cheerful. I hadn't lost my mind, and I hadn't forgotten what was going on. I could still feel the cold hand of fate on my shoulder. I still knew that Harmony was missing, that there was a murderer on the loose, and that every minute that ticked by meant it was less and less likely that we'd ever find her alive. And I could still hear the dry whisper of my own fear, taunting me, threatening me, and saying, "Just you wait. Just you wait and see how this is going to end."

But the point was, it hadn't ended. Not yet, at least. It could have ended there at the elevator. After that talk with Mark, after that black sleeve, after that white hand, I had thought it was over. I had really thought it was over. I remembered the despair that had flooded through me when I saw the white skin streaked with blood and thought it was Harmony's skin and Harmony's blood. It was the worst thing I had ever felt in my life, worse than the day when I woke up and found out that my dad had left my mom, worse than the day when my mom had taken me to Child Protective Services, turned around, and walked away. I could still see her turning around, and it still hurt, but even then, even right when it happened, there was always the possibility that my mom would come back. Janet Daniels wasn't coming back.

And maybe Harmony wouldn't come back, either, but I didn't know that yet, and I didn't have to suffer through it until I knew. Or until the days turned into weeks, and the weeks turned into months, and the months turned into years without her, and I finally had to admit that, for whatever reason, I wouldn't see her again. But right this minute, Harmony had been missing only three-and-a-half days. The murderer had taken no particular care to hide his victims; if Harmony was dead, why hadn't the police found her body? Because she was still alive, I told myself over and over. And I had to do everything I could to find her. I felt like the condemned man who gets a 48-hour reprieve because the executioner has had a death in the family.

Detective Anthony had been talking to Marshall on the phone at the reception desk, explaining the scope of the search warrant and working through protections for privileged materials. He hung up, chuckling. "That Marshall Farr of yours is a smooth one," he said. "When he heard that the police would be in the building for the foreseeable future, he immediately decided that Mr. Piper deserved more than a church service and a few plates of smoked salmon, and he closed the firm for the afternoon. He's taking all your best clients over to the Seattle Tennis Club for a lubricated wake. I guess he didn't want them coming back here and being fingerprinted or strip searched or whatever it is he imagines that we do."

"Marshall is king of damage control," I told him. "When he was chair of the Hiring Committee, he hired a lateral to work on a high-profile case, and the guy totally screwed it up. We almost lost the client, and the partners were screaming for blood. Somehow, Marshall managed to convince everybody that the case was hopeless from the start, and that he had purposely sacrificed the lateral so that the 'real' partners wouldn't be tainted with a very public and humiliating loss. And you know, it worked. Within a couple of days, people were marveling at Marshall's strategy and nerve. A few weeks later, the Governing Committee announced that he was our new managing partner."

"What happened to the lateral?" Anthony asked.

"Oh, he was long gone by then. I think Marshall called him in the courtroom and told him not to come back."

"Why do you stay here, Jack?"

The concern in his voice caught me off guard.

"I don't know," I said after a moment. "I summer clerked here. I've spent four years here. I'm learning a lot. They seem to like me; they say they like my work. It means a lot to me to be around people who think I do a good job. And as for all the bad stuff, I guess I don't believe it would be any different at another firm. I guess I just don't know where else I'd go."

Anthony nodded. "Well, if you decide to get out of here, I want you to give me a call. There are a lot of places that I bet you haven't even thought of. The prosecutor's office, the FBI. The police department, for instance."

I must have looked startled, because he smiled. "By the way, you look exhausted. We don't need you here right now, and you probably can't get much done with us around telling you where to stand and not to touch things. Why don't you go home and get some sleep?"

I shook my head. "I can't. I got a new assignment at Mr. Piper's memorial service."

"You have got to be kidding," Mark said.

"Unfortunately not. And it's an emergency. Is it OK if I just work on it in the library? I'll stay out of everybody's way."

With Anthony's assent, I settled down in the library at one of the computer-equipped study carrels. I had thrown together emergency restraining order pleadings for this client before. I pulled up my previous pleadings. All I really had to do was figure out what was going on in this dispute, replace the fact section of the brief, draft supporting declarations, and find caselaw and rewrite the argument section to support issuance of the restraining order on these new facts. If everything went well, I was looking at ten to fifteen hours of work. That would give me plenty of time to take a break and go home and feed Betsy. If everything didn't go well, I would be working on this clear up to Jeremy's 8 a.m. deadline. Everything would just have to go well.

It took a lot of time on the phone with the client, but by 6 p.m., I had the fact section written and the supporting declarations drafted and faxed to the client for approval. I stretched and figured out how many hours I had until eight o'clock in the morning. Fourteen. Time enough for dinner.

I grabbed my coat and briefcase and dropped copies of the declarations on my secretary's desk. I sat down in her chair to write her a note about finalizing them and getting them signed before 11 a.m. As I pulled myself up to her desk, my feet hit something hard. I bent down and found three banker's boxes, each stuffed with the Brand files I had asked her to pull from Janet's file drawers.

I winced at the size of the Brand case: thirteen pleading files, three correspondence files, and one Harmony Piper desk file. I was going to have to go through all those pleading files to draft the final order, which had to list every pleading that had been presented to Judge Brady. I'd start with the cost bill instead of the final order, I decided. It would be easier to pull all the receipts from the correspondence files and Harmony's desk file than it would be to identify the hundreds of pleadings submitted during 14 months of acrimonious litigation.

I tucked the correspondence and desk files into my briefcase. If they were at home, I'd have an excuse to leave work early tomorrow. Once I got the restraining order pleadings filed, I'd just have to go home so I could draft the Brand cost bill. And I really would draft the Brand cost bill tomorrow afternoon - but not until after lunch and a nap. Good plan.

I put on my coat. On the way out, I stopped by Mark and Anthony to let them know about the Brand files my secretary had taken from Janet's desk. They were examining Janet's cubicle. I told them I was going home to Betsy, but that I would be back in a little while if they needed me.

"Couldn't this motion wait, Jack?" Anthony asked. "The night doesn't seem to be a healthy time for people at your firm."

"Under our motion to shorten time, we have to have the pleadings in by tomorrow at noon. The partner will need to review them beforehand. Then I'll need a couple of hours to finalize them and get them down to the court. I can't work on them at home. I need the library and the documents here."

"Is this another phantom emergency?" Mark asked, examining a green glass sea urchin on Janet's desk. "Like that snipe-hunt argument this morning?"

"No. The argument was for Marshall. He just doesn't pay attention to case schedules and deadlines and stuff. He figures that's what associates are for. But this temporary restraining order is for another guy, Jeremy Smith, who never forgets anything. And he expects us not to forget anything, either. If he says we have to file these pleadings by noon, then we have to file them by noon."

"Achk!" Mark had encountered Janet's cup of sharpened pencils. His exclamation of pain was followed by a string of creative curses. "You know, Jack," he said, as he sucked the puncture wound on his palm, "no offense, but I'm really starting to hate your firm."

I was way ahead of him there. As I drove home in the soft, moon-lit drizzle, I thought back over Anthony's question. Why did I stay at Piper Whatcom? I worked like hell, I didn't make all that much money, and the only partners I didn't dislike were those I actively despised. Rather to my surprise, I had had opportunities to leave, but for some reason, I still stuck around.

Loyalty? Cowardice? Inertia?

Stability, I decided. The firm had been there almost a hundred years. It would be there for the next hundred years, and probably a hundred years after that. If I played all my cards right and kept my socks up and my nose brown, there was a chance that I could stay there forever, that I could grow up and grow old and die as a well-fed, well-trained, mildly prosperous Piper Whatcom partner. There were better lives, but there were a lot worse ones, too. There was a lot to be said for stability.

And, then, of course, there was Harmony. There was a lot to be said for Harmony, too.

ALL GOOD THINGS

CHAPTER 22

M y house was suspiciously silent. No barking, no growling, not even a snarl. I paused outside the door. Betsy was either luring me into a false sense of complacency, or she was dead. Both alternatives were horrible to contemplate.

I flung open the door. No Betsy. Good heavens, she must be dead. I dropped my briefcase onto the hall table and rushed into the house. "Betsy!" I shouted. "Betsy! Come here, girl!" To my amazement, there she came, galloping toward me from the kitchen, ears flapping and tail wagging. I braced myself, but she didn't attack. She just ran in circles around me, barking and wiggling. Warily, I sat down on the floor and started to pet her. She snuggled into my lap, put her front paws on my shoulders, and licked my face.

The only reason I could imagine for this unprecedented display of affection was property destruction so extensive that even Betsy feared the consequences. I would get up and investigate in a while, but right this minute, I was busy cuddling my dog. There would be plenty of time later to respackle the walls or lay new carpet in the hall.

I shut the front door, leaned against it, and closed my eyes. Betsy squirmed over on her back. I tickled her under her chin. My hands buzzed with needles of pain, as if they were asleep. All the exhaustion, anxiety, horror, and despair of the past twelve hours seemed to swoop down on me again. The relief and euphoria I had felt when I realized that it wasn't Harmony's body on top of the elevator had ebbed away during the dark, wet drive back home. Now all I could think of was Harmony out alone in this cold, rainy October night.

Then I thought of Janet Daniels, and her long, dark plunge to oblivion. I shivered. I had never liked Janet, and I didn't mourn her at all, especially if she had been the person who had lured Harmony out of the building. Still, no one deserved a forty-two-story tumble down an elevator shaft. Was it suicide or murder? Mark and Anthony weren't saying. For Janet's sake, I hoped it was murder. I hoped she was dead before she fell.

Betsy seemed to sense my change in mood. She squirmed back onto her feet and faced me. She walked around to my side and dropped her head on my shoulder. I put my arm around her and massaged her ears with my other hand. Then, just for safety's sake, I reached up and locked the door.

I didn't want to get up. I didn't want to make dinner. I didn't want to go back to work. I just wanted to sit here in the dark with Betsy and try not to think. But I was afraid of disappointing Jeremy Smith. Actually, I was just flat afraid of Jeremy Smith. I waited until Betsy seemed restive but unsure of how to disentangle herself with dignity. Then I stood up and said, "Dinner, Bets?" She was off to the kitchen in a blur of orange fur.

I gave her a heaping bowl of kibble and a lot of praise for being such a good dog, then set about feeding myself. I didn't have any bread. No milk, either. I'd drunk the last of it that morning. There was a quarter of a carton of cottage cheese in the refrigerator with a use-by date of the next day, but I hated cottage cheese. Besides, Betsy was territorial about cottage cheese, which she considered her exclusive luxury breakfast fare. I didn't want to do anything to ruin her mood. So I dumped the last of the cottage cheese on top of Betsy's kibble and looked for something else to eat. They really ought to make Single Male Associate Chow.

The cupboard was bare. Finally, I found a can of chicken noodle soup propping open the basement door and decided to have that. I sniffed the soup skeptically as it was heating. It had a strong, medicinal smell. It had a strong, medicinal taste, too, I realized as I sipped a bit, and it was a peculiar pinkish color. I tipped it down the garbage disposal and sighed.

I sat on the floor again, held Betsy's food dish on my lap, and petted her while she crunched her dinner. At least one of us was enjoying herself. I passed the time consoling myself with warm, loving thoughts of the best meals I had ever eaten. That was something I owed to Piper Whatcom. Up until recruiting season of my second year of law school, my idea of a really great meal had been two peanut butter sandwiches instead of one. I wasn't prepared for the smorgasbord of law firm recruiting. I had eaten at the best restaurants in the city with one potential employer or the other, and after a few tentative moments ("I'll have the ham sandwich, please"), I had learned to enjoy them very much. The restaurants, that is. I had eaten better during those few weeks of law school recruiting than I ever had in my entire life - except for ten beautiful days last summer, when Harmony brought me dinner every night.

It was after my accident on the soccer field. I was out of the hospital but confined to bed to guard against pneumonia. Harmony had shown up around 5:30, laden with plastic bags from the Market. She had propped me up on the couch, brought me iced tea, and told me all the firm gossip while she grilled salmon and made scalloped potatoes.

She had come every single night to make me dinner: steak with fresh chanterelles, halibut with asparagus, even prime rib - which she served with mashed potatoes and dark, silken gravy. The only reason I didn't ask her to marry me right then was that I thought she'd say no.

It wasn't the food, I thought, as I let Betsy into the backyard so she could romp a bit. It was the time and effort and care that Harmony had lavished on me. No one had ever made something so special just for me before. I knew how busy she was. She was hurtling toward trial in <u>Brand</u> and spending most of her days preparing for, taking, and defending excruciating depositions. Yet she had shown up every night at 5:30, which was about the middle of her workday, and had spent two or three hours with me, cooking for me, talking to me, and trying not to make me laugh because she understood that it really hurt.

I had screwed it up, I thought sadly as I changed my clothes, dried Betsy's fur, and gave her a pat goodbye. I locked the door, got into my car, and started toward town, remembering. The first day I had hobbled back to work, Harmony had come by my office, given me a careful hug, and asked with a radiant smile, "So, what do you want for dinner tonight?" And I, thinking that she had been looking after me because of residual guilt about my accident, chafing at the thought of being anybody's charity case, and not wanting her to feel obligated anymore, had said, stupidly, "Oh, that's OK, Harmony, you don't have to. I'm feeling much better."

She hadn't said anything more about it, but her smile had dimmed, and she had changed the subject. She had never come over to my house again. And when I realized what I had done, how dismissive and ungrateful I must have sounded, and how hurt and awkward I must have made her feel, I couldn't figure out how to repair the damage. We were still friends, and we still enjoyed lunch, coffee, and gossip together, but I felt like a wall had gone up between us. It had driven me nuts, but I didn't know how to tear it down.

On the way back to the office, I stopped at Dick's Drive In and ordered two cheeseburgers and two orders of fries to go. In the lobby of our building, I stopped to talk to Frank, who was looking a little spooked behind the security desk. I was feeling a little spooked myself, I told him.

"Chris isn't feeling well, and I'm taking half of his shift besides my own," he said. "So I'll be here all night. Call me right away if you see or hear anything suspicious."

"Don't worry. You'll be able hear me scream even though I'm up on the 42nd floor."

He laughed, then stopped as the sound echoed around the empty lobby. He jerked his thumb toward the freight elevator. "Bitch of a way to go. Chris said they made you identify the body."

"Yeah. It took a few years off my life."

"You want to keep from losing a few more years?"

"Yeah."

He pointed to my blue and orange Dick's sack of cheeseburgers and fries. "Don't eat that. I had a friend who came down with appendicitis right after he'd gone to

Dick's, and when the doctors heard where he'd been, they wouldn't believe that it wasn't food poisoning until they actually did a blood test."

"Oh." I looked longingly but dubiously at the warm, greasy sack, which smelled of salt, charred meat, and marvelously crisp potatoes.

Frank reached for it. "Here, Jack, I'll throw it away for you."

I snatched the sack away. "Nice try," I said over my shoulder as I headed for the elevators. Then I turned around and dumped one cheeseburger and one packet of fries on his desk. Frank looked up in delight. "Hey, thanks, man," he said, stuffing his mouth with fries.

"We'll die young together," I said.

Up in my office, I devoured my remaining burger and fries without ill effects. I licked my fingers and got down to work. I wanted to get this done, get out of here, and get home to Betsy. She was being such a good girl, and her good behavior was so rare that I hated to miss it. I worked steadily and intently until midnight, when the lights in my office went out. Not a problem. All the lights in the office tower went out automatically at 12 a.m. and 2 a.m. to conserve power and save the guards and custodians from having to switch them off individually. Only dim backup lights in the library and elevator wells stayed on.

I yawned and stretched. All I had to do was get up, walk a few paces to the wall, and switch my office lights back on again. But it just seemed like too much trouble. The rain-softened aura of the city lights and a fat, peekaboo moon filled my office with misty silver. As my eyes adjusted, I found that I liked this diffused, soothing light. It gave just enough of a glow so that I could keep working in front of my blue, illuminated computer screen.

I tapped away for a while, but the cool shadows in my office were too seductive. Exhaustion overwhelmed me. I put my head down on my desk. I would rest for a minute and try to get my second wind. Or my third wind. Or maybe fourth.

I don't remember sleeping, but I must have dozed for at least a while. I didn't hear a knock, and I didn't hear the doorknob turn.

But when I woke up, the door was opening.

by Rosemary Reeve

CHAPTER 23

screamed. The door slammed shut. I sat there gasping. Had I dreamed it? I couldn't tell. Had I just scared the shit out of some hapless custodian? I didn't care. He had certainly scared **me**.

I jumped up and turned on the lights. Then I wedged a chair beneath the doorknob and called Frank.

"Are the custodians still cleaning the 42nd floor?"

"I don't think so. Why?"

I told him what had happened. He told me to stay put until he got there. Even though I knew he was coming, I still jumped when he rapped on the door. "Jack, it's Frank. You OK?"

I opened the door to the dark hall. Frank had a walkie talkie in his hand. I would have been happier to see a gun. He whispered: "The police will come in five minutes unless I call them back."

Five minutes? What was this five minutes crap? We could both be dead in five minutes. I started to voice my opinion, but Frank put his finger to his lips and gestured for me to follow him. Most reluctantly, I did.

The halls were quiet and very dark. The custodians had closed all the office doors, so not even the moon or the city lights could filter through. As we approached each door, I kept expecting it to burst open in a hail of bullets. But it didn't. We moved quietly down the hall. We saw and heard nothing - until we rounded the corner. Before us was a trembling lattice of light on the hall carpet. The pattern was beaming from the miniblinds on the conference room's glass door, and the blinds were swaying slightly. A shadow moved across the lattice. Someone was in that conference room.

Frank motioned for me to go back the way we had come and stand just around the corner. I could see the glowing door of the conference room reflected in the corner window, but I could also slip into the darkness of the hall without being noticed if I moved quickly enough. Frank flattened himself against the wall on the far side of the door. I had to admire his nerve. Then he reached around and hammered on the door.

"This is Security! Open this door immediately and come out with your hands up!"

I heard a kind of wail in the room. Then the door swung open and a big, gawky man came out with his hands in the air. His face was shadowed by the half-open door.

Frank caught the man around the neck and pressed the butt of the walkie talkie into his back. "What is your name and what are you doing here?" he demanded.

I heard a panicked squeak, and even before the man answered, I knew who it was. That prize ass Charlie Snow. Prankster, clown, and cutup. The bane of our first-year associate class. I had just made Frank play Dragnet and put the entire police force on red alert because Charlie Snow was up to his old tricks. I should let them drag him down to the police station just to teach him a lesson. No, on second thought, I had developed too much respect for the Seattle Police Department during the last three days to waste their time with Charlie.

Frank had Charlie pressed face-first against the wall and was pummeling him with questions. Could he prove his name was Charlie Snow? Could he prove he worked here? Did he have any identification? Did he have a grudge against Janet Daniels? Where was he Monday morning at 2:11?

Frank was good at this. Charlie was blubbering weakly that yes, he had identification, that no one liked Janet Daniels, and that he was home in bed at 2:11 Monday morning, which is where he would be right now if it wasn't for that asshole Jack Hart. I leaned against the wall, tapped him on the shoulder, and said, "What was that about Jack Hart?"

Charlie yelped. He looked wildly from me to Frank, as if he weren't sure which was more dangerous, me or the guy pressing the walkie-talkie against his back. I was an avowed pacifist if not a full-fledged coward, but I knew that my size, scars, and broken nose gave me the look of a prize-fighter. I hunched my shoulders for a more menacing effect and repeated my question.

"Jack, I am so sorry," Charlie stammered. "I didn't know you were in your office. I've been working on this document review assignment you gave me, and I couldn't find one of the client binders. I thought it might be in your office. I didn't mean to scare you. There wasn't any light under your door, and I really didn't know you were there. Honest."

Charlie was so wretched and sincere - and so sincerely wretched - that I felt bad. Through the half-opened door, I could see the piles of documents I had told him to review. I nodded to Frank, who holstered his walkie-talkie and went off to call the police and tell them not to come. When he saw that he had been terrorized by a walkie-talkie, Charlie regained some of his aplomb.

"If it's any comfort," he said with an uncertain grin, "when you screamed, you scared me so bad that I very nearly wet my pants."

"That's more than I needed to know, Charlie," I said, backing away. Then I looked at his tired, pale face and said, "Hang on a second."

I went over to Frank, who had just finished talking to the police. "Thanks a lot," I said. "You were great. I owe you at least a week's worth of Dick's burgers. I'm sorry about," I jerked my head toward Charlie, "**him.**"

Frank laughed. "That's OK. I'd rather get a false alarm than a bullet between my eyes any day. By the way, next time be a big spender and spring for the extra five cents to get onions on those burgers." He gave us both a little wave and disappeared into the elevator well, whistling merrily.

I shooed Charlie into the conference room. He went unwillingly, clearly thinking I was going to make good on my threat to hang him from the chandelier by his tie. I let him stew for a minute while I inspected the piles of documents on the marble table. He really was an ass, but he was doing a good and careful job on my document review. His privilege log was clear and detailed, and he had flagged responsive documents with tabs color-coded to each request for production.

He was watching me anxiously. I didn't have the heart to punish him anymore. "I'm sorry, Charlie," I said.

He blinked. That was not what he expected.

"I didn't mean for you to have to stay here late to get this done. I wish you'd told me that you needed more time. I could have tried to get an extension from opposing counsel."

When Charlie realized that I was serious and I wasn't toying with him, he blurted, "I would have got it done today, but Marshall said that we needed to honor Mr. Piper. We all went with him over to the Seattle Tennis Club, and I got quite thoroughly drunk in honor of Mr. Piper, out of the deepest respect, you know. I didn't remember that you needed these documents reviewed by Friday until, well, almost until Friday. But I'm nearly done."

I looked over the binders full of untouched documents. "You are?"

"Yeah. I mean, I will be done."

"When?"

"Oh, six or seven more hours. Maybe eight."

I patted him on the back. "Charlie, find a convenient stopping place, then go home and get some sleep. I'll call opposing counsel first thing and ask for an extension. I think I can still get him to agree. He's your standard jerk, but he'll need a favor from me sooner or later, and he won't want to piss me off this early in the case."

Charlie looked at me like I'd lost my mind, but he wasn't going to argue with the gift of a night off, no matter how deranged he thought the grantor. I left him to his documents, turned on all the lights up and down the halls, and attacked my brief with renewed vigor. I'd wasted almost thirty minutes in napping, terror, and skullduggery. That was .5 of an otherwise billable hour.

By 1:45, I was ready to go home. I printed out the pleadings, stamped them "DRAFT," put on my coat, turned out my light, and took the stairs two at a time up to Jeremy Smith's office. I arranged the drafts carefully on his immaculate desk. Then I went down the stairs and got an associate overtime parking sticker out of our receptionist's desk. The partners kindly made it possible for us to park free in the building from 6 p.m. to 6 a.m. Big of them.

I was walking into the elevator when I realized that I should have left Jeremy a voicemail about editing the pleadings. The facts required us to walk a delicate line, and I knew from bitter experience about Jeremy's penchant for overstatement. How do you tell a partner to rein in thirty years of exaggeration, embellishment, and ridicule? I didn't know, but I was going to have to do it. We didn't have the facts to support Jeremy's usual blunt instrument kind of argument.

I was walking away from the elevator and composing a tactful voicemail in my head when I saw the light come on in my office. I heard a metallic racket, as if someone had just knocked one of my big document binders off the shelf. Charlie! I regretted my earlier kindness. I really was going to dangle him from the conference room chandelier this time. By his feet, I decided.

"Charlie, didn't I tell you to go home?" I yelled. The noise in my office stopped. The light went out. What was the moron playing at?

I was almost at the door when I saw the gun. The person holding the gun was shrouded in the darkness of my office, but I could see the gun itself quite clearly. It was a serious steel gray, and it was pointed right at me. Then three things happened at once:

I flung myself against the wall.

The gunman squeezed the trigger.

And all the lights went out.

ALL GOOD THINGS

by Rosemary Reeve

CHAPTER 24

W
as I dead? No, I was way too scared to be dead. I rolled across the hall, as far away from my office as I could get. I could see the faint silhouette of the gunman in my office doorway. Then he stepped away and disappeared into the dark hall. I could hear his slow, deliberate footsteps. He was coming toward me.

The gunman zigzagged slowly from one side of the hall to the other. I guessed he was trying to find me so he could make sure I was dead. I didn't know what to do. If I made the slightest noise, he would know where to shoot. But if I didn't move, he surely would stumble over my body - step on my hand or stub his toe against my ribs - as he moved from side to side across the hall. And then he certainly would know where to shoot.

He was just a couple of feet away, over by the far wall. If I didn't do something, I was going to die. I decided to crawl forward, moving one arm and one knee every time the gunman took a step. Maybe any noise I made would be drowned in the sound of his walking. If so, I had a chance of surviving a few more minutes. If not, not.

I tensed, waiting for him. I heard the creak of his shoe as he lifted one foot, and I moved one hand and one knee forward, placing them on the carpet as silently as I could. Then I heard the creak of the other shoe, and I moved the other hand and knee, placing them just as silently as I heard his footfall. Two large steps for the gunman, six small inches for me. So far, so good.

The gunman took two more steps. I crept forward six more inches. From the sound of his footfall, we were a few feet apart and almost parallel. If he took three steps straight across the hall, he would run right into me. My only hope was if he was moving diagonally across the hall, moving forward and to the side at the same time. If so, I might be able to inch up just enough that he would miss me.

Step and crawl. Step and crawl. The gunman's foot came down just a few inches from my right ankle. I felt the indentation of the carpet. I held my breath. He stepped away from me. I didn't dare crawl. He was too close. He stepped again, and I inched forward. Step and crawl. Step and crawl.

I had made it. He was behind me. Each step and crawl put more distance between us. He was going slowly up the hall, and I was going even more slowly down it. I guessed he was heading for the main switch at the top of the hall, the one that would flood the hallways with light. I was heading for the document room kitty-corner to my office.

The document room was an internal office; there was no window against which I would be silhouetted. It was huge and honeycombed with shelves, cabinets, file carts, and enormous boxes - all places where I could hide. It also had a phone in it somewhere, although I couldn't quite remember where. I thought it was mounted on the wall. If I could open the door, creep in, and shut the door silently behind me, maybe I could call for help before the gunman realized where I had gone.

Step and crawl. Step and crawl. I was just two feet away from the document room door. Between me and the room was the shaft of moonlight beaming from my open office. To get to the room, I would have to cross that shaft. If the gunman so much as glanced behind him, I would be spotlighted for him in the darkened hall. He really wouldn't be able to miss me.

I paused at the edge of the moonlight, terrified of leaving my shield of darkness. If only the moon would go behind the clouds! It didn't. I forced myself forward. I was a goner if the gunman reached the light switch before I was safely inside the document room. Step and crawl. I was right in the middle of the moonlight. Step and crawl. I was halfway through it. Step and crawl. I was at the door.

I grasped the doorknob. It turned smoothly. Gently, very gently, I leaned against the door, letting my weight open it slowly as I disappeared inside. The door was halfway open. My head and shoulders were in the room. I was trying to sidle the rest of my body through the half-opened door when it happened.

One of the hinges squeaked. In that silent, darkened hallway, it sounded like a shriek. I heard an exclamation, and I jumped up blindly just as another gunshot filled the air behind me. The force of the report flung me into the room. I slammed the door. I scrambled for chairs, tables, file cabinets, anything to pile in front of it. I could hear the footsteps pounding toward me. There would be no time to try to find the phone.

The gunman was kicking the door. It shuddered and bowed under the blows. It would be only a few moments before my makeshift barricade gave way. I pushed a few more shelves in front of the door and struggled through the dark room, bumping into files and fumbling over boxes. There was another door in the room's far corner. If I could get out that door, I would be able to slip through another dark hallway into the back of the library. The library had plenty of telephones. It was my best bet.

I found the door and opened it with a pounding heart, expecting to be greeted by a gunshot. Nothing. I peered into the inky hallway. I couldn't see or hear anything. On the tips of my toes, I scuttled down the hall and through the back entrance of the library, just as all the lights came on in the hallway behind me.

I gasped as I opened the library door. A large blond man in a blue sweatshirt was coming toward me. I was paralyzed with terror for a moment - until I realized that I was looking at my own reflection. The backup lights in the library were dim but still bright enough to turn the high, arched windows into mirrors. Damn, damn, damn.

I couldn't go back into that bright hallway. If the murderer was at the hall switch, I would walk right into his line of vision. I had to keep going into the library. I had to turn off those backup lights somehow.

There was a panel of switches just before the library opened into space for the study carrels. If I could get over there, I could turn out the lights and call 911 from one of the carrel phones. I would be exposed for about ten feet, but I didn't have much choice.

I was about five feet from the switch when I heard the footsteps. I froze. Nothing happened. I glanced up. For a split second, I saw the reflection of the gunman in the mirror-like windows. A big man in black. If I could see him, he could see me. I hit the ground just as he aimed and fired.

I heard a tremendous shattering of glass but felt nothing except a rush of air. He had shot my reflection, not me. An enormous black hole gaped in the golden windows. I leapt for the light switches, and the entire library went dark.

Or almost dark. The moon was flickering weakly behind a mass of mottled black clouds. It gave just enough light so that every shelf and shadow looked like a man ready to pounce. I slipped between the last pair of shelves before the study carrels. I breathed a little easier. At my back were the CCH tax reporters, big black binders thick enough to stop a cannon ball. In front of me were the official NLRB reporters, a wall of massive, mustard-colored volumes. Even a bullet couldn't struggle through their small print. I was cloaked in the shadows of the huge books and high shelves. Unless the gunman turned on the lights or actually walked between the shelves, he couldn't see me.

I strained to hear the gunman's footsteps. There was a bank of light switches at the very front of the library. I heard a faint sound not too far away. Was the gunman moving toward the switches? No, I realized with alarm. He was moving toward me. I could hear him walking between the shelves, shelf by shelf, working his way slowly and deliberately to the end of the library – the end of the library, where I was cowering between the tax books and the NLRB opinions.

I inched toward one end of the shelf. I saw the gunman's shadow as he turned into another pair of shelves. He was only two shelves away from where I stood, weaving through them, looking for me. I considered my options. I couldn't get out the back way because I'd be exposed in the open for at least 15 feet. Even if he didn't see me, he'd hear me.

There was a passage on one side of the shelves that led to the front of the library. It was feathered with moonlight. If I tried to escape down it, the gunman was sure to see me or my shadow as I raced by him. I could slip into the study carrels, but they were moonlit, too. And if the gunman found the light switches, he'd have no trouble picking out my head or feet even in the maze of carrels.

There was no way out. I was cornered, and I was going to have to fight. I was going to have to take him down. I said a prayer, stretched my arms wide across the NLRB reporters, and waited.

by Rosemary Reeve

CHAPTER 25

I waited as the gunman walked to the end of the third-to-last row of shelves. I waited as he rounded the corner to the second-to-last row of shelves. I waited as he started to walk down the row.

I waited until he was right in front of me, separated from me only by the shelves and books. Then, with all the force I could muster, I shoved the books through the shelves with a tremendous crash. Books flew everywhere. The gunman cried out and crumpled under the onslaught of NLRB reporters. I kicked the shelves over on top of him and raced down the corridor.

I skidded to a stop in front of the elevators and pressed the button frantically. I could hear smashing and swearing from the library. It was coming closer. I hammered the button again. I heard feet beating down the corridor. I was ready to run when suddenly an elevator door shot open. I threw myself into the car and hit and held the close button. The elevator well plunged into darkness just before the elevator door slid shut. I pounded the button for the lobby, but I couldn't get the button to light or the elevator to budge.

I heard the gunman struggling and grunting on the other side of the elevator door, and I knew what he was doing. He was holding down the elevator call button. That's why the elevator wouldn't budge. It was confused. It didn't know whether it was coming or going. I splayed my fingers and ground my hand into the close and lobby buttons. Unless one of us let go, the elevator would stay right there with the door shut. If he let go, the elevator would plummet to the lobby. If I let go, the elevator doors would open, and he would kill me. I couldn't let go.

The gunman started kicking at the elevator doors. They shook and creaked, but they held. I kept a death grip on the close and lobby buttons as I fumbled for the emergency telephone. A long, thick-bladed knife stabbed through the crack in the doors and began to twist. The gunman was trying to pry the doors apart. I managed to knock the phone free and screamed, "Frank, it's Jack. Take all the elevators down to the lobby right now!"

I kept screaming in the general direction of the phone as I hung onto the buttons with one hand and grasped for the knife with the other. I had to wrap my hand around it to keep it from twisting the doors apart. Even with my hand cushioned by my sweatshirt, the knife sliced deeply into my wrist and palm. I somehow managed to hold it straight.

The elevator lurched, and wonderfully and miraculously, the car began to drop. Frank had heard my screams for help. I pushed desperately against the knife. If I couldn't get it out of the door, it would wedge against the ceiling of the elevator and stall the car. I shoved it over and over, cutting my hand anew each time. The gunman was holding the knife firm, still trying to twist the doors open. As the car dropped, my grip on the knife lifted me off my feet. I held my breath and let the knife take my weight. The shock and pain of the resulting cut were dizzying, but my weight knocked the knife out of the door. I went crashing to the floor of the elevator.

The car plummeted toward the lobby. I knelt on the floor, clutching my wounded hand in my sweatshirt, the rush and swaying of the elevator making me lightheaded and sick to my stomach. It seemed like such a long way down.

I remember landing at the lobby. I remember Frank's voice, calling me. I remember yelling his name. At least, I thought I was yelling. It sounded deafening to me in the elevator. I remember looking up and seeing Frank framed in the doorway. I remember Frank holding my arm. I remember seeing blood all over and hearing lots of sirens.

But after that, I don't remember very much. The knife had slashed my wrist.

ALL GOOD THINGS

CHAPTER 26

I came to in the hospital. A bright light dazzled my eyes, and my wounded wrist felt stiff and numb. There was an IV in my other arm.

Mark Oden leaned over me. He was unshaven and dressed in a sweat suit. His black hair stuck out in all directions. His voice was tense and tired: "Jack, who did this to you? Who was it?"

I tried to shake my head, but there was something over my nose. I had to lick my lips several times before I could speak. "It was a big guy wearing black. He was in my office, looking for something. Did you catch him?"

"No, not yet. Not that I know of, at least. We were just starting to search floor by floor when I left in the ambulance with you. Was he a stranger? Was he someone you recognized?"

"I don't know. I saw his reflection for just a second. I couldn't make out his face."

"Was he wearing a mask?"

"I don't know. I'm sorry, Mark. I really don't know. Didn't he show up on the camera in the elevator well?"

He moved his hand toward my forehead. I thought he was going to swat me, but he shaded my eyes against the light. "First, you've got nothing to be sorry for. It's a miracle you're alive. Second, no, he didn't show up on the security tape. He turned out the backup lights in the elevator well, and there wasn't enough light for the camera to register a clear image - just a lot of grunting and scrabbling and struggling. It sounded pretty bad."

"It was."

"Tell me what happened."

I told him, in a high, shaky voice that I barely recognized as my own. My voice seemed to ring in my ears. When I finished, Mark said, "Tell me everything you can remember about the man with the gun."

"I already told you. I barely got a glimpse of him."

"I know. Just tell me any impressions you had of him. A sound, a smell, something he said. Anything, even the smallest detail."

I thought about it, reviewing the whole horrible incident in my mind. "His shoes creaked," I said slowly. "He seemed to know his way around the place, but he didn't seem all that familiar with the library. He shot my reflection instead of me. And he cussed a lot when I kicked the shelves over on him."

"Do you remember the specific things he said?"

"No, just the roar of his voice. He sounded furious."

"What was the knife like?"

"It was really long, and the blade was wide and pointed. It was sharp on both sides. It looked like a dagger or a hunting knife."

"Not a gutting knife?" Mark asked, too quickly.

"Mark, I wouldn't know the difference between a hunting knife and a gutting knife. Why do you ask?"

He sighed and rubbed his hands over his hair, leaving it even messier than before. "There was a snafu down at the jail. They released Brand just after midnight."

"What?" I tried to sit up, but I got tangled in the IV and the thing over my nose. "How in the hell did that happen?"

"It was a mistake. They screwed up the date and time we brought him in."

I was speechless. He continued: "We've got units looking for him all over town. The thing is, we can't figure out why he would get into your firm, and we can't figure out how he would get into your firm."

"The custodians," I said, with a suddenness that surprised me.

"What?"

"I don't know why he would get into the firm, and I don't know why he would go to my office, but he could have come in with the custodians. They're independent contractors, not employees of the building, so there's no supervision. He could have offered to take someone's shift in exchange for using their pass card. Or he could have hidden in one of their trash carts and sneaked into a closet or something until he thought the firm was deserted."

Mark considered that. "Would you know Brand by sight?"

"I think so."

"Could he have been the man who tried to kill you?"

"They're both big men, but I don't know whether the guy with the gun was Brand."

"Would Brand know his way around your firm?"

"He should. He was there with his attorney for at least a week of depositions."

Mark got up and introduced me to Officer Sawyer, who mumbled a greeting and clasped my fingers with a clammy hand. Then Mark excused himself, and I tried unsuccessfully to make small talk with Sawyer. He answered my questions stiffly, in monosyllables. Finally, I leaned back against the pillows and shut my eyes as if I were exhausted, which, actually, I was. I was grateful to hear Mark's voice again. I opened my eyes just as he came into view. Sawyer got up and headed for the door without saying goodbye.

"They're already checking out all the custodians who were in your building, and they're on their way to search and dust the trash carts," Mark told me. "Even if Brand got in that way, though, it doesn't explain why he wanted to get in. Can you think of a single reason for Brand to break into your firm and try to search your office?"

"No."

"No evidence or records that he thought you'd have on him?"

"You mean from his discrimination case? No. Everything we had, his counsel could get through discovery. And if he thought we were illegally withholding something, he could ask the judge to compel us to produce it."

"Were there discovery battles in his case?"

"There are always discovery battles in discrimination cases. His had no more than usual, I think. Brand's attorney is such a 24-karat jerk, though, that I think that the discovery battles that they did have may have been particularly bad. If they got really bitter, you'll find the motions to compel in the Brand pleading files."

"What about the correspondence files you took?"

I had forgotten those. "They're still in my briefcase," I told him, then paused. Where was my briefcase? I tried to picture leaving my house last night. "I didn't take it back to the office with me. I left it home on my hall table. There might be some threatening letters from Boyd Tate. That's Brand's attorney. My keys are in my front pocket. Do you want to send someone over to my house to get them?"

"Will Betsy attack the person if I do?"

"Probably."

"I'll come over in a few hours to pick them up, after you've had a chance to soften her up." Mark stretched and groaned. "It just doesn't make sense. Why would he risk going to your firm?" He fell back in his chair and sighed. I tried to turn my head toward him, but I was tethered to the bed.

"Mark, what is this thing on my nose?"

"Oxygen. You're short on hemoglobin right now. You left far too much of your blood back at your firm."

"Am I going to be OK?"

"Yeah. Your hand looks like someone took a meat cleaver to it, but the doctor said the wounds are superficial. Only the cut that nicked the vein in your wrist went deep, and it seemed to miss most of your tendons and things. Try to wiggle your fingers."

I tried. I couldn't feel anything. "Am I wiggling?" I asked.

"You are. Wiggling up a storm. Your arm must still be numb from the shot. Don't worry. You'll be up and making obscene gestures in no time."

Someone yelled "Oden!" from the door, and Mark got up again. "They'll be discharging you soon. Someone is going to take you home, and I want you to lock your door, put Betsy on guard, and stay in bed until I come over to get the files. Understood?"

"Mark, I can't. I've got to get those restraining order pleadings out by noon."

"Anthony's already taken care of that. He called that big jerk you were drafting those pleadings for and told him you had been stabbed."

"He called Jeremy Smith? At home? In the middle of the night?"

Mark nodded.

I whistled. Anthony was one brave cop. "What did the Vampire say?"

"I got the impression that he thought it was imprudent and thoughtless of you to get attacked in the first place, but Anthony was very firm. This is one emergency that Jeremy Smith is just going to have to handle on his own."

"Wow," I said. I added, "Thanks." I had hated the thought of going back to that office. And I always hated the thought of working for Jeremy Smith.

Someone called "Oden!" again, and Mark headed for the door. Then he stopped and turned back to me.

His tone was even but intense. "You know, when I got the call this morning, they told me you had been shot. And I was so worried about you that I didn't even take time to comb my hair."

I managed to keep from saying, "I can tell."

"What I'm trying to say is, I am looking forward to arresting you and Betsy for disturbing the peace for many, many years to come. So watch it. Understood?"

I nodded as well as I could with the oxygen tube on my nose. "Understood," I said.

by Rosemary Reeve

CHAPTER 27

O fficer Sawyer ended up being my ride home. Neither of us seemed thrilled about it. I struggled to get into his car, clutching my prescriptions and a bag of sample antibiotics and pain pills in my one good hand. My other hand dangled uselessly, swathed in gauze and elastic bandages. Sawyer didn't even try to help. He stalked over to the driver's side, slammed his door, and sat there, fuming at my clumsiness and delay. Finally, I just launched myself into the seat. Look, ma, no hands. The car bounced and wobbled under my weight. Sawyer made a disgusted sound.

He didn't warm up on the way from the hospital. He grunted when I asked him questions, he wouldn't let me give him directions to my house, and he made a wrong turn that sent us hurtling south on I-5. He snapped at me when I tried to point out ways for us to get back north to Green Lake. I was losing patience. I was also worried about my house. Betsy had been alone since 8 o'clock last night. It was closing in on 4 a.m. Even a well-behaved dog gets restless after eight hours alone. Betsy was smart and funny and a lot of other marvelous things, but she was a long way from being well-behaved.

I was a long way from home. My arm was throbbing. I wanted to walk into my little house, take my pain pills, and collapse on my bed. Sawyer swore and swerved the car across two lanes of traffic toward the Tukwila off-ramp. Amazing. I was going to Tukwila in a police car - with a disoriented maniac with a gun. Once we were off the freeway, Sawyer seemed even more hopelessly lost. I was going to have to do something if I wanted to get to bed before it was time to get up. Fight fire with water, Harmony had said.

"Officer Sawyer, have I done something to upset you?"

"What?" I repeated my question. There was a long pause. Then he said grudgingly, "No, it's not you."

I was silent. Stillness was another technique I had learned from Harmony. She prodded deponents into the most amazing admissions just by looking at them gravely and silently until they could no longer bear her quiet gaze. I couldn't catch Sawyer's eye, but at least I could let the tension build up in the car.

The tension built. Finally, Sawyer burst out, "It's that asshole Oden."

I kept silent, but with difficulty. Mark Oden was my friend. A long ago, newly recovered, friend. Sawyer continued, warming to his theme: "We came in the same year. We were in the same class at the police academy, and we both took the detectives' exam at the same time, but he's the one who gets all the breaks. He's still a patrol officer, not a detective. But all of a sudden, he's Anthony's right hand on this triple murder. Meanwhile, I'm wasting my time chauffeuring lawyers around town. It's affirmative action, that's what it is. It's just not fair."

Affirmative action? Affirmative action for a guy with a nice Scandinavian name like Oden? Mark had black hair and dark eyes, but he still looked like a big white guy to me. I was too curious to keep quiet. "Is Officer Oden . . . is he . . . ." I cast my mind around for a possible protected ethnic derivation. There was only one that seemed plausible. "Latino?"

"Half, I think. He's a half-breed if I ever saw one. A mutt." Hey, I thought, my dog is mutt. I'm a mutt. You're a mutt. Everyone when you get right down to it is some sort of mutt.

Sawyer looked over at me and sneered. "But he gets all the breaks because he's 'disadvantaged.'"

"What?" I wasn't expecting that.

"You know, a poor little foundling. One of society's victims. His mother was his sister or something like that. And he was in and out of group homes and juvenile detention when he was a kid. A real hellion. Some of the older cops even remember busting him, and they won't have anything to do with him unless they have to. But not Anthony, of course. The minute he laid eyes on him, they were thick as thieves."

"Why?"

"Because he's another one of them, of course." He leaned toward me, sending the car shuddering up the shoulder of the road. "You know that Grange scandal?"

I nodded.

"I took a look at the records before they turned them over to the newspapers. Anthony was there, years ago. 'Anthony Clive Anthony.' There can't be two of those in the world, can there? No, they're one and the same. And ever since Oden arrived, Anthony's been falling all over himself to help him climb the ladder. All the best assignments. All the best shifts. Oden should be out in the rain in a bike patrol around the Market, but he'll probably end up jetting over to Japan on this Piper murder. It's just not fair."

I let Sawyer rave, only half listening. The old foster boys' network. Who'd have thought? Well, it explained why Anthony had been so nice to me. It explained why he had worried about me and sent Mark over with dinner to look after me. It explained why he had told the Vampire that he had to do the pleadings himself because I needed to get some sleep. I guess that was preferential treatment. Preferential treatment not because of who I was but because of what I was. What I had been, at least. Should I feel guilty for that?

No, I decided. Actually, it seemed only fair. Some kids went to prep school at Lakeside and ended up together twenty years later, closing deals in the moneyed mist of the Seattle Tennis Club's steam room. Some kids went to group homes. Some kids went to a bungalow in Tacoma with a big gorilla of a foster father. Some kids, heaven help them, went to the Grange. If there was anything to be gained from being a ward of the State - and I seriously doubted that there was - Mark and Anthony and I deserved it. In spades. In back hoes, even. So Anthony liked Mark because they had a lot in common and because he understood what Mark had gone through to get where he was. So what?

I considered telling Sawyer all that, but he was really seething now. I couldn't get a word in even if I wanted to, and I still couldn't figure out where the hell we were. He ranted on. He didn't like anybody. Blacks, women, black women, Asians, Hispanics, Jews. Poor people. Rich people. Gay people. Mormons. What had the Mormons ever done to him? I was afraid to ask. Everybody was part of a big conspiracy to keep him down. I really should introduce this guy to Brand.

As he vented, Sawyer's driving and navigation became somewhat less erratic. He was trying to wend his way through the warren of streets around Green Lake, but I started to recognize the scenery that whizzed by in the darkness. There was the park, there was the Co-op, there was the house of the nice elderly lady who didn't even get very mad when Betsy barked her cat up a tree. I knew where I was now. Meanwhile, Sawyer was becoming lewder, louder, and harder to ignore. When he launched into a coarse tirade about how he presumed Mark was repaying Anthony for his kindness, I had had enough.

"Stop! This is it," I yelled.

Sawyer skidded to a halt. He squinted up at the street signs. "No," he said, "we're clear at the other end of the street."

"I'll walk," I said, wrestling out of the car. Once I was securely on my feet, I bent down so I could look him right in the eye. "By the way, Officer Sawyer, I am a really good friend of Mark Oden's. We met years ago." I paused. "In a foster home."

I intended to slam the door with drama and righteous indignation, but my burdens and enfeebled condition hampered my swing. It didn't even close completely. Oh, well, at least it would torment him with that awful whistling sound until he pulled over and shut it properly. Sawyer gaped at me, then gave me the finger and sped off. He almost ran over my foot in his hurry to get away.

I walked slowly up the street toward my house. As the glow of my indignation faded, I began to regret jumping out of Sawyer's car. I was tired to the bone. My feet felt flat and clumsy, and there seemed to be too much distance from my eyes to the ground. The moon had disappeared, and it was palpably dark. The porch lights burned, and the black leaves wagged, crackled, and fell in the wind, but the rest of the neighborhood was wrapped in the darkness and quietness of good people asleep.

I was shivering and sweating. I stopped and mopped my forehead with the back of my bandaged arm. I groaned at the immediate waves of pain. I had to get home and take those pills. I kept going up the street, walking slowly and carefully and trying not to move my arm at all. When I started up the path to my house, I was almost faint with relief. My house was quiet. No snarling. No barking. Good. Maybe Betsy was asleep, and I would be able to get in without a struggle. I wasn't up to a struggle right now. Betsy would win, paws down, even before I opened the door.

My front light was out, and my porch was swathed in shadows. I made a mental note to replace the bulb. I cradled the pills and prescriptions in my wounded arm and fumbled for my keys with my good hand. I had my key in the lock and was just starting to turn it when one of the porch shadows moved. I gasped and jerked my head around.

A gloved hand closed over my mouth, and I felt something smooth and dangerous press behind my ear. This was no walkie-talkie.

A low, cold, and somehow familiar voice whispered: "Don't make a sound. Just open the door."

ALL GOOD THINGS

by Rosemary Reeve

CHAPTER 28

I was motionless with shock and fear. The pressure of the gun against my neck
increased. The cold, dry whisper again: "Open it."

My hands trembled as I worked the key in the lock. If I made enough noise
opening the door, I might wake Betsy. I didn't know whether a Betsy attack would be
a good thing or a bad thing. The person holding the gun might well shoot me out of
sheer surprise. But it was pretty clear that Betsy was my only viable line of defense.
I couldn't fight, not with one arm that was stitched up with string and held together
with staples and bits of tape. Please let my crazy dog bark her head off, I prayed. And
please let my crazy neighbor get mad and call the police. Please.

My shaking hand could not get the key to catch. I slipped it out to try again and
dropped the bunch in a sudden tremor of fear. Wrong move. The person with the gun
shoved me into the door, crushing my wounded arm between my body and the frame.
The pain almost felled me. The world reddened and swam before my eyes. I felt like
I was turning inside out.

The voice hissed in my ear: "Pick it up slowly. If you make a sound or try anything
else, you're dead."

I bent and felt blindly for my keys. Nothing. The gun ground into my temple. I
flattened my hand on the concrete stoop, patting desperately. I shifted my weight in
a panic and found a key where my heel had been. I straightened up slowly, and eased
the key into the lock, wiggling it and jiggling the rest to make as much noise as I could.
This time it caught. I heard the click and felt the loosening of the door. Please, I
prayed again, let Betsy bark like she's never barked before.

I turned the knob and opened the door. Silence. No barking, no snarling, no Betsy.
Just the inky darkness of my house. The person with the gun pushed me inside. I
dropped the prescriptions and pain pills on the way. Maybe someone would see them
fluttering on the stoop and get suspicious. If only I subscribed to the morning Post-
Intelligencer instead of the afternoon Times.

The gloved hand came away from my mouth, but the gun didn't move from my
temple. A narrow beam of light snaked over my shoulder and flickered around my
entryway. It came to rest on my hall table - and my briefcase. I swore to myself.
Brand! It had to be Brand. There must be something in the files I had taken home.
He couldn't find them at the firm, so he had tracked me down here. I was so angry

that I almost turned and lunged at him. If I was going to die anyway, I wanted at least to inflict some damage on my murderer.

A throb from my bandaged arm and an answering wave of nausea convinced me of the foolishness of such an attack. Some damage I could do! Maybe I could bleed on him, or possibly even throw up on him, but that was probably about it. He pushed me forward a few steps, so I was just beyond the hall table.

He whispered again: "Kneel down and put your hands behind your head."

I complied, cudgeling my brains. Was that Brand's voice? I wasn't sure I had ever heard Brand speak. Yet it was a definitely a man's voice, and it was definitely familiar. I strained my ears. I heard him behind me, rummaging through my briefcase. I heard a smooth, sliding sound. He must be pulling one or more of the files out of the briefcase. I heard the rustle of papers. It had to be Brand. Who else would want those files?

Then the hopelessness of my position struck me, and I gave up trying to figure out who he was and what he was doing behind me. There I was kneeling on the maple floor that I had so lovingly restored, so weak that I could barely keep my hands behind my head, just waiting around to be shot. As soon as whoever it was had whatever he wanted, I had no doubt that he would kill me. He would probably kill me down in the basement, so as to muffle the sound of the gun.

Well, maybe I couldn't get away, but I could make it hard for him. I debated between rushing him and trying to flee into the darkness of the house. I decided to flee. Maybe I could clobber him over the head with something or stab him if I could get into the kitchen.

I was just about to jump and run for it when I saw her. I could make out only the outline of her tense orange body. She was crouched and ready to spring. Betsy. Bless her mad little heart. Bless her mistrust and her paranoia. Bless all the practice she had had attacking me.

Betsy was a few feet away and inching closer, moving silently on the pads of her feet. She stopped suddenly. My briefcase snapped shut, and whoever it was took a step toward me. The hair rose on the back of my neck. Whoever it was started to whisper again, but his voice was lost in the surge of air and fur. Without a snarl or even a growl, Betsy hurtled over my head, a sleek orange missile. I heard an exclamation and then a shriek, followed by a tremendous crash.

I scrambled to my feet. Betsy was growling now. Growling and snapping and slavering. She sounded like a pack of furious hyenas. What a dog. Whoever it was was cussing and grunting. I heard the tearing of paper or cloth. I couldn't decide whether to join the fray, turn on the light, or try to call the police. I chose the police. I was stumbling down the dark hall when someone or something rushed by me and sent me tumbling to the floor. Someone else trod on my lacerated hand. I screamed. Then I grabbed the person's foot and twisted as hard as I could. I was gratified to achieve an answering scream. I was less gratified to receive a kick in the mouth as the person shook me off.

The back of my head slammed against the hardwood floor. I was stunned for a moment. Then a hand groped my face, and I realized that whoever it was was trying to figure out where I was so he could finish me off. I rolled away from the hand and collided with Betsy, who was huddled by the kitchen door. There was something in her mouth. I canvassed it with my one good hand. It was at least one file. I tried to tug it from her mouth, but she held it fast.

The intruder was fumbling around my hallway and living room, trying to find me and Betsy. Or a light switch, I guessed. Well, he wouldn't find one of those any time soon. My house's obscure placement of light switches was a design flaw, but a fortunate one, in retrospect. I tried to crawl past Betsy to the kitchen. She wouldn't budge, and my bad arm made it difficult to pivot around her. I suppressed a hiss of irritation. I needed to get into the kitchen so I could get to my bedroom - and my phone.

Then the realization hit me, and I nearly screamed aloud with fear and frustration. My phone was sitting in a Bartells' shopping bag in the backseat of my car. My car was parked in the underground garage of my firm. And my firm was miles away in downtown Seattle. What with the body and the elevator and the restraining order, I had completely forgotten about installing the new telephone I had bought on the way back from Mr. Piper's memorial service.

I hugged my oddly still and silent Betsy and forced myself to calm down. It was not easy. We had no way of calling for help without giving away where we were and getting ourselves shot. We had no weapons. We had no way of getting out of the house without whoever it was hearing a floorboard squeak or seeing us silhouetted against the open door.

For the second time that morning, I was going to have to fight.

For my life.

ALL GOOD THINGS

CHAPTER 29

The gunman was coming closer. I tried to think myself back into the intent, instinctive trance I had been in earlier that morning. In the dark halls of my firm, I had synchronized my movements and even my breathing with my stalker so I was silent and invisible. But that was before I had a slashed wrist, a blood transfusion, and a shot of some potent but jittery and rapidly disappearing pain killer. I didn't trust my ears. I didn't trust my reflexes. I didn't and couldn't trust my wounded arm. What defenses did that leave me? Basically, Betsy, darkness, and surprise.

As if she knew I were relying on her, Betsy slipped noiselessly into the kitchen. That left me with darkness and surprise. I struggled to figure out where the gunman was. I was trying so hard to hear him that I was surprised when I actually saw him. Or saw part of him, at least. He was framed in the arched entrance to my living room. A drizzle of gray, pre-dawn light from the open front door briefly glazed his arm and chest. He was wearing something dark and dull. Against him, he clutched one or more of the files he had taken from my briefcase. Was it Brand? It could be. I couldn't tell.

I raised myself onto my haunches, steadying myself in the shadows of the kitchen door. If a soundless leap would work for Betsy, maybe ambush would work for me, too. The gunman moved a little closer, the faint light from the doorway dappling across his dark pants. In a few more steps, he would be right across from me. I would lunge from the side and tackle him.

I concentrated hard on my plan. I was startled when Betsy cuddled next to me. I felt for the file in her mouth, but she must have put it down somewhere in the kitchen. In the file's place was something long and smooth. She let me take it from her. It was one of her much cherished, much gnawed bones. Poor little girl. She was trying to save the thing that made her feel most secure. I tried to put the bone back in her mouth, but she wouldn't take it. She kept nosing it back into my hand. I was simultaneously touched and disappointed. What a loving but useless goodbye present. Then my thumb snagged on a jagged edge, and I almost cried out at the tearing pain. I fingered the bone carefully. In her efforts to dislodge its marrow, Betsy had chewed the bone into a dagger: long and sharp and barbed at the end. If I could sink that barb into the gunman's stomach - or better still, his crotch - it would hurt like hell.

The gunman was almost in place. I rubbed Betsy's jowls and kissed her forehead on the soft, silky spot between her ears. This was a rotten way to say goodbye. We'd just have to make sure it wasn't going to be goodbye, I told myself, with a bravado I didn't feel.

I was summoning my strength and my courage for my desperate leap when Betsy sailed right over me. I saw her arc, swift and silver, in the gathering light. She hit the gunman's chest, but she had started too far back and had squandered too much momentum. I heard her claws scrabbling for a hold on the cardboard file. I heard a horrible slap and a yelp and saw her tumble, ears over paws, fur gleaming and eyes flashing, into the faint pool of light before the door. She righted herself almost immediately and coiled to spring again, but she was too tempting an illuminated target in the darkness.

The gunman's arm came up. He was aiming at her. I lunged. I caught him around the waist with one arm, squeezing as hard as I could to knock the breath out of him. Together, we crashed into my living room and over the back of my sofa. In the confusion, the gunman threw me clear. I struck my head on the sharp corner of my coffee table and twisted on the way down. The gunman stomped on my stomach. I writhed upward and struck blindly with the sharpened bone. I was rewarded with high-pitched scream, but not the death-like crumpling I would have achieved if I had really connected with the goods.

I struck again. This time, my arm went wide, and I barely grazed his leg. He grabbed my wrist and pulled me up. I was bent backwards over the coffee table. I saw the glint of the gun as he aimed. So this was it. This was how it was going to end. Confused images flickered in my mind: Harmony, Mark, Marshall, my mom. Betsy. Lots of Betsy. Betsy sleeping, Betsy eating, Betsy watching TV, Betsy barking. Betsy jumping on my chest and launching herself bodily at the gunman. I didn't quite believe that that last image was for real until the gun went off, a deafening explosion in my little house, and I wasn't hit.

From the sound of shattering glass, I guessed that the bullet had struck my dining room light fixture. Betsy must have knocked the gunman over on his back. The room was silent. Had she knocked him out? There was no time to make sure. This might be our only chance to escape. I struggled up and groped for Betsy. She rushed by me, carrying a file in her mouth. She was bolting for the front door. I followed her, crouched and waddling, in a swift but undignified crawl.

Betsy raced through the front door. I was just a few paces behind her. I was right in front of the hall table when I felt something thud against my shoulder. The impact lifted me and slammed me across the table, crushing my wounded arm under my body. I opened my mouth to scream with pain, but nothing came out - except a trickle of something thick and metallic-tasting. I felt myself slumping and crumpling to the floor. I had no strength in my arms and legs. I couldn't catch myself.

When I hit the floor, the pain suddenly raged through my upper body. It stung like acid on a thousand cuts - on a thousand cuts inside me. Then, just as suddenly, the pain was gone. The world was shrinking rapidly, like a TV going dark, the image trembling and constricting until there was just one bright dot in the middle of the screen.

In my last little bright dot, I saw or heard or felt another shot. I heard Betsy scream.

And all the world went black.

ALL GOOD THINGS

CHAPTER 30

I was with Harmony.

We were sitting together, side by side, in an endless summer clerk committee meeting. The hiring chair was droning on about offering the clerks a glimpse of real-life courtroom practice. The recruiting coordinator turned to Harmony: "Are there going to be any interesting arguments next week?"

Harmony smiled at her and replied, "Well, Jack and I are planning on having a hell of a one."

Everybody laughed. I felt warm. It was the way she said it. Jack and I. As if we were partners. Jack and I. As if we were a team. Jack and I. As if she had taken my hand in front of a crowd of people.

Betsy had trotted into the room. Everyone was petting her and exclaiming over her sleekness and softness: Marshall, Humphrey Piper, Harmony, Charlie Snow, the recruiting coordinator, the hiring chair, Jeremy Smith, Dan Bradford. I was glowing with pride at all the praise. Jeremy Smith turned to me and said, "What a magnificent animal."

OK, that was it. I could make myself believe that Betsy had somehow waltzed into a Piper Whatcom committee meeting. I could make myself believe that Humphrey Piper had come back from the dead just to pet my dog. But no matter how much I wanted to, I could not make myself believe that Jeremy Smith would bestow uncoerced praise on any living creature, especially any living creature somehow connected to me. It had to be a dream.

But it was such a nice dream. I was about to burrow back into it when I heard the shot, repeated endlessly in echoes that seemed to reach even to my stomach. And then I heard Betsy scream. The scream didn't stop. It went on and on until I was screaming, too. Betsy. *Betsy.*

I saw Harmony leaning over me. She was all in white, and her lush black hair was piled on top of her head in a kind of crown. She laid a cool, smooth hand on my forehead and said gently, "It's all right, Jack. You're all right. It's all over now."

I was dead. I was with Harmony. Heaven.

My vision blurred. I blinked and saw my mother leaning over me. She was pasty white, and her hennaed hair stuck crazily away from her face, as if she were on fire.

She shook my arm with her pinching, grasping fingers and hissed, "Shut up, Jack. Your mutt is all right. People can hear you all over the hospital."

I was alive. I was in the hospital with my mother. Hell.

I took a deep breath and regretted it. The air seemed to burn all the way down. I forced myself to open my eyes and look around. My mother was glowering at me from above. Her face seemed to weave and ripple. One of us was chemically impaired, and for the first time in all our combined lives, it might possibly be me. Detective Anthony hovered on the other side of me, and Mark Oden was standing relatively still at the foot of my bed. I made myself concentrate on Mark.

"Betsy?" It was the only word I could say.

Mark understood. "She's OK. She got shot in the hind leg. Nice clean path, no damage to the bone. She's at the vet, and she'll be home in two days. Three, tops."

"Me?"

"You're OK, too, although you managed to rip out all your stitches, and you got shot in the shoulder. Right here." He turned and showed me on his own back. "It's possible that you'll be able to go home tonight. If it's OK with Detective Anthony, that is."

I turned my head toward Detective Anthony, who was looking at me disapprovingly. He ran his hand over his close-cropped gray hair.

"Jack, I don't know whether to nominate you for a citizen's commendation or to arrest you and take you into protective custody," Anthony said. "I really can't decide. Every time we let you out of our sight for a minute, something awful happens."

"I know," I said, with feeling.

"From now on, you are grounded, Jack. No going to work, no staying by yourself, no gallivanting around in the middle of the night. And definitely, positively, no hopping out of a police car and taking a moonlit stroll around your neighborhood because it's such a lovely evening. Got it?"

"Got it."

"There is a guard outside your door. I will keep an officer out there for as long as you are in the hospital. You may be discharged tonight, but I don't want you going back to your house, especially since Betsy won't be there to protect you. Is there anywhere you could stay for a few days?"

I considered. I had a college friend in Yakima, but he had just gotten married. I doubted I would be welcome, even if I could persuade myself to intrude. My law school roommates were scattered over the East and West coasts. My ex-girlfriend lived on Maui with a surfing champion named Wade.

"You have family nearby, don't you?" Anthony asked.

My mother and I both looked at him in horror. He could not be serious.

"No!" we exclaimed in unison.

My mother was shaking her head furiously. Her stiff red hair rustled like dying leaves. "It's impossible," she rasped.

Anthony raised an eyebrow. "Impossible? Why?"

My mother was never big on explaining herself. She rolled her eyes with irritation. "He just can't stay with me. He just can't."

"I don't see why not," Anthony said. "I understand that your apartment is in a secure building. We'll keep a car on watch outside. We'll have an officer stand by inside, if you like. I'm sure that nothing could be more important to you than the safety of your son, Mrs. Hart."

He had her there, I thought. What was she going to say?

What she said shocked me. She leaned across the bed and stared Anthony down. Her bloodshot eyes were fierce. She spat out each word as if she really meant it: "My name is *Ms. Boyden*, not Mrs. Hart. And nothing - *nothing*, Detective - is more important to me than the safety of my son."

Anthony smiled blandly. "Then we are agreed. Jack will stay with you. Thank you, Ms. Boyden."

My mother grabbed her purse. She stood up so fast that she knocked her chair against the wall. She pointed at me, breathing hard. "You can stay with me tonight, but that's it. You can't come until after 8 tonight, and you have to leave before 8 tomorrow morning."

We all looked at her in astonishment. She flounced to the door and flung it open. She was halfway out of the room when Anthony called, "Ms. Boyden?"

She stopped but didn't turn around. "What?"

"Officer Sawyer will take you home."

That was a mean thing to do, I thought, even to my mother. On the other hand, Officer Sawyer and my mother might really hit it off. Just so long as he didn't end up as my next stepfather. Or my next "uncle."

Once she was safely gone, I turned to Anthony. "What did you do that for? I'd rather be arrested than spend the night at my mother's."

"I know." Anthony winked at me, then looked very serious. "Consider it penance for being such an idiot last night." He slapped me on the feet with a file as he walked toward the door. "Get better, Jack."

Mark swung himself into Anthony's empty chair as the door closed behind the burly detective. Mark had found a moment to comb his hair, but his eyes were red and tired. He clicked his pen and opened his notebook.

"You want to tell me what happened?"

I told him, starting with the burnt-out porch light. I told him everything I could remember up to the moment of Betsy's scream. I didn't know what happened after that, but it turned out that Mark did.

"Your neighbor heard the noise and called us," he said.

I grimaced. "Did she say, 'It's that dreadful lawyer next door, always getting himself shot'?"

"Something like that. Right after she called, she saw Betsy dash out your door with something in her mouth. Then she saw a big man in black rush out and start chasing Betsy. She assumed she was witnessing one of your deranged games of keepaway, and she opened her own door to yell at you for disturbing the neighborhood. As if that would make the place more peaceful."

"And then?"

"And then she saw the big man in black aim a gun at Betsy and fire. That's when she realized it wasn't you. She screamed and slammed her door. Meanwhile, the nosy neighbor across your street saw the big man in black run up to where Betsy was lying and try to pull something out of her mouth. Your neighbor started flipping her porch light on and off and shouting that she had a gun and that she had called the police. Neither of those was true, apparently, but they had the desired effect. The guy with the gun bolted up the street."

He rubbed his red eyes. "A unit was there just minutes afterward, but we lost him. We think he got away down Aurora. Was it the same guy, Jack? The same guy that attacked you at the firm?"

"I don't know. They were both big and dressed in black. The guy at my house smelled, though, and I don't remember a smell with the guy at the firm."

"Smelled of what?"

"Sweat and something else. Sweat and aftershave, sweat and laundry detergent. Sweat and something stale. When I tackled him, my face was right in his belly. He was wearing a sweater or a sweatshirt. It was really soft."

"The shirt or the belly?"

"The shirt."

He wrote that down. "Anything else you noticed?"

"I thought it was Brand while it was happening. The guy went right to my briefcase. I thought it was Brand, and I thought that he must have been looking for his files at the firm and then tracked me down at home when he couldn't find them."

"Do you still think it was Brand?"

I was having a hard time putting one thought in front of another. Finally, I shrugged, and my shoulder started to throb. "I don't know. I guess I still do, but I can't figure out how he could know that I would have the files. And I can't figure out what he would want with them."

"Yeah, well -" Mark's voice broke off suddenly, and he looked away from me.

"Yeah, well, what?"

"Nothing. Forget it."

I was suspicious. I was more than suspicious. I was certain. "What did you find?" I asked in a low voice.

by Rosemary Reeve

There was a long pause. When Mark finally met my gaze, his eyes were sorrowful. "You promise not to freak out?"

I nodded, then sank into my pillow at the resulting waves of pain. Mark fussed with something beneath my bed and handed me a photocopy of a letter. "We found this in the last correspondence file," he said, "once we pried the file out of Betsy's mouth, that is."

The letter was on Boyd Tate's stationery and was dated Friday, October 20, the date of the Brand summary judgment hearing. Janet had date-stamped it: "Received HP/JWD Oct. 23." That would have been Monday. Such a long time ago.

I scanned the contents. They seemed perfectly straightforward and unobjectionable. Tate was simply requesting that Harmony expedite presentation of the final order and judgment so he could file Brand's notice of appeal as soon as possible. I didn't see the significance, except that for the firebrand Tate, the letter was a masterpiece of civility and restraint. I gave Mark a questioning look.

"Turn it over."

On the back of the letter, someone had printed three paragraphs in block capital letters. The message was faint but unmistakable. My stomach lurched. Filthy words. Filthier threats. I couldn't bring myself to read it all, but what I read left no doubt as to what the writer intended to do and how he intended to do it. Brand. It had to be Brand.

I shut my eyes very tight. "Mark, I am not freaking out."

"Are you sure?"

"Yes. But I think I would rather be by myself while I am not freaking out. If that's OK."

He took the letter from my hand. I felt him squeeze my good arm and heard the door close softly. I lay as still as I could in the dim room, hoping that sleep would erase what I had just read. I was dizzy with pain and fatigue, but sleep wouldn't come. I tried to think of Mark, of Betsy, of anything other than Harmony.

It was no use. Whenever I shut my eyes, I saw Harmony's trembling, tear-stained face, blue and broken in the security videotape. And then I saw those words, those foul, terrible words. They were plastered blackly over her, weaving and writhing and replicating - until they blotted her face from me and took her away.

ALL GOOD THINGS

CHAPTER 31

"Jack?"

Mark was standing in the doorframe.

"You OK?" he asked.

I felt calmer. I tried unsuccessfully to raise myself on my good elbow. "Yeah, I'm fine," I lied. "Thanks for giving me a couple of minutes to myself."

"More like a couple of hours, Jack," Mark said, sitting down beside me. I stared at the clock in amazement. It was almost four. I had no recollection of falling asleep, no sense of the passage of time. Mark noticed my confusion. "I tried to say goodbye before I left this morning, but you were already snoring. Did you sleep well?"

"Apparently. Did you find Brand?"

"Not yet, but we will. In the meantime, do you feel up to helping us out?"

"Sure."

"We found that letter I showed you this morning in the most current correspondence file. It was right at the top. You really couldn't miss it. The thing we can't figure out is why Brand - if it was Brand - didn't just rip out that letter and put the files back in your briefcase. He could have shut the briefcase, shot you, and split. We probably never would have realized that the letter was missing or even that it ever existed. We wouldn't have connected your murder to what would look like undisturbed files in your briefcase, especially if he tried to make it look like a robbery by taking something valuable from your house."

"There is nothing valuable in my house."

"Your wallet, then. You know what I mean. It still doesn't make sense."

"No," I said slowly. "It doesn't. So you think there was something else in those files? Something that Brand couldn't easily remove or easily find, so he had to try to take them all?"

"Possibly. If it was Brand. We've looked at every page, though, and nothing looks incriminating or suspicious to us. I know that you didn't work on this case, but would you mind looking through the files to see if something leaps out to your trained lawyerly eye?" He handed me four thick files, a couple of pens, and a pad of Post-its. "There might be something in these that's too subtle for a bunch of dumb cops."

"With the exception of Officer Sawyer, I haven't met a dumb cop yet," I said, thumbing through the first correspondence file.

"Ah, Sawyer's OK."

I held my tongue with difficulty. Mark looked at me and grinned. "Look, I know he's got it in for me, and I know he talks like a combination of Hitler and David Duke. And I've got a pretty good idea of why you suddenly decided to leap out of a police car and walk two blocks uphill in the middle of the night. You're not the first of Sawyer's passengers to get that sudden urge for exercise, by the way. But Sawyer's just scared. He knows he doesn't fit in, and he's looking for someone to blame. If everyone's against him, he's got an excuse for never getting things right. He'll snap out of it sooner or later."

"And if he doesn't?"

"Then you can defend me when I clobber him."

"Deal." I hesitated. I wasn't sure how he was going to take my next question. "Has Detective Anthony tried to help you at the police department?"

"So that's what Sawyer told you about me," Mark said.

"Among other things."

Mark stretched and put his head on one side. "Well, Detective Anthony has done as much as he can for me. He's kind of taken me under his wing and showed me the ropes. He looks after me. He advises me. He and his wife have me over to dinner almost every week to make sure I'm OK and that I'm eating. But up to now, we've been in different bureaus. He's a detective and I've been in patrol. He doesn't have any control over my beat or my shift assignments. He did request that I work for him on this case, though, and my sergeant assigned me to him for a couple of weeks."

"Why?"

"Because you and I know each other. He figured that you'd be more likely to talk to me than to talk to him."

"So your job has been to pump me for information?" I struggled to keep the offense out of my voice.

He gave me a sympathetic look. "No, Jack, not really," he said. "Anthony thought you'd be more relaxed with me than anyone else. And when you're relaxed, you remember things better and can see connections more easily. Do you think you would have figured out that Harmony's tennies and soccer shirt were missing if you'd had Sawyer breathing down your neck the whole time?"

"No."

"Well, then," he said, turning up his palms. "See? I'm a good influence on you. Nothing sinister about it."

I thought that over. "OK." I decided to drop the whole subject. I tapped the Brand files. "If I find something in these, how do I get in touch with you?"

"Just tell the officer outside your door. And, anyway, I'll be back at 7:30 to take you to your mommy's for the night."

"Don't remind me," I shouted, but he was gone.

It was kind of soothing to have a task to do. I raised my bed and arranged the files on my rolling table. When the nice lady came with my dinner, she clucked, "Oh, aren't you a busy bee," and left my tray on the night stand. "There, hon, that way you can just nibble at it while you work."

I took a tentative mouthful of the lasagna: chewy noodles in a sweet, greasy sauce, mortared together with solid ricotta. Maybe the hospital employed the lunch lady from my junior high school cafeteria. I glanced at the rest of the dinner and felt almost sure of it: garlic bread, canned peaches, a carton of milk, and a stiff glob of tapioca pudding under chalky whipped topping. But at least the lasagna was warm. And I was starving. I wondered what Betsy was eating tonight, off in her doggie hospital. I wished I could call her on the telephone and make sure she was OK.

I took a bite of the spongy garlic bread and got back to work. The correspondence between Brand's attorney and Harmony was wild. Boyd Tate's letters were barely readable, littered with errors and thick with accusations. He must have dictated and signed them without the benefit of proofreading. It was the only explanation for quasi-sentences like this: "Mr. Brant and have numerous object shuns to your so-called motion, including." Including what? We would never know.

Though Tate's literacy was questionable, his ability to be a pain in the ass was without doubt. He accused Harmony of withholding documents, of using her feminine wiles to "tit late and be witch" his client, and of scheduling motions without his permission. Since when did you need opposing counsel's permission to schedule a motion?

Even buffeted by Tate's idiocy, illiteracy, and abuse, Harmony never lost her cool. I was taking my task seriously, but I couldn't help enjoying myself while I was reading her letters. She was so unflappable. She sounded like a patient but firm British governess, kind but wily. Tate had faxed her a letter on April 15 saying that Brand would be unable to be deposed that day because he was upset about the death of his golden retriever, Buddy. Harmony had replied with a pleasant letter resetting the deposition and extending her condolences.

Five months later, Tate had faxed Harmony a letter saying that Brand would be unable to attend the final day of his deposition - which was on the last day that discovery was allowed - because of emergency surgery on his golden retriever, Buddy. Harmony had responded with a brief fax of her own:

> I am delighted to hear of Buddy's dramatic - if not miraculous - recovery. Although I sympathize with Mr. Brand's desire to be with his dog as Buddy struggles back to health, today's discovery cut-off date compels me to insist that the deposition take place at 10 a.m. as scheduled.

I think Buddy will understand. Should Buddy not understand, however, I suggest that we appear before Judge Brady at 10 a.m. to ask him whether he is willing to extend the discovery cut-off to accommodate emergency surgery on a recently deceased retriever.

Those jerks. Brand and Tate had stumbled into the firm at 9:55, looking sheepish and resentful. With tremendous self-control, Harmony had not asked either of them about Buddy. She confessed to me later, however, that she had woven as many canine references as she could into her questions: You were **barking** up the wrong tree, weren't you, Mr. Brand? And you wanted to nip that misunderstanding in the **bud**, eh? But that **dog** wouldn't hunt, would it, Mr. Brand? You were just chasing your **tail**, correct? So then you went to **fetch** the knife?

Harmony said Tate had seethed through the entire deposition, apoplectic with rage but unable to object without - on the record - implicating his client or himself in the shameless Buddy deception. I had read the transcript afterward and had laughed myself silly. No wonder Brand and Tate had staggered out of the conference room with such sunken eyes and scarlet faces.

Then I thought of how Brand might have channeled his anger against Harmony. I thought of those vile, hateful threats. I couldn't bring myself to read any more of those letters. They tormented me. Harmony's letters made me lonely for her. Tate's letters made me fear for her. The specter of Brand throughout them all made me despair of seeing her again.

I pushed aside the correspondence files and started looking through Harmony's desk file. It was a tidy collection of the minutia that builds up in every case: concise memos of telephone conversations with her client contacts, documentation of legal research that hadn't gone anywhere, copies of invoices and receipts. Nothing struck me as suggestive or suspicious.

I was about to close the file when I noticed how bulky the front cover seemed. I felt in the pocket and drew out a thick printout summarizing the attorneys' fees and costs incurred in the <u>Brand v. Crabfest</u> litigation. My pulse quickened as I looked at the date at the top: October 20, 2:50 p.m. Harmony must have run this printout on Friday, right after she returned from successfully arguing the summary judgment. Prompt and efficient as always, she must have been working on the cost bill.

I skimmed the printout. It summarized fees and disbursements by month, by attorney. Harmony had neatly circled the expenses Crabfest could recover from Brand. Prevailing employers had a very limited right to recover fees and costs from unsuccessful discrimination plaintiffs, but it looked to me that we could ask for at least a couple of thousand dollars for court reporters, copying costs, and the expenses of taking an out-of-state deposition.

I followed Harmony's neat circles down the printout, mentally adding up the tally. On the last page of the printout, I stopped. Harmony had circled the by-attorney breakdown of the number of hours we had billed on this case last month, during September. There was a question mark by it in the blue-black ink she used in her fountain pen.

I looked closer at the figures. Something was wrong. Harmony had broken her back on this case during September. The discovery cut-off had been on September 15 and the dispositive motion deadline had been on September 22. She had been in depositions up to the fifteenth, and then she had worked night and day so she could file the summary judgment on the twenty-second. And after that, she had been busy preparing witnesses and drafting motions *in limine* because she and Marshall had really expected that they would have to go to trial. I guessed that during September Harmony had spent at least 150 hours on this case. Maybe even 200 hours.

But according to the printout, Marshall Farr had spent 12.5 hours on Brand v. Crabfest during September. Humphrey Piper had spent 5.6. Charlie Snow had spent 4.8.

But Harmony didn't appear anywhere on the breakdown. According to the printout, Harmony Piper had not billed a single hour during September on the Brand v. Crabfest litigation.

ALL GOOD THINGS

CHAPTER 32

Mark interrupted my puzzling over the printout. It was time to go to my mother's for the night. Oh, joy. Before we left the hospital room, I showed him the Brand printout that didn't list any hours for Harmony for September. He wrinkled his brow and shook his head.

"If I had had any sleep last night, I might understand this by myself," he said. "I didn't, though, so you are going to have to explain it to me."

"I don't know what it means, either," I admitted, easing the T-shirt he had brought me over my bandaged hand, bandaged shoulder, stitched forehead, and bruised stomach. "But I'm sure this printout is wrong, and Harmony was sure it was wrong, too. You can see her question mark right next to the by-attorney breakdown."

"Does this have anything to do with Brand?"

"Probably not. It might have something to do with Janet, though." I combed my hair over the gash in my forehead. "Janet would be responsible for entering Harmony's time each week. If she fell down on the job and didn't enter any of the time that Harmony spent on Brand during the entire month of September, Harmony could have made trouble for her. It might have given Janet a motive to get rid of Harmony. To shut her up."

"You think Janet killed or kidnapped Harmony because she was afraid that Harmony would report her for entering her time wrong?"

When he put it like that, it did sound implausible. Besides, Harmony would never report anybody for poor job performance, even the chronically late and lazy Janet. I was just so eager to think that someone other than Brand had been responsible for Harmony's disappearance. I had no trouble picturing Janet as a murderer, but at least she wasn't a rapist. Probably.

"No, I guess not," I said lamely, following him out into the hospital parking lot. "But it doesn't make any sense."

"No, it doesn't." Mark unlocked the door and helped me into the passenger seat. He fastened the seatbelt around me because I couldn't use my left hand. "But you know, a lot of things about this case don't make any sense. I've spent most of the day trying to wrap up loose ends, and even when I get an answer, none of them makes any sense."

"Like what?"

"Well, in the first place, we can't get a clear read on Janet Daniels' time of death. She was dead when the murderer threw her down the elevator shaft - and probably she had been dead for quite a while. We think she was killed early Wednesday evening and thrown down the elevator shaft early Thursday morning, but we're not sure because the elevator didn't really start to malfunction until late Thursday morning. So that's one puzzle."

I had no light to shed on that dilemma. "What else?"

"The Oregon police caught up with the florist clerk who was touring with her band."

"Juliet?"

"Juliet, our lady of the flamboyant handwriting. And Juliet, our lady of the good memory. She remembered because of the romantic message on the gift card, the lavishness of the order - and the unpleasantness and inflexibility of the orderer."

Unpleasant? Inflexible? "You mean Jeremy Smith ordered those roses?" I asked in astonishment.

Mark threw back his head and laughed. "Close but no cigar. Wrong gender."

"Janet Daniels?" I said.

"Yep. Juliet remembers feeling sorry for Harmony for having such a bossy girlfriend. Janet made quite an impression on her."

I was shocked. Janet sent the roses? That must have been why she had taken the envelope from the gift card. She was trying to make it hard for the police to trace the florist. That evil, conniving, sneaky bitch. I was so angry I could have pushed her down the elevator shaft myself. I started to say as much to Mark, but he stopped me.

"Never tell a policeman that you could have killed someone, Jack," he said. "People can get the wrong idea. Besides, there's more. We figured out where Janet has been living."

"I thought she lived in Leschi."

"She owns a house in Leschi, but she didn't really live there. She didn't have any food in her refrigerator."

"That doesn't mean anything. I don't have any food in my refrigerator, either."

"Yes, I noticed that. But she also didn't have any clothes in her closet, and she had her mail delivered to the office."

"So where did she live?"

"You know that new building of condominiums on the waterfront? The blue one with the silver windows and the sort of biosphere dome on the top?"

"Janet lived there?"

"Janet lived there - in the penthouse."

"How on earth did Janet buy a penthouse condominium on the waterfront?"

"She didn't. Someone else bought it. It's in Harmony's mother's maiden name, actually. It's part of the trust properties, so it's Harmony's now. We tracked down the realtor. She remembers meeting with the buyer only once, but she identified him without any problems - a little weaselly guy with shining silver hair."

"Humphrey Piper? Janet was Humphrey Piper's . . . ?" I couldn't bring myself to say "girlfriend" in connection with the fearsome Janet Daniels. Instead, I waggled my hand and raised my eyebrows suggestively. "That's impossible."

"Why? She was, as Brand put it, still a looker."

"She wasn't his type. She was twice his size. She was his own age. She was his daughter's secretary."

"Well, Mieko was his secretary, at one time."

"Really?"

"Yeah. That's where they met. She was Mr. Piper's first secretary when he opened your Tokyo office. She neglected to tell us that when we interviewed her. She made vague allusions to family connections and meeting Mr. Piper at tea with the prime minister. Well, she did have tea with Mr. Piper and the prime minister, but she was there as Mr. Piper's secretary. Didn't Harmony tell you that her latest stepmother was her dad's ex-secretary?"

"No. Harmony's very protective of her dad. She thinks he can do no wrong. Could do no wrong, I mean. She wouldn't have said anything negative about him, especially not something that would make him sound like he was a dirty old man. Which he was, apparently. But back to Janet. Were she and Mr. Piper . . . ?" I waggled my hand again.

"We don't know. None of her neighbors remember seeing Mr. Piper, but they could have been discreet. The penthouse has a private elevator up from the garage. She had some kind of claim on him, though. There were quite a few calls between them over the weekend, including one to her from Japan that we think he made just three or four hours before he died. She kept calling his hotel even after we think he was already dead. He also paid her about ten grand a month, besides letting her live in that fabulous condo. That's more than he paid any of his other girlfriends. His friend in Fukuoka, for example, only got about $4,000 a month. According to the Japanese police, Miss Fukuoka is twice the looker that Janet ever was."

We were at the police garage. I knew the drill by now. We drove in, hopped - or, rather, Mark hopped and I hobbled - into another car, and drove out. Mark continued: "The condo is really cool. It's got everything you could want in it: a home theater, an exercise room - and a computer."

"A computer?"

"A computer. We checked the condo's phone bills, and guess what we found?"

"A call to our firm's computer network early Monday morning?"

"Bingo. Someone in the condo - presumably Janet - dialed into your computer network at 1:38 a.m. Monday, October 23. She must have logged in with Mr. Piper's passwords. Could she have gotten those?"

"Sure. She could have called Systems and said he had forgotten them or made up some other excuse. Or, if she'd done any work for him recently, she'd probably know his passwords. I think she was kind of his ad hoc secretary when he was in the Seattle office." I shook my head in disbelief. "So Janet sent Harmony that phony message about Mr. Piper's not being able to give Harmony the money. How did she know what to say? How did she know it would upset Harmony so much?"

"I don't know. But we know that that's not all she did. A couple of minutes after she dialed into the Seattle network, she called Harmony's office. The call lasted about twenty minutes. That would bring us up to about 2:05 a.m."

"And Harmony left the office in tears at 2:11 a.m."

"Yep. And Brand says he saw Janet at the Pipers' security gate with someone in the passenger's seat at 2:45 a.m."

I shivered. The mere mention of Brand's name sent chills down my back. "So if Janet lured Harmony downstairs, picked her up, and took her home, how does Brand fit into this?"

We were at my mother's apartment building in the Regrade. "I don't know, Jack," Mark said, helping me out of the car. "But we're getting closer, OK?"

I nodded. I was too tired to pursue the subject further, anyway. Just the brief conversation and the struggle into and out of the two cars had left me sweaty with pain and fatigue. Mark showed me where the unmarked police car was stationed. There was also a police officer in the vacant apartment next to my mother's. He buzzed us through the front door.

"It's not Sawyer, is it?"

"No. Although I understand Sawyer got along great with your mom."

I groaned. I groaned again as Mark helped me up the stairs. Why did my mom have to live on the third floor? By the time we got there, I was spent. I leaned against the wall while Mark knocked on the door.

No answer. Mark knocked again. Nothing. Mark looked at me with a raised eyebrow.

"At this point," I said, "I usually jingle the change in my pockets or make some loud reference to my checkbook. If that doesn't work, I just give up. I've never barged in on her."

"I gave your keys to Officer Murdoch next door," Mark replied. "I'll go get them and let you in."

I stopped him. "Please, please don't," I said. "Really. I'd much rather sleep with Officer Murdoch next door."

"I'm sure Officer Murdoch will be delighted to hear that." Mark and I jumped. Neither one of us had heard my mother open the door. She stood there in the doorway, a disembodied white face swathed in the darkness - dark apartment, dark red hair, dark robe, dark, clingy nightgown. She could not have achieved a creepier effect if she had tried. Maybe she had. You never could tell with my mom.

"But since I have gone to all the trouble of making up the hideabed, you might as well stay here." She moved back just enough that Mark would have to brush against her to get inside. He wisely pushed me in ahead of him, and my mother retreated, sniffing.

A dim orange lamp burned beside the hideabed. It made the room into a carnival of fantastic shapes and shadows. Mom shut the door, and Mark looked around him with alarm. He seemed to feel trapped. My mother ignored him, waved me toward the hideabed, and pointed regally toward an open door at the end of the hall. "That is the bathroom. You can freshen up if you need to. But don't turn on a lot of lights or go around opening and closing doors. I have a terrible migraine, and I am going to bed."

Ah. I *see*. "That means she needs to sleep something off," I whispered to Mark, who handed me the duffel bag of necessities, pajamas, and clean clothes he had brought from my house. He shook my good hand and whispered back, "Good luck, man. I'll be here to get you at 7 a.m. sharp."

"Could you make that 6?"

"I'll do my best. Scream for Murdoch if you get scared."

"Don't worry. One whiff of Brand and I'll be screaming my head off."

"Brand nothing," Mark said, walking to the door. "I'm talking about **her**."

I hated to see Mark go, but I was nearly asleep on my feet. I locked the door, washed my face, brushed my teeth, took my pills, and slipped into my pajamas. It took me a few minutes to figure out how to turn off the orange lamp by the hideabed. It was a glowing, glass globe clutched in the grasp of a gnarled brass claw. I poked and prodded at the claw, trying unsuccessfully to find a switch hidden in a talon or a button in a knuckle. Where did my mother pick up awful things like this? Quite by accident, I put my hand on the globe itself, and the light started to dim and flicker until just an ember of red smoldered in the center. Then it faded, and the room was dark.

I settled into bed. I was surprisingly comfortable. As my eyes adjusted to the night, I could see around the apartment. To my right were the big, arched windows that opened onto a veranda overlooking the garden. Mom loved that veranda. That's why she had wanted this apartment. I think she fancied the thought of lounging romantically on the veranda in one of her flowing, see-through nightgowns. To my left was the kitchen. Right in front of me was the door to Mom's sewing room. The sewing room was really just a big, old-fashioned closet, but it had a window for light and air, and Mom stored her material on the shelves and hung her works in progress on the metal bars that lined the walls.

I yawned and sank deeper into my pillows. Mom was a good seamstress. She probably could have been a fashion designer if she hadn't started drinking. That was what she had wanted to be - long ago, before she met my dad and made what she called The Biggest Mistake of Her Life. That would be me. The biggest mistake of my life, too, Mom, I thought sadly, slipping into sleep.

I was just on the border between reality and dreams when I heard the creak of a hinge. I couldn't tell whether it was in the apartment or in my mind. After a few moments of silence, I decided I had imagined the sound and sank back into the warm confusion of the hideabed.

Then I heard the sound again. This time I was sure it wasn't in my mind. I held my breath and listened. I heard it again. A door was opening. It was opening slowly, but it was opening. I raised myself on my elbow and saw the door to Mom's sewing room. It had been closed when I went to bed, but now it was open just a crack. There was a sliver of moonlight beaming across the carpet.

Not again. I opened my mouth to scream for Murdoch, but someone or something beat me to it. There was a roar, like a hurt or angry animal. The sewing room door flung open. Something small and lithe leapt from the doorway onto my bruised stomach. What the hell was going on? Did my mother have a dog? In this posh, expensive, no-pets apartment? That I was paying for?

I had had a lot of practice with attacks like this. I flung my good arm around the critter and rolled until I was on top of it. It was pinned between me and the bed.

The critter offered no serious resistance. But like Betsy, it might be biding its time and lulling me into a false sense of security. I fumbled for the sheets without letting it up. Somebody was giggling. I pulled the sheets off the critter just as I managed to turn on the orange lamp with a whack of my bandaged hand.

I sat up, startled.

It was no critter.

I was looking into the surprised but smiling face of a blond-haired, brown-eyed, snub-nosed little boy.

by Rosemary Reeve

CHAPTER 33

I let the little boy sit up. I got myself under control and edited out the various swear words that had flooded into my mind.

"Who are you?" I asked the little boy.

He crooked his fingers into claws and roared at me. "I'm a Tyrannosaurus Rex." Then he dropped his hands into his lap and looked around the disheveled hideabed. "That was fun," he said. "Can we do it again?"

I was trying to think of a logical reason why we couldn't do it again when my mother burst out of her room, trailing her black robe over her black nightgown. She looked like a big, red-haired bat. She grabbed the little boy's arm.

"Jimmy! What are you doing out of bed?"

"I got up to see Jack, Mommy. You said I could see Jack, Mommy. You said so."

I looked from one of them to the other. Jimmy? Mommy? Mommy? Jimmy?

Mommy was trying to drag Jimmy off the hideabed. She succeeded only in pulling him to his knees. "I said you could get up and look at Jack once he was asleep," she hissed at him. "Now you've ruined everything."

She leaned over the bed to give him a swat on the behind, but he darted away from her. The slap fell soundly on my already injured stomach. I buckled onto the bed. The mattress jerked up under my weight and hit my mom in the knees. She lost her balance and tumbled on top of me. Involuntarily, I said a seriously bad word. Jimmy immediately repeated it.

We were all thrashing around and trying to extricate ourselves from the bedcovers when I became aware that we were not alone. An appalled-looking policeman was standing open-mouthed in the hallway, seemingly unable to decide whether we needed rescuing or arresting for unnatural practices. Officer Murdoch, I presume.

My mother uncoiled herself from the bed and sashayed toward him, managing to shed her robe in the few steps to the hall. Murdoch looked even more alarmed.

"Officer, I am so sorry we disturbed you," my mother purred. "You see, my little boy hasn't seen his big brother in ages. He didn't mean to, but he woke Jack up. And Jack, well, Jack overreacted. He thought someone was trying to attack him."

She gave a false, silvery laugh. I said another seriously bad word, but this time, I said it only to myself. I was gratified when her glimmering laugh ran ashore on her harsh, gin-scoured throat.

She swallowed and tried again. "So, I just had to come in and referee. But don't worry, Officer, I've got everything under control."

She tried to take his arm, but Murdoch was unbending. My heart warmed to him a little. "Are you all right, Mr. Hart?" he asked.

"Yes, I am, Officer Murdoch. Thank you. I didn't know that my little brother was here." Or that he existed, I added to myself. "He was pretending to be a Tyrannosaurus Rex, and it took me by surprise."

"I wasn't pretending. I **am** a Tyrannosaurus Rex," Jimmy insisted from behind me. I realized he was peeping around my shoulder.

Murdoch walked over and took Jimmy by the hand. "I don't know, little feller," he said, squatting down so he could stare Jimmy in the eye. "You look more like a Triceratops to me."

Jimmy considered that for a moment. "What does a Triceratops look like?" he asked.

"Oh, they're much, much handsomer than that warty old Tyrannosaurus Rex. They've got three horns on their head. Right here." He pointed to his left temple. "Here." He pointed to his right temple. "And here." He tapped Jimmy gently on the nose.

Jimmy was sold. "Cool!"

"But the thing about Triceratopses is, they need a whole lot of sleep. So what do you say that we put you and your brother here back to bed?"

"Is Jack a Triceratops too?"

Murdoch gave me a keenly appraising glance. "No, I'd say that Jack is just a nice old Brontosaurus. He's big, and he's slow, and he wouldn't hurt a fly." No description, I thought, had ever captured me so well. "But Brontosauruses need a lot of sleep, too, especially when they've had the kind of day your brother has. So let's go to bed. OK?"

Jimmy went without a fuss. At the sewing room door, he paused and looked back at me. "What happened to your head?"

A herd of unconvincing lies stampeded through my mind. I settled for something that was more or less the truth. "Someone pushed me, and I hit my head."

Jimmy was immensely concerned. "Someone **pushed** you?"

"Yes, someone did."

"Well, if he pushes you again, you tell me, and I will spank his bottom," Jimmy said, nodding vigorously. He brightened up. "And then I'll eat him."

My mother swooped down on Jimmy and ushered him into the sewing room. She didn't want Murdoch to see that Jimmy was sleeping in an oversize closet. Murdoch helped me untangle the sheets and blankets and put them back on the bed.

"So, how long have you known you had a little brother?" he whispered.

"About as long as you have," I whispered back. "It came as a complete surprise."

Murdoch nodded sympathetically. "Your mother is a remarkable woman," he said.

I looked at him warily. He had seemed sane enough until then.

He grinned at me. "Although I don't know what the remarks would be."

I grinned back at him with relief. He winked and started down the hall. "Yell if you need anything, kid," he said. "I mean, anything at all."

Murdoch was almost out the door when my mother swooped back into the room. "Officer Murdoch," she called after him, "could we get you a blanket or a thermos of something hot to drink? It must be cold over there."

"Thank you, ma'am, but I am well provided for." He paused. "My wife saw to that."

Then he was gone, locking the door from the outside. My mother pouted. It just wasn't her night. She was trying to slip down the hall to her room when I stopped her.

"Wait a minute. What about Jimmy?"

"We'll talk about it in the morning, Jack."

"We'll talk about it now."

She made a show of fussing over me. "Look, you're so tired. You've been through so much. We'll talk about it tomorrow. You can stay as long as you like, now that you know."

"Very kind of you. But I want to know a lot more than the fact that he exists, dramatic though that may be."

She let out a long, drawn-out martyr's sigh and sat down at the table. "OK, but I'll need a drink."

"You can have a glass of water. I want the truth."

She rolled her eyes at me and refused the water. "His name's Jimmy Boyden. He's almost four. He's your half-brother."

"Who's his father?"

"Someone I met almost five years ago, of course. No one you know."

"Do you even know his name?"

My mother slapped me. It was just like old times. "Of course," she snapped. "But he didn't want Jimmy, and I couldn't take care of him by myself. So Jimmy's been staying with his grandmother - his father's mother. He visited me for a weekend every month."

Visited, she'd said. "But he lives here now?" I guessed.

"His grandmother died," she said heavily. "A little while ago. I haven't been able to find his father. He's been staying with me ever since. I didn't know what else to do."

I looked with dismay around the tiny, overheated room. A child. A child in this cramped, one-bedroom apartment, crammed with crystal balls and astrological charts and all the other spells, totems, and familiars that comprised my mother's spiritual life. The apartment would have been a nice enough place for a young professional who spent most of his time at the office. It would have been a nice enough place for a retired lady who enjoyed being alone with her books, kitty, and TV. And it was a nice enough place for my mother to do the odd palm reading and slowly drink herself to death. But a child! A little boy. Where did he have to play? It was too cold and wet to spend much time in the garden. Did he have any friends at all?

"He can't stay here," I said. "This apartment is too small. Doesn't your lease require one-person occupancy?"

"It's OK. I've fixed that with the landlady."

"How?"

"I told her Jimmy was your son, and that you didn't want him anymore."

"You told her what?" Well, at least that explained the landlady's silent treatment of me when I had gone to pay the rent. "You can't go around telling people things like that."

"But it worked like a charm. She was so appalled, she said it was OK for him to stay here so long as nobody complains. I just have to keep him quiet and away from all the other residents."

I put my head in my hands and moaned. "You're hopeless," I said. "You don't even understand that you've done anything wrong."

She thumped me on the shoulder where I had been shot. It was all I could do to keep from screaming.

When I composed myself and looked up, I saw that she was crying. "I am doing my best, Jack," she sobbed. "I got a job. A real job, before you start rolling your eyes. I'm a waitress at the Olympic Broiler on Pike and Second. I haven't even had a drink while he's been here. And I haven't done - I haven't done - I haven't done anything that you wouldn't approve of for a very long time." She turned her face away from me, rubbing her eyes and wiping her nose.

A job. I was floored. No drinking. I was even more floored. No doing whatever it was I would disapprove of. I was totally floored. It was always possible that she was lying, but she looked relatively sober. Usually it was the drink or the drugs that gave her enough imagination to lie. Then an awful thought occurred to me. "What does Jimmy do while you're out waitressing?"

"He stays here, of course."

"Alone?"

"Of course alone. I can't afford day care. I can't afford a babysitter. I can't take him with me, can I? That's why I asked you for the money."

"For expenses," I said softly.

"For expenses," she said.

She told me how much day care cost. I was amazed. What with her rent and my mortgage, I could never afford that. Not if Betsy and I wanted to continue to eat peanut butter sandwiches in the lavish manner we so enjoyed. The obvious solution - moving

Jimmy and my mother into my house and using the money that I would have paid for rent for day care - was unacceptable for any number of reasons. Chiefly, because I would rather die than cohabit with my mom.

My head, my shoulder, and my stomach were pounding. My mother was crying. What a successful conversation. I got up awkwardly. "Look," I said. "We'll figure something out. Just let me sleep on it, OK?" She didn't answer. I walked down the hall and got into bed. I knew when I was beaten.

Then I heard her voice, small and sad in the dark apartment. "Jack," she said, "I'm sorry I didn't tell you about him."

"Yeah," I said, pulling up the covers. "Yeah, me too."

by Rosemary Reeve

CHAPTER 34

A pang of conscience struck me as I sank into bed. If Brand really was after me, I was putting Jimmy in danger by staying here. I had no problem with putting my mother in harm's way. My mother was a survivor. If there was ever a nuclear war, I was going to find her and stand next to her. I was sure we'd both be fine. But Jimmy! He was just a little boy. He wouldn't understand that this was deadly serious, not a game or a frolic or a let's pretend. He might pull his leap-to-the-bed routine right as Brand burst in to blast me away.

I had to get out of here. I was rallying my strength to get up and get dressed when I suddenly fell asleep. The pain pills were more powerful than my guilt and fear.

I woke to a squall of rain crashing against the big arched windows. For one terrible moment, I thought it was Brand. I hurled myself out of bed and staggered toward the door. I didn't care that I was exposed in the middle of the room. Anything to lead Brand away from Jimmy. Then another squall hit the windows, and I realized that I was running from the rain. I stood there in the hallway, feeling simultaneously foolish and relieved. I was irrevocably wide awake.

I got myself a drink of water. The kitchen clock said it was just after five. Not too bad. Usually, I got up at six so Betsy and I could go for a run and bond over cottage cheese before I went to work. I missed Betsy. Maybe I could go see her today.

I showered and dressed. Then I checked on Jimmy. He was fast asleep, one arm curled around a battered white teddy bear, the other flung across the covers. His bed was small, but it almost filled the sewing room. A few toys and books were scattered on the shelves. I had to get him out of here and into a real home. But how?

I closed the sewing room door quietly and set about folding up the hideabed. In my weakened and injured condition, it took a while. I lay down on the sofa to catch my breath. Something was nagging at me. Something I had forgotten. Something not quite right. I concentrated for a while, then gave up. It would come to me eventually.

I turned on the orange light and rummaged in the stack of newspapers by the sofa. I was surprised that my mom even took the newspaper, until I saw the little red circles dotting the help wanted section. So she wasn't lying. At least not completely. She really was either looking for or in possession of a job. I scanned the circled ads:

waitresses, receptionists, sales clerks. I shook my head. The salaries were modest, and the work was hard. My mom would never make it.

But at least she was trying. I allowed myself a moment of petty envy. My mom had never tried to get a job when I was little. She had never stopped drinking, stopped drugging, or stopped whatever else it was she was doing so she could take care of me. She had left me with bureaucrats and taken off, like she was dumping an inconvenient puppy at the pound. I remembered the conviction in her voice when she had stared Anthony down and said that nothing was more important to her than the safety of her son. Clearly, she had been talking about Jimmy. What about me, Mom, huh?

I pushed the self-pity out of my mind and thought about Jimmy. He looked a bit like me - except far more handsome. His eyes were glossy chocolate instead of my wavering hazel, and his hair was sparkling blond instead of my indecisive ash brown, which looked blond or brown or both. He had a cute little snub nose with a smattering of freckles, while my sadly crooked schnoz was located almost - but not quite - in the center of my face. If I were my mom, I'd love Jimmy more, too, I decided. Then I resolved never to think of it again.

I looked back at the newspaper. In the dim light, it reminded me of the printout with the <u>Brand</u> fees and disbursements; the jobs my mom had circled looked like the costs Harmony had marked for us to recover: the court reporters, the copying costs, the expenses from the out-of-state deposition. The out-of-state deposition. I sat up on the couch. I was such an idiot.

Harmony had gone to Spirit Lake, Idaho, to take the deposition of one of Brand's former co-workers. The guy's name was something like Cumming or Cummings. He was a loony, someone who'd come back from Vietnam with a great deal more hate and whole lot fewer brain cells than when he went. He and Brand had fought in the same company, and years later, had ended up together at Crabfest Seafoods. Cumming had quit in violent rage when Brand was fired, and Brand had listed Cumming as a potential primary witness of Crabfest's alleged racial discrimination against Caucasians.

Could Brand be hiding out with Cumming somewhere near Spirit Lake? It was possible. Cumming was a slippery character. Harmony had had a terrible time finding him so he could be deposed. Tate wouldn't give her Cumming's real address, insisting that he lived "somewhere" near Coeur D'Alene, but that neither he nor Brand knew exactly where. Harmony had tracked Cumming from temporary residence to temporary residence all around northern Idaho. Finally, she had nabbed him in Spirit Lake with the help of the Veterans' Administration.

Harmony's paper trail on Cumming - all the addresses where he had lived or stayed for the last couple of years - would have been in the <u>Brand</u> correspondence files. Could that be what Brand was looking for in my office and then my house? I grabbed the phone.

Neither Mark nor Anthony were at the police department when I called, so I took my mother's keys, locked her door, and went to talk to Murdoch.

"Anything wrong, kid?" Murdoch seemed as calm and kindly as he had last night.

"Officer Murdoch, I think I know where Alfonse Brand might be hiding."

His eyebrows shot up. "Where?"

I told him about Cumming, about the deposition in Spirit Lake, and about how evasive Tate and Brand had been about where Cumming lived. He thanked me and sent me back to my mom's apartment with one of his wife's spicy pumpkin muffins. He said it was my reward for being helpful.

I settled back on the couch and ate my muffin while I skimmed through the newspapers for the last few days. I had been so immersed in work and so worried about Harmony that the news of the outside world came as something of a shock. It reminded me of the reorientation period I had needed after my first semester of law school. The world seemed to have undergone a sea change since I had embarked on learning about writs, consideration, replevin, and breaking bulk. There were new starlets on all the talk shows. All the music on the radio was different. Politicians who had been the hope of their respective parties when I had entered law school all seemed to be disgraced or dead by the time I read the newspaper after my first exams.

Now I concentrated on the metro sections, looking idly for stories about the murders of Mr. and Mrs. Piper and Janet Daniels. Nothing. Oh, well. It had been a big news week. A suspicious plane crash in Argentina had killed more than a hundred people. A traveling church group from Tacoma had escaped the crash almost unscathed, and the newspaper was full of interviews with the local survivors. They sounded terrified and sickened - but grateful. One said, "I'll never complain about getting the middle seat again." The people next to her in the window and aisle seats, she added, had been killed on impact.

There also had been a new round of revelations about the Grange, which I read with a horrified fascination. At the bottom of the story was a quote from our managing partner, Marshall Farr, who was representing a consortium of the media in getting access to the Grange's records. Marshall was livid that it was taking so long for the state to find and produce the documents:

> "Some people say, 'It's been 40 years already. What's a few more weeks?' To them I say, that for these shameful deeds and wanton neglect to remain hidden even one more day is an obscenity almost as reprehensible as the crimes inflicted on these poor children. Justice delayed is justice denied."

by Rosemary Reeve

Nice soundbite, I thought, turning the page. I wonder which associate wrote it for him.

I was about to lay down the paper and catch a bit more sleep when Mr. Piper's obituary caught my eye. I skimmed the column. Humphrey Piper had served in World War II and had earned his undergraduate degree from the University of Washington and his law degree from Harvard. He enjoyed scuba diving, yachting, flying, and tennis. He was preceded in death by his parents, Humphrey and Elizabeth Piper, his first wife, Elayne Westcott Piper, and his son, Humphrey Piper III, who had died in infancy. I blinked with surprise. I didn't know that Harmony had had a brother. I let the paper drop, shaking my head. It looked like Harmony was the only Piper left.

Please let her still be alive, I prayed. Please let us find her. Please let her be OK.

It was almost 6 a.m. I hoped Mark would be coming soon. To pass the time, I checked my voicemail. I had four new messages. I also had too many old messages. The voicemail lady said reproachfully, "Your mailbox is more than 75 percent full. Please delete unneeded messages or greetings."

I started with the new messages. I had two from Jeremy Smith. The first told me that he was not pleased with the draft pleadings I had left for him. When would I learn to stop pulling my punches, he asked. I groaned to myself. That meant he had reworked the pleadings with his usual edge of overstatement and blatant mischaracterization. We didn't have the facts to support his kind of creative writing. He was sure to blame me when we got sanctioned or laughed out of court.

As far as I could tell, Jeremy had left his second message just to be mean: "Well, Jack, I hope you enjoyed your day off. If you just can't manage to get to work, maybe you should consider a permanent vacation." Then he hung up. What a lovely man. I deleted both his messages. There was too much damage for me to try to repair it with a groveling voicemail.

The remaining two new messages were from opposing counsel in the case I was working on with Charlie Snow. He was wondering, first sarcastically and then downright nastily, when he would receive the documents he had requested. I groaned out loud. What with being chased around the library, shot at, slashed, hospitalized, attacked, and finally shot in my own home, I had completely forgotten to call the jerk and ask for an extension. I would have to deal with this today.

With a heavy head and a heavy heart, I started cleaning out my voicemail box. I pounded through the old messages, listening to a few words of each as I tried to decide which ones to delete and which to save. Then I heard Janet Daniels' voice, and I flinched at the memory of the last time I had seen her. Or seen her arm, at least. I backspaced and listened to the header: "Message from Janet Daniels, received 5:07 p.m., Wednesday, October 24."

It was the message Janet had left me about the missing file. Suddenly I realized what had been bothering me. It wasn't the out-of-state deposition in Spirit Lake, even though I was glad I had thought of that, and it might be important. No, something hadn't seemed quite right since I had talked to Mark on the way from the hospital to my mother's.

Mark had said they thought Janet had been killed early Wednesday evening. Janet had left me the message about the file at 5 p.m. on Wednesday. I had been in or around my office until about 7:30 p.m., and nothing on my desk had been moved by the time I left for the day. I remembered flicking my timesheet into my out box. It had gone in with a swish. Nothing but net. But when I had returned from court on Thursday morning, someone had fiddled with my desk. My stapler was in the wrong place. My stand of active files had shifted. My out box had been moved over a couple of inches - just enough so that I couldn't toss my timesheet into it from my desk.

I had assumed the trespasser had been Janet, looking for the file she had asked for. But maybe it wasn't Janet. Maybe Janet was dead by then. Who had been in my office? And what had he or she been looking for?

I punched the telephone buttons and let Janet's message play:

> Jack, this is Janet Daniels, Harmony's secretary. Look, Jack, something really important is missing and you need to find it for me. It's the correspondence file for East-West Partners, that's EWP. The client number is 19123-816. Look for the number first. If you can't find what you're looking for, look for the corresponding letters. You'll find it with the letters. It's really important, Jack. OK? Bye.

by Rosemary Reeve

CHAPTER 35

There was something strange about Janet's message. When I had listened to it
on Wednesday night, I had been rushing through and organizing my voicemails:
things I had to do right away, things that could wait, things that could wait but
probably shouldn't. It was triage - crude but effective - except that I hadn't really
listened to Janet's entire voicemail. I had just decided that it wasn't critical and
hurried on to my many other crises.

Now, in the dark and stillness of a rainy Saturday morning, the whole thing struck
me as odd. Janet had been an odd woman, but this message was odd even for her.
Why would she identify herself as Harmony's secretary? I knew who she was, and she
knew I knew who she was. Why had she called Harmony by her first name? She
always referred to her as "Ms. Piper," as if to underscore the significance of
Harmony's ancestry. What was all that mumbo-jumbo about numbers and letters?
The urgency in her last few words troubled me. "It's really important, Jack."

I listened to the message again. It was still odd. Again. Even odder. Again. The
oddest. I kept stopping on the words: "something really important is missing." Janet
didn't take her job seriously enough to consider a missing file really important. Oh,
she liked bossing people around, and she promulgated and perpetuated a myth that
she was fearsomely competent, but it was obvious from the moment you met her that
Janet thought she was too good to be anybody's secretary. And the way Janet showed
you that she was too good to be a secretary was to not be a very good secretary at all.
She had been more attentive to Harmony than she was to anyone else, but even
Harmony had ended up leaving a lot of Janet's work for the night secretary or staying
late - off the clock - to do it herself.

I had asked Harmony why she let Janet get away with it. She replied, in a lawyerly
evasion, "Janet is good at what she does." When I had pointed out that regardless of
whether she did it well, Janet still didn't do much of anything, Harmony had become
very quiet. She had seemed to be debating whether or not to tell me something.

Finally, she had closed the door and said, "Look, if Janet had been born thirty years
ago instead of sixty years ago, she probably would have been a partner at this firm by
now. But she never got that chance. Being a legal secretary was as close as she could
get. And Jack, I am not going to harangue her or pressure her for not paying her full

attention to a job that she hates. It's a job she never would have chosen if she had had a real choice."

I had thought about that for a long, long time. No wonder Harmony and Janet had gotten along so well. They had had an unspoken understanding. By overlooking her faults and shouldering the mess left by her shortcomings, Harmony was paying Janet back for Janet's missed opportunities, for Janet's paving the way. Where I had seen only Janet's arrogance and carelessness, Harmony had seen a debt to be paid. And she had paid it.

I shook myself. Harmony seemed to slip into my mind even when I was trying to concentrate on something else. I brought my attention back to Janet's message. If Janet didn't care enough about her job to get Harmony's photocopying done on time, she sure as hell wouldn't have gotten so exercised about a file. So what was she really talking about? What was really important? What was missing? What did I need to find?

Harmony.

I punched in the code that would make the voice tape play back slowly. This was an invaluable tool for deciphering the warp-speed messages left by Seattle's energetic and highly caffeinated lawyers. It also had the fringe benefit of making all the women callers sound languid and tranquilized, and all the men callers - even Jeremy Smith - sound affable, easygoing, and vaguely Southern.

As the slowed-down Janet drawled her way through the message, I wrote it down, word by word, in the margins of one of my mother's newspapers. Just before Janet said "bye," I heard a voice in the background. It had been indistinguishable at the normal speed, but slowed down, it sounded like a man's voice, not too far away. I rewound the message several times trying to decipher what he was saying, but to no avail. Maybe the police would have better luck. I hung up the phone and studied what I had written.

Janet had said to look for the number first, so I focused on it: 19123-816. It looked like one of our client numbers, with a five-digit client code to the left of the hyphen and a matter number to the right. But that matter number was impossibly high. Either Janet had said the matter number wrong, or the entire client number was phony.

The matter number should have identified the one of potentially many cases we were handling for that client. If we had really handled 816 cases for East-West Partners, it would be one of our biggest clients. I would have had to at least have heard of it before. But I had never heard anything about a client named East-West Partners. When Mark came, I would ask him to take me by the firm so I could check the master client list. I was willing to bet that East-West Partners wouldn't be on it.

I looked at the name next. The international/Asian flavor of "East-West Partners" suggested Humphrey Piper. He was our firm's Asian practice. Or he had been, at least.

I looked back at Janet's message. She had said to look for the numbers first and then "the corresponding letters." Not the name, "the corresponding letters."

"East-West Partners, that's EWP," she had said. I doodled the letters on the newspaper. I wrote them down the side of the paper, one on top of the other:

E

W

P.

Then I wrote them close together: EWP. It looked like a monogram. EWP. I wrote it with a flourish. EWP. Then, in a rush, I wrote underneath it, "Elayne Westcott Piper."

Harmony's mother. Humphrey's long dead, extraordinarily wealthy first wife. In whose name Humphrey had bought Janet's condominium.

I looked at it for a long time: Elayne Westcott Piper. Until I had read Mr. Piper's obituary this morning, I hadn't known Harmony's mother's name. Why did it look so familiar?

Then it hit me. It wasn't the name. It was the middle name. I remembered looking at a resume and seeing that middle name. I remembered interviewing the applicant with that middle name. I remembered spending far too much time as summer clerk coordinator keeping the clerk with that middle name in line and out of trouble.

Underneath Harmony's mother's name, I wrote, "Charles Westcott Snow."

by Rosemary Reeve

CHAPTER 36

harlie Snow? That goofy prankster? The clerk who had given me more trouble than anyone else during my two years as summer clerk coordinator? I ground my teeth. If I had been chased around the library, shot at, assaulted, and nearly killed by Charlie Snow, I was never going to live it down.

I thought back over the week. Charlie Snow had been in the office Wednesday evening, the night Janet was killed and thrown down the elevator shaft. That's when he had tried to frighten me in the library by pushing the book off the shelves. Charlie Snow had been in the office early Friday morning, when someone had gone into my office and then tried to kill me when I interrupted him in mid-rummage. In fact, Charlie Snow had admitted opening my door a few hours earlier, when he thought I wasn't there. Suddenly, Charlie Snow seemed to be popping up all over the place.

Had Charlie gone to Tokyo for the client seminar, where Mr. Piper had been murdered? I couldn't remember. It was unlikely because he was only a first-year associate. But, on the other hand, he wanted to do international litigation, and he and Dan Bradford got along like two snickering frat boys. Each was always trying to out-swear, out-drink, and out-gross the other. Charlie had spent a couple of weeks of his summer clerkship with Dan in the Tokyo office, and it was possible that Dan had brought him to the client seminar to reintroduce him to the area. I would have to check my e-mail. Our marketing director had sent out a list of all the attendees a couple of weeks before the seminar, so the people who were staying home could arrange client contacts and business development with the people who were going.

Charles Westcott Snow. Was he some long-lost relative of Harmony's mom, come to claim his share of the Westcott fortune? I tried to remember if I'd ever seen him with Harmony before. Maybe he had come to one of our soccer games while he was studying for the bar, but I think that was it. I didn't remember his having much if anything to do with Harmony, on or off the field. She had been in Alaska working on a natural resources trial when Charlie was summer clerking, and the Brand case had kept her so busy during September and October that she hadn't had much time to get acquainted with any of our new associates, including Charlie Snow.

Her work-imposed seclusion had irritated her. She and I had been summer clerk coordinators together the year before Charlie clerked, and she still took seriously the responsibility of welcoming and orienting new people to Piper Whatcom. As she had put it: "It's awful when you're so miserably overworked and exhausted that you don't even have time to tell the new kids what a great place this is."

I listened to Janet's message again, to check whether the voice at the end might be Charlie Snow's. I couldn't tell. It sounded like a man's voice, and it sounded like he was close by. That was all I could figure out.

I stretched and looked at the clock. It was almost 6:30. Mark should be coming soon. I called the police station again to see if I could entice him to hurry. I wanted to get out of my mother's apartment before she woke up. Nothing by way of solving her and Jimmy's housing crisis had occurred to me during the night, and I didn't want to face her without a plan. If I was unprepared with alternatives, I was afraid she'd try to weasel her way into my house.

Mark sounded rested and refreshed. He greeted me with a conspiratorial whisper: "Do you need to be rescued?"

"They're still asleep," I whispered back. "But I'd like to be gone by the time she wakes up."

"Who's 'they'? Your mother hasn't seduced Murdoch, has she?"

"Not yet. She tried, though. 'They' are my mother and my almost four-year-old half-brother. His name is Jimmy."

I heard a sharp intake of breath on the other end of the line. There was a silence. Then Mark said, "Is that even possible?"

"Yes, Mark, it is possible. You see, a mommy and a daddy love each other very much, and the daddy gets the mommy really, really drunk, and –"

"Shut up. You know what I mean. You're almost an old codger yourself. Shouldn't your mom be past her producing years by now?"

"She was fifteen when she had me. I'm twenty-eight, and Jimmy's almost four, so that means, let's see, that means . . . ." I squinted and tried to do the math in my head. I gave up. It was too early. "Oh, that just means that yes, it was possible."

"It means she was 39 when she had him."

"Well done."

"There's a calculator on Detective Anthony's desk."

I wanted to steer the conversation away from Jimmy. "Look, are you coming to get me pretty soon? I have a lot to tell you."

"Yeah, Murdoch called in your tip on Spirit Lake. We've got the Idaho police looking around up there."

"There's more. I was going through my old voicemails, and I found one from Janet the night she died." I described the message and why I thought it referred to the first Mrs. Piper and maybe Charlie Snow.

Mark said sharply, "You mean that big geeky guy who scared you when he opened your office door?"

"The very same big geek."

"I'll be there in ten minutes. Don't come down to meet me. I'll call Murdoch when I get there, and he'll open the front door."

While I waited for Mark, I rummaged around the apartment for paper and envelopes. I found some with a pentagram on them. Let's hope it didn't mean what I thought it meant. My mother, the devil worshipper. I wrote out a check for $100 and added two twenties from my wallet in case she couldn't cash the check until Monday. I wrote in big letters on the envelope: "For Food, Clothes, Babysitters, or Toys for Jimmy." I licked the envelope closed and added a P.S. on the flap: "Will Call Soon." That was as mushy as I got with my mother. I slipped the envelope under her bedroom door.

Jimmy's letter was harder. He probably couldn't read, so I drew little pictures here and there: "I'm sorry I had to leave before you got up." A sketch of Jimmy asleep with his teddy bear. "I will come back soon to play dinosaurs with you." A sketch of Jimmy with Triceratops horns, claws up and looking ferocious. "Maybe we can go to the zoo together." A sketch of the monkey cage with Jimmy in front. I signed it, "Love, Jack," and drew a passable, smiling Brontosaurus next to my name. Then I tore off the pentagram, stuffed the letter in the envelope, and put the envelope under the sewing room door.

Mark's knock was soft. I slipped silently out of the apartment. Murdoch handed me my keys, and I locked the door as quietly as possible. We didn't speak until we were outside. Then I shook Murdoch's hand and thanked him for watching out for me, and Mark and I got in the police car and headed toward the firm.

It took some courage to go back to that office. Mark looked over at me as we were waiting for the elevator. "You OK?"

"Yeah, why?"

"You're an unusual shade of green. Do you not want to do this?"

"The firm always affects me this way. I'll be fine."

Fortunately, the elevator that opened for us was not the one in which I had nearly bled to death. I was feeling quite cheerful and brave until we arrived in the darkened lobby of the 42nd floor. The backup lights were just bright enough to make everything look jumpy and shadowy, like in a haunted house or a bad dream. There was the marble floor I had skidded on as I raced from the library. There was the button I had hammered so frantically while I was praying for an elevator. And just around the corner was the hallway where I had crept for the document room door. Step and crawl. Step and crawl.

A shudder went down my back. Mark looked at me with concern. "This might be a good time to remind you that I'm armed," he said.

I forced a smile. "Thanks." I had no idea how awful it would be to come back here. What was it going to be like when I tried to go home? I swallowed hard and followed

Mark toward my office. He walked with his gun drawn, turning on every light along the way.

I flinched when I saw my office. It was smeared with fingerprint powder, and quite a few of my books and binders had been pulled off the shelves. "Except for the fingerprint powder, it was like this when we got here," Mark said. "Whoever it was, and whatever he was looking for, he wanted it pretty bad."

I averted my eyes from the mess and sat down at my computer. First I brought up our master client index. I typed in the number Janet had left on my voicemail. Nothing. I typed in the name. Nothing. I typed in the initials. Still nothing. I looked up at Mark, who was leaning over my shoulder. "East-West Partners isn't one of our clients," I said.

I toggled into e-mail. I had a screen of new messages, including one from Marshall Farr. Hell. I started to skim it, with rising surprise. It was the most contrite, apologetic message I had ever received from a partner. It began, "Are you still speaking to me?" He was truly sorry about the mix up over the argument, he wrote, but he wouldn't forget my willingness to jump in at the last minute to help out. Willingness, nothing, I thought to myself. I was tricked.

I read the rest of the message. Marshall said just to leave the cost bill and final judgment to him. He was going to try to negotiate a no-appeal settlement with Boyd Tate, Brand's attorney, and there was no use submitting the final paperwork until we knew whether Tate would bite. In the meantime, he said, I should take it easy. He was doing the "Marshall Farr grand tour right now," but he would treat me to a conciliatory dinner when he got back. "How does Rovers sound?" he asked. My mouth watered. Rovers was one of the best - and most expensive - restaurants in town. I had always wanted to go there.

"What's the Marshall Farr grand tour?" Mark asked.

"He means he's visiting our other offices," I told him. "Marshall runs a taut ship. When he became managing partner, he gave all of the branch offices six months to break even and one year to show a profit. He closed three branches that couldn't make it. I think they're all profitable now, but he's always dropping in on them to keep them on their toes."

I typed in a search command for our marketing director's name and brought up her e-mail about the Asian clients seminar. I paged through the list of attendees' names, and Mark leaned closer as I got to the "S"s:
Brent Sang
Kerry Seymour
Jeremy Smith
Charlie Snow.
Mark tapped the screen. "Bingo," he said.

ALL GOOD THINGS

CHAPTER 37

stretched in one of my visitor's chairs while Mark sat at my desk and called Detective Anthony. Mark gave a loud exclamation, and I looked up, questioningly. Mark put his hand over the mouthpiece.

"The Idaho police found Brand." Something in his voice stirred my nerves.

"He's not dead, is he?" All the rest of our suspects had mysteriously snuffed it hours before the police could apprehend them.

"Not yet. But he's in bad shape. He and Cumming were shooting up. They went too far. Cumming's in a coma, and Brand hasn't regained consciousness." Mark removed his hand and listened to Anthony. He turned to me again. "They found them in a cabin near Spirit Lake. Anthony says to tell you good work on that tip."

Mark started to talk to Anthony about extradition proceedings if Brand survived, and to describe the curious prominence of Charlie Westcott Snow in the events of the preceding week.

I stopped listening. Strange appearances of Charlie Snow notwithstanding, Brand was still the most likely suspect in Harmony's disappearance. He had a motive, he had a record, and he had admitted being at her house the night she vanished. If Brand was the bad guy, and if he died, how would we ever find Harmony? Or find Harmony's body, I thought, much to my surprise and dismay. I tried to reproach myself for my lack of faith, but optimism seemed in short supply this dark, cold Saturday morning. Harmony had been gone almost a week. We didn't have a clue where she was.

Or did we? Janet's words came back to me. "You'll find it with the letters." All right, Janet, I thought, let's suppose that Brand is not the person who snatched Harmony. If it wasn't Brand trying to retrieve that letter, what was that big, trigger-happy guy in black looking for, first in my office and then in my home? And who messed with my desk between when I left on Wednesday night and when I got back from court on Thursday morning?

I focused my thoughts on Charlie Snow. He had been in the office on Wednesday night. I had put my phone on speaker while I listened to my voicemail. Unless I had a visitor, I seldom closed my office door, so he could have overheard Janet's message. It might have been by accident, a particularly disturbing accident if Charlie had just murdered Janet and stuffed her body somewhere to await the plunge down the elevator shaft. Imagine having killed someone - which has to be an intense, stomach-churning business, no matter how mad or calloused you are - only to hear your victim's voice a few minutes later, as you attempt to stroll nonchalantly down the hall. Horrible.

Even if Charlie had heard Janet's message, though, how did he know what to make of it? He obviously didn't, I decided. There had been three separate incidents of searching, after all - four if you counted the attempt I had aborted when I screamed as my office door swung open. That didn't sound like a man who had a clear idea of what he was looking for. Suppose Charlie had heard just enough of Janet's message to make him scared and suspicious. He couldn't know whether Janet was simply speaking in code, or whether she actually had hidden some damning evidence for me to find. But he couldn't take the risk of being wrong. If there was anything to find, Charlie would know that he had to find it before I did.

I hadn't given much thought to the possibility that Janet had hidden something incriminating. Her message itself was so weird that it had occupied my mind trying to decode it. But what, really, had I gleaned from the message? Just that Janet was trying to tell me something and that it probably had something to do with Harmony's mother and possibly Charlie Snow. That wasn't much to go on - unless the message was an arrow that was supposed to point me to something else.

I snagged Mark's attention. He put his hand over the mouthpiece again. "Did Janet have any files for East-West Partners, EWP, or number 19123-816?" I asked.

Mark shook his head. "No. Anthony's been checking. There's nothing like that in the files we took from Janet's, Harmony's, or Humphrey's offices."

Mark went back to discussing search warrants for Charlie's apartment. I busied myself by looking through the files in my credenza, searching for anything remotely connected to a name like East-West Partners or a number like 19123-816. Nothing. I scanned for rhymes, anagrams, plays on words. Still nothing. As delicately as possible, so as not to cause a further avalanche, I checked behind each of the books remaining on my shelves. Still more nothing. I looked through my infamously untidy in-box, which was crammed with continuing legal education fliers, docket notices, and all the caselaw advance sheets that I was supposed to read - somehow - on my own time. There was nothing anywhere that evoked East-West Partners in any way.

I leaned against my credenza, stumped and frowning. Mark hung up the phone. "What's the matter?"

I stared at my bandaged palm, as if I expected the answer to the whole puzzle to magically appear on the smooth, white expanse. I sighed. "For someone who was trying to speak from beyond the grave, Janet left a hell of a hard message to understand."

"I think that was probably intentional."

"Why?"

"If Janet had been sure she was in mortal danger, she wouldn't have been pussyfooting around," Mark said. "She would have either called the police or told someone loud and clear what was going on. I think this message was kind of Janet's insurance policy. She knew she was going to do something dangerous, but she wasn't sure exactly how dangerous it was going to be. If everything went as she hoped, she could tell you the next morning that she had found the file, and you probably wouldn't have thought any more about it. So she didn't want to tip her hand or make you suspicious. In fact, even if we do find something she left us, I doubt it will be too explicit. If her blackmail threat was going to work, she'd want to be very careful about exposing her soon-to-be benefactor. At most, I think we'll find a clue at the end of this rainbow. Maybe not even that."

"You think she tried to blackmail her accomplice?"

"I think so. She doesn't strike me as the kind of person who would get cold feet. Besides, Mr. Piper's death cut off her gravy train. I'd guess she went out campaigning for another benefactor. She probably had more on her accomplice than he had on her, and she decided to try to make it pay."

I shivered. Unexpectedly, Janet's deceptively sweet face came to mind. Then I pictured her, bloody and broken, a collection of bits and pieces jumbled into a body bag in the morgue.

The morgue. I looked up, startled.

Mark took a step toward me. "What is it?"

"I'm not sure," I said slowly. "But if Janet left something behind for us to find, I think I know where it's going to be."

"Where?" he asked.

"In the morgue," I said.

ALL GOOD THINGS

CHAPTER 38

I explained what I was talking about during the elevator ride to the 46th floor. We were heading for Archives, which everybody referred to, grimly but colloquially, as the morgue.

Janet had said to look for the number first. Up to this point, I had thought she said to look for it first just because it was so obviously wrong, because it would show us that the client didn't really exist and clue us into her hidden meaning. Not even Janet kept her files in order by client number. Every attorney, secretary, and legal assistant I knew of alphabetized his or her files by the client name. Janet's files had been in somewhat loose alphabetical order, I recalled, but I figured that was due to her general sloppiness, not an overarching numerical scheme.

But there was one place in the firm where files were kept by number. We sent closed files to Archives, sort of a way station between active duty and off-site storage. I wasn't sure how long the files stayed in Archives, or how the Archives staff organized them, but I remembered once having to find a closed file in the middle of the night when I was working on a brief. After wandering aimlessly among the shelves for the better part of an otherwise billable half hour, I had stumbled on a block of files that all began with the number 38. And right there I had found the file I was looking for, which also began with a 38.

I punched in my access code and pushed open the heavy security door. The air inside was cool and still. Mark and I wandered among the tall shelves. The individual blocks of files were in numerical order, but the blocks themselves were scattered around the room with no discernable logic whatsoever: blocks of files beginning with 43 were next to blocks beginning with 89, and so on. I hazarded a guess that they were arranged according to the plan of our off-site storage facility.

"Either that, or by a secret code, your Governing Committee's birthdates and measurements, or a pact with Satan himself," Mark replied, shaking his head with frustration. "Where in the world do these files begin?"

Finally, we just walked up and down each row, one of us checking the files to the left, the other checking the files to the right. We were almost to the very back of the room when Mark made a triumphant noise. I wheeled around. Mark had found a block of files all beginning with the numbers "19." They looked like they were in numerical order. We checked for number 19123-816. Nothing. The files went from

19100 directly to 19205. Just in case Janet had misfiled it, Mark started at the end of the 19 row and I started at the beginning. We checked up and down the row until we met in the middle. Still nothing.

"I'm sorry, Mark," I said, straightening up and stretching. "It looks like I've led you on a wild goose chase. I didn't mean to waste your time."

"Not a problem," he replied. "I'm glad we checked it."

I was quiet. There were only three alternatives. One, there was no such file, and Janet was just speaking in code. Two, there was such a file, but Janet had secreted it somewhere else. Three - and worst - the murderer had beaten us to the file and taken and destroyed the evidence that might have convicted him and led us to Harmony. I rolled my eyes with frustration.

"Think we're too late?" I asked, dreading the answer.

"I don't know." Mark bent down and studied the row of files. "I can't be certain, but it sure doesn't look like anything has been shoved in or taken out of here. All the spaces between the files are pretty uniform. Nothing's jammed or gapping. I think I'll have this row dusted, though, just in case. Can I call from up here?"

"Sure." I pointed him toward the front of the room, where there was a long, narrow table studded with phones and computer terminals. When the archivists were there sorting and cataloguing files, it looked like NASA's mission control. "Just dial 9 to get an outside line."

I wandered around the shelves while Mark called the police station. I wanted him to feel free to talk in case he wanted to tell Anthony that I was dragging him down blind alleys. After all, I was. I was pretending to be captivated by a Northwest Chamber Orchestra poster on the back wall when I realized that I could no longer hear the murmur of Mark's voice. I walked to the front of the room and found him sitting on the table, his back against the wall and his feet propped up on one of the archivist's chairs. He was staring straight ahead.

"Comfortable?" I asked, sitting down opposite him.

He gave me an abstracted smile. "Humor me," he said.

"About what?"

"Who sits in all these chairs?"

"The archivists, usually. There are six or seven of them."

"And they work from 8 in the morning to 5 in the afternoon like normal people, not from 8 in the morning to 5 in the morning like you insane attorneys?"

"Pretty much, I think."

"So if someone needs a closed file during business hours, they don't just waltz in here, walk by all these nice archivists, and try to get it themselves, do they?"

I was beginning to see his point. "No. They'd never find it. I guess they'd ask the archivists to get it for them."

"And when someone wants to close a file, they don't walk up here and stick it on the shelf, do they? I mean, not only would it take them hours to figure out the right place for it, but wouldn't the archivists have to put it through an elaborate closing and cataloguing procedure?"

"I guess so. So you think, you think -" I paused, feeling like I was treading on his territory. "What do you think?"

" Janet left you that message just after five on Wednesday night. This desk was probably staffed from 8 to 5. She couldn't just walk in here and stick the file on the shelf when there where people up here, could she? No, I think she was waiting until after hours, when all the archivists would be gone, and she could have as much time as she needed to put the file anywhere she wanted. But something interrupted her. Something forced her hand. When does that man's voice come on the tape?"

I considered. "Right after 'OK' and right before 'Bye.' Actually, there's a little pause after "OK," then the man's voice, and then she immediately says, 'Bye.'"

Mark was pacing around the room. "OK, let's go back to Wednesday night. Let's say Janet has made a phony file and put whatever evidence she has in it. She's waiting for a chance to plant the file up here. Five o'clock comes. She starts to leave you the message. The murderer interrupts her. Her cubicle's on the corner; she wouldn't be able to see him if he came up behind her."

Mark took a menacing step toward me. I leaned back, nervously. He was so intense. "Don't do that, please," I said.

"Sorry." He sat down beside me and started swiveling in his chair. "So she's got the file, and the murderer is there beside her. He says something to her. Maybe he says they have to talk. Maybe he says it's urgent, that he's got the money she wanted or whatever, but that she has to come with him right away. What's the best way for her to make pretty sure you're going to get her phony file full of evidence without making the murderer suspicious?"

I thought for a moment, visualizing Janet at her cubicle, the file on her desk, and the murderer - a big, faceless murderer wearing black - leaning over them both. "She couldn't put a note on it for me, I guess," I said. "Most people know that Harmony and I are good friends. Janet doesn't work for me, and it would have looked suspicious if she had been sending me a file. What do you think she did?"

"I think she said something like, 'Oh, just let me tidy my desk,' which the murderer wouldn't mind at all. If he was going to kill her, he probably wanted it to look like she had left the firm in her normal way at her normal time. I think she probably dropped this phony file of hers in her outbox, with a quick note on it saying something like, 'Please close.' The murderer hardly would have worried about her closing a file, would he? And then, I think she went off with the murderer and never came back alive."

"And during the last messenger run at 5:30, the runner would have picked up the file and taken it to Archives," I said, excited.

"Right, and what would Archives do when they got a file for a client that didn't exist?"

"They'd send out an office-wide e-mail asking someone to explain the mystery of East-West Partners."

"Which you would see, and which would jog your memory about Janet's message. So you would come up here, claim the file, and find the evidence. From Janet's point of view, it was perfect. She could hide her file in plain view without making the murderer suspicious, and yet she could actually be pretty sure that Archives would bring the mystery file to your attention in a day or two."

I looked at him with admiration. "I haven't received any e-mails from Archives, so if there is a phony file around, I guess they haven't tried cataloguing it yet. It would either be waiting for them up here or in one of the runner's carts, waiting to be delivered to them."

"Wouldn't it have gotten here by now?"

"It probably should have, but I doubt much was accomplished on Thursday. Most people went to Mr. Piper's memorial service, and then Marshall closed the firm in the afternoon when he found out about Janet. And on Fridays, a lot of the runners get weekend fever and duck out early. Besides, stuff going to Archives doesn't take high priority. No one's really waiting for it, you know? But let's start looking up here just in case."

Mark checked the bins by the long table and computer terminals while I searched the archivists' in-boxes. Then I thumbed through several cartons of files stacked by the door while Mark examined all the counters and cubbyholes he could find. After about fifteen minutes of papercuts, we were both ready to take a crack at the mail carts.

The mailroom was dark and warm. I could hear the purr of the fax machines, which kept spitting out paper at all hours of the day and night. I pointed out the 42nd and 46th floor carts. "If it's still in the pick-up stage, it will be somewhere in the basket of the 42nd floor cart," I told him. "If they've sorted it for delivery already, it will be in the 46th floor cart in the hanging file marked Archives."

Mark checked under Archives. "Not there," he said, sitting down beside me on the floor and starting to sift through the materials in the basket of the 42nd floor cart. There were a lot of files in the basket, a lot of books, and a lot of interoffice envelopes. I held the envelopes gingerly with tissues as I peeked inside - just in case. We got to the bottom of the basket. Nothing.

Dammit. I leaned back against the warm fax machine. I was about to give up hope and admit that there either wasn't a phony file or that the murderer had gotten to it ahead of us when I heard Mark curse, then gasp. He had been tidily putting everything back in the basket. One of the files had slipped from his hands. I blinked at it as it fanned on the linoleum floor. It looked like it had come apart, but in reality, the file that had been stuck inside it had simply slid out intact.

We both stared at it. There it was, right on the floor. Its tab said "East-West Partners." Along the side was the number: "19123-816." And on the top was a sticky note, in Janet's angular handwriting. "Close File," it said.

Mark looked up at me. His eyes were shining.

"You are incredible," I said, and I meant it.

He shook his head a little. "No, I got one thing wrong," he said, in mock chagrin.

"What?"

He pointed to but didn't touch the sticky note. "I should have guessed that Janet Daniels wouldn't say 'please.'"

ALL GOOD THINGS

CHAPTER 39

I felt like the dog must feel when the hunter takes the duck away. Our mailroom was crowded with cops - Anthony, Sawyer, a couple of the criminalists I was starting to recognize, and a few other people I had never seen before. Anthony was on the phone, explaining the scope of the search warrant and working through protections for privileged materials. Other cops were talking together in low voices that I couldn't make out. Mark and I hovered on the outskirts of the group. It struck me as unfair. We were the people responsible for this whole production. We were the people who had found the thing, for Pete's sake. Right now, however, we couldn't even get close to the East-West Partners file.

Sawyer sashayed over to us, looking tremendously self-important. I watched his approach with suspicion, remembering all too well how much Sawyer resented Mark's working with Detective Anthony. Sawyer ignored me and turned pointedly to Mark.

"Anthony wants a complete check on the file and the cart before we have any civilians look at it," he said, putting an unwarrantedly pejorative stress on "civilians." "He says you're supposed to take Mr. Hart to breakfast and bring him back here in an hour. Mr. Hart is to review the file once its contents have been properly documented and secured." His voice rang with triumph. He smirked at Mark. Now look who's doing the chauffeuring duties, his expression said.

Mark didn't seem to mind at all. He smiled at Sawyer and said, "Great. Jack and I will be back in an hour. Tell Detective Anthony thanks for us, OK?"

Sawyer opened and then closed his mouth. It seemed to dawn on him that taking a witness to breakfast - even a witness as unpleasant and irritating as I was - might be preferable to crawling around a Piper Whatcom mail cart looking for fingerprints. As if to resolve any doubt in Sawyer's mind, Anthony looked up as Mark and I left the mailroom. "Good work, Oden!" he called after us. "You, too, Jack." There was a general murmur of assent from the huddled officers. Sawyer looked at us murderously and turned away.

"Poor Sawyer," Mark mused in the elevator going down to the lobby.

"Poor *Sawyer*?"

"Yeah. Now he's mad because I'm taking you to breakfast. But he'd be just as mad if Anthony had kept me behind and sent him with you. His whole life is a grudge. He never knows what's going on, but he's always sure that someone else is being treated better than he is."

"Harmony's had a couple of cases with plaintiffs like that," I told him as we got back into the police car. "She used to do mostly employment litigation. She defended one case where the plaintiff hadn't been promoted one year but had been promoted the next. The plaintiff said both decisions showed that the company was biased against women."

"How did the case come out?"

"During cross examination, Harmony asked the plaintiff how the promotion decisions showed gender discrimination. It was risky because it opened the door for the plaintiff to whine to the jury. Usually, you want your opponent to just sit there and agree with you during cross examination. But Harmony gave her the rope, and the plaintiff hung herself. The plaintiff said that when she didn't get the promotion, the company had been trying to keep her down because she was a woman. Then she said that when she did get the promotion, the company had been trying to overwhelm her with work and sabotage her with increased responsibility - also because she was a woman. A couple of the jurors laughed out loud."

"What did Harmony do?"

"She just looked at the plaintiff for a moment. And then she said, 'When you didn't get promoted, you were hurt and angry and you wanted to hurt the company back. And then when you did get promoted and the new job was a lot harder than you thought it would be, you wanted all the problems you were having to be someone else's fault, didn't you?' The thing was, Harmony didn't say it like she was accusing her of anything. She said it very, very gently, like she felt for her, like she was sad for her. After about five seconds, the plaintiff sniffed and said, 'Yes. Yes, I did.' And that was really pretty much it. Harmony moved for a directed verdict in favor of the defense, and the judge granted it from the bench."

"Harmony must really be something."

"She is. And thanks for using the present tense."

We were cruising down an unusually empty Fourth Avenue. The rain had slowed from a crashing torrent to a steady, soaking downpour. "Steve's Broiler OK?" Mark asked, parking the car in a puddle in front of Steve's dark windows and blue and white sign. I made encouraging sounds. We walked into the smoky interior, where the moist air was thick with the fumes of steaming coffee and frying bacon. Mark inhaled happily as we waited to be seated. "Since the Doghouse closed, I come here a lot," he said. "It's the only place in town where you can smoke a pack of cigarettes without lighting up."

Our waitress was a cute brunette with dimples and dangly, heart-shaped earrings. My hair fell back from my stitched forehead as I lowered myself unsteadily into the booth. The waitress clucked with sympathy at the sight.

"What have you been up to, handsome? Get a little rowdy last night?" She smiled at me. "I'd hate to see the other guy."

It had been a long time since anyone had called me handsome. I wasn't sure how to respond. "Thank you for the compliment," I said, returning the smile, "but in this case, the other guy is my coffee table."

"He put a hell of a dent in it, though," Mark chimed in.

The waitress laughed and patted me on my injured shoulder. "My hero," she said. My smile widened in a rictus of pain, which the waitress seemed to take as encouragement. She asked us what we wanted to drink, nipped away, and returned with our steaming mugs of hot coffee - and an unexpected butterhorn for me.

"On the house," she said. "It will give you strength."

When she had gone with our orders for French toast and pancakes, Mark grinned at me. "You heartbreaker."

"Shut up," I said, offering him half the butterhorn.

"I'm serious," he said, shaking his head at the pastry and dousing his coffee with cream. "You have that helpless look that appeals to women. Especially with your head busted up like that. That's why the waitress flirted with you instead of me - even though I'm clearly much more attractive."

We talked about the East-West Partners file as we attacked our breakfasts. "I think it was a real Piper Whatcom file," I told him. "It had all the file codes and office tabs on it, which would be hard for Janet to fake. I think she just put phony name and number labels over the ones that were already there."

Mark mopped up his maple syrup with the last of his French toast and nodded. The file had seemed too thick and dogeared to be a complete fabrication. He drained his coffee and glanced at his watch. "We've still got 35 minutes before we have to be back," he said. "Do you want to hang out here and keep flirting with the waitress, or is there somewhere else you'd like to go?"

"Is there time to see Betsy?" I asked.

Mark considered, then shook his head. "She's at Emerald City Vets. It's out in your neck of the woods. We could get there and back, but you wouldn't be able to spend any time with her."

"Not worth it, I guess," I said, disappointed. I missed Betsy.

"Plan B?"

"Why don't we just go back to the firm? I need to get some documents out today. Actually, I needed to get them out yesterday, but I completely forgot about calling to ask for an extension."

"I can't imagine why," Mark said. "Nothing like being stabbed, shot, and stomped on to sharpen your memory for important details like little bits of paper. Who's the numbskull you're working for now? Is it that awful Jeremy Smith again?"

"No. The partner I'm working for is Dan Bradford, but the numbskull who's putting the pressure on me is opposing counsel." I told him about the nasty voicemails demanding the documents. "If they're not on his desk first thing Monday, he's going to file a motion to compel and ask for sanctions - against the firm and against me personally."

"You're not up to working this weekend," Mark said, with real concern. "As soon as you've looked at that file and seen Betsy, I'm going to take you back to your mother's and make sure that you get some rest."

"I can't, Mark. I appreciate it, but I really can't."

"Isn't there someone else who could pitch in?"

"Charlie Snow, I guess, but - well, you know."

"Yeah, I know. Depending on what we find in that file and lurking around his apartment, Charlie may be otherwise engaged this weekend." He reassessed. "How much work are we talking about here?"

"Seven, eight hours to finish reviewing the documents, three or four hours to draft the objections, five or six hours to designate the responsive documents, three or four hours to copy them or get them copied. The copy center really ought to do that last bit, but they don't work on weekends. And even when they do work, they balk at 28 volumes of documents with instructions to copy a document here and there. So, of course, I end up doing it myself."

"Can you bill for that?"

I shook my head. Suddenly I was exhausted. The smoky room seemed stifling. "Let's get out of here," I said.

Mark had fed me last time, so I tried to pay the check for both of us. He objected. "Can't let you do that, man. It's against regulations to accept gratuities of any kind."

"It's not a gratuity. It's breakfast."

"Gratuities include meals and beverages. I'm not going to get kicked off the force for eating two pieces of French toast, even though they were extremely good."

We ended up splitting the check, but I left the tip - a nice, round 100-percent tip. I caught Mark's amused glance and said, "She was very efficient."

"That she was, handsome," he agreed. "And perceptive, too." On the way out, he asked casually, "What's the name of your numbskull opposing counsel on this document thing?"

I told him. "Why?"

"Hang on a second." He left me in the rock-walled entryway while he ducked back into the restaurant. He came out looking so pleased with himself that I was alarmed.

"What have you done?" I asked.

"I found the numbskull's address. He lives by Volunteer Park, and we have just enough time to get there and back."

"What for? I don't have the documents ready to give him."

189

"I know that. But I think your favorite numbskull needs a little visit from the police." He chuckled at my horrified expression. "Don't worry. It's all perfectly legal. You need rest, and when you're not resting, we need you to be available to work with us on this case. I'm just going to explain to the numbskull why you won't be able to get those documents to him for a while."

Mark's assurances notwithstanding, I still had grave concerns about our visit to the numbskull. My misgivings intensified when Mark pulled up in front of a lovely house on lovely, tree-lined Aloha Street and told me to scrunch down so the numbskull wouldn't be able to see that I was in the car.

I obeyed but peeped through the window as he strode up to the porch and rapped commandingly on the door. He didn't quite hammer on it, but his knock was insistent and authoritative. It would be impossible to sleep through it and mighty hard to ignore. Maybe they taught recruits to knock like that at the police academy.

The door swung open. The numbskull stood there in his bathrobe and slippers. Even from my cramped vantage point, I could see the apprehension in his face. Mark disappeared into the lovely house for a few minutes. When he emerged, the numbskull was shaking Mark's hand desperately. He seemed to be thanking Mark over and over.

"What happened in there?" I burst out when we had turned the corner and it was safe to sit up again. "What did you do to that poor man?"

"Not a thing," Mark replied. "Not a damn thing. I just told him that you had been shot and seriously injured and would be unable to return to work and get the documents to him until you had fully recovered and finished assisting us in our investigation. And he was very nice. He thanked me for coming by and said that you shouldn't lose a minute's sleep over the documents. In fact, he wished you a speedy recovery and said he doesn't really even need them until next month."

"He did?"

"Yes, he did."

"Wow," I said. "Thank you."

"You're welcome," Mark said, ruffling his black hair. "The police are here to help people get along, Jack. And you would be surprised how many people are cooperative if you give them half a chance."

And if you carry a gun and have the power to arrest them, I thought.

As if he read my mind, Mark looked over at me and smiled. "Of course, I may have asked just a few innocuous questions that may somehow have led him to believe that I suspected him of being the person who shot you."

"You didn't!"

"Oh, just the basics. Nothing out of the ordinary. Where were you in the early morning of Friday, October 27? Did anyone see you while you were asleep alone in your lovely home? No one? Oh, I *see*. Do you have anything against Mr. Hart? Have you pressured or threatened Mr. Hart during this litigation? Do you know of any reason why Mr. Hart would be so concerned about your not receiving your documents on time that he would insist on staggering into work right after he was released from the hospital?"

He winked at my speechless face. "I really got him with that last one. He had to say that he was sure the only reason you were so concerned was that you were a very responsible and dedicated attorney. And since we'd got to something we agreed on, I just made him say a few more nice things about you, shook his hand, and told him I was glad to see that you had such a good friend, even among opposing counsel, and that I was sorry that I had bothered him for no good reason. That's when he started thanking me all over the place. We parted the best of friends."

I was simultaneously stunned, appalled, and touched. I started to stammer out a few inadequate words of surprise, scolding, and thanks, but a beep from the Mobile Data Terminal interrupted me. Mark pushed a few buttons and brought up a message from Anthony: "Are you on your way back with Jack?"

Somehow Mark managed to type back a response and drive at the same time: "Yes, sir. We're about five minutes away from Jack's firm."

"Don't come to firm," Anthony sent back. "Come to department instead." The screen flickered while the rest of the message came up: "We've arrested Charlie Snow."

by Rosemary Reeve

CHAPTER 40

harlie sat with his head in his hands in the cramped interrogation room. He
didn't look up as I came in. I didn't want to talk to him. I was so full of rage
that I didn't trust my voice. I sat down as far away from Charlie as I could get.
I was so repulsed and angry that I didn't trust myself to be within striking distance of
him.

When Mark and I had arrived at the police station, Detective Anthony had showed
us what the police had found in Charlie's shabby studio apartment on the south edge
of Capitol Hill:

- A sizeable stash of pot, meth, and pills. No wonder Charlie
  acted like such a loon sometimes.
- An assault rifle. "It's not the gun we were looking for,"
  Anthony had said, "but if he's got an illegal firearm, he
  probably has some legal weapons as well."
- A binder full of news clippings about the Pipers. Some of them
  were photocopies, some were slick pictures from microfilm,
  some were freshly cut and mounted newsprint. The last entry
  was Mr. Piper's obituary, the same one I had read the day
  before. There was a thin red line underneath Harmony's
  mother's name: Elayne Westcott Piper.
- A folder full of birth certificates, death certificates, marriage
  licenses, wills, and genealogy charts. Charlie Westcott Snow
  was Harmony's first cousin, from the disinherited side of the
  family. Elayne Westcott and Emily Westcott had been sisters,
  twin daughters of Harvey Westcott. Harvey's will cut off Emily
  and left everything to Elayne. Harvey had died in 1963. Emily
  had married Benjamin Snow and had Charlie a few years
  afterward. Charlie was an orphan. Emily's death certificate
  said she had died in childbirth. Benjamin Snow had killed
  himself in 1970.
- A manila envelope full of photographs. There were a couple of
  shots of the Pipers' house, from several different angles, and a

lot of posed pictures of Mr. Piper, which Charlie might have taken from our marketing department. They looked like something we'd use for client proposals or brochures. Charlie had pictures of Harmony's little red Honda, front and back. He had several pictures of Harmony, too, which looked like candid shots from our firm picnic this summer. We had invited the former clerks who were studying for the bar. Charlie was in two of the pictures, lurking suspiciously in the background. One picture had the three of them: Harmony and Mr. Piper smiling at each other by the volleyball net; Charlie keeping a wary eye on them from the other side. Charlie must have swiped the picnic pictures from the lunchroom bulletin board. At the very bottom of the envelope was a black and white photograph of an Asian man who looked familiar. It was Mr. Yamashita, the man who had cried at Mr. Piper's memorial service.

- A pocket diary, swarming with notes in Charlie's sloppy handwriting. From August on, Charlie had documented his observations of Humphrey and Harmony Piper - both in and out of the office. He must have been stalking them. He knew that Harmony and her stepmother went to the Japanese Presbyterian Church overlooking Lake Washington every Sunday. He knew that Mr. Piper worked out at the Washington Athletic Club whenever he was in Seattle. During the latter part of August, he had written on ten consecutive days, "Harmony to Market, then to JH's GL. Back PWH by mid-evening." Harmony to the Market, then to Jack Hart's in Green Lake. He must have been spying on her - and on me - as she shopped for and made me dinner.

I had spent about an hour reviewing the evidence from Charlie's apartment. Now I glared venomously at him across the interrogation room table. He was too far away to hit, but not too far to spit at. I didn't want to be here. In fact, I wanted to be anywhere but here. Anthony had insisted. Charlie had refused to tell the police anything until he talked to "his attorney," Jack Hart. Anthony had told me to give it a shot but not mislead him. Whatever they got on Charlie, and however they got it, they wanted it to stand up in court.

I sat silently in the stuffy room until I had control over my voice. I rehearsed what I was going to say in my mind until I was sure I could get it out without actually lunging across the table and throttling him. I cleared my throat. Charlie looked up with a start. I saw the relief flooding into his pinched, pale face.

"Jack!" he cried. "I knew you'd come." He began to get up from his chair, as if he were going to lumber toward me. I stopped him with an upraised hand.

"Sit down," I hissed at him. He sat, alarm tightening his silly mouth. "Listen to me. I am not representing you, Charles Westcott Snow. There is not one chance in hell that I would be your attorney. Not one chance. This is not a privileged communication. When you are done talking to me, I am going to walk out that door and tell everything you said - everything, Charlie - to the police. You got it?"

He nodded weakly.

"So do you still want to talk to me, or should I make it easier on both of us and leave right now?"

He was silent.

I got up and stalked toward the door. Over my shoulder I said, "They'll get you a public defender. I think they may be willing not to seek the death penalty if you tell them what you did with Harmony."

Charlie squeaked with anguish. I glanced back at him and saw him shaking his head, his hair plastered to his forehead with sweat and his eyes wide and glassy with horror. In spite of myself, I couldn't walk out on him. I couldn't go through that door. Not yet.

"Where is she, Charlie? Where's Harmony?" My voice surprised me. It was soft and quiet - not gentle, exactly, but soft. I was just too tired and hurt and sad to bully him anymore. The thought that Harmony might have been murdered just because Charlie hoped he was going to inherit some money washed over me like a dark foam, smothering my rage with such deep regret that I could barely breathe. Just for money. The best, kindest, smartest person I knew. Gone forever, just for money.

I stared at Charlie without really seeing him. I knew what it was like to need money. I knew what it was like to be poor, really poor, to go to school every day in thrift shop clothes that never looked or smelled right, to wonder which bill I would be able to pay and end up not being able to pay any of them, to never be able to buy the convenience, freedom, courtesy, and security that even middle-class people take for granted. I knew what it was like to face people's judgments every day. I knew what it was like to see people's faces register pity, repulsion, or fear when they saw me or talked about me. I knew what it was like to be a problem to be solved. Or ignored. Or denied.

Real poverty takes everything away. You can't even walk down the street without being reminded, over and over, that you're nothing, that you'll always be nothing, and that there's nothing you can do about being nothing. When you're really poor, everything you see is just something else you can't have.

by Rosemary Reeve

I had faced real poverty for years. I would never be able to forget its staring, terrible eyes. But I would have faced real poverty every day for the rest of my life if it meant I could have spared Harmony from Charlie Snow. I would have paid him anything to keep away from her. Hell, I was such a soft touch that I probably would have emptied my bank account for him if I had had even the slightest inkling he needed money. So would Harmony.

I sucked in the sour air. Of course. Harmony wouldn't have been able to stand the thought of her full first cousin, orphaned, disinherited, and living in what was probably a crackhouse in the bad part of Capitol Hill. Charlie must have approached Harmony for money. That explained her phone call to her father. The maid who had overheard their conversation had got it a little wrong. Harmony must have wanted money, all right, but for her long-lost cousin, not herself. And Mr. Piper had refused, so Charlie had killed him at the client seminar. And he had taken Harmony - or had had Janet take Harmony for him. But why? To pressure her for more money than she was willing to give him? To force her to change her will?

I didn't know, but if Charlie had snatched Harmony for money, there was a possibility that she was still alive. I plunked down in the chair next to Charlie. I leaned close to him.

"You are in a hell of a lot of trouble, Charlie. If you don't tell me right now where Harmony is, I am going to walk out that door and let them do whatever they like with you. They've got four murder charges to pin on somebody, and I can almost guarantee that they're going to pin them on you."

Charlie went even paler than before. Tardily, I remembered that there hadn't been any stories in the newspapers about Mrs. Piper's and Janet's deaths. Maybe the police were trying to keep them as quiet as possible. I had to be careful about what I gave away.

"If Harmony is still alive, and you tell me where she is, I promise you that I will help you defend the three murder charges. I'll give you money for a lawyer. I'll work for you myself for free. Anything. I don't care about the other people. All I care about is Harmony. If you give me Harmony, I'll help you."

Charlie looked at me wildly with huge, terrified eyes. When he spoke, his voice was broken. "Jack, if I had any idea where she was, I'd tell you. But I don't. I don't know anything. I didn't take Harmony. I didn't kill anybody. I didn't kill Harmony. I don't even know her."

"Oh, you kept that diary of yours just out of idle curiosity?" I yelled at him. "You have everything in there except Harmony's favorite ice cream. You must have followed her around 24 hours a day."

Charlie's shoulders slumped. He craned his neck back and let his mouth drop open. He looked like he was drowning. "I kept a lookout for her and her dad because I was trying to get to know them, trying to figure out where they went so I could be there,

196

trying to figure out what they liked so I could like it, too. I wanted to become familiar with them, friendly with them, before I told them who I was. I wanted them to like me enough to want to help me."

"I don't believe you."

"It's true. That's why I applied to Piper Whatcom. That's why I summer clerked here. When I found out that Harmony was up in Alaska and Mr. Piper was going to be in Tokyo that summer, I could have screamed. That's why I invented an interest in international litigation and got myself sent to Tokyo for two weeks."

"And did you ingratiate yourself to Mr. Piper while you were there?" I didn't even try to keep the sarcasm out of my voice.

"I couldn't. He was in Korea the first week and Taiwan the second. I've never really had a conversation with Mr. Piper. I've only said three words to Harmony in my whole life."

I remembered seeing his name on the Crabfest bill. "That's not true. You worked for her on the Brand case."

"For a couple of hours, yes. I cite checked a brief for her. She told me what to do, and I said, OK. I handed it to her and said, Here. She told me I had done a good job, and I said, Thanks. Three words, Jack, that's it."

He got up and started pacing around the room. "Look, I admit I went into your office on Wednesday night. When you called me by my middle name there in the library, I got scared. I had put my full name on my resume when I applied for my clerkship. I thought that if Harmony or Mr. Piper saw it, it might help me get in the door. I haven't used my middle name at the firm since then. Like I said, I wanted Harmony and Mr. Piper to get to know me and like me before they found out who I was. I didn't think it would be a big problem until now."

"Now?"

He grimaced. "What with Mr. Piper's dying suddenly, Harmony's not coming to work, and the cops' being all over the place, I figured that it might not be a such a good idea to leave something around that people might use to figure out I was one of Harmony's relatives. I didn't want to end up dead or arrested." His voice shook on the last word. "I looked around your office until I found your summer clerk stuff. I took the resume with my full name from your binder and replaced it with one that just said Charles Snow. And I promise you, that's all I did."

I thought that over. "You might have done that to cover up your motive for killing Mr. Piper and kidnapping Harmony," I said.

"And if I had, would I leave you alive? Someone who had seen the resume? Someone who called me Charles Westcott Snow whenever he was pissed at me? Which is always? Someone who might call me Charles Westcott Snow in front of anybody, even the cops? If I was the cold-blooded murderer you think I am, I would have killed you in a minute."

I bored my eyes into his. "Maybe you tried," I said.

His blank look was masterful in its weak blue innocence. For the first time, I started to believe him. If he was hiding his guilty knowledge of his attacks on me, he was good actor. "What about Friday morning, when you opened the door to my office?" I asked. "You were lying about looking for a binder of documents. You hadn't touched three-fourths of the binders you had in the conference room. There's no way you would have come to my office looking for more."

"You're right. I was lying. I was going to look for your hiring committee correspondence file. I had talked to the hiring coordinator on Thursday morning to see whether anyone else would have documents with my middle name. And I had found out that the summer clerk coordinator kept all the hiring correspondence. I was going to tear out any letters with my full name on them."

I rubbed my eyes. Charlie was starting to make sense to me. Doubts began to crowd into my mind. Even if Charlie had been the gunman at the firm, there would have been no reason for him to go to my home and try to take the Brand files. If he had gone there to kill me, he would have just marched me into my basement and put a bullet through my head. I groped for a question to ask him.

"You lied to the security guard," I said, a little weakly. "When he asked you where you were at 2:11 a.m. Monday morning, you told him you were home in bed. You would still have been in Japan then."

Charlie exhaled in irritation. "Yes, I was still in Japan, but I didn't think of that there in the middle of the night with some nutcase pressing me against the wall and shouting questions at me. Would you remember exactly where you were at 2:11 on Monday morning if you thought you had someone behind you with a gun in your back?"

I thought that over, glumly. It made sense.

Charlie put his hand on my wounded shoulder. There was no malice in his eyes, no knowledge of or delight at causing me pain. I could have sworn that he didn't know I was injured. "Think about it, Jack. You've always been fair with me. You spent a lot of time with me teaching me how to behave at the firm. I know you don't like me, but you recommended that the hiring committee offer me an associate position because you thought I did good work and I was smart."

I blinked at him. How did he know that?

He smiled grimly at my surprise. "The recruiting coordinator told me. So if I'm so smart, would I kill the only family I have, the only people who could help me? I'm smart enough to know about estate planning, Jack. I'm smart enough to know that a bright attorney who's worth as much as Harmony would have a will, and that all her money would be neatly distributed with contingent beneficiaries and residuary clauses and nothing left to go to long-lost relatives she didn't even know she had."

"You could have kidnapped her and tried to force her to change her will."

198

"And lead the police right to my doorstep? That wouldn't be very smart, would it? Can you imagine the headlines? 'Heiress killed on Thursday - changed will in favor of Charlie Snow on Wednesday.' I might as well just jump off the Space Needle with a big sign saying, 'I killed my cousin.'"

I couldn't think of anything to say. Charlie took my silence for suspicion. "I didn't touch her, Jack, I swear to you. I didn't touch anybody."

I shut my eyes and leaned back in my chair.

Damn it all to hell. Charlie was a silly ass and a manipulator and a sneak.

But the worse part of it was, I believed him.

by Rosemary Reeve

CHAPTER 41

My head was swimming. I sat silently in the interrogation room while Charlie babbled on beside me. I wasn't listening to him anymore. I was thinking about Harmony. If Charlie hadn't taken her, who had? Janet was dead. Mrs. Piper was dead. Brand was lying unconscious in some Idaho hospital. Every time I thought we were getting somewhere, we ended up back at the beginning.

I put my elbows on the table and cradled my aching head in my hands. Charlie was almost in tears, dithering about his innocence. He grabbed my injured shoulder, put his face close to mine, and shook me. Through the resulting thunderclap of pain, I could just make out what he was saying.

"You have to get me out of here, Jack," he pleaded, shaking me again. "I won't go to prison. I can't. I'll kill myself first. I won't go back there."

He took his hand off my shoulder. I crashed back into my chair, trembling with pain. I pulled myself together, piece by piece. What did he mean, "back there"? Without knowing it, I had used Harmony's technique of silence to prod Charlie into saying more than he intended to.

I got up slowly and faced him. Charlie was taller than I was, but he slouched enough so that I looked him right in the eye. I took a step toward him. He took a step back.

"Back there?" I said.

He started, and for the first time, looked self-conscious. He didn't answer.

"You've been in prison before?"

"No, of course not," he burst out.

"So what did you mean, 'back there'?"

Still no answer. I started to shrug, then thought better of it as my shoulder throbbed. I threw up my hands in a gesture of indifference. "Suit yourself," I said, walking toward the door. "I'll find out from the cops."

I was almost to the door. Charlie blurted, "It was a long time ago."

I stopped and looked back at him. Charlie continued, weakly, "I was a kid. My dad died. I bounced around a little, but I ended up at that big place on First Hill, the one they're investigating now."

I gaped at him. "At the Grange?"

He let out a long, shuddering sigh. "At the Grange," he said. "It may not be prison, but I bet it's the closest thing to it. I won't go through that again, Jack. I promise you, I will kill myself first."

Two conflicting impressions hit me in rapid succession. First, I felt so sorry for Charlie that I couldn't speak. I remembered his panicked squeak when I had pulled his tie through the shelf. I remembered his almost hysterical fear when Frank had slammed him into the wall outside the conference room. I remembered the horror on his face when he had looked wildly from me to Frank. Which one of you, his expression had said, is going to hurt me worse? It was the expression of someone who had been hurt too much, too often, too long. I almost reached out my hand to pat Charlie on the shoulder and tell him that everything was going to be OK.

Then the second impression hit me, and I couldn't move. Charlie wasn't a victim anymore. He was a victimizer. There's a lot of room in a law firm for victimizers, but Charlie just wasn't good enough at it yet. He hadn't learned that in a law firm, an associate can be malicious only if he never gets caught or if he can convince everyone that it's the other guy's fault. Charlie knew how to be a jerk, but not a clever jerk. That's why I had spent half my time last summer trying to save his sorry ass. Cruel practical jokes, vicious gossip, nasty e-mail bandit messages that really hurt people, that hit them in places they couldn't defend: Charlie had done them all. He had run me ragged trying to apologize for him, cover up for him, rein him in.

I knew the odds. I was determined to beat them, but I knew them. Boys who have been abused grow up to abuse. Boys who have been molested grow up to molest. What had Charlie grown up to do? I tried to imagine what it would be like to have grown up at the Grange - always afraid, always alone, always crushed under the silence, the snitching, the certainty that no one would believe you if you complained and that no one would help you if you tried to get away.

I didn't need to imagine how hard it would be for Charlie to have struggled through high school, through college, through law school, through the bar. I had done that myself, and sometimes I still dreamed about it. It was always the same dream. I was on a high ladder above something terrible. Sometimes it was a tangible threat - spiders, or snakes, or men with huge forearms webbed with swelling veins. Sometimes it was just an abyss, an immense, colorless nothingness into which I knew I would fall, and out of which I knew I would never emerge. Every paper, every test, every project was another rung on that ladder. The higher I climbed, the happier I was to put more and more distance between me and the nothingness below. But I was also more and more afraid. As I climbed through school, as I climbed through my career, I was more and more terrified of falling back where I had been.

My bad dreams couldn't be anything compared to Charlie's, I thought. Even the initial disclosures from the Grange had been shattering. I looked over at him. His face was gray and rigid. He looked like someone who was staring into hell - and not for the first time. How would I react if I had grown up like Charlie, only to learn that my cousin had lived in wealth and privilege only a few miles away? How would I feel if I had fought every step of the way through law school and into my first good job, only to see my Harvard-educated cousin cruising along ahead of me, soaring toward partnership? How would I feel if I had to take assignments from her? Suck up to her? I remembered the weird resentment in his voice: "I've never really had a conversation with Mr. Piper. I've only said three words to Harmony in my whole life."

Was that it? Resentment, retaliation, revenge? All those photographs, those clippings, that surveillance. They smacked of feeding his grudges until they consumed him. Maybe this whole nightmare had been Charlie's way of evening the score. Charlie's mother and father had died, and Charlie had disappeared into the untold tortures and privations of the Grange. Now Harmony's stepmother and father had died and Harmony had disappeared - into what? I simultaneously wanted to murder Charlie and sit down on the floor and howl for the waste of it all.

I settled for scouring Charlie's eyes for any clue of what was going on. He looked back at me anxiously, but beyond the fear, I could see nothing. It gave me the creeps. It was true that I didn't see any malice, any triumph, any hatred, any revenge. But the thing was, I didn't see anything at all in Charlie's eyes. Just the same emptiness that was at the bottom of the ladder in my worst dreams. It was like someone had taken everything away from Charlie, and he wasn't ever going to get it back.

I couldn't look at that terrible blankness any more. I stumbled toward the door, thrashing Charlie away as he tried to clutch at me. Charlie was calling my name. He started to scream as Mark Oden pulled me through the door. Charlie was still screaming my name as Mark slammed the door shut behind me.

by Rosemary Reeve

CHAPTER 42

"Do you think he did it?"

I had told Mark and Detective Anthony everything that had happened in that awful room. They had listened gravely and silently. When I had finished, Anthony had patted me on my uninjured shoulder and asked Mark to take me outside so I could get some air.

The storm had dwindled to a shower so fine that it felt less like rain falling than like mist rising from a dark, cold lake. The breeze blew clouds of vapor around me. I felt clean and cool in the wet, gray air.

I looked over at Mark. He was waiting patiently for an answer to his question.

"I don't know," I told him. "I have a hard time believing that Charlie could pull off something so elaborate. Charlie does mean, hurtful things sometimes, but he's such a goon about it that he always gets caught."

"Janet could have helped him plan it."

I tried to imagine Charlie and Janet in cahoots. I failed.

I tried to imagine Charlie and Janet even having a conversation. I still failed. I shook my head.

"Maybe Janet would have helped if she thought he would inherit Harmony's fortune and give half of it to her," I said, "but I can't believe she'd risk so much as breaking a nail to help Charlie get revenge on the Pipers. She'd cut off her income by doing that. Look at that condo. Mr. Piper paid her pretty darn well, and she wasn't in business for her health."

"I know."

"And even if she was involved," I continued, "two things still don't make any sense to me."

"What?"

"One, I don't understand why Charlie would come to my house to get the <u>Brand</u> files. And two, assuming it was Charlie, and assuming he was there because he wanted to polish me off to make sure I wouldn't blurt out his full name at an inopportune moment, I don't understand why he didn't just shoot me right off the bat instead of waiting while he looked in my briefcase."

Mark took a big gulp of the soft air. "I can give you some possible answers," he said, "although I'm not sure they're even close to correct."

"Shoot."

"OK, if Charlie overheard you listening to Janet's message, he probably figured out that Janet had hidden something for you. So he searched your office on Wednesday night and didn't find anything. He had a day to think about it some more and wanted to try again early Friday morning. But you foiled his plans, first by screaming when he opened the door, and then by coming back to your office after he thought you had gone."

"So since the police were all over the office, he decided to track me down at home?" I asked. Mark nodded. It still didn't make any sense to me. "But why would he think I had taken the file or whatever home?"

Mark shrugged. "I'm not sure. I think he's nuts enough to believe he could . . . well, persuade you to tell him what you had found and where you had put it."

"You mean torture me?"

"Something like that. Or drug you, possibly. It would explain why he didn't kill you right away. It would also explain why he picked up the Brand files when he saw your briefcase sitting there. He couldn't be sure how Janet would have disguised her clue. He probably wanted to look through them or ask you about them - when you weren't in a position to refuse."

A sudden gust of wind chilled me. Mark turned his back to the draft. His hair ruffled out in the wind. "So now what do you think? You seem to know him better than anyone. Do you think he did it?"

I hesitated. Everything Mark said made sense. Charlie was a sick puppy, no doubt, but a murderer? It didn't ring true. I shook my head in frustration. "He just seems like too much of a geek."

"I know. He does, doesn't he? It's hard to believe he'd have the . . . ." He groped for a word and shrugged. "Horsepower for something like this."

"The geek defense," I said.

Mark rolled his eyes. "I've heard less convincing things from defense attorneys." He sighed. "Sometimes even when they were defending me."

"What's going to happen to Charlie?"

"We arrested him on the drugs and weapons charges. Until he makes bail, we'll hustle to see whether we can tie him to any of the crime scenes. Hair, fibers, the rest. If we get any matches, they'll charge him with one or more of the murders."

"He's really scared about going to jail. He says he'll kill himself."

"I know. That's what Anthony went to work on. They'll keep a suicide watch on him. They'll check him every fifteen minutes. Nothing will happen to him, Jack."

The thought of jail brought something else to mind. "Have they strip searched him yet?"

Mark gave me an odd look.

"I'd like to think I inflicted at least a little damage on him during my two battles," I explained. "After all, I did kick a shelf over on him and gouge him in the groin with one of Betsy's bones."

"Ah. I don't know about the family jewels, but as I understand it, he wasn't fully dressed when they went to his apartment. He had some bruises on his side and back. Not bad ones, but some. He said he got them playing basketball with Marshall Farr. Is that possible?"

"It's more than possible. Marshall throws his elbows like a windmill."

"When was the last game?"

"Wednesday, probably. Marshall and a bunch of other guys play once a week at lunchtime."

"Do you play with them?"

"Not anymore. I used to, though, before I broke my ribs."

"How did that happen?"

I told him about my glorious stint as goalie and how my career was cut short by the soccer ball from hell. He looked at me with disbelief. "I swear, Jack, you need a priest, a chaperone, a doctor, and a bodyguard to follow you around."

I clapped him on the back and smiled. "That's what you're here for, isn't it?"

Back on the fifth floor of the Public Safety Building, Anthony put me to work. The police had called in an emergency team of interpreters to decipher the contents of the East-West Partners file, most of which was in Japanese. I skimmed their quick translations. Most of the correspondence concerned a loan workout for Midori Ltd., one of our large Japanese clients. The translators had found a block of letters toward the top, however, that had nothing to do with the workout or Midori. I guessed that Janet had taken the Midori file from the secretary who sat next to her, whose attorneys all focused on international finance, and put the other letters inside.

I concentrated on the other letters. Most of them had been written in Japanese, but a few had been in Chinese and Korean. They were addressed to the presidents or chief executive officers of some of our biggest Asian clients. They were all from Mr. Piper. Beneath his name was written "President, Piper Consulting, Inc." The letters were essentially bills. They were written in a respectful yet somehow self-aggrandizing tone, as if Mr. Piper was emphasizing his own importance by flattering his correspondents. They outlined the consulting work that Mr. Piper had performed for their companies during the month. Each letter summarized the fees for the work in a discreet, apologetic, and syrupy paragraph near the bottom. I drew in my breath as I paged through the letters and looked at the fees. $21,034, $40,890, $10,769. Mr. Piper was charging his consulting clients his PWH billable rate - $500 an hour.

I took a closer look at the consulting services that Mr. Piper had been providing. Maybe they lost something in the translation, but they sure didn't look like consulting services to me. "Negotiation of executive buyout in purchase-sale agreement of

Taramoto Enterprises." "Telephone conference with Mr. Dong re: enforceability of noncompetition covenants vis a vis U.S. temporary employees." "Analysis re: benefit of creating Foreign Sales Corporation for Taramoto manufacturing division." These weren't consulting services. They were legal services. And all of us - partners included - knew the Piper Whatcom rules. If you had any spare time or energy at the end of your fourteen- to eighteen-hour day, you were welcome to write books, sell real estate, or become a mad inventor and keep all the money you made on the side. But any money you made from the provision of legal services belonged to the partnership of Piper Whatcom & Hardcastle. Consulting services, my ass. This wasn't consulting. This was a con.

And it wasn't a little con, either. Most of the letters were from a one-month period. I tallied the fees for the month and came up with more than $80,000. If Mr. Piper had charged his - that is, our - clients more than $80,000 every month, he would have grossed about $1 million every year, in addition to his Piper Whatcom salary of a million or more. With no overhead, no equipment expenses, and no salary costs except for what I imagined was a regular blackmail payment to Janet Daniels, no wonder Mr. Piper could afford to live in a lavish mansion in Magnolia, scuba dive in Aruba, and fly his private plane all over the world.

I turned to the last letter and started. It was addressed to Mr. Yamashita, the older gentleman who had spoken so movingly at Mr. Piper's memorial. It was a bill for $100,000 for 200 hours of work on the Brand v. Crabfest Seafoods litigation during September. According to the letter, Crabfest was a Yamashita, Inc., subsidiary. The letter listed all the work that Harmony had done - all the depositions she had taken, all the pleadings she had drafted, all the motions she had argued. But it credited all the work to Humphrey Piper, not Harmony Piper, and it billed the work at Humphrey's $500 hourly rate instead of Harmony's $160 hourly fee.

I let the letter fall back onto the stack. Poor Harmony. She adored her father. She went to law school to please him. She went to Harvard to further his legacy. She went to Piper Whatcom to be close to him all the time. I didn't expect anything of my mother, so she never disappointed me. But Harmony had expected a lot of her dad.

I pushed the letters away. I had a pretty good idea of how Humphrey had orchestrated his fraud, how Janet was involved, and how Harmony had accidentally discovered it. I just needed a crack at our computer system to prove it.

ALL GOOD THINGS

CHAPTER 43

had learned how to use our computerized billing system out of sheer desperation. My secretary was well-intentioned but overextended; often, the demands of the three partners she worked with took precedence over my modest associate needs. Once she had gone shopping for a birthday present for one of their wives instead of entering my hours for the week. After I had been reprimanded for missing the billing deadline, I had figured out how to enter my own time.

I brought up the billing history for Crabfest Seafoods. I started at the beginning of the year, scanning the monthly by-attorney breakdowns for Mr. Piper's name. For work done from January through August, we had billed Yamashita, Inc., Crabfest's parent company, for a lot of Harmony's time, a little of Marshall Farr's time, and a smattering of the time of assorted other associates, including Charlie Snow. From January through August, there was no time whatsoever billed for Mr. Piper.

I paged down to the billing history for September. It listed the figures I had seen earlier when I had reviewed the Brand billing printout in the hospital. For work done during September, we had billed Yamashita, Inc., for 12.5 hours of Marshall Farr's time, 5.6 hours of Humphrey Piper's time, and 4.8 hours of Charlie Snow's time. This was the first time all year I had seen an entry for Mr. Piper. There was no time listed for Harmony.

I checked the dates on the September billing summary. The work in progress printout had been prepared on October 4. The billing attorney would have had a week to edit the work descriptions or write off any time that seemed unwarrantedly high, duplicative, or misspent. The final bill had been mailed to Yamashita, Inc., on October 18 - the day before the beginning of the client seminar.

I glanced at the photocopy of Mr. Piper's letter to Mr. Yamashita. It was dated October 6. I toggled into our billing auditor, a chronological list of all the entries to our billing system - whether initial inputs, corrections, or deletions - and started scanning the entries between October 4 and October 6.

It was not easy work. The columns of light blue figures wavered and swam before my eyes. It was like looking for something underwater. I blinked and looked over at Mark, who was sitting in one of my visitor's chairs, reading the summer clerk files I had kept on Charlie Snow.

"You need to take a break?" Mark asked.

"No, I'm OK," I said. "It just all blurs together after a while."

I turned back to the computer screen and kept scanning through the columns. Near the bottom of the sixth page, I found what I was looking for. On October 5, Janet Daniels had transferred 200 hours from Yamashita's billing number to a non-billable client development number. She had written off the 200 hours that Harmony had spent on the Brand litigation during September.

I double-checked the billing history of a couple of the other clients for which Mr. Piper had been providing "consulting" services. For each of them, I found the same pattern. There were no entries for Mr. Piper on the by-attorney monthly billing breakdowns. But as I checked the billing auditor, I found that Janet had transferred enormous amounts of time from the client numbers to client development. I compared Mr. Piper's letters with their corresponding monthly entries. In each case, the hours written off matched the time Mr. Piper had billed that month for his consulting.

I took a deep breath. Who would have thought that Mr. Piper was a crook? All this time, he had been charging his clients directly for the work he did for them. All that money should have gone to the firm, but he had pocketed it under the guise of doing consulting services for some of our biggest Asian clients.

The police would have to check each of his clients' accounts carefully, but the basic scheme was already clear. Mr. Piper worked hard for his clients and kept his time just like the rest of us. But instead of allowing the hours to be billed through to the clients, Mr. Piper had had Janet Daniels write off his time to client development every month. The written-off hours wouldn't go on the clients' bills. As far as Piper Whatcom was concerned, it would be as if the work had never happened - except that then Mr. Piper had turned around and billed the clients directly. The clients had received the services they were paying for. There was no fraud there. It had been the firm Mr. Piper had wanted to hurt, not his clients.

I wondered why no one had ever questioned why all of Mr. Piper's time was written off every month. There were two possible reasons. First, Janet had transferred the time to client development, not the official write-off number the partners used to keep track of non-billed hours. It was conceivable that no one had noticed the wholesale write-off. More likely, however, someone had noticed the write-off and thought it was just fine. Mr. Piper's reputation was for fawning client development, not bare-knuckle lawyering. With tens of millions of dollars flooding into the firm from Mr. Piper's Asian practice, Piper Whatcom could well afford to float someone who spent his days generating work for everyone else instead of billing his own hourly quota. People at the firm - me included - just assumed that Mr. Piper had devoted his time to playing golf with bigwigs and sucking up to titans of industry. I was actually kind of surprised to see that he had done real work - and a lot of real work, too. Maybe that was the secret of his extraordinary client development skills. He had worked hard for his clients himself, and from the enormous fees they had paid him, it looked like they had really appreciated it.

In a weird way, it must have been sort of a symbiotic fraud. Everyone must have felt they were coming out ahead. Mr. Piper had earned a million or so extra dollars each year, and he must have enjoyed the satisfaction of cheating the firm that had removed him as managing partner. The firm had soaked up the tidal wave of business that Mr. Piper had generated through his hard work and individual attention and hadn't even questioned what storm had stirred the sea. Mr. Piper's clients had received top-level legal services from a senior partner at the top of his game. And I bet they had enjoyed the feeling of prestige and pampering when Mr. Piper had said something like, "You know, I'm going to take this case on personally. We'll have all the resources and expertise of Piper Whatcom behind us, but I want to handle it myself - through my consulting company." What was it that Mr. Yamashita had said at Mr. Piper's memorial service? He had said he was thrilled when **Humphrey** had offered to be his company's outside counsel. Not Piper Whatcom, but **Humphrey**.

All in all, it was a well-mannered, almost beneficent con job - except that the one person who would not look upon fraud with the least degree of allowance had discovered it. Poor Harmony. It was kind of ironic that the only reason she had discovered her father's scheme was that Janet was a lousy secretary. The computer code for Mr. Piper was "PIPEHU." The computer code for Harmony was "PIPEHA." I imagined that Janet had zipped through Mr. Piper's bills pretty quickly. There would have been a lot of them, and the work would have been tedious. As she was zipping through, Janet must have misread PIPEHA for PIPEHU and written off all Harmony's September work on Brand by mistake. That's why on the Yamashita bill for September, there was no time listed for Harmony Piper, but there was an entry for work by Mr. Piper. It was the only time Mr. Piper had showed up on the Yamashita bills all year.

I thought about how horrified Harmony must have been when she had figured out why none of her time had showed up on the Yamashita bill for September. No wonder she and her father had had such an angry telephone conversation the weekend before he died. The hotel maid who had interrupted Mr. Piper with his tea had gotten most of it right. Mr. Piper and Harmony may have been arguing about millions of dollars, but I guessed that Harmony was insisting that Mr. Piper repay every cent to the firm. Three million dollars would have been about accurate. It looked like Mr. Piper had grossed about a million dollars a year, and he had been in charge of our Asian operations just over three years.

Poor Harmony. She must have felt so hurt and betrayed. I sighed deeply. Mark snapped the file closed and looked up at me.

"Find what you were expecting?" he asked. I had shared my suspicions with him on the way from the police station to my firm.

"Yeah. Mr. Piper was embezzling. Janet was helping him. And I think Harmony found it out when she got back from winning the Brand summary judgment and printed out the billing history so she could work on the cost bill. She's awfully smart, and it wouldn't have taken much poking around the billing system before she figured out what had been going on."

"Poor kid."

I nodded and sighed again. The exhilaration of the chase had evaporated. I had felt vigorous and engaged when I had been on the trail of Janet's clues and Mr. Piper's fraud. Now I just felt tired and frustrated. Janet's clues weren't worth much as far as I was concerned. So they had led us to Mr. Piper's embezzlement. So what? I didn't care about Mr. Piper's embezzlement. I wanted the clues to lead me to Harmony. I wanted them to lead me to Harmony **now.**

Mark seemed to share my funk and frustration. "Find anything interesting in Charlie's files?" I asked him.

"No. Nothing you hadn't already told us. He sounds awkward, mixed-up, and a little twisted, but he doesn't seem to have a lot of follow through, energy, or imagination."

"So where do we go from here?"

"I'll call Anthony and tell him what you found. You be thinking about Janet. My gut says she's the key to the whole thing."

I groaned but obeyed. We switched places. While Mark talked to Anthony, I sat in one of my visitor's chairs and studied the newspaper on which I had written Janet's message. I went through it line by line, scanning it desperately for any hidden meanings I might have missed.

"Look for the number first." Well, we had done that. And looking for the number first had led us to the East-West Partners file with Mr. Piper's letters. Were there any other numbers we should have looked for? Could Janet have meant anything else by "Look for the number first"?

It beat the hell out of me. I puzzled over it a few minutes, then shook my head and moved on to the next line. "If you can't find what you're looking for, look for the corresponding letters." Well, I definitely couldn't find what I was looking for. Every lead we had chased toward Harmony seemed to have run right into the ground. Corresponding letters, Janet had said. Look for the corresponding letters.

I had assumed that she meant the letters corresponding to the name of the file, East-West Partners. That had given us EWP, which was both the abbreviation for East-West Partners and the initials for Harmony's mother, Elayne Westcott Piper. That's what had led us to Charlie Westcott Snow, Harmony's first cousin. Charlie was disturbed and obsessed with the Pipers, there was no doubt about that. But both Mark and I suspected that Charlie wasn't really up to this sort of tangled plot.

I rubbed my eyes and studied the line again. The word "corresponding" bothered me. Was there something else that the letters could correspond to? I traced back through the message. The only apparent antecedent was "number," in the sentence "Look for the number first." How could letters correspond to the number?

I racked my brains. The only thing I could think of was the change in our staff and associate rankings. The partners used to give us letter grades - A, B, C, etc. This year they had changed to numbers: 1 meant outstanding, 2 meant good, 3 meant satisfactory, and so on. The new system was supposed to decrease associate competition, but of course, everyone knew it was a wolf in sheep's clothing. How hard was it to figure out that 1 stood for A, 2 stood for B, and –

Geez. 1 stood for A.

I quickly wrote the alphabet down the side of the newspaper, then wrote the numbers from 1 to 26 beside it. It looked like this:

A 1

B 2

C 3

D 4

E 5

F 6

G 7

H 8

I 9

J 10

K 11

L 12

M 13

N 14

O 15

P 16

Q 17

R 18

S 19

T 20

U 21

V 22

W 23

X 24

Y 25

Z 26.

Then I set about decoding the number. 19123-816. That would be AIABC-HAF. AIABC-HAF? I pushed the paper away from me in disgust. Great. I had traded an incomprehensible number for an incomprehensible word. So much for the idea that Janet was speaking in code. I was about to turn back to the message and take a look at the next line when I remembered searching through Archives with Mark. We had found a block of files that began with "19." They had been grouped by themselves, away from the files beginning "13" and the files beginning "15." "19" must have meant something as a unit, not as a chance configuration of "1" and "9."

I looked back at my code. 19 stood for S. 12 stood for L. SL. Spirit Lake. The hair on the back of my neck rose. 3 stood for C. It had to mean Cumming, Brand's loony friend from Vietnam. The Idaho police had found Brand unconscious in Cumming's cabin. Spirit Lake, Cumming. My hands felt cold.

816 - supposedly the matter number. There wasn't any letter corresponding to 81. It had to be 8. 8 stood for H. What about the 1 and the 6? I tried it as 16. 16 stood for P. HP. Harmony Piper. I stared at it in disbelief. The answer had been in front of us all along. SLC-HP. Spirit Lake Cumming-Harmony Piper. But the Idaho police had torn apart Cumming's Spirit Lake cabin without finding anything connecting him or Brand to Harmony.

The click of the telephone receiver snagged my attention. I glanced up at Mark, who had been talking to Detective Anthony. Mark sat down in my chair. He looked suddenly old and tired.

"What is it?" I asked.

Mark looked straight ahead. His eyes looked dull and shallow. "Two things," he said.

"What?"

"Number one, Brand died of the heroin overdose. He never regained consciousness."

I took a deep breath. "And number two?"

Mark looked down at his hands before replying. "Number two, Anthony got a call from a police lieutenant he knows in Utah. They found a body that matches the description we sent out on Harmony."

I put my hands over my face, as if that would keep Mark's words from reaching me. But it didn't work. Utah, I thought miserably.

SLC-HP.

Salt Lake City-Harmony Piper.

by Rosemary Reeve

CHAPTER 44

I t was late afternoon when Mark, Anthony, and I buckled into our seats on the plane to Salt Lake City. Anthony let me have the window seat so no one would bump my wounded wrist and shoulder with a beverage cart or a low-swinging piece of overhead luggage. I stared numbly out the window, trying to keep my mind blank so I wouldn't have to think about where we were going and what I might find there. We roared through multi-colored strata of clouds on our ascent. The first layer was black and purplish, like a new bruise. Then we passed through a spectrum of milky blues and grays, rising quickly into a haze of rose and gold. Finally, we broke through the mist entirely and left Seattle behind us, a dark, wet, secret city swept under a carpet of flaming clouds.

We followed the Cascade mountain range for a while, white peaks stabbing through the puffy crimson blanket, then banked and headed East. The sun was at our back. We flew in its pool of light for few minutes, the rose and gold and red around us gradually fading as we met the approaching darkness. Soon, even when I craned my neck, all I could see of the sunset was a smoldering line on the far horizon. The line narrowed until it was just a flicker of fire across the sky. Then the darkness sealed the sky behind us, and we hurtled into the night.

There was nothing more to look at outside. I turned my head around and stared at the seatback in front of me. The occupant had reclined, and the seat was just inches from my nose. I felt panicked and claustrophobic, as if the whole cabin were shrinking in on me. I stole a look at Mark, who was crunched uncomfortably in the middle seat and trying to read the newspaper without hitting me in the nose or putting out Detective Anthony's eye whenever he turned the page. Maybe this wasn't such a great idea after all.

Anthony had been reluctant to let me accompany them to Salt Lake City. I pictured his troubled green eyes. They had looked almost gray when he put his hand on my arm and said, slowly and seriously, "Mark and I can do this, Jack. We've got Harmony's photographs. They'll send us Polaroids of the DOA. We can wait for a dental examination, if necessary. You don't have to come."

But I had insisted. If Harmony was dead, I wasn't going to believe it until I saw her body myself. Besides, I couldn't stand the thought of some ghoulish dentist poking through her mouth, examining her fillings against her X-rays. Identifying

Harmony's body was one last thing I could do for her. I could give her back her name even if everything else had been taken from her.

I forced my mind to go blank again. It was surprisingly easy this time. I don't know how long we flew in silence. The cabin was dark and quiet. The individual reading lights shone like fireflies over the rows ahead of me. I had almost convinced myself that I was alone on the shore of a cool black lake in the middle of a hot and lazy summer night when Mark suddenly slapped down the newspaper and swore so loudly that a passing flight attendant gave him a wan and stricken look.

Anthony looked up from the documents he had been studying. "What's the matter, Oden?"

"There is no justice," Mark said through clenched teeth.

"What do you mean?" I asked.

Mark handed me the Metro section and tapped a story near the bottom. "Read that," he said, pointing. "Starting there."

I read. I let a moment of pure rage pass over me. When I gave the newspaper back to him, I was horrified to see that my hands were shaking. "Mark's right, Detective Anthony," I said. "There is no justice."

The story was yet another interview with members of the Tacoma church group who had survived the suspicious plane crash in Argentina. In the accompanying photograph, these survivors looked sickeningly familiar. The adults from my second - or was it third? - foster home. Even after all these years, she still had long, straight blond hair. Even after all these years, he still had thick forearms webbed with swelling veins. You couldn't tell from the picture, but I guessed that he still had one leg shorter than the other and he still got his kicks from beating up his foster kids. Mark's and my former foster parents had survived the Argentina plane crash and were milking it for all it was worth on page B-1. In the story, they thanked God for sparing their lives so they could continue His work of saving errant and abandoned children. The Times reported, piously, that the couple had opened their home to more than fifty foster children over the years.

Those poor damn kids, I thought. I looked over at Detective Anthony, who was tut-tutting his way through the story. He handed the newspaper back to Mark with a sad smile.

"Maybe they've changed since you and Jack knew them, Mark," he said.

"Fat chance," Mark replied, too quickly. He added, "I mean, fat chance, sir." He tried again. "People like that don't change, Detective Anthony."

The sad smile again. Anthony's voice was gentle: "Why not, Mark? You changed, didn't you?" Then Anthony bent back to his documents before Mark could reply.

We flew on in silence. I don't know whether I slept and dreamed that I wasn't sure whether I was awake, or whether I stayed awake and just wasn't sure whether I was asleep, but our landing in Salt Lake City took me by surprise. So did Salt Lake City

218

itself. I'm not sure what I was expecting, but I was taken aback by the wide, glittering streets, the thin, dry air, and the height and closeness of the mountains. The night was cold and moonless, and the mountains seemed purple, vast, and very near against the blue-black sky.

Anthony's friend Lieutenant Siddoway picked us up at the airport. Mark and I sat in the back of Siddoway's unmarked car and strained to hear snatches of the murmured conversation up front. I saw Siddoway jerk his head in my general direction. "Husband?" he asked Anthony.

Anthony shook his head. "Close friend."

"Poor bastard."

Their voices droned on, even lower than before. I caught little bits here and there. The woman they had found was Caucasian, about five feet tall, about 125 pounds. Black hair. Pretty? Yes, very pretty. Exotic-looking, too. Not a face you would forget. How old? She looked young, Siddoway said. They had thought she might even be under 20, but you couldn't be sure with girls, could you? No, Anthony agreed. You couldn't.

I felt a surge of hope that was almost immediately extinguished. Harmony did look young. When she pulled her hair back and was severely suited and high heeled, you could tell she was at least over 20, but I remembered how she had looked chasing Betsy around my living room. Hair flying, T-shirt hanging out, white tennis shoes kicking at the air: she could have passed for fourteen.

I forced myself to focus on Anthony's and Siddoway's conversation. They had found the body underneath an overpass near the airport, Siddoway said. I shuddered. We were still pretty near the airport. She had been bludgeoned: a few hard blows on the back of the neck. She didn't suffer long. She was already dead when someone had tipped her over the bridge onto the scrub brush below.

I hung my head. I took deep breaths and made my mind go blank again. It was becoming almost second nature.

Everything came suddenly and cruelly into focus when we reached the medical examiner's office up by the hospital, and they started bringing out the clothes. Up to this point, I had been dimly aware of the goings-on around me, but only in a distant, detached way, as if I were idly watching a duplicated but uninteresting program on a display of television sets in a department store. But now all I could see was the black coat that a plump, kind-faced woman was handing me. The coat was made of a smooth, woven wool, heavy and fluid in my hands. I made a show of looking it over carefully, but I already knew it was Harmony's. I could smell it. Her perfume on it was faint but unmistakable. I handed it back. I nodded. "It's hers."

The shirt was next. My stomach turned over when I saw the flash of purple. The next instant, the heavy cotton T-shirt was in my hands. The soccer league logo was on the pocket. Around the cuff, just like a bracelet, was embroidered "Piper #5." I caught Mark's eye. "Yes, it's hers," I said. I swallowed hard. "It's her soccer shirt."

by Rosemary Reeve

The rest of the clothes blurred before my eyes. The jeans just looked like jeans. The white tennis shoes just looked like white tennis shoes. I shook my head. "They could be hers. I don't know," I said. I also failed to recognize the watch. But when the kind-faced woman brought out the single earring, I moaned aloud. Harmony wore her diamond earrings almost every day. They had been her mother's. I didn't even have to take it out of its plastic bag. I buried my face in my hands and nodded. "It's hers," I said through my fingers.

"We recovered only one earring from the body," I heard Siddoway say. "But the other easily could have been lost in her murder or her fall."

When I looked up again, the clothes and the kind-faced woman were gone. Mark put his hand on my good shoulder. I could feel everything narrowing around me. It was time for me to identify, as Siddoway put it, the deceased.

I fixed my eyes on the back of Siddoway's bald head as we walked into the cold room. I didn't want to see anything I didn't have to. The room smelled of disinfectant and something sickly, raw, and primitive. Every nerve and muscle in my body wanted me to run away.

I steeled myself to stay put. Siddoway and someone else were opening something and pulling something out right next to me. I stared straight ahead, unseeing. I heard a zipper opening. It caught for a second, and I shuddered at the sounds of someone wrestling with it. Then the catch gave way, and the zipper buzzed open a few more inches.

Silence. Anthony put his hand on my back. "Whenever you're ready, son."

I closed my eyes and pictured Harmony sitting across from me at the Happy Teriyaki, laughing and gesturing wildly with her chopsticks to emphasize a fine rhetorical point. I lingered over the image, memorizing how straight she sat, how lustily she ate, how impatiently she brushed her hair out of her eyes. I wanted to make sure that the look of her dead face wouldn't be the only way I could remember her.

I opened my eyes and looked down at the dead woman. They had pulled back the body bag so I could see her face and neck. Her hair was black and straight. Her wide, frozen eyes were blue. Her skin was pale and very clear.

She was a beautiful, beautiful girl.

But she wasn't Harmony.

ALL GOOD THINGS

by Rosemary Reeve

CHAPTER 45

"**A**re you sure, Jack?"

Of course I was sure. I was positive. But I didn't blame Detective Anthony for being skeptical. I had glanced at the woman in the body bag, seen that it wasn't Harmony, turned on my heel, said, "It's not her," over my shoulder, and walked out of the room. In fact, I had kept on walking until I reached Siddoway's unmarked car, out in the hospital parking garage overlooking the city. I was leaning against the car now, surrounded by three worried policemen.

I scanned their faces. Mark looked concerned but hopeful. Anthony looked tense and dubious. Siddoway's face was a mixture of pity and blatant disbelief. I addressed myself to Anthony.

"Yes, I'm sure that the girl in there isn't Harmony," I said.

Anthony looked off into the glittering distance, then back at me. "I'm not doubting you, Jack. You know that none of us wants that to be Harmony in there. But you're tired and hurt, and you've been under a lot of strain. Besides, sometimes people can look very different after death. You're used to seeing Harmony dressed up, with makeup on, and her hair done. Is there any chance that you could be mistaken?"

I pretended to give the matter mature reconsideration. "No," I said, after what I figured was a suitable interval. "It's just not Harmony, Detective Anthony. I'm sure it isn't."

"You positively identified the clothes she was wearing. And you barely glanced at her face," Siddoway objected. "I'm sorry, son, but she's your girl."

Frustration raged through me. I wasn't mad at Siddoway. I wasn't mad at anyone except whoever it was who had taken Harmony away. Unfortunately, Siddoway was right in front of me, and the person who had taken Harmony wasn't. I snapped at Siddoway, "I know what I saw."

Both Mark and Anthony looked startled at the sharpness of my tone. Siddoway gave me a mocking, slanted grin. "Oh? And just what did you see, kid? You must have looked at her all of three seconds."

My brain didn't have the faintest idea how to respond. It had absorbed only the gestalt negative: It wasn't Harmony. My mouth, however, was already answering. After three years of law school and four years of practice, I didn't know much, but I knew how to talk.

"I saw that her eyes were the wrong color," I said, my voice thin and bitter with rage and worry. "Harmony's eyes are dark blue. Sometimes they seem almost black, but I've never seen them look that pale blue, that kind of turquoise. They're also the wrong shape. Harmony's eyes are almond-shaped; the dead girl's are more round. Harmony has straight, even teeth, but the girl in there has gaps between hers, especially right here at the side." I tapped my teeth. "Harmony's face is oval. The other girl has a wide forehead but a pointed chin. They both have pierced ears, but the holes are in different places. The girl in there also has two holes in her left ear, and Harmony doesn't. And wouldn't. She's way too much of a lady. And there's a little round scar on the side of the other girl's right nostril. I'd bet she wore a nose ring there at one time. I can guarantee you that Harmony has never, ever worn a nose ring."

I paused. Mark was looking at me with amusement mixed with pride. Anthony and Siddoway were open-mouthed.

I glared at Siddoway. "Is that enough to convince you, or should I go on?"

It was enough. Siddoway silently got in the driver's seat, and we were underway. During the ride downtown to the police station, I kicked myself for lapsing into anger and sarcasm. It certainly wasn't Siddoway's fault that Harmony was missing. I had lashed out at him just because I was desperate and frustrated. I felt bad. I also felt stupid. From a practical standpoint, I needed to keep Siddoway enthusiastic about the case. An unknown girl had turned up dead in Salt Lake City wearing Harmony's clothes. Whoever she was, she must have had something to do with Harmony or someone who had been with Harmony since Harmony disappeared early Monday morning. We needed the cooperation of the Salt Lake police, and all I had done so far was insult them.

When we arrived at the police station, I cornered Siddoway and apologized for my outburst. He forgave me gracefully. "It's OK, kid. Anthony told me you had been through a lot lately," he said. "Besides, I thought you were kind of impressive up there."

"I thought I was kind of obnoxious up there," I said lamely.

Siddoway winked at me. "I didn't say you weren't obnoxious, kid. I just said you were kind of impressive. And you were - in an obnoxious sort of way."

Siddoway handed me a pad of paper and a pen. "Here's your chance to be impressive again. Somehow your girlfriend's clothes ended up on a dead girl in Salt Lake. You need to help us figure out why and how."

Harmony wasn't my girlfriend. I started to protest, then thought better of it. Siddoway smiled at my discomfort. "Sorry, I meant your 'close friend.' Your close friend whose face you happen to have memorized, right down to the piercings in her ears. Anyway, it's your job to think of any connections whatsoever between Salt Lake City and your close friend, your firm, her friends and family. Just write them down, no matter how innocent or unrelated they seem. If your firm does work here, write it down. If your friend has ever been skiing here, write it down. There's got to be some link, and we're not going to be able to find your friend unless we find that link first. And find it fast, too."

I settled down with the pad of paper and let my mind wander. I started with our Salt Lake office. It was brand new, the first office we had opened since Marshall Farr became managing partner. The office was small - just two partners and one associate - and struggling. Marshall had given them one year to break even and two to show a profit. They were still in their first year, but I had heard they were hemorrhaging money. I wrote "SLC office new but in trouble" on the paper.

Brent Sang was the sole Salt Lake City associate. He had transferred to Salt Lake from our San Francisco office and was up for partner this year. The dismal prospects of the Salt Lake City office would hurt his chances, I thought. I remembered his brown-nosing speech at Mr. Piper's memorial service, his frenzied handshaking and backslapping as he worked the room. I had thought then that Brent must have been grateful to Mr. Piper for dying at such a convenient time. Was it too convenient? If Brent had killed Mr. Piper and kidnapped Harmony, he would have removed Harmony - a serious and favored contender - from the pool of associates up for partnership, prevented Mr. Piper from influencing the rest of the partners to admit Harmony to the partnership, and provided himself with a rare opportunity to brownnose firm-wide at Mr. Piper's memorial service. Not bad for a day's work. I jotted "Brent Sang - clearer road to partnership" on the paper.

What about other people at Piper Whatcom? We had a few expatriate Utahns in the Seattle office, mostly partners but a few associates. I added their names to the paper. I knew that we were handling some complicated contract negotiations out of the Salt Lake City office, but I didn't know what it was all about. The closest I ever got to transactional work was cleaning up the mess afterwards when the deal went sour. There's a reason litigators call corporate work "pre-litigation." I wrote "SLC office - contract negotiations" on the paper.

I paused, stumped. I didn't know whether Harmony had any ties to Salt Lake City. I didn't know whether she skied. I didn't know whether she had ever even visited the city. I chewed the end of my pen. I was about to give up and show my lamentably short list to Siddoway when an old and battered memory started to rise in my mind, like the slow float of a corpse. I did know of a link between Janet Daniels and Salt Lake City. About two years ago, Janet had screwed up on filing an administrative appeal with the Utah Public Service Commission. She had sent the documents by overnight mail to arrive on the deadline, but she had forgotten to put the required ASCII disk in the envelope so the Commission could load our documents into their computer system.

Jeremy Smith had been livid. He had nabbed me in the hall and ordered me to fly to Utah that morning and deliver the disk in person. He had backed me into the elevator and was shouting his parting instructions when Janet interrupted him. There was no need to panic, she had said, glaring at Jeremy. She had e-mailed the ASCII documents to someone in Salt Lake City, who had downloaded them onto a disk and taken the disk to the Commission. Everything was taken care of. Then Janet had swept out of the lobby, leaving two very frazzled and irritated attorneys in her wake.

So who was Janet's contact in Salt Lake City? It would have had to be someone she was pretty close to - at least close enough to trust with a task that could save her job. Had she turned to this person to save her job now, when she was afraid that Harmony would divulge her role in Mr. Piper's embezzlement? It was worth checking out, at least.

I went over my list with Anthony and Siddoway. Anthony raised an eyebrow when I told them about Janet's possible contact in Salt Lake City. "Can we find out who she e-mailed the documents to, Jack?" he asked.

I paused, considering. The message would be long past purgatory. We could retrieve even a purged e-mail if the system hadn't already written over the memory involved, but it would take some time and a lot more expertise than I possessed. Besides, it had happened more than two years ago. Even if I could get one of our computer wizards out of bed and into the office, there was no guarantee that he or she would be able to find anything.

Anthony was looking at me expectantly. "Even if it still exists, it's going to be hard to get the e-mail back," I told him. I turned to Siddoway. "But do you have a computer with a modem that I could use? If we reimbursed Janet's contact for mileage to and from the public service commission, we probably passed the cost onto the client. The name of the contact may have shown up on the client's bill."

A few minutes later, I had tapped into the Seattle network. I retrieved the client number from the master index and brought up the billing history. I searched for the word "mileage." There were a whole lot of disbursements for "mileage." I searched for "Salt Lake." "Salt Lake" showed up all the time, in description after description. Finally, I just went back two years or so and skimmed through the monthly expenses and disbursements. Mark sat down beside me and read over my shoulder.

We both saw it at the same time. Two years ago in November, we had billed for reimbursement for the amount we had paid to a carrier for telecommunication charges, the cost of a computer disk - and mileage to and from the Utah Public Service Commission. The bill had the carrier's name and her address:

Lydia Keddington, 249 S. Carden Street, Salt Lake City.

by Rosemary Reeve

CHAPTER 46

Lieutenant Siddoway was out of breath. "We've got a lead on our Jane Doe," he said to Anthony. "West High School student. I thought she looked young. A kid called 911 saying his girlfriend didn't meet him for a date last night and didn't show up for her work-study shift at a beauty parlor today. He's afraid to call her at home because she's grounded and her folks can be pretty tough. She was going to sneak out late Friday night to be with him. She fits our girl's description." He glanced at me. "Right down to the scar from the nose ring, Jack."

"Do you have an address for the missing girl?" Mark asked him.

"Yeah, 249 -"

"S. Carden Street," Mark and I finished for him. Anthony and Siddoway looked at us in surprise. Mark added, "Jack just pulled the address off his firm's bill. Janet's contact in Salt Lake City was someone named Lydia Keddington."

Siddoway looked down at the paper in his hand and nodded. "That's our girl's mom."

There was a frozen moment while we all realized what that had to mean. The air around us seemed to thicken. Anthony looked at Siddoway, and Siddoway looked at Mark. No one looked at me. Siddoway licked his lips. "This is it," he said.

The room exploded into activity. Siddoway seemed to be everywhere at once, alternating among yelling orders, muttering with somebody about warrants, and huddling with Anthony around a map. Anthony waved Mark over. I was left alone. I knew better to intrude, but I edged as close to the three of them as I dared. From Siddoway's yelling and Anthony's gestures, I figured out that they were sending cruisers to watch the house and block off the street. Siddoway would take a couple of uniformed officers into the house itself.

When the three of them headed for the door, I followed them. I was actually halfway into the car before any of them noticed I was there. "Jack!" Anthony said, turning around with alarm, as if he had forgotten I existed. "Jack, no. I'm sorry. You can't come with us."

"But Detective Anthony -"

"No, kid." It was Siddoway's turn. "No way in hell am I taking a civilian in there."

"I'll stay in the car. I'll keep down. You won't even know I'm there." They both shook their heads. "Look, I'm the only one of you who has ever seen Harmony. I know what she looks like. I know what her things look like. I know what her perfume smells like. I can tell you if she's been there." Siddoway and Anthony exchanged glances. They were weakening.

I tried again. I couldn't stand to just wait around at the police station while Harmony might be alive and in danger. "Look, I'll sign anything you want releasing you from liability," I said. Besides, it's not like I have a wife or anyone who's going to sue you if I get killed -"

"Shut up and get in the car," Siddoway burst out. "You give us any trouble, and we'll lock you in the trunk. Got it?"

"Got it," I said. I slammed the door, and we were off. A team of uniformed officers followed us in a police car.

Siddoway used his blue light and his siren at first but cut them off as we turned into a residential neighborhood. A police cruiser was parked sideways in the middle of the road, and the officer was out of his car, directing the slow, sparse traffic past the street. Siddoway maneuvered around the cruiser. He killed his headlights and drove slowly and quietly. The houses seemed large but shabby. The street was dark with overhanging trees and lined on both sides with parked cars. Down at the other end of the street was another police cruiser, also parked sideways and blocking anyone from entering.

Siddoway slowed almost to a crawl. He pulled off to the side of the road and crept onto the pavement until the car was hidden in the shadow of a precariously leaning fence. Just behind us was a vacant lot. I could see the lights of a maze-like apartment complex through the tall weeds. About a hundred yards ahead of us was a white, Victorian-style house. Its windows were dark, but the facade was half-illuminated by a light on the other side of the street. By craning my neck, I could see the number painted on the front porch: 249.

The police car with the uniformed officers slipped from behind us and parked in front of 249. Siddoway almost murmured into the radio: "Ready when you are."

On cue, two police officers emerged silently from the cruiser. They mounted the stairs to the house. I was too far away to tell whether they knocked, but a light went on upstairs. Then a light went on downstairs. Mark leaned over and whispered, "We'll be going in a few minutes. Whatever you do, stay down and stay in the car. OK?"

"OK, I whispered back. "Don't worry about me. I'll stay right here in the car."

I meant it when I said it.

CHAPTER 47

Light flooded the porch. The two policemen were clearly visible against the white house. One was pressed flat against the wall on the far side of the door. His gun was drawn, and he looked ready to spring. He had ginger hair, which shone very orange under the porch light. He reminded me of Betsy: tense, coiled, and ready to take a piece out of someone. The other officer stood in front of the door, his hand on his gun but otherwise unthreatening.

The door swung open. For a second, the porch light fell on the face of the person inside. I gasped.

"What is it, Jack?" Anthony whispered.

"I thought it was Janet Daniels," I stammered. Mark looked up at me sharply. "I know it's not Janet Daniels," I added, to reassure him that I wasn't delusional. "But that woman looked like her."

"A relative, I guess," Mark said. The two officers entered the house.

"Well, time to find out." Siddoway said. "Let's go, guys - except you, Jack. You just sit tight and keep down." Siddoway snapped off the radio. The three of them slipped noiselessly out of the car. I didn't even hear their doors close. Then they stole toward the house, Anthony and Siddoway in single file, gliding silently in the shadows of the overhanging trees. I couldn't even see Mark anymore. Then one of the shadows by the house moved a little out of sync with the night breeze. In an instant, Mark had sidled up the steps and into the house. A few minutes later, he emerged and nodded, and Anthony and Siddoway came up the stairs and went through the door.

There was nothing to do but wait. I kept my promise to Mark and scrunched down. I peered at the house through the gap between the front seats. Lights went on one by one. Every now and then, I saw a tall, broad-shouldered shadow on the shining blinds. The police must be searching room by room.

Another light flickered to life on the second-floor. The glow dripped down the battered roof of a small garage or shed right beside the house. I straightened up a bit. It would be easy to climb out of that second-story window and onto the garage roof. The roof sloped toward the ground at a gentle pitch. If the pretty girl in the body bag had sneaked out of this house to see her boyfriend, I bet this was the way she had come. It would have taken just a few moments to get out of the window and down the roof. The drop to the ground looked pretty short - no more than six or seven feet at the roof's lowest point - and there was a big tree next to it. She could have grabbed onto a low branch and climbed down if she was too scared to jump. Poor kid.

Well, that explained how the girl in the body bag could have gotten out of the house. But how on earth had she gotten ahold of Harmony's clothes? And why had somebody killed her? If her murderer was involved in Harmony's abduction, it made no sense whatsoever for him to dress the girl up like Harmony and dump her body in a place where it was almost certain to be found. Or did it? The girl looked enough like Harmony to make three really smart cops think I had lost my mind when I insisted that the body lying in the hospital wasn't hers. It wasn't so much that their features were similar; it was that unusual coloring: black hair and blue eyes. All Harmony's family was dead - except for Charlie, who claimed he barely knew her. The police couldn't call a doting relative in to identify her. Had the person who took Harmony killed the other girl and dressed her up just to throw the police off the scent?

I shivered. It was a possibility. It was a particularly gruesome and horrible possibility, both because of the callous sacrifice of the girl and because it would mean we were wasting precious time on yet another dodge. I searched my mind for other alternatives. It was possible that the girl had participated in Harmony's abduction, but if so, she surely wouldn't have left the house wearing her victim's clothes. It was also possible that someone in the girl's life had been involved in Harmony's disappearance, but that the girl herself had been innocent. If she had just stumbled over the clothes - stashed somewhere awaiting disposal - she might have decided to borrow them for her date. They were nice clothes, after all. Any girl would have liked the look of that stylish coat, that soft, thick shirt - and those diamond earrings. Those diamond earrings, I thought bitterly, were to die for.

The more I thought about that last alternative, the more plausible it seemed. Siddoway had said the girl was in high school. She was a minor, a teenager still under her parents' control. Weren't teenage girls notorious for borrowing their mothers' clothes? That was the impression I had gleaned from watching a lot of TV. And if the girl had been sneaking out to see her boyfriend, maybe she had wanted to make sure she wasn't recognized by her neighbors or her boyfriend's folks. What better disguise than to wear what she thought were her mother's clothes?

I visualized the girl slipping out of her window and onto the roof. An arc of light from the streetlamp just grazed the window pane. The girl would have been illuminated for several moments, at least until she took the few steps across the roof and jumped to the shadowy ground or swung down from the dark tree. If it was as cold Friday night as it was right then, the girl would have had the coat buttoned. If someone had been watching the house, the way I was then, they would have seen a small, pretty, black-haired, black-coated woman gleam briefly in the light and disappear.

I stared at the house, but I wasn't really seeing it. I was imagining the girl sneaking out of the upstairs window. Given the dark and the distance, she would have looked like Harmony to anyone watching from the ground. Was that why she had been killed? Had the murderer been watching the house and mistaken her for Harmony?

A movement or something ahead of me dragged me back to the present. I scanned the house anxiously. A few more windows were lighted, but I couldn't see anything else out of the ordinary. I sighed and rubbed my eyes. I couldn't even remember what had caught my attention. I tried to focus on the girl again. It didn't make any sense. Why would the murderer be watching the house? If Harmony's clothes had been in the house, the murderer must have been the one to put them there. Unless -

Unless. I had a flash of comprehension. I had assumed that the person who had murdered Mr. Piper had to be at least involved with the person who abducted Harmony. I had figured that Janet had lured Harmony into her car, incapacitated her somehow, and delivered her to the accomplice who had been responsible for Mr. Piper's death. But what if Harmony's abduction and Mr. Piper's murder had happened independently? What if, without knowing what the other one was doing, Janet had abducted Harmony, and someone else had killed Mr. Piper? Someone else who was involved in Mr. Piper's fraud, I thought. Someone else who stood to lose a lot if Harmony exposed her father's crime. Someone else who wanted to shut Harmony up permanently.

That would explain why someone might have been watching this house last night, waiting for an opportunity to either make sure Harmony was dead or to finish the job himself. And if he had seen someone who looked exactly like Harmony sneaking out after the house was dark, wearing Harmony's black coat and obviously trying hard not to be noticed, it would explain why he had struck first and asked questions later. I wondered if he realized he had killed the wrong girl. If he didn't, he would be long gone. If he did, maybe he was still close by, waiting for another chance -

Something ahead of me caught my eye again. This time, I realized what it was. I had seen flash of light from one of the cars parked in front of me. I remembered Mark's words of warning from a few days ago. Someone had been parked in front of my house the night Mrs. Piper was killed. My neighbor couldn't describe the person, but every now and then, she had seen a flash of light from the car. And now I had seen two sudden glints from a car that was parked just before the white, Victorian-style house. A house in which a girl who looked like Harmony had lived. A girl who had been killed wearing Harmony's coat, shirt, and heirloom diamond earrings.

I didn't know who he was. I didn't know why he had killed Mr. and Mrs. Piper. But I was pretty sure that their murderer was crouched and watching the white Victorian house. I was pretty sure that he was sitting in front of me, just three cars away.

ALL GOOD THINGS

CHAPTER 48

crept forward as far as I dared, wedging myself in the gap between the front seats. I braced my elbows on the console and peered through the windshield. Lieutenant Siddoway had pulled his car off the road and onto the sidewalk, so I had an angled view of the dark car ahead of me. It was a mid-size sedan, maybe a Buick or a Pontiac. I couldn't tell which. It looked relatively new. It was egg-shaped instead of boxy, and its surface seemed smoother and shinier than the finishes of the other cars parked up and down the street. The listing fences, overgrown gardens, and shabby houses showed that this wasn't a wealthy neighborhood. That dark, sleek, shiny new car was out of place.

There was another flash of light from the car. It was so faint that I thought I must have imagined it. But no, there it was again. A domed shape surfaced for just an instant and was gone. The top of the guy's head, I supposed. I guessed that the glints I was seeing came from his glasses. Charlie Snow wore glasses, but he was in jail. So did Brand, but he was dead. I didn't know who it was, but there was definitely someone hiding in that car.

I reviewed my options. I had promised Mark I wouldn't leave the police car. And as much as I hated having to sit here like a frightened child while the police searched the white house for Harmony, I really didn't want to leave the police car. I already had had two near-fatal run-ins with Mr. Piper's murderer. I didn't relish a third round, especially not when I was hurt, exhausted, and in an unfamiliar place.

I took a deep breath and tried to make myself relax. So long as the guy was inside the car and the police were inside the house, everything was fine. The guy couldn't have already taken Harmony, or he wouldn't still be here. And with all the police around, he couldn't get into the house to try to find her. Police cruisers blocked both ends of the street, so he couldn't drive away. I would just wait until Anthony, Mark, or Siddoway came back here. Then the police could surround the car and arrest the guy. Everything would be fine - if the guy would just stay put in the car.

I saw a movement in the car, then another and another. The guy's head was bobbing along the seat. I craned my neck and raised my head up as much as I dared. The guy in the car was moving from the driver's seat across to the passenger's side. What was the bastard doing? Then I saw the shadow lengthen on the right side of the car, and I knew what he was doing. Damn, damn, damn, damn, damn. He had opened the passenger door a crack.

What was I going to do? I stole a glance backward, but I couldn't even see the police officer who was directing traffic behind me. I could tell he was there because of the red and blue lights spinning behind me, but the road curved a little, blocking the policeman and his cruiser from my view. I could see the policeman who was directing traffic at the far end of the block in front of me, but if I made any signals in his direction, I was more likely to attract the murderer's attention instead of the policeman's. That was the last thing I wanted to do.

The right-side shadow lengthened further. I guessed that the passenger door was open about six inches. I saw a white hand grasp the door.

My eyes fell on the police radio. I didn't know how to use it, but I was going to learn. Right now. A dark shape was pouring from the car, slipping steadily into the shadows. I wriggled further into the front seat and started flipping switches and punching buttons and calling for help as loudly as I dared.

On the third try, I realized that I had been holding down the button that allowed me to talk but prevented me from hearing the return transmission. I shook my head and took a breath. The car door ahead of me was closing silently, as if by an unseen hand. I had to get control over myself. I whispered, "Please, please help me. There's a murder suspect in front of 249 S. Carden Street, and I think he's trying to get away." Then I let go of the button.

The answering voice was a woman's, tense with frustration and sharp with suspicion. "Identify yourself. This frequency is for law enforcement only."

"My name is Jack Hart," I whispered back. "I'm a witness in Lieutenant Siddoway's police car. All the police officers are searching the house at 249 S. Carden, but I think I've spotted a murder suspect right by the house. He just got out of a car. Please send help right away. There are two officers at opposite ends of Carden Street, but I can't attract their attention without alerting the murderer."

Silence. An evergreen branch jerked violently just two cars away from me. That had to mean the guy from the car was coming my way, creeping toward me in the shadow of the overhanging trees. I whispered one last desperate message. "He's coming right at me. Send help and don't respond, or he'll hear you."

I replaced the radio and retreated into the back seat. I crunched my six-four frame as small as possible into the tight crevasse. By twisting my neck to the right and peering around the front seat, I could just make out the trembling of the trees before me. The guy was still shrouded in shadows, but every now and then, I saw a hand or a leg as he moved slowly through the trees. He was just one car in front of me and still advancing.

I beat down an irrational fear that he knew I was in the car and was coming to finish what he had started Friday morning. He couldn't know I was there, I comforted myself. For all he knew, I had died at his hands up in Seattle. Besides, I was well-hidden. In the dark and the shadows, he wouldn't be able to see me unless he came right alongside Siddoway's car and happened to look in.

My reassurances rang false. What if he did come alongside Siddoway's car and look in? He probably would. Assuming he didn't know I was in the car and wasn't coming to kill me, I guessed that he was heading for the vacant lot just behind me, the lot that led to the maze of apartments through the block. Those long weeds and that crazy maze offered him camouflage and confusion, his best chances to get away. His path to the vacant lot would take him right by the car where I was cowering.

I scrunched down a little further. Where in the hell were the police? I was starting to wish that Siddoway had locked me in the trunk after all. At least I wouldn't know what was coming toward me.

The overhanging trees shadowed almost all of the sole car length between Siddoway's car and the approaching murderer. Almost, but not quite. There was a short gap where the trees gave way to the tipping fence. Siddoway had pulled so far up on the sidewalk that the guy was going to have to walk around our car to get to the vacant lot. In the time it took him to step out from under the trees and move into the shadow of the fence, he would be exposed in the open - right in front of our car. There wasn't much light, but there should be enough for me to see his face. It would be a brief glimpse, but it had to be enough.

I steeled myself to keep my watch through the crack between the front seat and the passenger door. I knew it was going to be risky. If I could see him, he would be able to see me. But I had to know. Even if it got me killed, I had to know who had torn my life apart like this. I had to know who had done this to me and Harmony.

I saw the guy's leg. I saw his other leg. He was almost to the end of the overhanging trees. I saw his hand. I saw his neck and chest. And then he stepped out from under the trees, and I saw his face.

I felt like someone had opened a trap door right under me. I stared numbly at his face, and then I stared numbly at the place where his face had been. I felt sick. The thought of Harmony with Brand or Charlie had been bad enough - they were two madmen consumed by insecurities, obsessions, lusts, hatreds, and revenge. But this might even be worse. This was someone I knew and trusted, someone I liked and admired, and someone I had thought liked me. Nausea burned my throat. I struggled to accept that this was the man who had tried to kill me twice in one night. The man who had stuffed Mr. Piper into his luggage, strangled Mrs. Piper, and thrown Janet down a 42-story elevator shaft. The man who had bludgeoned a lovely teenage girl and tossed her body off a bridge like a sack of cats.

The man coming toward me was my managing partner.

The man coming toward me was Marshall Farr.

ALL GOOD THINGS

CHAPTER 49

P ain, nausea, and betrayal sank to the bottom of my stomach. Rage seethed up. It surged along my muscles and nerves. It throbbed in the tips of my icy fingers. Forget groveling here in the back seat, my rage insisted. Jump him, hit him, knock him down. Pound his head against the pavement. Crack his skull. Make him pay for what he did to you and Harmony.

I took a deep, shuddering breath and felt it stoke the fires inside me. I took another and felt even less in control. The police, I thought. Where in the hell were the police? I did not intend either to get myself killed or go to prison for beating Marshall Farr to death. But I was incandescent with rage. Ten seconds ago, I had been praying that the police would come to protect me from the murderer. Now I was praying they would come to protect me from myself.

A movement at the side distracted me. Marshall was at the front of Siddoway's car, walking in the shadow between it and the leaning fence. Because Siddoway had pulled up on the sidewalk, there wasn't much room. Marshall was only a foot or so away from the side of the car. If he even glanced down as he approached, he would see me. And if he saw me, I figured he wouldn't waste any time getting rid of me. He had already tried it twice.

OK, then. I was going to attack Marshall in self-defense, not in revenge. That was perfectly legal. It was also perfectly necessary, as Marshall was only steps from the back seat. I turned the door handle and waited until his shadow fell over the seat in front of me.

I summoned all the rage and pain I had felt a few seconds ago. I pictured Marshall with all the other people I had once trusted and who had betrayed me - my mom, my dad, my case workers, my mob of foster parents. I let all the hatred I had suppressed, ignored, or denied all my life rush pell-mell into my veins. And then I threw the car door open with all my might.

The unusual weight of the door and the scream and crunch from behind it confirmed my timing. I had smacked him backward about six feet. He was lying on the ground. One hand was over his face; the other was fumbling in his jacket. Not that damn gun again. Oddly, the thought of the gun just made me mad, not scared. I was too hurt and angry to be scared.

I jumped out of the car and nearly lost my balance on the soft, wet leaves underfoot. Using the open door as a blind, I stole across to the vacant lot, where the leaning fence petered out into slabs of lumber and other rubble. I grabbed a two by four, stepped over the ruined fence, and waited on the other side.

I heard the squeak of the car door. Was Marshall going to try to steal a police car? Then I heard footsteps coming toward me. He had had to close the door to get around it. A few more footsteps squished in the wet leaves - then stopped. Only three more steps, and I would have been able to whack him over the head with the two by four. But Marshall didn't move. I guessed that he wasn't going to leave the shelter of the fence until he knew who and where I was.

Well, I wasn't going to duck around to the front of the fence and risk getting shot, and it sounded like Marshall wasn't going to duck around to the back of the fence and risk getting whacked. So were we just going to stand here on opposite sides of the fence, like two feuding countries stranded in an unwinnable war? Apparently, we were. I wondered what Marshall would do if and when the police arrived. Where were the damn police? I suppressed a hiss of irritation. Probably only minutes had passed since I had radioed for help, but it felt like hours. Or even days.

I was listening so intently for footsteps that I failed to catch the rustling of the tree branches above me. It wasn't until I heard the click that I looked up. I looked up right into Marshall Farr's sculpted face, hovering over the fence like someone had stuck his head on a pike. His glasses were blank and white in the glare of the lights from the apartment complex. Damn, damn, damn, damn, damn. He must be standing on the trunk of Siddoway's unmarked car.

I saw the gun pointed at me. I was about two feet from the fence. If I lunged, I might be able to knock the battered wood fence over onto Marshall and topple him off the car. But would I even make it to the fence? I knew from experience that Marshall was a bad shot, but could he - could anybody - miss me from four feet away?

I decided to stall. "If you shoot me," I whispered, "the police will hear the gunfire, and it will lead them right to you."

Marshall looked almost amused that I was trying to talk my way out of this. He wasn't convinced. "I'll risk it," he said. "You're the only person who's seen me. You're the only person who can link me to that house." The gun came up. "Goodbye, Jack," he said.

I was just about to leap for the fence when I heard the second voice come out of the darkness. It was a strident, but almost peevish voice, husky with age but steely with indignation. I had heard that voice so many times before, but I couldn't believe I was hearing it now.

In the darkness, I heard Janet Daniels screaming. "Marshall, you stupid bastard, get down from there before you get us all shot. I've told the police everything. They're all around you. Put your hands up and get down."

Marshall's mouth dropped with horror and amazement. The hand holding the gun sagged. I leapt for the fence. I crashed it and myself over on top of Marshall. Marshall fell backwards onto the ground on the other side of the car. I slid down the flattened fence onto the trunk, scooted over it, and jumped off right on top of Marshall. I kneed him savagely in the groin. He screamed. He put up his arms to try to throw me off, but I was too heavy for him. I grabbed his wrists and forced them to the asphalt. I was deciding how I could hurt him further when I realized I was not alone.

Mark was standing over me with his gun drawn. Then another policeman came out of the darkness, and another. The two uniformed officers took Marshall by the arms and pulled him up, spread-eagling him over the back of the car. Mark helped me to my feet and walked me over to another parked car. We sat together on the hood and watched the two uniformed officers search and handcuff my boss. I could hear Siddoway's voice booming through the cold air. "Marshall Farr, you are under arrest for the murders of Humphrey Piper, Mieko Kodama Piper, Janet Wilma Daniels, and Brenda Baxter, and for the attempted murder of John Boyden Hart."

"Are you John Boyden Hart?" Mark whispered.

"Yes," I whispered back. "My mother was still in her Kennedy phase when she named me. I've always gone by Jack." I cleared my throat. "You haven't found Harmony yet, have you?"

Siddoway was giving Marshall the Miranda warnings. Mark sighed. "Not yet," he said. "But we found her purse and a duffel bag of socks and underwear hidden in Lydia Keddington's bedroom. There's a black wool dress hanging in Lydia's closet that looks like it would be about three sizes too small for her. If Harmony is still there, we'll find her. Anthony and Siddoway have been grilling Lydia and her husband. If they don't crack soon, we'll get permission to take the house apart if we have to."

I shuddered. Mark slid off the hood and faced me. "You OK?"

"Yeah. I'm really sorry I left the car. It's just that he was coming right at me. I thought he'd see me."

"I know. Dispatch told us you called for help. When I said stay in the car, I didn't mean you had to sit there like a pigeon if you were in danger. I'm just sorry you had to go through that. By the time we got out here, he was up on the car looking over the fence. We figured if we shot at him, we might hit you on the other side. So I tried to scare him down."

"You are one hell of a mimic, Mark," I said. "Even though I knew it had to be you, hearing Janet's voice like that gave me the creeps. I'm surprised Marshall didn't have a heart attack."

"Well, it scared him enough at least." He paused. "Remember how we were going to kill our foster father when we were kids?"

I remembered. "You were going to distract him, and I was going to clobber him with something heavy," I said.

Mark nodded. "It always was a damn good plan."

by Rosemary Reeve

CHAPTER 50

he officers turned Marshall around to march him to the police car. He threw me a look of such loathing that I was almost flattered. I stood and watched the cruiser disappear into the night. When it had gone, I noticed that Siddoway was opening the trunk of his car. He looked up and smiled at the alarm in my face. Then he slammed the trunk and tossed me a blanket. Until then, I hadn't realized that I was shivering.

"You did good, kid," he said. Mark took me to the house so I could keep warm.

On the porch, Mark paused. "There are a couple of things you should know," he said. "Lydia Keddington is Janet's niece. She and her husband have five children. The two little ones are their own - twin boys. Lydia's husband's brother is coming by to pick up the twins. The other three are - or were - foster kids. I started with surprise. "The oldest was Brenda, the girl Marshall killed by mistake. She was fifteen."

I flinched. I didn't even try to cover it up with a cough or disguise it with a sneeze. *Fifteen.*

Mark nodded grimly. "I know," he said. "And then there's Dwight, who's about ten, and Gabby, who's six or seven. Dwight and Gabby aren't talking. Well, Dwight's been cussing at us and calling us pigs, but that doesn't really count. Gabby just sits still and looks at her hands. Siddoway's getting a social worker in here to take them." He ushered me into the house. "I thought you'd want to know."

Mark pointed me to the living room of the big white house and went off to check the progress of the search. I glanced around. The room was cluttered. Stacks of yellowed newspapers lined the walls. There was a broken vase in the fireplace and a bunch of chipped glass grapes on the coffee table. The sofa was a rusty mustard. When it was new, it probably would have been called something like harvest gold, but I imagined that the harvest was long past for the Keddington family. The green carpet was scarred with grimy, well-worn paths - one to what I guessed was the kitchen, the other between the sofa and the TV. An oniony smell of greasy dinners hung over it all.

The computer stood out against the general air of obsolescence and decay. It was by no means the latest model, but it looked like the most current and expensive item in the house. I walked over to the desk and examined it more closely. There was no printer, just the computer, terminal, and modem. The computer was a 286 IBM-clone - identical to the computers Piper Whatcom had offered for sale to the staff and associates when we had upgraded to 486s a few years ago. A gift from moneybags Aunt Janet, I thought. She could have bought the whole system from PWH for a hundred bucks.

I stretched and let the blanket fall from my shoulders. After the crispness of the night air, it was stiflingly hot in the house. Now that my shock, anger, and fear had dissipated, I was feeling the effects of my final escapade with Marshall. My hand and shoulder throbbed viciously. There were fresh spots of blood on the bandages around my wrist. One by one, new bruises were announcing themselves across my body.

I hobbled over to a shiny blue recliner, sank into it, and let myself wilt against its worn velour. I closed my eyes and tried to process everything that had happened in the few hours since we had left Seattle. A frightened sniff brought me back to the present.

"You can't sit there," said a little voice.

I opened my eyes and looked around. A black-haired little girl wearing faded Princess Jasmine pajamas was standing in the hall between the living room and the kitchen. This had to be Gabby. Gabby was shifting from foot to foot and looking at me anxiously.

"You'll get in trouble if you sit there," Gabby said. "Only Mr. Keddington gets to sit there."

She seemed so worried about it that I scrambled out of the chair. I went over to her. She was shivering in the draft from the front door, and her round face was drawn with exhaustion. I held out my hand.

"Thanks for the warning," I said. "I'm Jack Hart."

After a moment of deliberation, she took my big warm hand in one of her small cold ones and gave it a quick shake. She released me and snatched back her hand as if she were afraid she might catch something. "My name is Gabriella Lopez. People here call me Gabby."

Something in her voice convinced me that she was not enamored of the nickname. "May I call you Gabriella?" I asked her.

Again the deliberative pause. "Yes," she said finally. Her voice was faint and dull. She was swaying with sleepiness.

"Gabriella, it's cold in the hall. Why don't you come with me and sit in the living room where it's warm?"

"I can't."

"Why not?"

"Because the policeman told me to wait here and not move a muscle."

"How long ago was that?"

She shrugged and dropped her eyes. The passage of time was not her concern. She was doing exactly what she was told, and as long as she did exactly what she was told, no one could get mad at her, no one could punish her, and no one could blame her for anything. I had seen this before. I had experienced this before. Some foster kids went nuts, like Charlie. Some foster kids went bad, like Mark. And some foster kids went inside. They just kept their heads down and did everything they were told until there wasn't anyone to tell them what to do anymore. Like Gabriella. Like me.

"How about if I picked you up and took you into the living room?" I asked her. "You wouldn't have moved a muscle, but you'd be nice and warm. OK?"

A very, very long deliberative pause. "OK," she said.

I went into the living room and got the blanket I had dropped. I wrapped it snugly around her several times so she wouldn't feel manhandled when I picked her up. Then I carried her into the living room, managing to suppress my groans as she leaned against my injured shoulder. I nestled her down on the sofa and tucked the blanket around her. "Feel better?"

"Uh huh."

"Good." Questions were storming through my mind: Had she seen Harmony? Did she know where she was? Did she know how she had gotten here? I reined myself in. Gabriella and I were barely on a first-name basis. She would clam up immediately if I pressured her. I sat down at the other end of the sofa and stole a glance at her. Her eyes were closed, but I was pretty sure she wasn't asleep. I figured the best way of drawing her out was to do something else I shouldn't do. Kids are sticklers for rules. If they have to obey them, they want everyone else to suffer, too.

I went over to the TV and started flipping through the channels. Infomercial after infomercial clicked by without a protest from Gabriella. Apparently, TV was not restricted in this house. I walked around the room, touching and slightly displacing the few pictures and photos on the walls. No warning from Gabriella. I looked over at her suspiciously. Maybe she really was asleep. Touching the pictures had always been a major no-no in all my foster homes.

One of the photos held my attention. It was a snapshot of children clustered in front of a tinsel-blasted Christmas tree. There were two cute little boys, maybe two years old, at the front of the picture. Then there was Gabriella, her round face still and unsmiling, her liquid brown eyes focused on something a long, long way beyond the photographer. Beside her was a thin, defiant-looking kid with dark skin and close-cropped hair. Must be Dwight. And behind Dwight was a lovely blond girl with a heart-shaped face and round, turquoise blue eyes. I realized with a start that it was the girl I had seen lying in the body bag in the hospital. But up at the hospital, the girl's hair had been black, not blond.

I turned back to Gabriella with a renewed sense of purpose. I had to get her to talk. I went over and turned on the computer. I had been avoiding touching the computer in case the police needed to use it as evidence of a link between Janet and her niece, but desperate times call for desperate measures. I sat down at the desk and cracked my fingers, as if I were going to dive in and start typing on the keyboard. Almost immediately, I heard Gabriella's warning voice behind me.

"You can't touch that."

I halted my hands in mid-air and jumped as if I were surprised. "Why not?"

"Because it was a present from Mrs. Keddington's aunt, and only Mrs. Keddington gets to use it."

"Oh." I shrugged with disappointment. "Geez, you can't do anything in this house."

Gabriella's expressionless eyes met mine. "It's not so bad," she said. "There are just some things that only the adults can use."

"What happens if you use something you're not supposed to, Gabriella?"

Silence. I had gone too far. I tried again. "Do they punish you? Hit you? Yell at you?" I decided to risk it all. "Lock you up?"

A long silence. Then she said, "They don't hit you."

All children are natural lawyers. It's the literalness of their minds. "But they do something to you, Gabriella?"

She nodded slowly. "What do they do?" I asked, fighting to keep the panic out of my voice. "What do they do to you when you do something wrong?"

She looked right into my eyes. This little kid could give Harmony a run for her money when it came to quiet and disquieting stares. I looked right back at her. Then she crooked her index finger at me, beckoning me.

I went over to her and knelt down beside the sofa. She reached up and whispered in my ear.

"The Punishment Room."

CHAPTER 51

"**G**et away from her!"

Dwight had stalked into the room. His thin face was twisted with fury. He wedged himself between me and Gabriella. "You get away from her, you fucking pig."

"I'm not a cop," I said without moving. I held out my hand. "My name's Jack Hart."

Dwight batted my hand away. "I don't care what your fucking name is." He glared at me, but I saw the flash of anxiety in his eyes. Things were not working out the way he had planned. I hadn't budged, and I hadn't even blinked at his anger, his insults, or his language. Dwight was going to run out of ammunition really fast, I thought.

I turned to the little girl. "Gabriella, have I done or said anything to hurt you or upset you?"

Gabriella thought it over. "No," she said. She shoved her foster brother in the back. "Dwight, you're squishing me. Get off."

I got to my feet and moved away so Dwight would feel that he could preserve his honor yet do the same. After a moment of indecision, he unsquished Gabriella. He stood a few feet away from me, scowling, his arms crossed over his scrawny chest. I sat down at the other end of the couch and patted the place between me and Gabriella. "Gabriella and I were having a nice conversation before you came in," I told him. "And if you want to stay, you are more than welcome, but Gabriella and I are going to continue having our conversation whether you are here or not."

Everyone hates to feel he's going to be missing something. Arms still folded, Dwight marched over and sat down on the sofa. His back was stiff and straight, but his legs dangled, and his feet didn't touch the floor. "Gabriella was telling me about the Punishment Room, Dwight," I said. "Have you ever been in the Punishment Room?"

Silence. I turned to Gabriella. "Gabriella, where is the Punishment Room?"

She started to answer, but Dwight cut her off. "Don't tell him anything, Gabby," he snapped, turning on her furiously. "He just wants to find Brenda. He just wants to take Brenda away from here."

Find Brenda? Take Brenda away from here? What the hell was the kid talking about? I sought out Gabriella's eyes, but she had bowed her head and was studying the backs of her little hands. She seemed terrified by the thought that she might have done something wrong. Dwight glowered at me. I decided it was time to go for bust. "Listen, you two," I said, swinging myself off the sofa and sitting down on the coffee table so I could face them. "You guys are my only hope." They both looked up in surprise. "My best friend in the whole world disappeared last week. No one has seen her since Sunday night, and I am really, really worried about her. I think she might be in your Punishment Room. I need you two to help me find her."

Dwight was silent. Gabriella whispered, "You're not supposed to sit on the coffee table."

I scooted off the coffee table and sat cross-legged on the floor in front of the sofa. Then I stared at Dwight and Gabriella silently and just let the tension build.

It built. Finally Dwight said, "Your friend isn't in there. Brenda's in there."

I knew full well that Brenda was in a body bag up in the morgue, but I wasn't going to tell them that. "Why did your foster parents put Brenda in the Punishment Room?" I asked.

"Because she dyed her hair black to look like that lady from Seattle."

Gabriella suddenly giggled. "What is it, honey?" I asked.

For just a moment, Gabriella smiled. It changed her whole face. "Brenda always thought she had the best hair because it was yellow," she said. "But when she saw the lady from Seattle, she decided she wanted to have hair like me." She pushed her fingers through her marvelously glossy, straight black hair. Her gesture was artless and heartbreaking, a little flourish of poise and exuberance in a life full of silence, solemnity, and down-cast eyes.

"I don't blame her," I said. "You have beautiful hair." Gabriella glowed. "Why on earth would your foster parents not want Brenda to have beautiful hair like yours?"

"Because they didn't want the lady from Seattle to take her away. And they were right, because the day after Brenda dyed her hair, a man came to the door looking for her. And Mr. and Mrs. Keddington said that we couldn't tell anyone about Brenda trying to look like the lady from Seattle. They said we shouldn't even talk about the lady at all. They said if the man found Brenda, he'd try to take her away. They said the lady from Seattle would claim to be her mother, and that they wouldn't be able to keep her because she and the lady looked so much alike." Gabriella stopped and gulped. "You're not going to try to take Brenda away, are you?"

My heart twisted for them. The thing that had frightened me most as a foster child was being separated from the kids I had come to regard as my siblings. When Mark was shipped off to the group home, I couldn't sleep for a month. No one had ever filled Mark's place, but there were other kids I had known and grown close to - and then lost. It was like losing your family - again and again and again. Eventually, I had wised up and just stopped getting attached to the other kids around me, but these kids weren't old enough for that sort of armor. I should have realized that when

Dwight had come storming into the room to protect Gabriella. They were going to take Brenda's death awfully hard.

I would let the social worker deal with that, I decided. I had to concentrate on Harmony.

"I promise you that I'm not trying to take Brenda away from you," I assured them. "But I need you to show me where the Punishment Room is so I can ask Brenda if she's seen my friend. And if Brenda says no, then I'll just move along to the next house. But I can't leave until I've talked to Brenda. And I can't leave until I'm sure that my friend isn't in that Punishment Room."

Dwight and Gabriella looked at me dubiously. Finally, Dwight said, "We'll show you, but you won't be able to get in."

"Will Brenda be able to hear me if I yell?"

"Yeah, but you'll have to yell really loud."

"I can yell really loud."

"We'll help you yell," Gabriella offered suddenly. My praise of her hair was really paying off.

I patted each of them on the cheek. "You guys are the best," I said, and I meant it. They both accepted the compliment and the caress. They wouldn't have if I hadn't meant it.

They led me to the door of a dark and musty-smelling basement. The stairs were rough, uneven wood. I hesitated and looked with concern at their bare feet. "Do you two have any slippers?"

They shook their heads. "Wait here," I told them, going off to look for Mark. Mark produced their shoes with amazing speed. Dwight pulled his on by himself. Gabriella put her feet up in my lap so I could help her. They each took one of my hands.

With Mark shadowing us from a few feet behind, Dwight and Gabriella led me into the basement.

CHAPTER 52

Dwight and Gabriella were as good as their word. Dwight led me to a squat, bolted door beneath the rough staircase. It was hidden behind stacks of huge plastic tubs filled with wheat, beans, and something that looked like and probably was peanut butter. Food storage, Dwight said.

Mark hammered on the door with his no-nonsense policeman's knock, I slammed it repeatedly with my fist, Dwight and Gabriella kicked it, and all four of us screamed at the top of our lungs - except that Mark and I screamed "Harmony," and Dwight and Gabriella screamed "Brenda."

We all made a lot of noise for a long time. Then I tried to shut everybody up. It was harder than I expected. The screaming seemed to unleash something pent up in the kids. Dwight and Gabriella kept yelling and kicking the door long after Mark and I were straining to hear signs of life from within the closet.

Finally, everyone was quiet. And then we all heard the noise from the other side of the door. It was heartbreakingly faint, but I heard a few muffled thuds and then a muddy and distorted cry. I couldn't make out what she was saying, but I knew that voice. "It's Harmony. She's in there," I gasped to Mark.

Mark shouted for help, and suddenly the dim, damp, cramped basement was overflowing with policemen and policewomen. Somebody snatched Dwight and Gabriella and took them upstairs. Every step of the way, they screamed for Brenda. Then they started screaming for me, and I couldn't stand it. I hurtled up the stairs and saw them struggling with a thin, sandy-haired guy in an olive turtleneck. The social worker, I guessed. He had a young face but old eyes.

Gabriella launched herself at me. She almost knocked me backward down the stairs. I flung my arms around her, twisted, and landed heavily on the top step. She was sobbing. I held her on my lap and rocked her until she could take a breath. She gasped and choked, then buried her wet face against my shoulder. Dwight stalked over and started tugging my arm. His face was rigid with anger and fear.

by Rosemary Reeve

"If it's your friend in the Punishment Room," he demanded, "then where is Brenda?" When I didn't answer, he started pushing at me. "Tell me! Where is Brenda?"

Over Dwight's shoulder, I locked eyes with the social worker. He pressed his thin lips together and shook his head. A hell of a lot of help he was going to be. Most reluctantly, I met Dwight's burning gaze. I wasn't going to lie to him, but I couldn't bear to tell him the truth. I ended up just mimicking the social worker's gesture of defeat. I squeezed my lips together and shook my head at Dwight: a few tight, stiff, helpless jerks back and forth. I must have conveyed more than intended to, however, because I saw the tears flood into his eyes. Dwight looked down at Gabriella, who had her arms around my neck and was quieting by degrees. He looked back at me. His head snapped up. He took a couple of noisy, shallow breaths. He folded his arms tight across his narrow chest and suddenly sat down beside me on the stairs. I wriggled an arm from around Gabriella and put it lightly across his shoulders. He leaned against me for a few minutes, his small body taut and unbending against mine. Then he straightened up. He brushed himself off and put his hand on Gabriella's back.

His voice was husky but perfectly controlled. "C'mon, Gab," he said, as if she were just late for dinner or something equally inconsequential. "It's time to go."

I hugged them both and gave each of them one of my business cards. It had my work telephone, my home telephone, my e-mail address, and my fax number on it. Piper Whatcom believed in total attorney access, 24 hours a day, 7 days a week. I might as well get some good out of it. I cupped their grim, shadowed faces and tilted them toward me so I could look them right in the eyes.

"This is my number at my law firm. This is my number at home. If I'm not in either place, the firm will page me for you. You can call any of those numbers collect," I assured them. "That means I'll pay for it. You just have to tell the operator you want to make a collect call. I want you to call me if you need me, or if you're scared, or if you just want to talk to me. OK?"

They both nodded solemnly. The sandy-haired social worker let out a disapproving tsk and shook his head. His expression was transparent: Nothing good could come of lawyering up foster kids. I thought of giving him a conciliatory, grown-up smile, but decided against it. I hated social workers. They had never done me any good. Maybe they would do Dwight and Gabriella some good yet, but it was hard to make myself believe that as I watched the skinny, sandy-haired man take the two kids by the shoulders and march them away. Gabriella looked back at me just before she got in the social worker's car. I caught one last glimpse of her shy, secret, unsmiling face - and then she was gone.

I took a deep breath and hurtled back into the basement. I would feel sick about Dwight and Gabriella later. Right now, I had to focus on Harmony. I almost crashed into Mark at the bottom of the stairs. We stood together and watched the Salt Lake police work to free her. The police had removed the hinges from the closet door. A couple of beefy guys were lifting the door out of its frame. They shouldered the plank and carried it toward me, blocking my view of the closet as they approached. The bare basement bulb glared on the thick wood. The big cops leaned the door against the wall next to me and turned away.

I looked at the door in horror. The back was padded with a smothering layer of insulation. That's why it had been so hard to hear Harmony in the closet. Someone had clawed away the insulation along the bottom of the door. The ragged edges were stained a rusty brown.

I blinked and looked up in time to see a small, white shape in Lieutenant Siddoway's arms. It had to be Harmony. Her head was thrown back, and I could see her black hair hanging down. Her neck looked long and somehow broken. Anthony was wrapping her in a dark blanket and calling for a stretcher. Siddoway let her down on the stretcher, and men and women in uniforms crowded around her. All I could see were their backs and butts - and one small white foot sticking out from the crowd. I kept my eyes on that little foot. I strained my eyes for movement.

Mark put his hand on my back. He was trying to push me toward the stretcher. I resisted. If Harmony wasn't OK, she would need every one of those men and women in that throng of police and EMTs. No way in hell was I going to jeopardize her by getting in their way. And if Harmony was OK - and I was praying that she was - how in the hell was I going to explain to her what I was doing in Salt Lake City in the middle of the night in Janet Daniels' niece's basement? Harmony and I were friends, but that was all. She didn't know how I felt about her. I didn't know whether I wanted her to know how I felt about her. I had been ready to take on anyone and do anything to rescue her. But the thought of facing her now made me extremely shy.

Mark was watching me closely. I leaned toward him and spoke in his ear: "I don't want to get in the way." A pucker appeared between his eyebrows, but he nodded. We flattened ourselves against the wall. People with tubing, bandages, and other intimidating medical implements ran around and through the crowd surrounding Harmony. I saw Harmony's toes wiggle. Then her whole foot moved. It looked like she was flexing the muscle in the leg. Flexing it slowly and painfully, maybe, but flexing it of her own accord.

Suddenly, the hive of people rose and lurched in my direction. They were carrying Harmony out of the basement. Mark and I shrank further against the wall, but the basement was too cramped to allow everyone easy passage. The crowd eddied and swarmed around us. Without moving an inch, I found myself standing right next to the stretcher. The EMTs carrying the stretcher had to wait for a moment while the two big cops moved the padded door out of the way again.

I blanched at the sight of Harmony's hands. They were battered, swollen, and crusted with blood. Black infection lines shot up her bare arms. I stole a look at her face. Her skin was dead white. Her eyes were closed. She was wearing an oxygen mask, but I could see all too clearly the new sharpness of her cheekbones, the purplish half-moons like bruises beneath her eyes. A gash on her temple was black with clotted blood.

The EMTs bumped the stretcher as they tried to maneuver Harmony up the stairs. At the sudden movement, Harmony opened her eyes. For a fraction of a second, her gaze was as blue and unfocused as a baby's. Then she cast her eyes in my direction, and I could see her eyebrows rise and her stare rivet on me. I could actually see the color deepen in her eyes, like a clear sky gone suddenly intense and electric right before a summer storm. I saw the light come into them. It wasn't like a flash, or even a spark. It was like a steady light coming out of the darkness: a lantern you could move toward after a long, nocturnal journey; or a lantern moving toward you, carried high by someone coming to find you after you had been lost for a long time.

Harmony held my gaze until the EMTs moved her onto the first few stairs. Then her eyes closed, and she seemed to sink deeper onto the stretcher. I watched her from the bottom of the stairs as they eased her out of the basement where she had been a prisoner. Minutes later, I heard the wail of a siren as they took her away.

When I looked around, Lieutenant Siddoway was standing a few feet from me. "Well, did we get it right this time, kid?" he asked.

"Yes," I replied. "Oh, yes, you did. That's definitely her."

CHAPTER 53

I t was Sunday morning, and we were back where we started. The ambulance had taken Harmony to the University of Utah Hospital, the same medical campus where Brenda was lying somewhere in a body bag, her pale turquoise eyes frozen open and staring at nothing. I thought about Brenda's boyfriend, the kid who had called 911 because Brenda hadn't shown up for their date. Had they brought him in to identify her? Had they shown him the clothes that he wouldn't recognize? Had they shown him the face that he would? I asked Lieutenant Siddoway. He pressed his lips together and nodded, a few, sharp, helpless bobs of his head. He didn't look me in the eye.

Mark, Anthony, and I slept fitfully in the padded chairs of the glassed-in waiting area while the doctors checked and treated Harmony. A doctor woke us around 5:30. Ms. Piper was weak but alert, she told us. She was suffering from dehydration and pneumonia, and several of the wounds on her hands were severely infected. They were giving her fluids, nourishment, and antibiotics intravenously, and they wanted to keep her in the hospital for at least 24 hours to make sure her body could fight off the infections. We had to be careful about tiring her out, she said, but if we wanted to talk to her for a little while, she thought that this would be as a good time as any.

Anthony thanked her but was obviously concerned. "I'm afraid that what we have to tell Ms. Piper will be very upsetting to her," he said. "Would it be better if we let her rest for a few hours?"

The doctor smiled at him, but her face was shadowed. "Normally, I would ask you to wait," she said, "especially since I understand that you have to tell her that her father and stepmother have passed away. But the problem is, Ms. Piper very much wants to talk to her father. She asked every doctor and nurse to dial the phone for her. Everyone made up some excuse or the other, but she's quite ingenious. Her hands are bandaged, and the arm nearest the phone is immobilized with the IV, but she managed to reach over and dial the operator using a pencil. So she already knows that there's no answer at her home in the middle of the night, and now she's very, very worried about her stepmother as well." She paused and rubbed her temples. "You do what you think is best, Detective. There's no good way to learn that your parents are dead. But I can guarantee you that Ms. Piper won't be getting much rest in the interim even if you wait to tell her."

She nodded to us and hurried down the hall. Anthony scanned our faces. He passed his hand over his gray hair and sighed. "No time like the present, I guess," he said. At the door, he paused and shook his head. "This never gets any easier."

Harmony's eyes were closed. Mark and Anthony loitered behind the curtain separating the empty bed from Harmony, unwilling to disturb her. Mark threw me a beseeching glance. I walked over quietly and sat down in the chair beside the bed. She opened her eyes almost immediately. I saw the warm, steady light rise in them again.

"Jack." Her voice was hoarse and broken.

"Hi." I bent over and kissed her very gently on the forehead, steering clear of the gash in her temple. Her skin felt hot and dry under my lips.

"How did you know where I was?"

"It's a long story," I said. I stroked her hair away from her face. Her eyes glowed. "I'll tell you later, OK?"

"OK." Her eyelids drooped, as if they were just too heavy to keep open. She blinked and refocused on me with an effort. "Jack, I need to call my dad and my stepmom. I tried them at home, but there's no answer. They must both be in Japan. I called the hotel in Tokyo where my dad usually stays, but he's not there. Could you ask the police if they found my purse? I've got Mieko's mom's number in my address book. She'll know where Mieko is, at least."

I didn't know what to do. I kept waiting for Detective Anthony to jump in, but he seemed willing to let me carry the ball. Harmony noticed my hesitation. "Please, Jack. I really need to talk to my dad."

I put my hand on her arm. I saw the fear come into her eyes as I shook my head.

"What is it?" She was trying to sit up. "Jack, what's going on?"

"Harmony, look -"

"What has happened?" She was even paler than before. She was sitting bolt upright, struggling with the tubes and bandages around her. Her eyes were burning in her ashen face. "Tell me!"

"Harmony, you can't call your dad."

"Why not?"

I started to answer her, but Anthony interrupted. He moved from behind the curtains. "Ms. Piper?"

She jumped at his approach. "Yes?"

Anthony showed her his badge. "I am Detective Anthony of the Seattle Police Department. This is Officer Oden."

She nodded at them. "Yes, I saw you in the basement."

"Ms. Piper, there is no gentle way to do this. I am terribly, terribly sorry, but I have to inform you that your father and your stepmother are dead."

She didn't say a word. She didn't make a sound. But she shrank from him as if he had slapped her across the face. I sat down on the bed just behind her and pulled her back against me. I could feel her trembling through the thin blanket.

She put one bandaged hand to her forehead, a plump, white paw against her black hair. "Was it a car accident?" she asked him, without looking up.

"No, Ms. Piper."

Her head came up so sharply that she butted me in the nose. I could see her reflection in the mirror over the sink. There was pure horror in her face. "Did my father kill himself?" she demanded.

"No, Ms. Piper. He didn't kill himself. Your father and your stepmother were murdered. Your secretary was also murdered. And had you not been kidnapped by your secretary's niece, we believe that you would have been murdered, too."

"Me?"

"Yes."

"But why? Why would anyone want to murder my father? Or Mieko, or Janet? Or me? Do you know who it was?"

"We have a suspect in custody."

Harmony was trembling so violently that it was actually hard to keep hold of her. I tried to ease her back onto her pillows, but she jerked out of my grasp. The IV apparatus clashed and shuddered. She flung her arm impatiently against it. She was almost out of the bed. "Who is it? Tell me who it is."

Anthony looked at her sadly and doubtfully for a moment. Then he said, "It's Marshall Farr. We're quite sure he killed your father and your secretary. We're quite sure he tried to kill you. We're less certain that he killed your stepmother. I think it's far more likely that your secretary killed your stepmother, but we may not be able to prove that."

I looked up at Anthony in surprise. That last bit was news to me. He caught my eye and nodded almost imperceptibly, but Harmony saw the gesture. A long, hard shudder went through her body. Then she climbed back into bed and pulled the covers up to her chin. Her eyes traveled slowly around the room. Her gaze rested on me for a few moments, and she said my name - quietly and almost to herself - as if she had forgotten I was there. I rearranged her wrist so that the IV could drip freely into her vein. Her arm was cold and limp in my hands. When I had finished, she said my name again. It was like it had just occurred to her. After a long pause, she looked at me and said, "Thank you."

Anthony cleared his throat. "Ms. Piper, at some point, we're going to have to through this step by step with you, but it doesn't have to be right now. Why don't you try to get some rest?"

Harmony turned the full force of her blue eyes on him. Her gaze was still and smoldering. "You need to ask me some questions?"

"Yes, we do, but it can wait -"

"No, it can't. It can't wait," she said. I could feel her fighting to control herself. When Anthony paused, uncertain, she added, almost softly, "I have my whole life to cry, Detective Anthony." He acknowledged that fact with a gentle bob of his head. Her voice hardened. "I will tell you anything you want to know. But in return, I expect you to tell me everything I want to know. Do we have a deal?"

Anthony blinked at her. I could tell that Harmony was not exactly what he and Mark had expected. Then he sat down in the chair on the other side of the bed, and Mark perched on the window sill and snapped open his notebook.

"Deal," Anthony said.

by Rosemary Reeve

CHAPTER 54

"We need to know what led up to your disappearance, Ms. Piper," Anthony said. "Why don't you start with the Brand summary judgment? First of all, why didn't you tell anyone about the argument?"

"You mean why didn't I tell anyone I was going down to argue it, or why didn't I tell anyone we won?"

"Both."

Harmony reflected. "Well, I didn't make a big deal about the argument itself because we were pretty sure we were going to lose. And I didn't tell anyone that we had won because it would have sounded like I was bragging. Besides, there wasn't much of anyone around to tell. Marshall was in Japan for the client seminar, and Jack was up in Bellingham at a deposition. I was going to draft all the final paperwork and leave it for Marshall with a note, but I got kind of upset."

"Why?"

"The argument itself was a little upsetting," she said. "Mr. Brand is excitable. He's been bad through the whole case. One minute he'd be sending me poetry, the next, he'd be threatening to have me disbarred. His counsel got him on Prozac, and that seemed to help. He was just uniformly sullen after that. But he was really scary after the argument. He yelled at me, and Judge Brady had to clear the courtroom. I ran all the way back to the firm."

"Why didn't you let Judge Brady call a police escort for you?"

She grimaced. "I should have. I was stupid. But Judge Brady is an acquaintance of my dad's. He knew me when I was a little girl. I'm still short, and I still look like I'm about twelve. It's hard enough to get judges to take me seriously, even without letting them think that I'm frightened or I need to be protected."

"But you were frightened, and you did need to be protected."

"Yes, I was. I did." She sighed. "But Judge Brady didn't need to know that."

"What did you do when you got back to the firm?"

"I barricaded my door and called my dad in Japan. He was at one of his atrociously early breakfast meetings, so I left a message. I tried to call my stepmom, Mieko, but she wasn't home and she wasn't at the tennis club, either. It was only 3 or so in the afternoon, but I was beat. I had stayed late the night before, cramming for the argument, and I'd been putting in a lot of time on an appellate brief and my partnership applications. I decided I'd just draft the <u>Brand</u> cost bill and final judgment and order, and then go home and go to bed."

"And did you?"

"I started to, but well, that's when I got upset. I printed out a billing history on <u>Brand</u> so I could do the cost bill, and I found something strange. None of the time I had billed on the case during September showed up on the history. As I looked back, I saw that until September, there wasn't any time billed for my father. I knew that he had worked on the case from the beginning, when he was advising the corporate parent in Japan. But I couldn't find any record of his charges. I was puzzling over it when my dad called me back. He was out of his breakfast meeting, just taking a bathroom break in his hotel room."

She seemed to choke. I thought she was going to cry. Mark slid noiselessly off the sill and fetched her some water. She looked at him gratefully, then drained the cup.

"I told him we had won the summary judgment, and he was thrilled. I told him that Mr. Brand had screamed at me, and he was horrified. And then, just because I was puzzled and frustrated, I told him that someone had screwed up our charges on <u>Brand</u>. And he didn't say anything at all. I thought maybe he was upset about it, so I started babbling that I would figure it out and take care of it, that he didn't need to worry. And he said, 'No, Harmony, don't you do that.' I said it was no trouble at all, that I would talk to Accounting that afternoon. He said, kind of louder, 'No, Harmony, I mean it. Don't do that.' We went back and forth like that for some time. After a while, I started to get suspicious. Finally, he told me what he had been doing." She looked unhappily at Anthony. "I guess you need to know what he had been doing?"

Anthony nodded. "I'm sorry, but yes, Ms. Piper."

"He had been embezzling money from the firm." She covered her face with her bandaged hands, then added hastily, "My father was managing partner of Piper Whatcom for seven years, Detective Anthony. Some people thought he overextended the firm with new offices and new hires. When the Governing Committee voted him out and replaced him with Marshall Farr, Marshall took credit for saving the firm. It really hurt my dad, Detective. I know that doesn't excuse him for doing something dishonest, but it really did hurt him. The way he saw it, first he had put the firm in a position to do work all over the world. And then he had developed the clients so that the firm had work to do all over the world. But Marshall took all the credit for the firm's success. It was horrible for him.

"He told me what he had done. He said he didn't cheat any of his clients, and he didn't take fees for anybody else's work. He just skimmed the charges for his own time, but he worked a lot and he billed out at around $500 an hour. He said it came to about a million dollars a year for the three years he'd been in Japan. I told him he had to give the money back, that he should take the money out of my trust fund if he had to." Her voice broke, and she shook her head from side to side, as if she were trying to knock the memory out of her mind. "I told him I'd go to Marshall if he didn't pay the money back. I wouldn't have squealed on him. I didn't mean it, but I said it." She stopped, unable to go on.

Anthony patted her arm. His voice was gentle. "How did he respond?"

"He was furious," Harmony told him. "He yelled at me. He was so upset, he even dropped the phone. And I yelled at him, too. Finally, I just hung up on him and left. He called me back at home that night, and we talked some more. He was still mad. Then we talked a couple of times on Saturday. Finally, we agreed that he would tell Marshall about the embezzlement when Marshall arrived at the client seminar from Sapporo. That was the last time I ever talked to him." Her voice trailed off.

"But you received an e-mail message from him later?" Anthony prompted her.

"Yes, I did. It was really late Sunday night or really early Monday morning. I had been at work all day because I had an appellate brief due on Monday. I'd kind of been avoiding you, Jack, because I thought I'd end up telling you about my dad if I talked to you. I didn't want anybody to know about it, not even you." She looked around at me, her face hot with embarrassment. "Especially not you," she added.

Harmony turned back to Anthony. "I was finishing up my appellate brief when I got the message from my dad. He said that he just couldn't do what he had promised, that he didn't have the money to pay back the firm, and that he would take care of it in his own way, in his own time. He asked me not to do anything. I couldn't believe it. I couldn't believe that he would go back on his word like that, and that he didn't even have the courage to call me up and tell me in person. He knew how upset I was about it. He knew that in a few days, I had to submit my partnership applications and sign that all my fee credits and hour reports were all true and correct. And he knew that they weren't. No matter how mad he was at the firm, I couldn't understand how he could do that to me. I couldn't understand how he could put me in that position."

"What did you do, Ms. Piper?"

"I threw his photograph against the wall. I deleted his message. I just wanted to blot it all out. But when I went to pick up the photograph so I could throw the frame away, the phone rang, and I cut myself on the broken glass. I thought it must be my dad, calling to apologize and let me know it was all a mistake - but it wasn't. It was Janet. She was calling to tell me that she wouldn't be in that day. Lydia - her niece - was visiting with her kids, and she had broken her arm on the Underground Tour. She thought she saw a rat and fell backwards, or something. Janet was going to drive her and the kids back to Salt Lake City, and then fly home."

She took a deep breath and let it out slowly. "Janet could tell I was upset. She asked me what was going on, but I wouldn't tell her. She pressed me pretty hard. She kept saying, 'I can tell you're in pain, and I can't stand to see you suffer like this.'"

She lowered her voice in an extraordinary Janet Daniels imitation. Mark and I exchanged surprised glances. Another mimic. Unfortunately, Harmony saw us and misinterpreted our meaning. Her face was pale, but her cheeks were red. "I know what you're thinking," she said. "This is the part of the story where you see how gullible I am."

"You're not gullible," Anthony put in quickly, glaring at me and Mark. "You were awfully vulnerable that night, though. I assume Janet took advantage of that?"

"I think she did. I hope you'll be able to tell me why she did it, but she pulled all my strings. She wouldn't get off the phone. She kept telling me how tired I was, and how hard I had been working, and how much I needed a vacation. I couldn't even answer her, or argue with her, or anything. I just kept agreeing. I was so tired. I was so tired of being there. And I was so hurt and so angry. You know, I never even really wanted to be a lawyer. I definitely didn't want to work at Piper Whatcom. But my dad wanted it so much, and he was so proud of me. At least, I thought he was."

Anthony looked puzzled.

"Did Janet tell you that your dad wasn't proud of you?"

Harmony gave him a sad, tight smile. "No, Detective Anthony," she said. "Janet told me that my dad wasn't my dad."

"What?" I couldn't contain myself. "And you believed her?"

"Yes, I believed her," Harmony replied. "And it knocked the wind out of me. She was probably right, Jack. From the time I was old enough to notice things like that, I realized that it was odd that I had thick, black, straight hair when both my mom and my dad had hair that was fine, blond, and curly. My eyes and skin are the same color as my mom's were, but that's all, and I don't look anything like my dad."

Lucky you, I thought, picturing Mr. Piper's overall ferrety expression.

"If you already suspected that Mr. Piper wasn't your biological father, why did Janet's mentioning it upset you?" Anthony asked her.

Harmony paused. "It was like Santa Claus," she said finally.

"I'm sorry?"

"When I was little, I knew there was no Santa Claus. But I didn't want my dad to know that I knew there was no Santa Claus because he seemed to enjoy it all so much - you know, hanging up the stockings, looking for Rudolph's nose in the sky, leaving out milk and cookies on Christmas Eve. Just in case my dad didn't know that there was no Santa Claus, I didn't want to spoil it for him. This was the same kind of thing. If he didn't know, I wasn't going to bring it up. And if he did know, and it didn't matter to him, then I definitely wasn't going to bring it up. He'd always acted like my dad, and that was enough."

"Do you know who your biological father is?"

"I think so. His name is Higuro Yamashita. He's half Japanese and half Swedish or something, and he lives in Tokyo. He lived with my parents about thirty years ago. He moved in about ten months before I was born. He always used to send me birthday presents and special gifts on Girls' Day. That's a Japanese holiday. When I graduated from law school, he managed to get tickets to the ceremony somehow. He came up and gave me a big hug right in front of my dad."

"What did Janet say that upset you so?"

"She asked me if I was crying because I had found out that one of my dad's clients was actually my biological father. I was stunned. I had never told anyone what I thought, and I couldn't imagine my dad's telling anyone, either. Then she said that my dad had told her that he wasn't my real father, but that he went along with the charade because my mom's will named 'Harmony's father' as trustee of my money. Not 'Humphrey," not 'my husband' - just 'Harmony's father.' And it does, you know. When she said that, it all made sense. It made sense that he would go back on his word to me, that he would do something so wrong without caring how it affected me. I thought that it must all have been a lie for all those years. I thought that he must have never cared about me at all - that he only cared about keeping control of my money. My mom didn't leave him anything at all - even the house is in trust for me."

She wiped her eyes fiercely with the back of her bandaged hand. "What happened then?" Anthony asked.

"Janet said she'd come and get me. She insisted. She said she was worried about me. When I hung up, I looked down and found out that I had been bleeding all over my dad's picture and a book I had been using for my brief. I slammed the book closed and pushed it away from me. I couldn't stand to see my dad's face anymore." She took a deep, shuddering breath. It knocked and rattled in her lungs. Her eyes looked dark and hollow. "And now, I guess I won't. Not ever. Not ever again."

Anthony cleared his throat and patted her arm again. "Would you like to take a break, Ms. Piper?"

She nodded without looking up. Anthony and Mark rose quietly and headed for the door. I started to follow them, but Harmony stopped me.

"Please, Jack," she said. "Please stay."

by Rosemary Reeve

CHAPTER 55

After the break, everything came out in a rush. Harmony had grabbed her purse and coat and wrapped the broken glass and frame in tissues so the custodians wouldn't cut themselves. She had thrown the rubbish in the big bin in front of the freight elevator on her way to the loading dock. She had gone via the freight elevator so Frank, the security guard, wouldn't see that she had been crying and ask embarrassing questions. She knew the elevator's security code because she had had to use it during her natural resources trial in Alaska, when she was in charge of transferring 172 boxes of documents and exhibits from the Seattle office to the trial site.

On the way to Magnolia, Janet had persuaded her to take a few days off and help her injured niece drive her kids back to Salt Lake City. "All I wanted to do right then was run away," Harmony explained. "I couldn't stand the thought of betraying my father by exposing what he had done, and I couldn't stand the thought of betraying the firm by not exposing what he had done. When Janet offered me the chance to leave town for a few days - for a good reason no one could really criticize - I jumped at it. My appellate brief was done, and I had blocked out the whole week for trial preparation in Brand. Since we had won summary judgment, I didn't have much of anything pressing to do."

Janet had taken Harmony home so she could pick up a few things for the trip. Harmony had tossed a few T-shirts, some underwear, a pair of Levi's, and her tennis shoes in a duffel bag. Because she routinely stayed so late at work, she already had makeup and a toothbrush in her purse. She had wanted to change her clothes in her bedroom and wake her stepmother to say goodbye, but Janet had insisted that they leave right away.

"She told me she would take care of everything," Harmony said. "She said she'd call Mieko first thing in the morning, that she'd tell everyone at work where I had gone. She said she'd put my brief in final form, have Jeremy sign it, and serve and file it by Monday afternoon. She told me not to worry about a thing. She said I should just forget about the firm and my dad and enjoy the drive and a few days in Utah. She said I shouldn't even check my voicemail; that she would give Lydia her cellular phone so she could call us if something important came up." She looked a little sheepish. "I guess that should have made me suspicious. She wasn't normally a generous person.

But she was being so nice to me, and she seemed so concerned. Besides, the thought of leaving the firm and the whole mess with my dad for a few days was just - well, it was just wonderful. I felt like I had been let out of jail. Even though I was tired, it felt magnificent to leave Seattle behind me and drive away as the sun was coming up."

With five kids crammed into Lydia's station wagon, the drive to Salt Lake had been long, loud, and harried - but fun. "The kids were so cute," she said. "Especially Gabriella. She's six. She wouldn't talk to me at first, but by the time we hit Oregon, I knew everything about everyone in her class. Then Dwight moved up front and started criticizing my driving. He said I drove like a girl. And I said, well, I am a girl. And he said, yeah, but you don't have to drive like one, baby. Tom and Tyler - the twins - sang the Barney song for about 150 miles. It was excruciating. But they really were adorable."

"What was Brenda Baxter like?" Anthony asked.

Harmony wrinkled her nose. "Barbie-doll Brenda? Brenda is a teenager. She'll probably be very nice when she grows up, but she was a pain in the neck the whole way. She wanted to know where I got my dress and how much it cost. She asked me who made my shoes. She wanted to know if my earrings were real and how much they were worth. She told me she worked in a salon and could do wonders with my hair if I'd let her cut it. She asked me if I had a boyfriend. Then she wanted to know why I didn't have a boyfriend." She stole a brief glimpse at me. I hoped my face didn't show the relief I felt. "I guess I sound ungrateful, since she got me out of there and all, but Brenda was difficult."

"What do you mean, since Brenda got you out of there?"

Harmony's eyes widened. "I mean, since Brenda told the police I was in that closet."

"How do you know Brenda called the police?"

"She rapped on the door when I was in that room. She put her face down to the crack, and I pulled the insulation off the bottom of the door so I could hear her. She said she'd call the police if I gave her my earrings. So I gave her my earrings. I pushed them through to her underneath the door."

Anthony couldn't hide his surprise. Harmony said hastily, fearing she had gotten Brenda in trouble, "She can keep the earrings, Detective. I know she kind of had me over a barrel, but a deal's a deal."

Anthony nodded. He didn't tell her that Brenda had taken the earrings but had somehow neglected to call the police and had gotten herself killed by swiping Harmony's clothes. I felt a surge of anger toward the dead girl. Maybe it was for the best that Dwight and Gabriella were out from under her influence.

It had taken them two days to drive from Seattle to Salt Lake City. They had stayed overnight with Lydia's sister in Oregon. Whenever Harmony had gotten close to a phone - whether at Lydia's sister's house or during a bathroom break - one of the children would have a crisis, and Harmony's services as an enforcer, mediator, or medic would be urgently required. Lydia had insisted on paying for all the gas, leaving Harmony to wrestle the kids in the lavatories - conveniently out of sight of the attendants and cashiers who might be questioned by the police. After they arrived in Salt Lake City, Harmony had crashed and slept late on Wednesday. Later, Lydia and her husband, Paul, had taken Harmony and the kids for a drive and a hike in the mountains, a lovely day amid the autumn leaves, and then had a cookout of hot dogs and toasted marshmallows by a beautiful canyon river.

"I had a glorious time," Harmony told Detective Anthony. "The kids were running around the fire, the river smelled so good, and the air was perfectly clear. When we got back to Salt Lake, I thanked Paul and Lydia, and told them I would fly back to Seattle the next day. They made me some hot chocolate, and we sat around the living room and talked. When I went to bed that night, I was feeling so much better, and so relaxed. I thought it was the best day I had spent in a long time. I went right to sleep - and then I woke up in that closet." She paused and looked down at her hands. "All I had on was the T-shirt and underwear I had worn to bed. I was so cold. There were two juice boxes on the floor beside me. I screamed, I tried to kick open the door, I tried to claw off the joists under the stairs and kick one of the slats free. But I couldn't."

I shuddered at the thought of that squalid, freezing cell. There was a reeking drain in one corner. The sloped ceiling looked barely high enough for her to stand. The wood across the stairs had been raw, splintered, and stained with blood.

Harmony let her hands fall into her lap. "That's the end of my story, Detective. Except that when you opened the door, I had never been so glad to see anyone in my whole life."

Anthony gave her his sad smile. He put his hand on her arm. "We were mighty glad to see you, too, Ms. Piper. We had almost given up hope."

She returned the sad smile. Then she settled herself back on her pillows and said, "Your turn, Detective Anthony."

by Rosemary Reeve

CHAPTER 56

Detective Anthony rubbed his eyes. "There's a lot we're still working on, Ms. Piper," he said. We'll probably get a couple of plea bargains out of this, and then we'll have more nailed down. But I'll tell you everything I know and everything I suspect, OK?"

"OK."

"There were a couple of people who didn't want your dad to come clean about what he had been doing. One was Janet Daniels. She had been helping your dad embezzle – and she'd been making a tidy profit out of it, too. From what Jack turned up and from our examination of your stepmother's computer, it looks to us like Janet wrote off the time your dad worked, and your stepmother prepared bills in Japanese, Chinese, and Korean to charge your dad's clients directly."

Harmony's eyebrows shot up. "Is that why my dad married Mieko? So she could draft the bills for him?"

"Probably. She was his secretary in Tokyo when he started this scam. I imagine she figured it out, and she wanted a piece of it. She spoke and wrote several languages fluently, and she was very useful to him."

"So is she the second person who didn't want my dad to come clean?"

"I'm sure it would have been inconvenient for her. But the day before his death, your dad made several phone calls from his hotel room. He called Janet Daniels, he called your stepmother, and he called Marshall Farr. Marshall was up in Sapporo, scouting out the possibility of opening another office in Japan. And we think that the person who really didn't want your dad to come clean was Marshall Farr."

"Why? The firm was losing millions because of what my father did."

"Yes, but the firm was making even more money by having your father in Asia. Compared to what they had made and what they stood to make, the amount your dad embezzled was seed money. This is what I think happened. Your dad wasn't going to go back on his word. He was going to come clean, just like he promised you. But he hated the firm, Ms. Piper. And I think he probably hated Marshall more than he hated anyone else. It must have been torture for him to hear Marshall taking the credit for saving the firm when he thought that the firm's success was due to all the work he had generated in Asia.

"We found an outline of your dad's keynote speech for the last day of the client seminar. Your dad's laptop disappeared from his room, but there was a backup copy of the document in his personal directory on your Tokyo network. It's very rough, and at first it didn't make any sense to us. When Jack discovered the embezzlement, things started to fall into place. Reading the outline in the context of the embezzlement, it looks like your dad intended to tell all the Asian clients exactly what he had done and why he had done it. If he was going to go down, he was going to take the firm with him. I don't know a lot about doing business in the Far East, but it seems to me that trust, personal integrity, relationships, and respect are pretty much the name of the game. You know a lot of your dad's clients. Do you think they would keep doing business with your firm if they knew that your firm had screwed over your dad, your dad had embezzled funds, and your firm hadn't bothered to investigate or prevent the embezzlement because they were making out like bandits riding his coattails?"

"No," Harmony said. "If a firm couldn't keep its own house in order, my dad's clients wouldn't want it mucking about in their affairs. The firm would be tainted. We'd lose all the business."

"I thought so. And I think Marshall thought so, too. Jack told us that Marshall was a master of damage control. The worst possible damage from Marshall's point of view would to lose all the Asian business that's been keeping Piper Whatcom afloat. Everyone would have realized that it was your father's Asian clients that saved the firm, not Marshall's brilliant management style. I think your father realized how much he could hurt Marshall by publicizing what he had done. He called Marshall in Sapporo. He probably said they needed to talk, making it sound urgent enough that Marshall went right to your father's room when he arrived in Tokyo. I think your father taunted him with the specter of exposing what he had done and of ruining the firm. And I think Marshall picked up the metal vase on the table and hit him over the back of the head. I doubt it was planned. I imagine Marshall was horrified when he realized your dad was dead. But Marshall's about twice the size of your dad. He broke his neck in two places."

Harmony closed her eyes and sank back onto the bed. For a moment, I thought she had fainted. Then, without opening her eyes, she said, "Go on, please, Detective."

"Marshall stuffed your father's body into his luggage - that big, orange suitcase he used when he was going to be on the road for some time. Then he cleaned up the room. He hid your father's things under the bed and in the drawers so it would look like he was gone. He phoned the front desk and pretended to be your father. He asked them to arrange porter service for his bag to the airport early Wednesday morning and left his tickets on top of the bed. It seems the hotel staff were accustomed to strange scheduling requests from your father. He was a very busy man, and he had - well, uh, _"

"I know he had a girlfriend in Fukuoka, Detective," Harmony said. "I assume there were more?"

"Yes, there were, Ms. Piper. As I said, your father was a very busy man. Anyway, we think that's how your father was killed. Marshall wiped off his fingerprints, joined a large group of clients and attorneys at a Tokyo bar, and didn't actually check into the hotel until much later that night. Your father's friend in Fukuoka discovered his body in his luggage on Wednesday morning."

Harmony's cheeks were wet, but she was nodding slowly. After a pause, she said with a quiver, "What about Mieko and Janet?"

"We assume your father's final calls to Mieko and Janet were warnings that he was going to spill the beans. Janet would have been horrified. She was making a lot of money off your dad's embezzlement, and if he came clean, it would only be a matter of time before the firm found out about her role in the crime. Your firm might pull its punches with a wealthy rainmaker partner, but it wouldn't have any compunctions about hanging a secretary out to dry. Janet knew she was in trouble.

"Janet figured that if she could get you out of the picture for a couple of days, she'd be able to talk your father into keeping quiet. I called down to the police station while we were taking a break, and Lydia Keddington gave a statement to Detective Siddoway about an hour ago. They arrested her and Paul for kidnapping and attempted murder, and they're desperately trying to cut a deal. She said she had taken the kids out of school to visit her aunt for a week. They stayed in Janet's house in Leschi. They got home late Sunday night from some excursion or other, and Janet called her in a panic. She told her that you had goaded your father into doing something very foolish, and she needed to get him out from your influence so she could have a chance to talk some sense into him. Janet insisted that Lydia take you back with her to Salt Lake, that she keep you away from telephones and out of sight as much as possible, and that she keep you safe in Salt Lake for a day or two. Janet paid her $2,000 a day for the job - for expenses, she said. It took Lydia and Janet a little while to map out the longest possible route and fake Lydia's injury, then Janet sent you that e-mail message that looked like it was from your dad."

Harmony sat up eagerly. "Janet sent that? Not my father?"

"Yes, Janet sent it. She waited a few moments to make sure you'd get the message, then she called you to make sure you were sufficiently upset. When you didn't seem sufficiently upset, she dropped the bombshell about Mr. Yamashita. I can't prove it, Ms. Piper, but I very much doubt that Mr. Piper confided in Janet that he wasn't your biological father. Whether he was or not, he'd hardly be likely to tell her. She was already blackmailing him about the embezzlement. He wouldn't be eager to give her any more ammunition against him. I think it was just a shot in the dark that hit home hard."

Harmony looked a little happier. "That makes sense," she said. "Thank you for telling me that."

"Sure." Anthony let her savor the small solace for a moment, then continued. "Anyway, Janet got you bundled off with her niece, then set about covering your tracks. She might have just left everyone guessing as to where you were, but Jack found the blood on your carpet and flipped out. He called us immediately. The last thing Janet wanted was police sniffing around, so she tried to make it look like you were off with a boyfriend. She sent roses to you with a cryptic message, and she arranged to have them delivered when she would be there and could suggest what had happened."

"Anybody who knew me even slightly would know that I wouldn't skip work for a boyfriend. Why didn't Janet just kill me?"

"I doubt she thought it was that serious a problem. She was, as you know, a very forceful woman. I imagine she thought that with you out of the way, she could bully your father into backing down. After you returned in a couple of days, you would find your father thoroughly bent to her wishes. And I think she knew you well enough to realize that you wouldn't turn in your dad. You wouldn't have, would you? Even if he wasn't your biological father?"

Harmony shook her head. "No. I guess that's a bad thing to say to a policeman, but no. I wouldn't. I wouldn't turn in my dad."

"I imagine Janet thought that she was going to be able weather this storm and keep sharing in your father's embezzlement. And she might have been able to, too, if Marshall hadn't killed your father. That must have been a nasty shock for Janet. It was also, I imagine, a nasty shock for your stepmother, although they reacted to it in very different ways. My impression of your stepmother was of a rather soft, self-indulgent woman. She might have written the fraudulent letters for your father, but she was genuinely shocked and frightened when Oden and I showed up to tell her husband had been found dead under extraordinarily suspicious circumstances.

"Janet was tougher. We found fibers from Janet's coat in your father's study. We think that Janet went to your house Tuesday evening, after she had learned of your father's death. My guess is that the women quarreled over what to do. Mieko probably wanted to tell us about the embezzlement. Janet probably did not. A scraping from under Mieko's nails matched Janet's blood type. We'll get DNA reports in the next little while, but we think Janet strangled Mieko to keep her quiet. We also know that Janet took the fraudulent bills from your father's study. She took the evidence that linked the write-offs of his time with the bills for Piper Consulting."

Anthony stretched and sighed. "If that had been all she did, it would have taken us a very long time to crack this case. But her next step was infinitely riskier. Marshall was back from Japan and looking for you. In fact, he sent Jeremy Smith home in the middle of the client seminar to look for you. It must have been an unpleasant surprise for both of them to arrive back in Seattle and realize you had disappeared. If it's any comfort, Ms. Piper, you probably drove them wild with worry and suspicion. As long as you were alive, there was the possibility that you would divulge your father's embezzlement and ruin the firm. Besides, you knew that your father had intended to talk to Marshall as soon as he arrived from Sapporo. Marshall wouldn't have wanted you to tell us that. It would have put him with your father uncomfortably close to the time of the murder."

"Is that why Marshall was outside my house late Tuesday night?" I asked. "He thought I knew where Harmony was?"

"Yes. He knew you and Ms. Piper were close friends. He thought you might lead him to her. That's why he offered you the day off on Wednesday, too. He intended to follow you. You didn't really believe that bullshit about his being concerned about your well-being, did you, Jack?"

Well, actually, I had believed it. I flushed. Harmony patted my hand, a small, white paw touching me as softly and quickly as a butterfly. "Jack's a sweet, trusting soul, Detective Anthony," she said in my defense. "You have to really work at it to make him hate you."

"That's not true," I protested. "I hate lots of people."

Anthony turned to me with a genuine grin, not the wry, lopsided smile I had always seen before. "I **do**," I insisted.

"Be that as it may, Jack," Anthony said, "Marshall probably thought he could follow you to Harmony. But when he was listening in to your phone calls, he heard you leave the message that you needed to talk to me about Mieko. And that's when he made his fatal mistake. He went to your house, Ms. Piper, to see what your stepmother knew about the embezzlement and your disappearance. We found a few strands of Janet's hair in the alcove off your father's study. We think Janet hid there when Marshall arrived. She could have seen him drive up from the study and slipped into the alcove before Marshall entered the house. Marshall found your stepmother dead and probably searched the study to make sure nothing there would lead us to your father's embezzlement. We assume that Janet watched him from the alcove, put two and two together, and figured out who had killed your father.

"That's when Janet made her fatal mistake. She tried to blackmail Marshall to replace the money she had been getting from your dad. But Marshall was altogether a different kind of operator than your dad was. He bludgeoned her and threw her body down the freight elevator shaft. She landed on top of the elevator car. We found her the next day, when rigor mortis subsided and one of her limbs fell against the sheaves and messed up the elevator. When you announced to Paul and Lydia that you were going back to Seattle, they were very frightened. Janet had ordered them not to let you go. They couldn't contact Janet. She was already dead, although they didn't know that. They panicked, drugged you, and stuffed you in that closet. They may have left you a couple of juice boxes just in case, but my guess is, they would have left you there until you died. They just did not know what to do. All they knew is that they didn't dare to let you go."

Harmony was biting her lower lip. The sun was rising from behind the mountains, and the sky was streaked with plum and gold. In the early morning light, Harmony's eyes looked steady and almost black, like low coals. Anthony handed her a tissue. She covered her whole face with it, as if she were trying to block everything out. Her shoulders sagged. "That's the end of my story, Ms. Piper," Anthony said.

Harmony balled the tissue in her fist. She was quiet for a few moments. Then she said, "How did you know it was Marshall, Detective Anthony?"

"A couple of things made us suspicious. I'd expect a case like this to be crawling with reporters. But I didn't get one single call from the media. There wasn't a single story - in the newspapers or on TV. I ran into a couple of the usual eager beavers around the department, and they told me there was a news blackout from above, from their editors and publishers. In exchange for the media's keeping everything quiet, Piper Whatcom was going to write off all the media consortium's legal fees from the Grange litigation. While we were interviewing people from your firm, we asked a few innocuous questions and found out that Marshall was in charge of the Grange litigation. We figured he must have been the one to offer the media that deal. I wondered why he wanted to keep the firm out of the news so badly. And I wondered what else he'd do - or already had done - to keep the firm's name clean.

"There were other things, too. Janet left us some clues. We think she was interrupted while she was trying to leave us a major clue. She hid a folder full of your dad's letters for Jack to find and started to leave him a voicemail that was just weird enough to get him thinking. We assume that the voicemail was supposed to point him toward Marshall, but Marshall interrupted her right in the middle of it. You can hear his voice on the tape, and then Janet breaks off very suddenly.

"Even so, Janet managed to point the finger at him. She was a devious woman, and she never relied on one scheme when two would do. She knew how you had found out about the embezzlement - the Brand case. I think she told Marshall that he needed to get an associate to cover the Brand summary judgment argument. Marshall didn't pay attention to schedules or deadlines. He didn't know you'd already won. So he roped poor old Jack in on it - sent him down to court on Thursday with 35 minutes to prepare for the alleged argument. The whole thing looked suspicious to me. Marshall might forget things, but he wouldn't remember an incorrect date. If he thought the argument was on a certain day, it had to be because someone had told him it was on that day. And unless you were pulling his strings somehow, the only person who could have done that was Janet Daniels. Her little plan worked, too. Just like she expected, Jack followed the trail and figured out that there was something very odd about your hours on Brand. And from there, Jack led us to the embezzlement."

Harmony threw me a look that I couldn't read. Anthony followed her gaze and smiled. "And the final clue was that Jack was still alive."

"What?" Harmony and I said together.

"After your father's memorial service on Thursday, Jack left Marshall a message telling him you had already won the summary judgment. When Marshall got that message, that's when he realized that Janet had led him into a trap. He probably didn't know exactly what was so suspicious about the Brand case, but he was right to be concerned. He had to get the Brand files away from Jack before Jack stumbled over what you had stumbled over. Unfortunately, Jeremy Smith had given Jack an emergency assignment before Marshall got Jack's message. Jack was at work until almost three in the morning, and then Marshall tried to search his office. When Jack came back unexpectedly, Marshall tried to kill him. He may have thought that Jack had recognized him. He may also have thought that if Jack lived to tell about someone's searching his office, it would tip us off to the importance of the Brand case.

"Anyway, he shot at Jack three times without hitting him. I knew we couldn't be dealing with anyone who knew how to handle a gun. A couple of our other suspects did know how to shoot. Alfonse Brand, for example, had been in Vietnam. I knew he wouldn't have missed Jack from fifteen feet. But Marshall got some sort of deferment from the draft. He taught English to underprivileged kids on Mercer Island or something. I figured we were looking for a novice criminal. Marshall fit the bill."

"He hit me once," I protested. "He got me in the shoulder and Betsy in the leg." Harmony started and looked over at me. I could see the fear in her face. "Betsy's going to be OK," I assured her.

"What about you? Are you going to be OK?

"Oh, yeah, I'll be fine." She didn't look convinced. "Like Detective Anthony said, Marshall's a bad shot."

"Actually, we think it was Jeremy who tracked you down at home, Jack," Anthony said. "We've arrested him - in fact, Jack, we let Sawyer arrest him as a sort of tribute to you - and we expect that he'll sell out Marshall pretty soon. We're almost positive he was mixed up in this. For one thing, the bullets in the firm and in your house came from two different guns. For another, we don't think Marshall could have escaped from the firm in time to get to your house. We had officers in the building until after you were shot. But before I realized Jeremy was involved, I called him to let him know you wouldn't be able to finish those pleadings because you had been stabbed."

"Stabbed?" Harmony was sitting up. I tried to hide my bandaged hand, but she pounced on it. The half-dried blood looked exceptionally gruesome on the white gauze. "Oh, Jack," she said. "Jack, I am so sorry."

I withdrew my hand and shook my head. "No reason to be."

"Well, I'm sorry, too, Jack," Anthony said. "If I hadn't called Jeremy, he wouldn't have realized that Marshall had screwed it up and decided to finish the job himself. I doubt Marshall would have dared to call him from wherever he was hiding in the building. But we're pretty sure Jeremy was the man who attacked you at your home. That touch of sadism he showed, making you kneel down and wait to be killed, slamming you against the door to punish you - it all sounded exactly like Jeremy to me. The blood we took from Betsy's teeth is his type. We'll have to wait for the DNA report for an exact match, but he has a mammoth hickey on his neck that he's having a hard time explaining. Plus, you said he smelled. Have you ever stood close to Jeremy?"

"No. I don't even like being in the same room as Jeremy," I said. "Even the same firm is too close for me."

"He reeks." It was Harmony's contribution. "I shared a condominium with him in Alaska last year. By the end of the trial, all my clothes smelled like him. I was forced to buy a whole new wardrobe." She paused, thinking it over. "What did Jeremy get out all of this, Detective?"

"He was going to be your new managing partner, Ms. Piper, and he and Marshall were going to split the origination credit on all your father's clients. They would have doubled or tripled their salaries. I don't think that's why Marshall killed your father, but it was an unintended benefit."

Harmony sank back onto her pillows. She looked spent. Anthony pulled her blankets up over her, as if he were tucking her in. "This has been too much for you," he said. "I'm so sorry. You get some rest, OK, Ms. Piper?"

"OK." She closed her eyes, and Anthony got to his feet. At the movement, she sat up. The blankets fell away. "Detective Anthony?"

"Yes?"

The plum-colored light was filling the room. "I'll never be able to repay you for what you did for me," she said to him. She turned toward the window sill, where Mark was looking pink and pleased against the gold-tinged clouds. "Or you, Officer Oden. I can't thank either of you enough." She lifted her bandaged paws regretfully. "I wish I could shake your hands. You saved my life. If you hadn't been so wonderfully clever, I would have died in that horrible room."

Anthony's sad smile melted. He reached down and patted her on the shoulder. "No charge, Harmony," he said. Then, in a different tone, he added, "Besides, we really weren't all that clever. In fact, for the longest time, we thought it was Jack."

"**Me?**" I was aghast. "Why on earth would you think it was me?"

"Well, everyone - and I mean everyone - Oden and I talked to told us that you two were getting pretty close until a few months ago. We thought maybe there had been some sort of break up or jealousy or something."

So the whole firm had noticed the distance that had come between me and Harmony after my accident. How embarrassing. I had been such an idiot. I didn't dare to look at Harmony. I kept my eyes on Detective Anthony. He shook his head at my horrified face. "Plus, Jack, I could not figure you out. I've never had a witness jump right into a case the way you did. You kept finding things for us to do, people for us to suspect, and weird things we needed to investigate. I couldn't decide whether you were an evil genius -"

"Or a nice dumb guy?" I ventured.

"Or too good to be true," he finished. "I kept telling Oden I was going to arrest you just in case, but he wouldn't hear of it. He said he knew you when you were a kid, and he knew there wasn't any evil in you. So in exchange for his promise to keep a close eye on you, I let you muck about as much as you wanted. And I'm glad I did. We wouldn't have found Harmony in time without you. But even after you had nearly been killed trying to help us, there was one last reason that made me keep wondering about you."

"What?"

"I think Harmony knows," he said.

I turned to Harmony and saw her eyes widen. She leaned back, blinked, and said, "Oh."

"What? What does Harmony know? What's going on?" I fumed. "What does everyone know except me?"

Harmony was bright red, and this time it wasn't because of the morning light. "Well," she said, "in April, my dad and I changed our wills. We had never gotten around to adding bequests to Mieko. We were there in the attorney's office, and I was looking at my residuary clause. I decided I really didn't want to give all my money to Harvard, which was how my dad had it set up since when was I kid. So I left everything to my dad and then to Mieko. And if they both predeceased me, everything went to you."

"**Me?**" I leapt to my feet. Now I was completely aghast. "Why in the hell would you leave your money to me?"

"Because I like you. I like you a lot more than I like Harvard."

"You loved Harvard."

"I know. But I like you more. So I just added a codicil leaving everything to you instead."

I sank back into my chair. Anthony offered me a tissue. Mark brought me a glass of water. I waved them away. Harmony was watching me closely. "If you hadn't found me, you'd be worth a lot of money right now," she said. She gulped a little. She said, almost to herself, "Disappointed?"

"No." I was stunned by disbelief. "No, of course not. Don't be ridiculous." My head swam. I pressed my hands to my temples, and the pain brought me back to reality.

"Harmony, if we hadn't found you, those two clowns would have given me the chair," I told her.

Her cheeks were pink and glowing. I put my face close to hers. "You almost got me executed," I said. "Promise me you won't ever pull a stunt like that again."

She settled back into bed. There was a tiny smile on her solemn face. "I promise, Jack," she said.

ALL GOOD THINGS

by Rosemary Reeve

CHAPTER 57

t was 5:30 a.m. the day before Thanksgiving. I turned off my alarm clock and
mentally ticked through my schedule. I had a million things to do. I had a
conference call at 7, my semiannual performance review at 11, lunch with Mark at
12, a busy afternoon, and an evening of housecleaning and laundry-doing ahead of
me. Harmony was coming home from Japan the next day, and I wanted the house to
be decent - just in case. We were all going to Detective Anthony's for Thanksgiving
dinner, but there was always the possibility that Harmony might come over to my
place afterward to spend the night.

We had fallen into that habit. It had started on Halloween, the day after we
returned from Salt Lake City. I set the snooze alarm, punched my pillow, and let my
mind wander back to Halloween. It had been a wonderful day. Betsy and I had ladled
out bowls of Snickers and Sweet Tarts to the pint-size ghosts, witches, Power Rangers,
Batpersons, and fairy princesses that prowled our neighborhood. All the children had
exclaimed over Betsy's enormous collar, one of those plastic, funnel-like affairs
designed to keep her from licking her wound or ripping out her stitches. I had told
the kids it was Betsy's costume, claiming variously that she was supposed to be an
Elizabethan lady-in-waiting, a satellite dish, and a cheerleader's megaphone.

"Who's the cheerleader, then?" one of the Power Rangers challenged me.

"Well, I am, of course," I replied. I towered over him from a great height, bent
down, and said, "Rah!"

My mother brought Jimmy by so he could enjoy Halloween in a safer neighborhood.
He was too little for a purchased costume, and my mom apparently hadn't felt like
sewing anything, so she had dressed him in green pants and a green sweater and taped
a sign on his chest: "I am a frog. Ask me to hop." He started hopping madly the
minute he saw the candy in my hands. I handed him the whole bowl, then fetched the
special treats I had bought him and stuffed them in his sack. He didn't even notice.
He was entranced by Betsy. It was mutual. She curled around him and licked his face
and hands, as if he were her puppy and she were washing his paws. When my mom
finally extricated him to take him home, Jimmy was slick and dripping from Betsy's
maternal ministrations.

Betsy and I were ready to hobble off to bed when I heard a soft knock. I scrounged
up the last of the candy and opened the door. Harmony was standing on the porch.

"Trick or treat," she said.

I put down the candy and held out my hand. She slipped her rebandaged hand in mine and stepped inside. Then she put her arms around my waist and hugged me for a long time. I couldn't tell whether she was crying. I didn't dare to let her go so I could check. I just held her. I just held her, patted her, and made soothing, sympathetic sounds. Finally, I heard something muffled deep in my chest and released her. She didn't meet my eyes. "Don't I get a Snickers?" she said.

"You get anything you want," I told her. "You know that."

I led her into the living room and settled her down on the couch. Her hands were shaking. "Last night," she told me, "I was so tired, it didn't matter where I was. I didn't even have a chance to think about my dad or Mieko. Once we got back from bailing out Charlie, I just lay down on my bed and went to sleep. But tonight, I couldn't even get past the portraits in the entryway. I tried to go in the back door, but everything I saw reminded me of them, of everything that's happened. I don't want to stay there alone tonight, Jack."

I understood. My first night back, Betsy and I had sat on my front porch for an hour and a half before we plucked up the courage to go inside. And nobody had been murdered in my house. "Why don't you sleep here tonight?"

"I'd like that," she said. "Just sleep, I mean," she added hastily, in case I got the wrong idea.

I didn't get the wrong idea. I tucked her into my guest futon in my spare bedroom - otherwise known as Betsy's sunroom - and stumbled wearily to my own bed. After a moment of indecision, Betsy followed me, limping slowly and painfully along the hall. I was immensely flattered. She and I were slipping into sleep - her snores amplified by the funnel around her face - when I heard the sobbing in the sunroom. Betsy and I looked at each other. I didn't know what to do. Poor Harmony. She was obviously trying very hard to be quiet, but I could still hear her, even under what sounded like layers of blankets. I didn't want to intrude on her grief. I didn't want her to feel like she had to put on a brave front. But I couldn't stand to hear her cry.

I scooped up Betsy and carried her into the hall. She limped to Harmony's door and scratched on it. Then she made soft, sweet, pleading noises. I heard Harmony's footsteps on the maple floor. I saw the arc of light from the opening door gleam on Betsy's fur and thumping tail. I saw Harmony's arms fall around her, and heard her tear-choked voice say, "Oh, Betsy." I saw Harmony bury her face in Betsy's neck. Then Betsy trotted inside the room, Harmony shut the door, and I went back to bed. Harmony was in good paws.

After that, Harmony and Betsy spent every night together in the sunroom. And Harmony and I got used to living together - in the platonic sense of the word. It was a lot like my first few weeks under the same roof with Betsy. Harmony didn't inflict property damage, but she had her good days and her bad days. Sometimes she was warm and engaging - fully there, with me, right in the moment. Sometimes she was so far away I couldn't even talk to her. Sometimes she'd seem to be there, and we'd be carrying on a perfectly intelligent, often witty and delightful conversation - and then I'd notice the look in her eye, as if it was shadowed by a long trauma that wasn't over yet. Wasn't over by a long shot.

But I knew the drill by now. We watched a lot of TV together: the end of football season and the beginning of basketball. She'd sit on the couch beside me - just out of reach. Betsy would sprawl between us, and sometimes our hands would meet as we petted her. I laid in a supply of Cheetos, and I was delighted when Harmony overcame her fear of Day-Glo orange food coloring, moved closer to me, and dived in. After ten days with her - ten weird but wonderful days - I didn't ever want to let her go.

But I had. She had been in Japan for a little over a week now. She was going to meet up and fly home with Detective Anthony, who had left a few days later to resolve the jurisdictional niceties that arise when an American is so inconsiderate and uncouth as to kill another American in a perfectly respectable, four-star Tokyo hotel. While Anthony apologized for the stupid gaijin, Harmony was going to collect her father's ashes and visit with Mr. Yamashita, who had left her 38 voicemail messages in the days after Mr. Piper's death.

The snooze alarm buzzed me from my recollections. I yawned and stretched. It was almost 6 a.m. I had an hour to get to work. It was a rush, but I made it to the firm with 15 minutes to spare. As I walked to my office, I was aware of more than a few unfriendly stares. The week before, The Regrade Dispatch's "Police Beat" column had broken the story of the murders and Marshall's and Jeremy's arrests, and all the other media in Seattle had jumped on the bandwagon with a vengeance, as if they thought the ferocity of their coverage could somehow atone for their earlier conspiracy of silence. The goings-on at Piper Whatcom had been front-page news ever since. Even The National Law Journal had run an article about us, coyly titled "The Pied 'Piper' of Seattle." Then the tabloid TV shows got hold of a picture of Harmony, and the airwaves were filled with stories about the exotic, mysterious young heiress who had brought a powerful law firm to its knees. I tried to shield her from it as much as possible, but she knew what was going on, and it hurt her.

"Today, 'Hard Copy,'" she had said, glumly turning off the TV after a lurid teaser interrupted a perfectly good football game. "Tomorrow, The Enquirer."

I hadn't said a word to the press - and not because I hadn't had the opportunity. When the reporters figured out I had accompanied Mark and Anthony to Salt Lake City, I had had to change my telephone number and shoulder my way through TV crews camped in front of my house. They didn't intimidate me. In fact, some of their pretty, blow-dried correspondents - male and female - turned a little pale when Betsy and I lurched out of my little house for our therapeutic, vet-ordered walks. We both looked big, battered, and menacing, and we could have beaten and bitten the hell out of them if we'd had to. We didn't have to. They parted in front of us like a perfectly dressed, perfectly coiffed sea. But even though in person the reporters were relatively respectful of my silence, they still showed their videos of me every night on television. I hadn't said a word - I wouldn't say a word - but in my coworkers' minds, I was cryptically but irrevocably implicated in the fall of the firm of Piper Whatcom & Hardcastle.

And it was going to be a quite a fall. We had already closed our Tokyo office. Our Asian clients were defecting in droves. We had enough existing business to keep us afloat for a couple of months, but the Asian clients had made it very clear that our services would not be required in the future. As it faced its inevitable demise, the firm was turning on itself, chewing off its own limbs to try to escape the steel trap.

Staff and associates would get the ax first. We hadn't done anything wrong, but we were easy to fire, and we were expendable. The savings on our aggregate salaries would give the firm a few more months of miserable existence. Then the partnership would blow apart, and the few partners who still had clients might band together. They might survive, but no one was going to come out of this unscathed. Emotions were running high, and everyone was looking for a scapegoat. Who better than the big, scary-looking guy they kept seeing walking his dog on TV? I wasn't looking forward to my performance review.

I finished my conference call and forced myself to turn to my review packet. Ever since a tax associate had gone berserk and thrown a Dictaphone at her reviewer during a particularly exacting evaluation, Piper Whatcom had given associates an opportunity to look over our written comments before we met with our inquisitors. My packet was suspiciously thin. Usually, they were bursting with minute dissections of our performance, personalities, and potential. Once Jeremy Smith had written a two-page criticism of my choice of ties. Not this time, I thought grimly. I thrust my hand into the envelope and pulled out a single sheet of paper. It had my name at the top and my billable and fee-credit statistics - and pretty impressive statistics, too, if I said so myself - in columns right below. There was one line under "Comments":

"Jack Hart is not a team player."

There was a star next to it. Down at the bottom, there was another star. Next to that, it said, "Recommended termination."

That was it. That was my review. You'd think they could have come up with something a little more creative than that team player crap. I ripped the sheet in half and left it accusingly on my desk. I dictated a terse letter and a notice of withdrawal from representation of my current client matters. I tossed the tape on top of the torn review. Let the bastards forge my name.

It was disturbingly easy to clean out my desk. Some associates plundered the firm's form files when they left, but I wasn't up to industrial espionage. I tossed my Black's Law Dictionary into my briefcase. A couple of books from law school went in next. Then Jimmy's picture. A coffee mug from Prison Legal Services, for which I worked pro bono. A thank-you gift from Motorhead, a Lucite cube imbedded with a shrunken version of the verdict form awarding them more than $6 million in damages. It had been my first trial. A beautifully detailed model Cessna, a gift from a client for whom I had successfully defended a forfeiture claim on his beloved airplane. I wrapped it tenderly in tissues and nestled it into the pocket of the case.

I put on my coat, snapped my briefcase shut, and lifted it with disbelief. Could that be it? The artifacts of four years of blood, sweat, and tears were in my briefcase, but the bag was lighter than when I took home even an average night's work. So much for my brilliant career. I paused at the doorway and looked out the window. My office had a lovely view of Mount Rainier, but today the giant mountain was hiding behind layers of clouds. I knew it was there, but I couldn't see it.

As I waited for the elevator, I treated myself to one last look at Seattle from the 42nd floor reception area. Even on a close, rainy day like today, the view was spectacular. I could see Lake Union and Lake Washington. I could see the vast and beautiful Sound. The water was slate blue and wreathed in mist. Every now and then, a shaft of sunlight broke through the heavy clouds and pierced the fog, a round patch of opal on the dark water.

The elevator door shot open. I steeled myself and stepped inside. It was the elevator in which I had nearly bled to death, but they had torn up and replaced the carpet. The new rug was plush and springy under my feet as I plummeted down the shaft. I inspected the car carefully on the way. Not a trace of my blood remained.

I didn't know what to do with myself. It was only 10:30, and I wasn't meeting Mark until noonish. I had a most unusual desire to talk to my mom. Sometimes she made me feel better simply by comparison. I walked down to the Olympic Broiler - past the sign that touted the place, somewhat ominously, as "An Adventure in Good Eating" - and asked to see Marta Boyden. I got a blank stare in return. OK, Mary Boyden then, I said, thinking maybe she was going by her real name. I got an even blanker stare. Marti Boyden? I asked, racking my brains for an alias she might have used. Marta Hart? I tried describing her, realizing that I was being profoundly unflattering in my word choice.

Nothing. Wherever my mom was working - if she was working - she had never been a waitress at the Olympic Broiler. So why had I been paying for babysitters for Jimmy every day? Damn, damn, damn, damn, damn my mom. An even worse thought pushed my irritation from my mind. Given my suddenly reduced circumstances, Jimmy and my mom were going to have to move in with me until I could get another job. That was sure to put the kibosh on Harmony's habit of sleeping over. I ground my teeth. My mother had a lot to answer for. So did that bastard Marshall Farr.

I was so happy to see Mark coming toward my table at Bruno's, a great little dive on Third Avenue. He was bursting with news. Jeremy Smith had finked on Marshall in exchange for a reduced sentence. Mark brought me a copy of his confession. I skimmed through it while Mark went to select his lunch from the multi-national cafeteria line: Mexican food at one end, Italian at the other.

According to Jeremy, Marshall had called him in a panic from Sapporo and instructed him to fly back to Seattle and find out what Harmony Piper knew about an alleged embezzlement from the firm. Later, Marshall had told him that he had offered Mr. Piper every deal imaginable to keep quiet about the embezzlement - including raising his salary to match the fees he skimmed - but that Mr. Piper had thrown the offer in his face and vowed to ruin the firm. Marshall had told him that Mrs. Piper was already dead when he arrived at the Pipers' home. Marshall had killed Janet Daniels because she threatened to expose him as Mr. Piper's murderer, but it was Jeremy who had thrown her body down the elevator shaft. They had thought that splitting up the task would allow each of them to arrange an alibi. Jeremy had suggested to Marshall that he take the <u>Brand</u> gutting knife - a foot-long dagger designed for slitting open large, flat fish like halibut - from the document room in order to throw suspicion on Brand. That was what had slashed my wrist. Jeremy admitted shooting me and Betsy in my house but claimed he had meant only to wound us to prevent us from following him. Right. He had told Marshall about Janet's niece in Salt Lake City, but he claimed to know nothing about Brenda Baxter's murder.

I handed the document back to Mark and dug into my enchiladas. "Is this going to put Marshall away?"

"It will help a lot - if the jury believes Jeremy. His credibility is sort of up for grabs at this point. But I talked to Siddoway this morning, and they got two real breaks on Brenda Baxter's murder. They found Harmony's other earring way down in a crevice in Marshall's rental car. He'd vacuumed the trunk, but the earring was so far down he couldn't see it. And they also found someone who remembers seeing a car fitting that description parked on the shoulder of the overpass a few hours before Brenda's body was found below."

"Oh." I couldn't think of anything else to say. I was suddenly so tired that I wanted to push the food away and put my head down on the table. I let the fork full of steaming meat and cheese fall to the plate. Mark looked up at the clang.

"You OK?"

"No."

"Tell me about it."

It all came out. The firm. My mom. The thought of living with my mom. The bitter injustice of having to lose Harmony as a roommate and replace her with my mom. The miserable prospect of trying to keep calm and find another job while my mom was on my back every minute of the day. The sheer impossibility of finding another job when I had shown up on TV every night that week, branded the dangerous loner who - somehow - had destroyed his last employer. When I finished, Mark shook his head.

"I am so damn sorry, Jack," he said.

"Yeah, me too." I looked around at the checkered plastic tablecloths, the walls that were stuccoed and studded with clusters of exposed bricks, the dark brown lattice hung with plastic greenery. Bruno's was a dim and smoky little hole, but the food was delicious, and the owners were warm and friendly. More than once, I had seen them give a homeless person a hard-earned ten or twenty out of the cash register or promise a panhandler a good meal if he or she would come back after the lunch rush. It was the perfect place to hide from the buttoned-down posturing of Piper Whatcom. "You know why Harmony and I used to like to come here, Mark?"

"No, why?"

"Because no one else from Piper Whatcom would deign to eat at a place like this, so we could talk freely without worrying about being overheard. We were always so afraid to say what we really thought. And now that it doesn't matter if I'm overheard, and now that I can say anything I want to about Piper Whatcom, I am so tired and hurt and sick of it all that I can't even think of the words."

"I can think of a couple of appropriate words."

"This is a family restaurant, Mark." I groaned and put my head in my hands. What a pain in the butt this was going to be. Happy Thanksgiving, one and all.

Mark handed me my fork. "Eat," he ordered. "Then we'll do anything you want to this afternoon."

"Don't you have to go back to work?"

"Nope. I was on 4 a.m. to noon today. It's quitting time for me - for both of us, I guess. If I can change out of my uniform at your house, we could go on a pub crawl."

I hmmmed noncommittally. I drank about a beer a month - for medicinal reasons - and I had already met my November quota.

"We could go to a movie."

I hmmmed again.

"OK, wise guy, what do you want to do?"

"Shoot a rack of pool at the 211 Club, let Betsy off the leash at Magnuson Park, have crab and fresh oysters at Ray's Boathouse - out on the deck, even in the rain - and swing back by the Regrade and scare the hell out of my mom. And then I need to clean my house."

Mark raised an eyebrow in admiration. "John Boyden Hart," he said, hoisting a steaming forkful of shredded chicken in my direction, "you are my kind of guy."

ALL GOOD THINGS

by Rosemary Reeve

CHAPTER 58

Mark and I had a wonderful afternoon. Relaxed and full of crab, we went right home from Ray's Boathouse. I was too tired to confront my mom with her lies about working at the Olympic Broiler. If she was going to move in with me, there would be plenty of time for us to go for each other's throats. Besides, I didn't want to mess with her karma. She was going to spend Thanksgiving Day with Jimmy's father, and I imagined she was even then casting love spells and plotting her astrological chart. If she and Jimmy's dad reconciled, maybe she'd move in with him instead of me. I was adamantly in favor of anything that might keep her out of my house.

The next morning, Mark, Betsy, and I showed up early at Detective Anthony's Craftsman bungalow on Queen Anne Hill. My job was to fetch and carry, set up chairs, assist Mrs. Anthony with the cooking, and plan the most advantageous football schedule. Mark's job was to set the tables, build the fires, and pick Anthony and Harmony up at the airport. Betsy's job was to avoid being eaten by the Anthonys' brace of enormous Rottweilers. Mrs. Anthony glanced at Betsy nervously as we came in. I feared that I had misread the invitation and started apologizing for bringing my dog. Mrs. Anthony shushed me.

"Tony said Betsy could hold her own against our two dogs, but keep her on the leash for a little while, dear," she said. "Buster and Peanut are actually very sweet, but they get territorial when there's another dog around."

Buster and Peanut were approaching Betsy cautiously, one on either side of her, ears forward, legs stiff. Betsy ignored them. "I think they'll be OK together, Mrs. Anthony," I told her. I lowered my voice. "Betsy has no idea she's a dog."

Betsy followed me into the kitchen and stayed there while I peeled and diced 20 pounds of potatoes, and Mrs. Anthony put a mammoth pot of water on to boil. I sloshed hot cream and melted butter around and mashed the spuds while she made a stockpot full of gravy. Then she tossed off her apron.

"We've finished our bit, Jack," she said. "We do the birds, the stuffing, and the potatoes and gravy, and everyone else brings the accompaniments and does the dishes. Come and have a rest."

We lounged in the living room with the dogs around us. Buster and Peanut were tired of being ignored and were vying for Betsy's attention. Buster brought her a squeaky toy. Peanut tried to nip her tail. Betsy looked at them pityingly and walked away. Much to Mrs. Anthony's surprise, Betsy turned on the television with a swat of her paw and settled down in front of it. Soon Buster and Peanut joined her, one on either side. They seemed more interested in her than in the football game, but Betsy didn't take her eyes off the set.

I liked Mrs. Anthony a lot. She was almost as tall as her husband and was as gregarious as he was reserved, with a wide-open face and a generous mouth. She put her feet up on the coffee table and regarded me benignly. "You're a good cook, Jack," she said. "Harmony is a lucky girl."

I could feel myself turning red. I carefully addressed only her first statement. "I really don't know how to cook at all," I told her. "But I like to mess around in the kitchen. Usually, though, I don't have time. Betsy and I eat a lot of peanut butter sandwiches."

Wrong thing to say. Both Betsy and Peanut heard their names and rushed over to investigate. Not one to be left out, Buster followed, just on the off chance that I had said "Buster" instead of "butter." Suddenly, I was surrounded by dogs. Peanut put her paws on my knee and nuzzled my hand. Buster jumped onto the couch beside me and thrust his face into mine, as if he were near-sighted and wanted to take a closer look. And Betsy, who, aside from exceptional moments of heroism, had spent the last five months treating me as a regrettable necessity, suddenly decided that I was her territory, and that she didn't like two other critters moving in on me. She launched herself over the coffee table and onto my lap. Then Buster and Peanut decided that they, too, wanted to sit on my lap. They pounced at the same time, and I crumpled under their weight. I couldn't even breathe. Everywhere I turned, there was a dog.

Mark chose that moment to usher Detective Anthony and Harmony into the living room. The three of them stood on the other side of the coffee table and roared with laughter. I managed to shove the dogs off my lap and tried to stand up, but Buster caught my sweater in his teeth, and Peanut hit me in the back of the knees. I sat down heavily on the sofa. Betsy jumped on top of me, put her paws on my shoulders, and licked my face. Then the other two piled on again. Mrs. Anthony finally shooed Buster and Peanut away, and Harmony distracted Betsy long enough for me to escape the impromptu love-in.

Harmony looked great, especially for someone who had been on an airplane for hours. She was wearing a black silk dress, with a white silk scarf tying back her hair. She looked crisp, definite, and fresh. She wrapped her arms around me and leaned luxuriously into my chest.

"I missed you," she whispered.

"I missed you, too," I told her. "And you can see how your absence has affected Betsy. You must never leave us again."

She shut her eyes and rested her head against my shoulder. She started to say something, but it was drowned in the clamor of arriving guests. With the dogs at my heels, I introduced Harmony to Officer Murdoch and Vera, his round, beaming wife; Officer Sawyer and a sniffly, pained-looking woman I took to be his girlfriend; and a few of the other policemen and policewomen I had come to know. Then we all settled down to some serious eating. People had brought interesting side dishes like scalloped onions and Brussels sprouts with chestnuts, but I focused on the heart of the meal: turkey, mashed potatoes, gravy, and stuffing. Lots of stuffing. I put one cranberry on my plate for good measure.

Harmony ate just as heartily as I did. She perched beside me, teetering with her laden plate, and filled me in on her trip to Japan. Mr. Yamashita could not have been nicer to her. He had told her a lot about her mother, someone she barely remembered. He had begged her to stay in touch with him. She was thinking it over. She wanted to get to know him, but even visiting with him for a few days had made her feel disloyal to her dad. She had brought her dad's ashes back in her carry-on luggage. "In the spring, when the weather's warmer, I'm going to scatter them over Priest Lake," she said. "He loved going there. I thought of scattering them somewhere in Japan, but I just couldn't. I couldn't stand to let him go that soon."

I put down my plate. Only the cranberry remained. I moved closer to Harmony. She took my hand. "We need to talk," she said.

The living room was hot and loud. We slipped onto the Anthonys' porch, unnoticed by everyone but Betsy, Buster, and Peanut. We wouldn't let the dogs follow us, so they sat in a row behind the sliding door and watched us through the glass.

It was dark and wet outside. Rain was pouring off the porch lid. Harmony took my other hand and faced me. "Jack, I'm not going back to your house tonight."

"I cleaned the bathroom, Harmony," I said.

She smiled but was not deterred. "I mean it. I already asked Mark. He's going to take me back to Magnolia instead. I need to be able to stay in my own home, Jack. It's important for me not to be afraid of it anymore. Do you understand?"

I understood. "Sure," I said.

"If I don't go back there and deal with everything that's happened, I won't ever feel like I have a home again."

"Harmony, I understand," I said. "Don't worry about it." I turned to go back into the house, but she held me fast. Her eyes searched mine. "Jack, there's another reason, too."

I waited. I suspected I wasn't going to like the other reason.

"I don't want to lead you on, Jack," she said. "You're too nice a guy for that."

I knew it. I knew I wouldn't like the other reason. Suddenly, it hurt to have her touch me. I shook off her hands. "Ah," I said. "I *see*."

I spun toward the door. She threw her arms around me and pulled me back. She was surprisingly strong. "No, you don't see," she insisted, and there was such pain in her voice that I looked down at her anxiously. I saw the tears spring into her eyes. "Jack, I am just now starting to realize that my dad is dead. I know it sounds stupid, but when I wake up in the morning, it takes me a few minutes to realize that my dad's gone, that Mieko's gone, that most of what I believed about myself and about my family is gone. And it's not just first thing in the morning, either. When I was in the Narita airport, I actually bought some of the rock candy my dad likes. It's this little pink and blue crystally stuff, and it tastes like perfume. My dad loves it - loved it. When Detective Anthony asked me what it was, I said, 'Oh, it's just a little present for my dad.' Then I realized what I'd done, and I started to cry, right there in Duty Free. I don't have any idea when and how I'm going to come out of this, and I don't expect you to sit around waiting for me to pull myself together. You deserve a lot more than that, Jack. You really do."

She was fighting to control herself. I put my hands on her shoulders and held her steady. When she raised her eyes to me again, they looked slate blue, like the dark water I had seen from my firm that morning. She bit her lip. "In a lot of ways, I feel like I'm still down there in Salt Lake City," she said. "I feel like I'm in a lonely room, where no one can find me. No one can get where I am."

I moved my hands up to her temples and stroked her hair. She let her head rest against my hands for a moment. Then she straightened up. "But this time, I have to get out of the room myself," she said. "You can't come charging to my rescue anymore."

I thought that over. When I was through thinking it over, I took her in my arms and kissed her. She was startled, but she kissed me back. We held each other for a long time. Finally, she pushed me away. She looked exasperated. "Did you hear a single word I said?" she asked.

"I heard every word," I told her. "I have just two questions. Is this the 'I like you as a friend but I'll always think of you as a brother' speech? Or is this the 'I've been through hell and I need some time' speech?"

She almost laughed. It turned into a sob, but it started out as a laugh. I saw that steady light come into her eyes. Her face was soft and sad as she put her hand up to my cheek. "It's the 'I've been through hell and need some time' speech," she said. "You know it is. I love you, Jack. But I can't guarantee you anything. I don't know from minute to minute how I'm going to feel. And I don't know if this is ever going to end."

"It will," I said. "I promise you."

"All I can promise you is that it's going to take me a long time. I'm talking major, major time here, Jack."

I cupped her face in my hands and worked my fingers into her hair. I kissed her forehead, then her nose, then her mouth. I tilted her face up to me and bent down so I could look her right in the eyes.

"Harmony," I said, and I meant it more than she could know, "all I have is time."

The End

BOOK CLUB QUESTIONS

Spoiler: Some of these questions may reveal elements of the story.

Thank you for featuring *All Good Things* at your book club. Here are some questions to get you started. Enjoy your discussion!

1. When were you sure you knew who the murderer was? Were you right?
2. What was the most significant clue to the murderer's identity? Why?
3. What did the Seattle setting add to the book?
4. How did the retro timeframe affect the story?
5. Harmony Piper is presumably missing from the first page. How is her character developed?
6. Discuss whether Jack was a reliable narrator. Was there any point at which you doubted him? When/why? Share examples.
7. Discuss the perspectives of the police officers and whom they appeared to suspect. Did that change throughout the book? Share examples.
8. Discuss how themes of abandonment and abuse are developed in the book. How do the characters differ in their response to difficult backgrounds?
9. Discuss the significance of foster care/fostering.
10. What does the character of Betsy add to the story?
11. How realistic was the depiction of the lives of young associates at a large law firm? What seemed exaggerated (besides – one hopes – the murders)?
12. Discuss Jack's interactions with the children in the book – including Jimmy. How does he develop rapport with the children? What interview/negotiation tactics does he use?
13. Discuss Jack's interactions with Mark. Does their relationship change during the book? In what ways? Share examples.
14. How are authority figures portrayed? What does this add to the story?
15. Would you like to read other books by this author?

If you have a question for me, you can reach me at:

https://www.goodreads.com/goodreadscomrosemary_reeve

by Rosemary Reeve

"The best way to thank an author is to write a review."
-Nathan Bransford

Thank you so much for reading my book!
If you enjoyed it, please leave a review online, and please look for other Jack Hart mysteries on Amazon and the Kindle Store.

All the best,

Rosemary Reeve

The Jack Hart Mystery Series:

All Good Things
No Good Deed
Only the Good
Dead Weight

http://amazon.com/author/rosemaryreeve

https://www.goodreads.com/goodreadscomrosemary_reeve

CPSIA information can be obtained
at www.ICGtesting.com
Printed in the USA
LVHW032311260319
611967LV00002B/334